My Own Dear Brother

MY OWN DEAR BROTHER

HOLLY MÜLLER

BLOOMSBURY

NEW YORK · LONDON · OXFORD · NEW DELHI · SYDNEY

Bloomsbury USA
An imprint of Bloomsbury Publishing Plc

1385 Broadway	50 Bedford Square
New York	London
NY 10018	WC1B 3DP
USA	UK

www.bloomsbury.com

BLOOMSBURY and the Diana logo are trademarks of Bloomsbury Publishing Plc

First published in Great Britain 2016
First U.S. edition 2016

ISBN: HB: 978-1-63286-533-5
ePub: 978-1-63286-535-9

Library of Congress Cataloging-in-Publication Data is available.

2 4 6 8 10 9 7 5 3 1

Typeset by Integra Software Services Pvt. Ltd.
Printed and bound in USA by Berryville Graphics Inc., Berryville, Virginia

To find out more about our authors and books visit www.bloomsbury.com.
Here you will find extracts, author interviews, details of forthcoming events,
and the option to sign up for our newsletters.

Bloomsbury books may be purchased for business or promotional use.
For information on bulk purchases please contact Macmillan Corporate
and Premium Sales Department at specialmarkets@macmillan.com.

For Mr Ballinger

Prologue

Every year the saint came to the house. When Ursula was eight she and her brother Anton knelt on the window seat and looked out from the living-room window. The saint's white beard glinted in the porchlight; his tall bishop's hat nearly touched the lintel and in his fat-fingered hands he clutched the curling golden staff and ancient book. His cheeks were dark like smoked ham, eyes half buried by pudgy lids – burnt currants peeping from an over-risen cake. Breath plumed from his purplish lips. Ursula looked for feet below his robes. Was he touching the ground or did he hover just above it? She couldn't see Mama or Papa in the open doorway, only the yellow light falling on the steps and dirt outside, with their shadows cast long and dark within it.

Ursula's older sister, Dorli, was dusting the ornaments in the living-room cabinets and pretending not to care about the visitors. Her eyes betrayed her by their constant nervous darting towards the door. Ursula wondered if Saint Nikolaus knew they were watching and she supposed he did because he knew everything and could see inside their heads. In his book would be a list of all she'd done wrong; nothing could be hidden or denied. He was magical – worse than God Himself, because he came into the house. She peered into the shadows of the yard. Against the snow she could just about discern black figures, some capering to and fro, some crouching, others lumbering near the edge of the vegetable border. The dark outlines were tall and broad – a few stood still, like tree stumps, watching. She readied herself to draw away from the window should one of them step into the light. Mama's voice trilled with mirth, joined by Papa's low rumbling laugh. The top of Saint Nikolaus's hat nodded, a gilded tulip.

'There are so many,' said Ursula.

'They're going to let them in.' Anton climbed from the window seat.

'And we all know whose fault it is,' said Dorli.

Anton went along the hall to the kitchen. Ursula followed, ears straining to hear beyond the shuffle of her own feet and Dorli's that came close behind, beyond the voices at the door, and out to the dark areas of the yard. Soon it would begin. She dreaded the first sound.

Ursula and Anton sat at the kitchen table while Dorli half-heartedly dried a dish. The clock on the wall loudly measured the seconds and Jesus on his wooden cross gazed regretfully at them from beneath the thorns on his brow.

Yesterday Ursula had been caught thieving sugar at the grocer's – fingers in her mouth, wet with saliva, disgusting as a gypsy brat. She shifted on the hard chair and absentmindedly smoothed the back of her hand where Mama's wooden spoon had cracked against the bones in five angry strokes.

Then, from the yard at the front of the house, perhaps from the living-room window where she and Anton had been moments before, it came – rattling, harsh like cutlery in a drawer, but deeper, louder, continuous. A tremor passed through Ursula's insides – her breath shortened. She glanced at Anton then fixed her gaze on the bleached wood of the table, following the deep grooves of the grain, finding the knots that were like eyes, the one that had fallen through and left a clean round hole. She would have liked to hide under the table if it didn't make her look a fool in front of him. The rattling began again, and a heavy dragging sound, the hollow clonk of metal on wood. Something clattered on the other side of the kitchen wall. Then came a tap-tap at the glass. And finally the sound Ursula had dreaded most that made the hairs rise on her arms. It was worse than screech owls, worse than the strange coughing of stags at night in the woods, worse even than the almost-human screams of the fox; a gibbering, swelling high note that rose to a frantic pitch and squealed there for an eternity, then died away to silence. The sound was repeated just outside the kitchen window. Ursula's heart thumped and she swallowed all her saliva away; Anton's jaw muscles flickered with concentration. The shutters, which would normally be closed, were hooked open to expose them to the night. She daren't turn her head, though she had to force herself not to, knowing what was looking in, its dreadful face against the windowpane. Dorli wiped her hands on the cloth and hurried into the pantry to hide. She closed the door behind her.

'Coward,' said Anton.

The tapping ceased. There was a period of quiet. The house waited. The children waited. The fire crackled in the stove but it brought no feeling of warmth or safety, only a picture in Ursula's mind of Hellfire, of eternal burning. The windows glowered and breathed chill air. Voices rose in the hallway as Mama ushered the saint inside.

'They're in the kitchen,' she said.

'Should I bring my companions?' Saint Nikolaus's words echoed theatrically in the hall.

'Yes,' Mama replied, also pointedly loud. 'I think you should.'

Immediately there was a fearful din – the metallic scrape and jangle came swiftly down the hallway towards the closed kitchen door; growls and guttural cries ricocheted up the stairwell, grew loud and close to the door panels. Ursula imagined coarse fur brushing against her winter coat that hung on its peg; there was the clack of hooves. The handle turned by increments. She looked at Anton in panic.

'You don't have to stay,' she whispered.

'I won't let them take you.' He gripped her hand.

The kitchen door opened, the empty frame a ghastly space from which only the worst of things could come. Black figures stepped into view, the ones Ursula had seen in the yard; the group of Krampuses. They pushed through the doorway – so many, crushing, crawling, tongues hanging like dogs'. She wanted to look away but couldn't, took in their revolting movements, the baskets swaying on their backs, horned heads and eyes bulging as big as onions, the crimson tongues long as neckties but thrusting outwards, thick and stiff. She hid her face in her hands. Straight away they crowded near, chains dragging on the tiles with a dry, scouring sound. She curled downwards into her chair. They began to prod her, sharply, roughly, on her shoulders and arms; foul breath, fiery with alcohol, blasted on the back of her neck where her hair parted in pigtails. She smelled their rancid pelts.

A voice spoke from near the kitchen doorway. It was the saint. 'You', he announced, 'are a thief!'

Ursula peered from between her lashes, the saint a gaudy shape a few metres away, red, gold and white. She avoided looking at his small, black eyes, the unhealthy, livid face. She felt a disturbed twist in her belly, a different type of fear.

'On your knees!'

She fell from her chair, bashing her kneecaps against the floor. She bowed her head. 'Dear Lord,' she began. But she couldn't think. She couldn't form a prayer. They would take her. They were going to take her now – she felt them grasp her arms.

'You must be punished,' said the saint. 'It is wrong to steal and lie and sneak.'

At this she was tugged and shoved from side to side; there was a keen swishing noise and she knew it was the Krampuses lashing the air close to her ears with their cruel sticks.

'Stop it!' said Anton from somewhere near by. He'd left his chair, trying to reach her.

Ursula opened her eyes to look for him. One of the Krampuses was beside her, its face pushed close, the rigid point of its tongue curled as if to lick her cheek. She raised her hands. I repent, she thought – her voice had deserted her. Sticks sang in the air and sharp pain lashed the backs of her calves. She contracted into a ball, her face close to the stone floor. Blows fell on her back. She was gripped about the arms and middle and lifted.

'Get off!' her brother shouted. 'Put her down!'

The Krampuses panted heavily with the pleasure of their task and Ursula was hoisted high in the air. Would they dash her on to the flagstones?

'Take her! Take her!' said the saint with glee.

And so they did.

Part One

1

Summer in Austria was hot and oppressive, full of baking mornings that burned knees and ears like crackling, and afternoons that darkened abruptly into night beneath storm clouds, accompanied always by a sudden strong wind that drove scraps of straw in anxious cartwheels along the road. Dusty fields of maize and rye, and gardens hemmed in by five-foot fences to keep out the marauding deer, were wetted and then dried again in a perpetual cycle as clouds broke their undersides on the Alps in the south and spilled their bellies across the country. There were several storms like this each week – the rain fell like buckets of bath water, cleansing and warm on the skin; in the mountains marmots shot to their burrows at the first pulse of thunder, and chamois bolted. Forked lightning tore the sky along its seams and speared the ground. The goats and marmots had good reason to run.

After a downpour the sun returned and the tall firs that shielded Ursula Hildesheim's house were peaceful once more, releasing their pale souls to heaven, or so it looked as the vapours rose from them, their trunks streaked rust-red with rain. The Hildesheim place was similar to many other Austrian homes, though poorer and barer than many of their neighbours', clad in pine with foundations of stone, a dark bulky structure leaning with age, top-heavy with balconies and overhanging eaves, a shipwrecked galleon marooned on the flood plain of the River Traisen. They had what Mama called a 'measly smallholding', enough to feed them and keep them working in all their free time, with one cow named Edi, a few goats for sausages and caged rabbits for stews. Trout swam in a concrete channel near the cherry trees, heads to the current. It was an unchanging place, other than the slow slump of the house into the earth, the greying and splitting of the cladding and sag of the roof, and the thickening of cobwebs in the sheds. The only thing that had altered in Ursula's memory was that Austria was called the Ostmark since the Germans came and the region where she lived was no longer Lower Austria, but the Lower Danube. Also, many of the men had gone to war, including her papa.

'Poor Herr Hildesheim,' complained the people of the nearby village of Felddorf where Papa had lived since boyhood. 'He'd be ashamed to see how his children run wild. That woman. Doesn't spare time for church – a high days and holidays type.' And somehow Mama, having had the audacity to hail from a large town and style her hair in curls rather than coiled plaits, was blamed for the Hildesheim poverty – despite the fact that she worked long hours on the neighbouring farm – for Ursula's muddy, bare feet and light fingers, for Papa's failures: drinking, gambling and debts.

Walking home from school along the track Ursula escaped into surroundings where mud and barefootedness were usual, where no one watched her with distaste, and where the only thing she could hear was the toot of the train as it came along the valley, the summoning clang of the church bell, birdsong, wind in branches and Mama's long yell across the hill when it was time to eat. Occasionally she dallied in Felddorf when there was a dance at the Gasthaus and the soldiers on leave played their trumpets and drums so she could hear a tune spill out on to the street, or catch sight of a courting couple. She'd sit between bushes in the flower border, hidden from view, and study the way their fingers moved, twining together like plaits of straw then untwining and twining again, a wordless message. If she was lucky they'd kiss and she'd watch their lips and jaws and cheeks move in slow and lingering rhythms, the touch of their noses, the glisten of tongues, the pink of their faces, their bodies pressed tight. It would be blissful, she thought, to know such feelings – tenderness, a warm touch, romance; to be a woman. Even imagining, she was moved, and a leaping started inside her like March hares. Dorli said she was still a child until she started her monthlies. Ursula prayed they'd soon come. Perhaps they would – Dorli had started at Ursula's age, which was thirteen.

She befriended Schosi Hillier on the day the letter came. It was January 1944 and Papa had been missing since Stalingrad. The Party didn't know whether he was dead or a prisoner in Russia, and they said to hold on because it wouldn't be long until the final victory.

'I hope they're right,' said Mama, who hated the war and said it only made things worse for everyone. 'It's gone on long enough. We need your papa home.'

While Ursula and Dorli prepared dinner in the kitchen and Anton removed clinker from the stove, a nervous postal worker handed a black-edged envelope to Mama at the front door. He kept his eyes on the snow-covered ground and his cap in his hands.

'Lord, help us,' said Mama, turning and coming inside.

'Papa's fallen,' said Anton, whispering close to Ursula's ear, as though answering a question in a school test. He went off to fetch his new pearl-inlaid letter opener. Ursula thought about when Opa died and he'd been put into the ground in a way that had seemed unceremonious despite the doleful prayers and the flowers that had covered his cheap coffin; he was lowered quickly and earth tossed over him, dug under like manure, not like a man who'd walked and talked and carried her around on his shoulders. She supposed that Papa had been treated in much the same fashion, in some faraway place. Mama sliced the envelope, her hair still twisted in the pins she wore at night to make it curl. Her skin had turned as white as porcelain and her hands trembled so violently that it looked as though the letter was stuck to her fingers and that she was trying to shake it off. She read and a flutter of laughter escaped like a moth into the room. Ursula looked sideways at her sister, who was sixteen and usually stepped up for things like this but Dorli had frozen beside the workbench where she was in the middle of making bread rolls. She didn't move at all, her hands ghostly with flour and shreds of dough, holding them carefully above the mixing bowl as though even then it mattered whether she dropped something on the floor. Ursula wanted to knock the bread mix on to the flagstones. Couldn't her sister forget herself this once? Ursula knew that there were sobs and awful cries filling the room and that Anton had walked out of the house, but everything had become muted as though she was buried under a mountain of blankets.

Schosi Hillier was standing on the track near the gateway when Ursula went out looking for her brother. She knew who Schosi was – he lived in the small house near the woods and had a job at Herr Esterbauer's farm where Mama worked. She'd seen him going back and forth across the fields. Once or twice his mother, Frau Hillier, had joined the Hildesheims and walked with them to church on a feast day. But the boy was left at home. He couldn't speak or else was so shy that he wasn't worth bothering with. He hid behind his mother's skirts, despite being far too old.

'He's a blessing and a curse to his mother,' Mama sometimes said. 'They've nothing at all. We must thank God, Uschi, for what we've got.'

When Ursula saw him lingering there, uncertain and ungainly, his coat far too big and hanging like a sack, she remembered that his papa had been killed too. Not so long ago the black-edged death cards had been handed out by Frau Hillier.

'Seen Simmy?' Schosi called. His voice was hoarse and he stuttered like a woodpecker – he wasn't dumb after all.

'Who?'

Schosi didn't look at her; his eyes darted into the corners of the yard. 'My cat.'

'Your cat? I haven't seen it.' She wondered why he chased after it. A cat only returned if it wanted to.

'Came down this way.'

'Sorry.' She continued across the yard, the snow mashed with mud from boots and wheelbarrows and carts.

Inside the cowshed it took a moment to discern the shape of Anton's legs dangling from the hayloft trapdoor.

'Toni.' She kept her voice soft because she knew he was angry. As she waited for his reply she sensed someone standing behind her. It was Schosi, blinking shyly from beneath his thick dark fringe. She turned back to her brother. 'Come down.'

'No,' he said.

She began up the wooden ladder, not caring that Schosi might see her underwear because he wasn't like other boys. She reached the top and sat on the edge of the loft platform so that her legs hung beside her brother's. His hair stuck up in a tawny shock from his forehead as though he'd been trying to pull it out and his skin glistened with a faint sweat that gave him a feverish look. The letter opener was embedded in his hand.

'It doesn't hurt,' he said. He kept the hand carefully in his lap. There wasn't much blood and the letter opener looked unreal, the way it poked from the top of his hand, the tip of the blade, when he turned it to show her, just bursting through the skin of his palm like a tiny beak emerging from an egg. She held his good hand and rubbed the cold skin.

'Why did you do that?' she said. She tried to stop the tears coming.

'Can I play?' called Schosi. He rested a foot on the first rung of the ladder, peering unseeingly into the darkness of the trapdoor above.

'Not today,' said Ursula. 'Come back tomorrow.'

Schosi hesitated then walked away. She heard him talking as he went and she thought it was strange because there was nobody there.

Anton said, 'Why's *he* here?' without much curiosity, his voice faint.

Ursula hugged him and touched the hair at his temple. He closed his eyes; a rose glow shone prettily on his lids; his breath came fast.

'Why do you have to hurt yourself, Toni?'

'I told you, it doesn't hurt.'

Schosi was waiting for them in the shelter of the firs when they emerged after breakfast. Ursula and Anton laughed to see his peculiar figure and called out, 'Looking for your cat again?' and, 'Don't cry! He's just gone mousing!' Schosi came as far as the gate then drew a scrap of cloth from his pocket. He twisted the fabric around his forefinger before releasing it and letting it spin. He stared at the swirl of cloth then repeated the trick. Ursula watched him, perplexed.

'He's cuckoo,' said Anton, tugging her arm. 'Come on. Leave him to it.'

But Schosi followed them.

That day they were allowed to roam; they didn't have to go to school because Papa was lost and Mama didn't care about the time or coming back for dinner. She'd bandaged Anton's hand but hadn't bothered to beat him or confiscate the letter opener. Anton was jubilant because he was sure it was worth something. He said that digging for bodies with the Hitler Youth had its perks because if you found money or anything valuable you could keep it. He'd shown Ursula his stash after returning from a week's rubble shifting – a gold ring, an ornate key, a pocket watch and some Reichsmarks hidden in his bedroom drawer. Also, a fire-blackened photo of a soldier posing in front of bleached pyramids beneath a searing sun.

'I'll go there one day,' he'd said, studying the photo. Ursula had looked crestfallen at the idea of his leaving for the other side of the world. He'd pinched her face until she smiled. 'Of course, I'd take you.'

The three of them played stick racing from the footbridge. There was just enough water flowing between the ice sheets that shelved from the stream's edge. By the time Schosi grasped the rules Ursula was tired of the game. He excitedly clattered back and forth in his heavy boots, laughing. Ursula and Anton shared a look – he was a fool, there was no doubt about that. Afterwards, they collected the home-made bows from the shed and chose a pine tree as their target. Anton was a deadly shot and within moments hit the bull's-eye. Schosi squatted near by, collecting ice from the long grasses to put in his mouth; he didn't try to join them but watched Ursula as she took her turn, an open gaze that flickered away as soon as she looked at him. He muttered to himself and played with the scrap of fabric, coiling it hard so that his fingertip turned bloodless white, or else pressed his wristwatch to his ear, his mouth stretching and trembling. Ursula was unnerved by his crouching, muttering, twirling – why did he make such expressions? His lips pressed together and outwards in a quivering line, as though barely able to contain the energy within, his eyes round as marbles fixed on the incessantly spinning cloth. His mother didn't let him go freely about, perhaps for shame, or perhaps because he was dangerous. She knew he didn't go to school and that the Hitler Youth didn't want him either. Anton said he'd completed only one year after kindergarten, then disappeared, never to be seen in school or about the village again. Now he was fourteen, Anton's age.

'Why aren't you in school?' Ursula kicked at the ground, filling the air with powdery flakes, which engulfed Schosi.

'I got a job.' He hunched good-naturedly against the miniature snowstorm.

Mama had told them he kept Herr Esterbauer's scythes thin and keen with his whetstone. 'He's soft on the lad,' she'd said. 'Or perhaps it's someone else he's soft on.' Mama enjoyed speculating. Herr Esterbauer had only his senile mother for company, and his vast fields and fine barns. Who might he fall in love with? Who'd be the lucky woman to become his wife? Schosi's mama was the current wager. They were a lonely pair and deserved one another.

At five o'clock the sun deserted the children's game and the sky became a freezing lid, threatening snow. Schosi was blue-lipped and Ursula's hair beneath her woollen scarf was damp from exertion, it having been her job to run back and forth to collect arrows. A squirrel scuttled in rapid, tail-jerking bursts amongst the needles at the base of the tree. Anton took aim, stretched the bowstring to capacity.

'No!' Schosi shouted, rising part-way to his feet. Anton jumped; the bowstring snapped. The squirrel flashed upwards.

'Damned idiot!' Anton flung down the broken bow. Schosi crouched and covered his head. Ursula ran after her brother who marched homewards. She looked back at Schosi who stayed beside the pine, squatting and twining his cloth against the white hill.

'She hasn't eaten?' asked Ursula.

Dorli shook her head then went to hang their wet coats above the Tirolia.

Ursula was relieved to find that Mama in this instance played her part, even if she'd so often hissed and wailed at Papa when he was home for not caring about her and for treating her badly and he, swollen with rage, had kicked her shin so hard that it split like an overripe plum. Other village women fasted and stayed in bed when their husbands died, and were spoken of respectfully for it.

Dorli said grace before beginning a dinner of stew and dumplings. Ursula sent vague prayers to the crucifix that crouched in the top corner of the room, about feeling grateful and being sorry for her sins. She ate with her usual speeding urgency to prevent Anton snatching what remained of her meal. She wanted to be less scrawny and to fill out her 'perished-looking face', which was what Herr Esterbauer had said about her when she'd gone to meet Mama at the farm. Her mouth and hands grew messy and she accidentally dipped one of her unravelling pigtails into her bowl – but Mama wasn't here to overlook her and knock her elbows off the table-edge. She made believe that they were orphans alone in the house, not going to school, not sweeping the floors, not bothering with all the childish, repetitive things that must be done: blackberry picking, grass cutting and gathering twigs for the fires. She didn't have to go to Junior League meetings to be laughed at in her ancient uniform, which used to belong to her sister. Anton hunted with traps, his bow, his gun, they were together all the time. Ursula's life was full of unexpected things.

Dorli clattered her spoon into her empty bowl long before Ursula was done; her dexterity with cutlery was unparalleled and somehow she remained neat. 'You can wash the dishes,' she said, stretching and tilting on her chair, her stomach and breasts straining the buttons of her dress. She loved to be boss – being an orphan with her around would be no fun at all.

The clock in the living room chimed seven as they cleared the table, a bright sound that faded despondently in the silence that emanated from upstairs, from behind the closed door of Mama's bedroom. Anton was morose as, leaning against the work surface, he watched Ursula wash plates, the wound on his hand leaking blood through the bandage. He didn't chatter as he usually would. Had it been like this in Schosi's house after his papa fell? Ursula found herself wondering. Did that odd boy really understand about death? She tried to picture the Eastern Front or Stalingrad but she didn't know what they looked like. In her mind Papa floated vaguely somewhere, dressed in furs and blasted with endless blizzards. She was used to missing him – the only thing that was different was that now she knew he wouldn't come back. He'd stay as she'd imagined, marching across colourless Russia, his outline blurred by flying snow.

2

Two nights later an SS man banged on the door with a gloved hand. Ursula woke at the sound and came downstairs to see him standing on the doorstep in the light of Mama's lantern. She loitered behind her mother, nervous but curious. The SS worked at the camp in the centre of the village, a place that had about it such a forbidden and horrifying atmosphere that she never looked for long through the bristling barbed-wire fence at the mouldering huts within. Now and then prisoners came out into the village to mend a wall or dig a grave, the SS making free use of their batons. Other prisoners were taken daily to the munitions factory to do the worst of the labour, or to farms. They passed amongst the people of Felddorf, spectre-like in thin prisonwear, their shoulder bones sharp as the ploughshares that they pushed with weakened arms up and down the fields, their misfortune too brutal, too alien, to be contemplated.

'Gnädige Frau,' said the man standing straight as a pole, his buttons winking in the amber lantern-glow and the shining peak of his hat catching snowflakes like a stiff black tongue. 'My name is SS Corporal Loehr. There's been an escape from the camp. Twenty-six Russians.' He clasped his hands behind his body. 'Dangerous men. They must be captured as quickly as possible. It's known they're hiding in the immediate area, perhaps in your barn.'

'Criminals?' whispered Mama as she peered into the yard beyond. Ursula could see only darkness outside and she watched the SS man carefully as he nodded and turned briefly to follow Mama's gaze, his face emerging from shadow – a red nose, tight with cold, and large womanly eyes blinking with troubled concentration. He turned back to them.

'A party of your neighbours are scouring the woods. One mentioned that you have a rifle here. Are you prepared to use it?'

Mama wrapped her shawl tightly about her – she blinked several times. 'Yes,' she said. 'One moment.'

She hurried to the scullery where Papa's gun hung across wall-mounted hooks. Ursula half hid behind the open door, feeling exposed in her nightwear. She daren't look at the man in case he spoke to her. Mama's lantern receded and disappeared into the back of the house. SS Corporal Loehr sniffed once or twice but was otherwise silent. Mama returned with the gun and some cartridges bulging in her apron pocket, broke the gun over her knee and fumbled the cartridges into the barrel. Her face was alive with something close to gladness, the misery of the last few days all but gone. Dorli materialised; she'd stuffed her hair up in pins.

Two striding figures appeared near the gate, hats pulled low. It was Herr Esterbauer, Mama's employer, and Herr Adler, the local Nazi Party inspector.

'We'll search the barns,' said SS Corporal Loehr. 'Flush out any unwanted visitors.' He saluted briefly. 'Gnädige Frau, it's cold. Take time to dress yourself. We appreciate your patriotism and courage.' With this he turned and walked to the centre of the yard, gesturing to the two men. Ursula saw the gleam of a pistol in his hand.

'Get inside. And stay there.' Mama elbowed Ursula then propped the rifle against the wall and ran to the coat-stand. She hastily and rather clumsily fastened her winter jacket. Anton was sitting on the stairs in his pyjamas.

'What's happening?' he said.

Mama waved him to be quiet. She grabbed the rifle and she and Dorli left.

'What is it?' Anton called again. He received no answer as the door thudded at their back. He bounded upstairs. Ursula followed, gripping the banister to propel herself. Upstairs, Anton writhed into his clothes, arms thrashing as he pulled a shirt over his head and a jumper too. Ursula hurried across the landing to the room she shared with Dorli to find her things in the wardrobe. She yanked long socks up over her knees and wriggled into her petticoat and skirt.

'So?' Anton cried breathlessly. 'What did the man say?'

She hesitated. It was a rare treat to be possessed of knowledge and to have him question her so intently.

'Well?'

'He said that criminals have escaped from the camp.' She buttoned her woollen cardigan straight over her vest. 'Bolsheviks. They're checking the barns in case they're hiding there.'

'Obviously Bolsheviks!' he said, and she felt foolish because the camp was designated for prisoners from the East – Red Army, Russians predominantly, a few Poles and Czechoslovakians.

Anton finished dressing and raced downstairs. Ursula knew he was going to get the old rifle. He was infatuated with it and had spent secret hours oiling and preparing it. He'd shot a sparrow from the top of the barn the previous week while Mama was still at work. It had rolled pathetically down the snowy roof and lodged in the gutter, one wing tip protruding like a final plea. Ursula followed as quickly as she could. She stopped to pull on her boots then opened the door. Mama had told her to stay but she couldn't wait here. She dreaded the sharp bark of Herr Adler who didn't take kindly to disobedient children, and whose inspections of their home made her guilt-ridden and afraid, but even a dose of his fearsome temper seemed preferable to being left alone. From inside the shed came a clatter. She slipped out and across the frozen yard. Anton had pulled the old hunting rifle from its concealment amongst a tangle of hoes and rakes and knelt with it on the floor, a box of cartridges scattered on the concrete. He blew into the sights, cocked the chamber and loaded, his movements practised, fluid. When he'd finished he stood. 'Go back in,' he said.

'I don't want to.'

'Well, you can't come with me.' He left the shed, jogged to the barn and went inside; the high door was open and there was bleating from the goats and the voices of several people. A moment later the adults emerged, the men in front, Mama behind with Dorli and Anton.

'Check the Hillier property!' SS Corporal Loehr made a swoop with his arm in the direction of Schosi's cottage. 'Herr Esterbauer, go with them!' The corporal set off with Herr Adler. 'We'll call at the Fingerlos place.' The Fingerlos house was along the track towards the village, home to Ursula's only and part-time friend, Marta. She watched Herr Adler run behind the corporal with the heavy-footed inefficiency of a plump man. She was struck by how like a hog he looked, with his ruddy neck bulging over his coat collar and merging with his darkly flushed cheeks, eyes black and small and his swollen hands and feet. As ever she experienced a faint sickening as she looked at him. She feared for the camp inmate who might be caught by him. Just before the men disappeared from view, SS Corporal Loehr shouted something over his shoulder and his voice echoed between the walls of the outhouses – about being 'vigilant', and shooting 'immediately'.

Herr Esterbauer, Mama, Dorli and Anton exited the yard through the field gate with a lantern between them and Anton darted ahead with the gun slung low in his hand, graceful, like the spear of an Indian brave. The beam of the lantern was eclipsed and Ursula was in complete darkness. Nerves clenched in the pit of her stomach. In the dank shed, mice – or worse, rats – scuttled erratically amongst the boxes. She set off with the feeling of a devil at her heels, clambered the gate, snagged her socks on the rough wood, jumped and landed in a deep drift. The others had trampled the snow and formed a path she could follow but she soon lost their tracks once properly into the field. She tried not to think about the stories she'd heard of Russian prisoners turning to cannibalism in the camps. They were an animalistic people, with violence in their blood. Gory images rose in her mind and painted themselves on to the darkness, red-ringed mouths, clawing hands, burrowing to find her insides. Her panic deepened. She would come to no good. She'd be pounced on and pinned to the ground. Her body filled with hot sparks of fear; a sense of the inevitable weakened her limbs so that they lost power and her steps grew slower. She gasped aloud – she had a sense that she'd run before through snow like this, in terror, amongst muffling drifts, under a black sky just like this one. The strength-sapping paralysis in her limbs was familiar, an echo. She told herself briskly to be calm, to control her thoughts. She forced herself to move faster, wallowed onwards, the cold air hurting her lungs and the snow so deep that her legs were almost entirely submerged with each step.

After a while of arduous running, and of staring into the night and scanning for a sign of the others, she glimpsed movement and vague shapes up on the hill, the tiny glitter of a lantern. It must be Mama and the others; an escaped Russian wouldn't have his own lantern. A loud crack came, the air splintered with its echo. A gunshot. Ursula knew it immediately. There was another report and another. The shots came from the valley below, from the village. Could it be Anton's rifle? No, he was elsewhere, heading for the Hillier cottage. It occurred to her that he might be in danger, that he wasn't invincible despite his own belief. Hadn't the SS man said that the convicts were armed? She looked frantically again for the lantern and when she found it, a blinking speck in the dark, it seemed impossibly far ahead. She ran faster, falling often, her hands throbbing from cold and from plunging through the frozen crust of the snow. She must keep her head, she told herself again, and found that she was able to remove herself in part from her sweating, thrashing-along body, the fury of the moment, the fierce cold, the painful bite of ice in her tired lungs, the din she made on the night-time hill, allowing her to run without stopping, without constantly turning to check who followed.

At the brow of the hill, trees huddled black to her right and she could hear the burble of the river in its icy channel. She decided on the longer, open route along the edge of the woods and continued down the far side of the field. She kept to the right path by referring to the position of the trees, the section of field seeming far longer than she remembered. She prayed to God to protect her, to protect her brother. She'd be good for ever if He'd have mercy on them now.

Eventually, the forest curved away so that she knew she was at the top of the sloping field that overlooked the valley of Herr Esterbauer's land, and amongst the trees below would be the Hillier place. There was a pinprick of light. The lantern again or the cottage. She sped into a clumsy gallop down the incline, hoping she didn't meet any logs or wires. Her knees buckled when she ploughed into an unexpected snowdrift and her hand struck something hard and sharp as she fell. She cried out and scrambled to her feet. Her fingers pulsated with pain and she held the hand to her body and kept running as best she could. The ground levelled and became uneven; there were the pale outlines of birches dividing the field from the next. She guessed that she now travelled along the rough cart track that led to the Hillier house.

Suddenly it was before her, squat and dark. She stopped. Chinks of light were visible, edging the shutters. The front gate stood open; the snow on the path was disrupted. She heard movement in the lean-to at the side of the house and ducked below the level of the fence. It was only Herr Esterbauer who came out, his heavy tread groaning and squeaking the snow. He went to the front door, pushed it open while softly knocking, met by Frau Hillier who wore a thick coat over her nightgown.

'Nobody else,' he said.

Frau Hillier nodded and he passed her and went into the house. She remained for a moment, staring around her small front garden, hunching her shoulders as if she wished for a scarf. Her round face, usually soft and calm, was hollow with worry. Beyond her in the kitchen Schosi sat on a chair twirling his scrap of cloth. The door closed and Ursula was in darkness again.

From behind the house came a cry – Ursula was sure it was Anton's voice – then shouts and finally a shot, loud and shocking. Ursula ran towards the sound, down a narrow path between a sheer weed-covered bank and the side of the building, which she guessed would lead to the back yard; it felt like a tunnel and she saw nothing ahead except dull flickering. At the end she stopped; light moved on the ground near her feet in a swaying rhythm; the shadow of an unseen object swung large then small. She pushed her stomach flat to the cold render and peered into the yard. Herr Esterbauer crouched with his rifle in hand – he must have come straight through the house. Mama and Dorli leaned from the back door, Dorli brandishing a poker. From the strut of the porch a hastily hung lantern threw light back and forth in waves. Herr Esterbauer stared at someone who lay on the ground in front of him. Ursula struggled to see, gripped with a horrible fear that it was Anton. But only a pair of legs and bare bloodied feet were visible. She emerged into the yard. Herr Esterbauer swept his rifle round to face her. She halted.

'Get away!' He gestured for her to go back the way she'd come, along the tunnel.

She didn't move and blood rose in her cheeks. She'd never disobeyed someone like Herr Esterbauer before, not directly. His deep voice resounded in the small yard, his face was creased into furrows, his grey moustache, dusted with frost, looked peculiar against the shining red skin that flashed bright at every upswing of the lantern, his wrinkles deepening and swooping. She tried again to see the figure obscured by the farmer's thick body and bulky snow boots.

'Toni? Is it him?'

'Go, Ursula!' said Mama, glaring at her in a way that promised a beating. Herr Esterbauer stood so that Ursula saw the head and shoulders of the man on the floor; he was a stranger with a hard face full of bones. Relief arrived, quickly followed by revulsion – the bulging, overlarge eyes showed white between partly-closed lids, like peeled eggs sunk into the sockets, and the snow around his head was melted away by a dark stain. His hair was shaved apart from a stripe down the centre, which was the regulation cut for prisoners in the camp. An inmate. They'd found one.

'Where is he?' she managed, still staring, appalled, at the bleeding prisoner who must be dead, she thought. She'd never seen a dead person before.

Herr Esterbauer pointed into the woodshed. Anton sat on the shadowed ground with his back against the woodstack, his rifle on the floor beside him. 'He's fine,' said the farmer.

Anton got to his feet, holding his own wrist. He came into the yard and stopped near to where the stranger lay. He gazed down at the man's torso where a black-looking wound pasted the thin shirt to the skin beneath. He stared as if mesmerised.

'Come!' said Herr Esterbauer with a curt wave of his hand, trying to shoo Anton onwards. 'Inside! I'll fetch SS Corporal Loehr. He'll deal with this.'

They filed through the back door into the cramped kitchen, Anton and Herr Esterbauer eventually following behind. Schosi and Frau Hillier sat together on an overstuffed armchair beside the Tirolia. Schosi looked up when Ursula entered, blinking owlishly, and she was struck by how strange it was to be in the normal, drab kitchen, with such distress thudding in her veins, with such horror outside. Frau Hillier told Schosi to get down and he dropped to the rug and folded his legs, pressed his watch to his ear. Frau Hillier examined Anton's injured arm, washed the cut then tied a bandage. When it was done Anton sat where he could rest the soles of his boots against the stovefront. Ursula pulled a stool close – her own hand was only bruised from her fall in the snow.

'Are you all right?' she asked.

'It was a piece of glass. He took a swipe at me.'

'Horrible! What a horrible thing!' The anger arrived quick and hot. 'What an animal!'

He shrugged in agreement.

'So, you had to shoot him?' She lowered her voice, afraid almost to say it aloud. She could barely believe that her brother had killed a man not moments before, blown a hole in his chest. It was frightful, that wound, the thin body; she couldn't stop thinking of it.

Anton nodded, his gaze cool and distant so that she knew not to ask anything more. She drew back and pretended not to watch him; it was difficult to tell what he was thinking, whether he was shaken and needed comfort, or whether he felt guilty. He looked quite normal, the petulant set to his lips, jaw protruding, skin tight and eyes glazed from the dry heat of the fire. He'd done what he'd always wanted to do – he'd fired his gun at an enemy. She supposed he'd been heroic. But worry wormed in her belly and made her restless. The poky Hillier kitchen was filled with an oppressive hush. Even Dorli was quiet and the adults cooperated in making drinks, speaking in undertones and glancing often at Anton, perhaps protectively, or nervously. Ursula felt another shudder of fear, picturing again the scene that was just beyond the closed and draughty door – Anton made no fuss, was stoical, was so much braver than she. She should try to be more like him. She caught the eye of Schosi who watched her. He clambered to his feet, clumsy amongst the extra chairs that had been carried in.

'Don't worry,' he said in his stammering voice, unbuckling his watch and handing it to her.

She took it, not knowing why he gave it to her, though it did make her feel comforted somehow. She inspected the watch: inscribed on its back in tiny scrolling letters was the name *Ludwig Hillier*. An unpleasant smell rose from the cracked leather strap, pungent and sour. Schosi retrieved the watch then held it to her ear, his movements careful, a slight tremble tickling against her hair. The minuscule tick was faint, almost too faint to hear amidst the clatter of crockery made by the adults.

'No.' She pushed him away, embarrassed. 'I don't want it.'

He contented himself with standing near by, fiddling with the watch and muttering his papa's name.

Hot drinks were served. Herr Esterbauer put a hand on Frau Hillier's shoulder. She let it rest there for a few seconds then dislodged it. Mama tinkled her teaspoon against her mug because it was too silent.

'I'll be off.' Herr Esterbauer touched Frau Hillier's shoulder again but she was stiff and unresponsive. 'Promise not to go outside tonight. It's not safe.' He went to get his hat. Dorli nudged Ursula and gave her a knowing, sidelong look. Ursula ignored her, more concerned about Anton who still sat immobile, facing away from them all, his drink untouched. 'Stay inside and lock the doors,' added Herr Esterbauer. 'There'll be more of them roaming about.' He squashed his hat on to his head. As he passed Anton he said, 'You stay out of it. You've done enough.'

Frau Hillier got up and followed the farmer to the door. She whispered something to him low and fierce. Herr Esterbauer shouldered his gun and was gone.

When she returned, Frau Hillier went to the sink and leaned over the basin. Her hair concealed her face and her arms trembled. Perhaps she'd vomit, thought Ursula. Dorli began biting her fingernails. After a while Mama said, 'Can we stay here tonight? I'm afraid to walk home.'

Frau Hillier didn't reply. Ursula hoped she'd refuse because she didn't want to sleep in a house with a dead man freezing solid in the yard.

'Are we just going to leave him?' said Frau Hillier. She turned round. 'All night?'

'It's terrible, isn't it?' said Mama. 'But you did well, Toni,' she added, directing her comment at Anton with some force.

'Yes, it *is* terrible!' Frau Hillier's tone was a fierce dart.

'Someone has to deal with it,' said Dorli. 'They're criminals – we must defend ourselves.'

'It's not Christian,' said Frau Hillier. 'It's not right. God is for the whole world. God is for everyone. Not just for Austria. Not just for us.'

Mama shook her head minutely. 'You ought to be careful,' she said.

'What about it?' Frau Hillier snapped. 'You're going to report me?'

'No. Not I.' Mama glanced askance at Dorli and then at Anton who still stared blankly at his boots. Frau Hillier was quiet for a minute then she collected the dirty mugs and cups and put them in the basin. She filled hot-water bottles and put a brick to heat on the stovetop for Schosi, because, she said, he had to give up his hot-water bottle for Ursula seeing as she was a lady. As Frau Hillier came past the table Mama held out her hand as a peace token and after a tiny hesitation Frau Hillier took it and then Mama stood and they hugged and cried. Some time later they lit a lantern to carry up into the loft and Frau Hillier checked that all the doors were locked and that chairs were pushed firmly beneath the handles.

3

Ursula woke before daybreak. Mama was dressing, a dim outline at the edge of the mattress in the Hillier attic. She hauled the covers from Ursula's legs as she buttoned herself into her winter underwear. Ursula sat up. Beyond Mama and across the floor was a bright square of yellow light, the edges of the closed trapdoor illuminated from below. She hadn't slept well. Tough stalks had poked from the straw mattress and plagued her all night long, or else the stuffing had slid from under her body so that she lay uncushioned on the floorboards. The unfamiliar house had creaked and emitted abrupt startling cracks that jolted her from sleep, and in her wakefulness Ursula's thoughts had travelled repeatedly to the dead man in the yard and her brother firing a gun into his living flesh, that black wound, the man's skin grey in the moonlight, frost creeping on to his clothes and clouding his eyeballs, the snow darkening around him until the whole yard was inky with blood.

Sunlight glowed milky and bright through the smeared front window as Ursula clambered down the ladder into the hall. Frau Hillier was at the Tirolia, filling a washbowl from the water chamber, Schosi at her elbow; Anton and Dorli were at the table. Frau Hillier threw a rag into the water and Schosi went to it, obedient. He made a rough attempt at wiping his face – his mother finished the job with a brisk scrub behind his ears and beneath his fringe. When Schosi sat beside Anton at the table Anton moved his chair away.

'What's wrong with him?' Anton asked coldly.

'I beg your pardon?' said Frau Hillier, hanging the damp rag above the stove.

'Your son – what's wrong with him?'

Frau Hillier turned, her round eyes, similar to Schosi's in shape and colour, focusing sharply on Anton. 'Nothing.'

'Why's he not in school then?'

'I took him out. He's not suited to it. He's very shy.' Frau Hillier handed Schosi a crust of bread, which he began to chew. 'You're better at work, aren't you?' Schosi nodded. 'He's a hard worker.'

'Well,' said Anton, 'he's been coming to our place and hanging about so he can't be working that hard.'

Ursula caught the spiteful note in Anton's voice. She wondered whether he was angry because of his arm being cut and bandaged as well as the wound on his palm from the letter opener. He did have to fumble about one-handed, and this morning he'd had to get help from Mama with his buttons and laces. That kind of thing always put him in a fearful temper.

34

The wariness in Frau Hillier's eyes dilated to fear. 'He's been coming to your place? When?'

'I didn't know,' said Dorli defensively.

'You're always out,' said Ursula. 'It's only been twice,' she told Frau Hillier.

'You shouldn't let him wander about bothering people,' continued Anton. 'He's not right in the head.'

Frau Hillier opened her mouth but said nothing.

'Anton!' Mama materialised in the doorway. 'That's enough!' She looked at Frau Hillier, apologetic. 'I don't know why he's being so rude.'

Frau Hillier flushed red and turned away. She began to get food out from the cupboard. She offered breakfast, flustered, but there was very little to share. Mama refused to eat, saying they would have something when they got home, and frowned disapprovingly when Ursula accepted a piece of bread.

Just as they were putting on their boots, there was a commotion outside, the whinny of a horse and voices. A moment later the door shook beneath a heavy fist. Frau Hillier hurried to the door. It was SS Corporal Loehr and Herr Esterbauer.

'Good morning,' said the corporal.

'Good morning,' said Herr Esterbauer, with a tip of his hat. 'We've come to remove the deceased.'

Frau Hillier nodded and the men set off for the back yard. Anton jumped from his chair and went eagerly to follow. Schosi copied him.

'Stop!' said Frau Hillier. The boys halted. The command in her voice was total. 'Sit down. You will respect the dead.'

No one said anything as the men scraped and shuffled in the yard – Frau Hillier drew her rosary from her apron pocket and ran the beads through her fingers. The men soon appeared outside the front window, their shoulders and heads visible; the corporal walked backwards, Herr Esterbauer forwards, a space between them where they carried the prisoner. They bent low out of sight beside the horse. After a moment the corporal mounted and Herr Esterbauer spoke to him briefly, then the two men raised their hands in the Hitler salute and the corporal departed. The horse trotted towards the village and Herr Esterbauer glanced into the window of the house before going off in the direction of his farm. Ursula balanced on the crossbar of her stool and craned her neck to see out of the window. There was the jiggling rump of the horse and the sharp outline of SS Corporal Loehr. From the back of the saddle extended a taut length of rope, the body of the Russian at the end of it, tied around the middle. The horse accelerated and the body dragged behind. The dead Russian didn't look like a real person, more like a wooden manikin, his entire frame rigid, arms and legs stiff as boards. He bounced and twisted – face up, then face down – ploughing unruly furrows in the snow.

'He'll break up in no time!' exclaimed Anton. He too had clambered on to his chair. Mama and Frau Hillier turned as one and pulled the children from their vantage points, their faces sick-looking and pale.

Soon afterwards Mama decided they should go home. Schosi followed them to the gate. He grasped Ursula's sleeve and tried to say something but his stutter got the better of him. She shrugged him off and then felt a little sorry. She smiled to make up for it, which seemed to delight him. He waved until his mother came and brought him inside.

—

'Herr Esterbauer's in love. Did you see the way he looked at her?' said Dorli once they were on their way, going via the field to avoid following in the path of the corporal's horse, not wishing to think what might be left along that route. They walked hurriedly, Mama a little way ahead, glancing nervously about. 'And he takes care of her boy at the farm even though he doesn't have to. Schosi's such a nuisance, but I suppose Herr Esterbauer's blind to it. That's love.'

'Do you think so?' said Ursula, not quite understanding how two such old and ugly people could be in love. They weren't anything like the courting couples she'd seen. Frau Hillier didn't even smile.

'Oh yes, I'm sure of it.'

'But she's fat,' said Anton flatly, 'and smells as bad as her idiot son. I don't want to think about her in the nip.'

'Anton, you're too much!' said Dorli, half offended, half entertained. 'I never thought about *him* in the nip either!' She giggled, drawing Mama's eye. 'Do you think they do it, then?' she whispered.

'I bet they roll about in the hay,' said Ursula, 'at the farm!'

Dorli clamped a hand to her mouth, eyes shining. It was good to joke, to forget the fretful and broken night.

'Don't talk like that!' hissed Anton. 'It's vulgar. I hate it when you speak like that.'

'I didn't mean it.' Ursula was instantly dismayed. She'd displeased him. But she hadn't been the only one – Dorli had spoken too and Anton himself. 'I was only playing,' she protested. But Anton refused to respond and strode vigorously along – he'd never been able to bear it if she was in any way crude. A crackle of gunfire came from somewhere ahead, difficult to place, echoing and indistinct amongst the rocky peaks of the hills, the salt and pepper of snow and pine forest. Mama stopped to wait for them, gathered them together with arms interlinked. They skied down the incline as they neared their house, boots filling with snow. Anton clutched Ursula's arm, his bandaged arm held protectively to his stomach, the old rifle across his back. They reached the gate just as more scattered shots came from the direction of the Fingerlos house. Dorli began to cry.

'Hurry!' said Mama, ushering them across the yard. They bundled into the house and Mama bolted the doors and all the shutters, blocking out the sun so that they had to light lanterns to be able to see. Mama gave them each tasks to occupy them and Ursula was soon situated in the chilly scullery pressing Anton's shirts. The thin squeak of the rollers, high-pitched and continual, did nothing to calm her but at least she was doing something with her hands. Her mind was free to wander again to that gloomy scene in the yard and to her brother's placid face, puzzling and unnerving because it showed her nothing. His furious whisper when she'd spoken coarsely. She was glad now to help neaten his clothes. It made her feel nearer to him.

They were just as anxious by evening and hungry. They hadn't been to the village for rations as they usually would and were making do with a scant meal of potatoes, greens and onions accompanied by a brass band on the wireless, and a report about the bravery of German troops. There was plenty of disdainful talk about the quailing disorganised Russians. Something was mentioned about the temporary retreat of the Wehrmacht in Eastern Europe; but victory was imminent, they would prevail, the

Russians were falling in thousands. And they fall outside in ones and twos, thought Ursula, the fatless vegetables half chewed in her mouth tasting suddenly revolting. Before they'd finished eating Herr Esterbauer arrived. He brought bread for them and news.

'Have they caught them?' said Mama. 'Is it safe to come out?'

'Did you see any shot?' said Anton.

Herr Esterbauer shook his head, and it wasn't clear which question he was responding to, or whether he simply meant that he didn't wish to answer. 'School tomorrow – everything will be as normal. Please come to work, Frau Hildesheim.' He sucked his moustache for a moment. 'But it's not over yet.'

After he'd gone, Anton said that Herr Esterbauer had probably seen men screaming for mercy and executions in the village and now he was going to rejoin the hunt. Ursula thought about when deer were flushed out of the forest in culling season, how they buckled and flipped in the sweep of the wooden hunting towers.

That night, Anton asked Ursula to come to him before sleeping. She crept along the balcony to his room, avoiding the planks that groaned or rattled loosely. She climbed into his bed to lie beside him and it was almost like normal again, like before Papa died, except that he spoke to her less. She smoothed his hair, the lantern at low wick. He shut his eyes, took her hand, rested against her. She watched his face, the pearlescent lids fragile and flickering, the shadow of his lashes forming a lattice on his cheek, the slope of his nose with its broad bone that cut close to the skin.

'Stay with me,' he muttered, his mouth squashed against her arm. She waited for him to fall asleep but it was a long time until his hand stopped gripping hers and he rolled away beneath the eiderdown.

Schosi waited while his mama got the belt; he cried and said he was sorry but she said she had no choice; she had to beat him for visiting the Hildesheim place.

'You can't go there,' she said as she came back into the living room. 'You know that.'

'Sorry,' he said again.

She rolled his trousers up above his knees and made him turn his back.

'Now, where are you allowed to go?'

'The farm,' he said.

'And you can go to the woodshed to feed the cats when you're home but nowhere else.'

He waited for the lash but it didn't come straight away.

'I don't like to do this, little mouse,' she said softly. 'I will only do three.' She paused. 'It's to keep you safe.'

She whipped the belt against his legs and he yelped. Pain flared on his calves and the smacking noise frightened him.

'Hush,' she said.

She whipped again harder then struck him a third time. Schosi wasn't sure if another lash would come. He couldn't count.

'All right,' said his mama. She turned him by his shoulders to face her. Several tears rolled down her cheeks. 'Sorry, Schatzi.' She took his hand. 'Now you stay here and say your prayers and think about what you've done. You're a good boy really but you must obey me.'

She went to put the belt away. Schosi looked at the painting of the Holy Mary that hung on the living-room wall opposite the portrait of the Führer, which his mama said was an ugly thing. He thought so too and averted his eyes from the stern and narrow face. Instead he looked at the vivid blue and gold of Mary's dress and knelt to pray and clasped his hands together. His legs were hot and sore. He asked Mary and Baby Christ to forgive him. He'd only wanted to make friends with the girl, Ursula. She was nice and smiled at him.

His mama came back and stroked his bowed head. 'Don't cry, my little rabbit. You're a big boy now so stop crying.' But she sniffed herself and patted her cheeks with the bottom of her apron.

After a moment Schosi turned to look at her. 'I want to have a friend,' he said.

She put her arms around him. 'But you do have a friend,' she soothed. 'Herr Esterbauer is kind to you. You're his favourite.'

Schosi nodded. But it wasn't the same as when he played with Ursula.

'And that brother of hers means you harm. You should avoid him.'

Schosi wiped his nose on his sleeve. He didn't like Anton – he was frightening.

'I'll make you something hot to drink,' said his mama and went off. 'Come into the kitchen to get warm, Schatzi. It's cold in here.'

He stayed kneeling for a while and thought about how the house wasn't only cold but silent too when his mama was at work. He was to go to the farm three times a week. On the other days he was to stay inside or go to the woodshed to see if the cats needed company and fill the log basket. He wept a little more. He wished he could see Ursula. Once or twice when she'd come to the farm she'd said hello instead of ignoring him like other people did. He'd enjoyed listening to her speak and the game of throwing sticks from the bridge. He liked her quick blue eyes that reminded him of chips of stone and her gold plaits covered in flyaway down. There were hairs on her legs too – little white ones like on the underside of a pumpkin leaf.

He went to the kitchen to join his mama and she gave him a cup of hot milk.

'I don't want to lose you, son,' she said, sitting at the table. 'There are bad people out there who don't understand, who think cruel things and don't care about you.' She squeezed his forearm. 'It's up to me to make sure you're safe.'

In the evening Herr Esterbauer called on his way back from the Hildesheims'. Schosi's mama answered the door and the farmer handed her a small pot and something wrapped in paper. They stood on the step for a while and Schosi watched them from the kitchen. Herr Esterbauer reached out to Schosi's mama and tucked some of her hair behind her ear. Then he leaned forward and kissed her. Schosi couldn't tell whether it was on the cheek or on the lips. She stepped backwards into the house and Herr Esterbauer stayed on the doorstep, looking ill at ease. The adults said a few more things, which Schosi couldn't hear, then Herr Esterbauer touched his hat and walked away. Schosi's mama shut the door and brought the pot and package to the table. In the pot was pork dripping – thick, grainy and delicious, and in the paper were six pieces of finest bacon.

Ursula was in a bad temper the following day when she and Anton walked to school, ice melting from the twigs, fat droplets puncturing the snow. The morning had been fraught and chaotic after another restless night of shallow sleep.

'He did his duty in a crisis,' Mama had said over breakfast. 'They're bad people. They're locked up for a reason.' She'd dabbed her eyes then screwed up her handkerchief and made a bony fist. 'And maybe your papa's soul can rest a little easier now.' Amongst her tears, Dorli's nagging and Anton's goading, Ursula had become preoccupied with the unjustness of the fact that everything she wore was no good. Cold wetness seeped through to her socks because her boots were full of holes. Her skirt was hastily darned in far too many places. She'd torn it again last week on a nail in the cowshed and Mama had made a hash of the repair, a large, lumpy patch of wrong-coloured thread that deformed the cotton and that Ursula would have to try to conceal with her hand once she arrived at school.

Marta Fingerlos ran from her house to join them, the bright flash of new leather around her feet and ankles, her dress devoid of clots of thread, and Ursula's misery deepened. She covered the blemish on her skirt with her satchel but even this was an embarrassment, the leather darkened and cracked with a long curling strap that hung like a tail. If only something of hers was smart. She anticipated with heavy heart the calls of 'Gypsy' or 'Ragbag'. Marta would abandon her at the school gates, as was agreed; it really was too much to ask her to become tainted as well.

'Hello, Anton!' Marta called, fluttering her fingertips. He didn't reply but instead sped up. He didn't like Ursula's friend who he said was a spoiled brat with a duty-shirking father who should be at the Front instead of pretending to be ill. Herr Fingerlos was well enough to keep a mistress and bastard in Lillienfeld so he ought to be well enough to fight. Marta registered the snub with a few blinks of her eyelashes then turned to Ursula. 'I heard you saw a dead man. What was it like?'

'Ever so scary.' Marta widened her eyes, thrilled. She had an endless appetite for drama and while Ursula could hold forth and entertain her or listen to one of Marta's own intrigues, then all was well between them. Marta nudged her in the ribs, eyes gleaming.

'You tell first, then I'll tell what happened to me.'

Ursula described the SS corporal and his pistol, the dark and frenzied dash across the fields, the sound of shots, her brother's brave battle one-handed against the knife-wielding prisoner who aimed to stab them all. 'He shot him straight through the heart,' she said as a final flourish.

'Really?' Marta gawped at Anton, who trudged ten metres in front, as if he might sprout claws and horns and turn and devour them. Then she insisted on hearing every detail about the body and the blood, which Ursula valiantly provided, ignoring the awful sensations that lingered in her, queasy and unsettling like a nightmare that remains in the morning.

Then Marta began her own story. 'The SS corporal came to our house too, and Herr Esterbauer killed two men in the field. Papa fired at shadows and thought the trees were people and shot at them. I've never seen him look so wild – he drank three glasses of schnapps afterwards.' Marta twirled her pigtails and chewed them like a baby, lips wet with saliva. 'Toni's very courageous,' she cooed, watching Anton. Ursula felt irritated. She wished Marta wouldn't call him Toni.

They reached the road – here the snow was churned oatmeal, frozen chunks turned over into the gutters. Workers moved towards the factory, abnormally silent. The newspaper seller didn't shout as loudly as usual. Marta freed her arm from Ursula's, widened the gap between them until it appeared they did not walk together at all. There were calls of 'Hey! Hey!' as several boys saw Anton and came to absorb him into their ranks. A football rolled from boot to boot, Anton's bandage snowy-white when he pulled up his coat to show them. Rudi was there, a friend of Anton's. He was Viennese, evacuated six months ago. He'd seen terrible things – bodies twitching in pieces after a bomb. His parents were dead. But he always laughed when he told about it so Ursula thought he mustn't care that much. Herr Adler, who housed Rudi, beat him as hard as he could but it did no good – Rudi stole and fought daily. Ursula dawdled, allowing Marta to increase still further the distance between them. Rudi was much like Anton, she thought. Her brother too brawled regularly. But he did it to defend the Hildesheim name.

At school there was a special announcement before lessons began. Herr Gruber stood in front of the class and clicked his heels together between sentences, which indicated the seriousness of the topic, and stared about from behind his crooked glasses.

'Today is a difficult day for the village,' he said. 'And the last thing we want is unruly children getting in the way. None of you are to leave the school grounds at break time and if you hear any disturbance don't go gawping at the fence, because you'll most likely see something you don't want to. Leave the authorities to get on with the job in hand.'

Herr Gruber said he'd appreciate there being no gossiping and unseemly behaviour. There was a war on and they should conduct themselves like respectable German citizens. He handed out their exercise books.

But, of course, at morning break there was tale-telling aplenty and huddles of children gathered around those with something to report. Ursula joined a knot of children, which included Marta.

'My mama saw a man this morning by the beehives in the orchard, looking for honey.' The girl who spoke was one of Marta's friends; she wore a dirndl that strained at the seams and Ursula wondered how she could be so fat in these frugal times. 'Mama shouted, "You! What are you doing?" and he ran away.' The girl looked around at everyone. 'He had on striped clothes so he must have been one of them.'

Another child, one of the youngest Siedler boys, was forced to tell all, though he looked tearful and as if he'd rather not.

'The SS man searched through the straw in our barn.' He was timorous in front of the gathered crowd. 'And Papa went through it with his pitchfork. He stabbed the Russian and I heard him screaming.' His lip began to tremble. 'He had a jar of dripping under his arm and his mouth was full of food he'd nicked from our larder.'

'See!' The older boys were triumphant. 'He must've been in their house. Imagine, a thieving Russki in your pantry, sneaking about while you're in bed.'

Ursula gasped involuntarily, imagining the stranger – desperate, violent. But then she remembered the dead man and how wretched he'd looked, the emaciated limbs brittle as tinder, not menacing at all, only sad and disgusting.

'Tell your story!' Marta instructed Ursula.

When Ursula shook her head, embarrassed by the assembly of faces that turned to stare at her, Marta told it for her, giving much emphasis to Anton's bravery. 'I mean it's lucky Toni is a good shot!' she exclaimed. 'The man was a criminal and quite mad.'

'They're not criminals,' said a sturdy boy with a bowl haircut who Ursula didn't recognise. 'Auntie says they're officers in the Red Army and that they're being murdered. Shamefully.'

There was a babble of surprise. 'What do you know?' somebody scoffed.

'They're thieves. They broke into houses.'

The sturdy boy turned to face the speaker. 'They're starving,' he said. 'Wouldn't you?'

There was uproar as the older boys began to argue. 'Commie! Russki-lover!' they cried. 'Auntie's a batty old witch!' In the upheaval the sturdy boy slipped away and Ursula saw him enter the school through the side door.

After the group had disbanded, she and Marta went to their hiding place, which was at the back of the school rubbish bins. Tucked between the bins and the wall they could play without being seen. This was a luxury not often bestowed by Marta. She brought out her paper doll, a game they were far too old for, but fun none the less. Ursula had forgotten hers in the bedlam of the morning, so they made do with one.

'Who was that boy?' said Ursula. 'The one with the bowl haircut. Is he new?' She'd liked his broad, healthy face with freckled nose and wide elastic mouth. His eyes were dark and slanted, like an animal of some kind. He was very beautiful.

'He's from Wiener Neustadt,' said Marta. 'He's come to live with his aunt. I think his family were killed. His name's Sepp.' She paraded the paper doll in the snow, sashaying its hips in a salacious manner. She'd pencilled breasts on to its dress-front. 'Oh, Sepp,' she said, in a honeyed tone. 'How lovely to see you.' Ursula reddened and folded her arms across her chest. She hated to be mocked. Marta could be cruel. Marta walked the fingers of her other hand towards the doll pretending they were a pair of legs. She used a deep voice, 'May I have the pleasure of being your Confirmation partner?'

'Don't be silly,' said Ursula. She prickled with embarrassment.

The doll and fingers danced, then pressed together for a kiss.

'Perhaps I'll have him as *my* partner,' said Marta. She flicked a glance at Ursula.

Ursula forced a smile. 'Perhaps,' she said. Of course Marta wanted him; she wanted every novel thing. And usually she got her way.

Marta discarded the doll and prattled on about preparation classes, the expensive lace on her Confirmation dress – her relative was a haberdasher in Vienna – and the delightful gifts she'd get from her mentor. All this would impress the boys, she said; her hand flopped about on its milky wrist. She eyed Ursula. Ursula adopted an uncaring look. She'd no interest in Sepp in any case, she told herself. She picked up the doll. She bent its leg into a jagged shape; she wanted to tear it. Instead she tossed it aside, deliberately beyond the shelter of the wall so that it caught a gust of wind and skittered off. Marta gave a cry and scarpered after it with hands outstretched. Ursula felt very slightly better.

Later that day there was shooting outside the school, not far away, and the class ran to the windows to see. Ursula saw droves of people hurrying. A small throng gathered and a few grey-clad SS men waved their arms and bellowed orders.

'Sit down!' yelled the teacher.

In dribs and drabs, the children returned to their desks. But they couldn't concentrate for the remainder of the lesson and the teacher was shaken and distracted. When there was another shot, startlingly loud, a boy stood up near the window and looked outside.

'There's blood on the snow!' he squawked.

Ursula's heart beat hard and she sweated. She looked at the girl who shared her desk, a dull child called Annaliese who'd been told that Ursula had fleas and was terrified of accidentally touching her. The girl returned the look surreptitiously then bent close to her exercise book as though inspecting every fibre of it.

The day was further disturbed when a loudspeaker, mounted on an army vehicle, drove past the school. The teacher's voice was drowned by the announcement that blared forth in High German.

Two dozen prisoners have escaped from the concentration camp. They pose a great danger for the population. They must be rendered harmless at once. None are to be taken captive – all are to be destroyed on sight.

This caused mayhem – even Herr Gruber went to the window and watched the van as it crawled the length of the road, repeating the threat of *Assistance – death. Concealment – death*. After a moment he turned round.

'Class dismissed,' he said in a quiet, croaky voice.

He went for his own coat as quickly as the children ran for theirs and there was pandemonium along the row of coat pegs. Everyone bolted, pushing, yelling and squealing, Ursula amongst them. Herr Gruber shouted for them to hurry home and to stay together in groups, his warning almost drowned by the uproar, a small vessel whisked away on the flood.

Outside, swastika flags on the fronts of houses billowed like flamboyant skirts as a military truck fired its engine and pulled away from the kerb. Beyond it, figures ran to and fro. Shouts rang near the Rathaus. Ursula stopped, seeing Sepp's face at one of the classroom windows – he and the older children were still inside. He gestured to her, pointing then beckoning. She turned to see the army truck roaring towards her, exhaust fumes rising and expanding. She scrambled to the verge. People stood along the road in the wake of the truck and stared after it. Anton appeared beside her, breathless, as the vehicle neared, the chains on the tyres rattling and crunching on stones beneath the snow. The back of the truck drew level. Dead men lay on the truck-bed. Some were naked or semi-clothed, some clad in the stripes of the camp – a confusing tangle of dirty skin and hair. It was unclear what was what or how many there were. Bare feet dangled over the sides of the truck and bounced as the vehicle went over a pothole. One of the men was alive and half sat, struggling to raise himself amongst the dead, his face bruised and swollen. His wasted arms failed to hold his weight – he fell back. Anton stared, tense and eager, then clamped a hand over Ursula's eyes and pulled her to his chest. She buried her face in his neck; her heart thudded and her whole body tingled with shock. She felt sick. It was awful; they were so pitiful and ugly. She remembered what Sepp had said. He'd said that the prisoners weren't criminals, but officers. He'd said that they were being murdered. And what else had he said? He'd used a word – a bold word, a defiant word. Shamefully. He'd said that the officers were being murdered shamefully. He'd spoken without caution. Ursula struggled to free herself from Anton's grip, to get another look, but he squashed her face with his hand so that she couldn't move. A smell like the butcher's shop wafted along the road, cloying and metallic, the same smell as Papa's old hunting clothes, or a gutted rabbit, or blood spurting in a hot jet across the farmyard, the pig's life flying out of a hole in its neck.

4

The car arrived at the house just after dark – obsidian black, faint light sliding along curvaceous panels and wheel arches. Ursula watched through the gap in the shutters – the small round headlights swept beams across the yard and flashed into her eyes; wide running boards flared along the length of the vehicle. The rest of the family were in the kitchen listening to the wireless – another broadcast about the war and the position of the Red Army. Ursula had tried to listen, but the Hungarian place names all blurred into one and she lost concentration. She only knew that the Russians approached and that everyone dreaded them. She had slipped away and taken one of Dorli's magazines into the living room, curled up on the window seat and immersed herself in the cheerful and resolute world of the League of German Girls. At the sound of an engine she started. At first she'd thought it was a plane overhead. No one drove a vehicle down their track. These days almost everyone rode bicycles and many had reverted to horse-drawn traps and carts. People dreamed of the day when they could start their motors again – tractors stood uselessly beside farms, trucks were covered with canvas, gathering leaves and bird droppings. There was very little fuel. The Hildesheim car had been pushed inside the barn and the cats slept within the torn upholstery.

Outside the window, the bumper of the extraordinary car gleamed as it halted beside the fence. The engine stopped, the lights extinguished and the yard was plunged into darkness. The driver-side door opened and a man climbed out. As Ursula's eyes adjusted to the light she could see that his upper lip was covered with a dark moustache. He wore a smart hat that tilted low over his brow. The black car, the smart clothes: Gestapo. Ursula tried to think if anything had been said, if Mama had broken the rules. She'd stayed home from work duty after Papa was killed, but just for a day. Sweat broke out on her palms. The man walked towards the house. She clambered from the window seat, crossed the floor and stood just behind the door of the living room, where she could spy through the crack at the hinge. His knock echoed along the hallway and Ursula heard her sister's voice, the bang of the kitchen door and the thud of hurrying feet. Dorli flashed by, housecoat flapping. She spoke through the panelling of the door.

'Hello?'

'Hello,' the man replied quietly. 'Can you please tell me, does Mali Hildesheim still live at this address?'

'Yes,' said Dorli. 'And who can I say is calling?'

'Fischinger – Fischinger Siegfried. I was a friend of Leo's. I've come to offer my condolences.'

'Oh,' said Dorli. After a moment's hesitation she opened the door.

'Hello,' said the man again. 'It's Dorli, isn't it?'

'Yes.'

'You probably don't remember me – you were very young. I've helped Leo over the years. Papers, accounts, that sort of thing.' Ursula caught a glimpse of gloved fingertips wafting nonchalantly up and down, the man himself still tantalisingly out of sight. 'I used to visit quite often. Such a lovely house. I've fond memories of it.'

'Oh, it's not a lovely house,' said Dorli, self-conscious. She took a step back into the hall. 'Come in and sit down if you'd like. I'll call Mama.'

Siegfried Fischinger came into the hall. Ursula thought her sister wasn't being very careful. If she'd opened the door herself she'd have made him wait outside.

The light flicked on in the room where Ursula stood and the bulb threw a triangular shadow behind the door. She darted to the window and climbed on to the window seat. Dorli asked the man whether he would take tea or coffee. 'Or schnapps maybe?'

'Wonderful, thank you.'

Ursula drew the curtains slowly, quietly. She was concealed. She leaned against the wall and drew her knees close to her body so that she felt small and safe.

Dorli's footsteps went off down the hallway and into the kitchen. There was a short blare from the wireless as the kitchen door opened and then closed again. There was no sound from the man at first. Then there was the slow click-clack of his shoes on the floorboards. His tread became muffled as he crossed the rug in front of the fireplace. Then the click-clack again as he strolled over to the bookshelves and the display cabinets. Ursula was tempted to peep out, thinking the man might have his back turned, studying the Czechoslovakian glasses and ashtray, the tiny bird made of silver and the shepherd and shepherdess. But she resisted. What if he'd pivoted on the smooth sole of his shoe and stood facing the window? Ursula let her breath in and out, shallow and slow.

Mama arrived after a brief delay. It had taken her some time to make herself presentable. They hadn't been expecting any visitors.

'Goodness me,' she said as she entered the room. 'Siegfried.'

The two kissed on both cheeks. Ursula offered up a thankful prayer that the man was clearly not here to arrest her.

'It's been such a long time,' said Mama. 'Seven years? Eight? I can hardly believe it. Come and sit down. Will you have a drink?'

'I already have one,' said Siegfried. 'Your daughter was most efficient.'

'Well, do sit down, please.'

The settle creaked.

'Take off your hat,' said Mama. 'Look as though you're staying.'

Ursula heard a rustle as Siegfried took off his coat, hat and gloves.

'But you'll have something to eat, of course?' said Mama. 'We have some bread or I could make a pancake. Sorry, I don't have much. You know how it is.'

'Gone are the days of your fabulous cakes. But no, I'm not hungry.'

'Are you sure? It's no trouble. It won't take a moment. A little bread. I have goat's cheese.'

She was making a fuss of him – Ursula supposed she was excited because hardly anyone came to see them any more.

'No, thank you, Frau Hildesheim.'

'But you always used to have a good appetite.'

'Yes, but I'm absolutely fine.'

Mama was quiet.

'So,' she said, after a moment. Her voice had worry in it. 'What brings you here? Not bad news, I hope?'

'No. Nothing bad. I just wanted to offer you my condolences about Leo. I thought I could perhaps make things easier, now that you're on your own.' Siegfried paused. 'I was very sorry to hear about it.'

'Yes,' said Mama.

'It must've been a terrible shock,' said Siegfried.

'It was, yes,' said Mama.

'It was a shock for me too.' Siegfried sounded awkward.

'Yes,' said Mama. 'I understand.'

'I'd very much like to do something to help. In his memory, as such.'

'Well, that's a kind sentiment,' said Mama politely.

'I know he kept his own books. I could help with his accounts.'

'Yes,' said Mama with a laugh. 'Almost certainly. He was useless with figures.'

'There're so many pitfalls, what with the contributions that're expected,' said Siegfried. 'Even from a small place like this. I could simply check that all would be in order if you were to be inspected.'

'Oh dear, yes.'

'Herr Esterbauer still rents the top field?'

'Yes.'

'Well, I could draw up some thorough documents, to ensure that there're no problems. I'm sure Esterbauer's an honest sort of chap but you never know. And as for Leo's estate, there may be ends that need tying. The inheritance, it goes to you of course. So, then—'

Siegfried stopped.

Mama made a small hiccuping sound.

'Frau Hildesheim,' said Siegfried. 'I'm sorry.'

'No, no.' Mama's voice was choked with tears. 'It must be done. It's just that I'm so thankful. For the help.'

'Of course. It's no problem.'

'It's kind,' said Mama. She made an effort to bring her voice under control. 'There's so much that Leo used to do. And though we've only a small place, I've needed all my time just to manage it these last few years. Herr Esterbauer's good to me, but I find it hard.' There was the sound of Mama getting up and then her footsteps. 'Leo's Will and other papers are kept in the bureau – you're welcome to look.' The roll-top lid rattled as she opened it. The bureau was where Papa had often stationed himself with an air of reluctant determination a few evenings a week, his dark head bowed before the reading lamp, gold light shining through his hair. He'd always shuffled and sighed in his seat. 'Leo's father left money, too,' said Mama. 'But it's hardly worth drawing out. It killed him, I'm sure of it – all his efforts reduced to a heap of useless paper.'

'Many people have faced the same, the country over.'

They talked on about money for a while, about the economy and the Reichsmark and how they'd had higher hopes for Hitler and what he could deliver. This kind of conversation when it'd been between Mama and Papa had always ended in Papa snarling something about the Yid leeches and Mama remarking that in their case it had more to do with his weakness for cards. Ursula's mind drifted to thoughts of the new boy, Sepp, with his strange opinions and careless mouth. She liked the name, neat but soft, short for Josef, a gentle name. He was a year older than she was, Anton's age. He had a friendly, handsome appearance, she thought. The shape of his eyes and the gloss of his bowl-cut dark hair were particularly nice. Her stomach lurched oddly as she pictured his broad cheekbones and strong brow, and somewhere in the pit of her a glow began. She wriggled, uneasy because of the intensity of the pleasure. It wasn't the same feeling as when Anton held her beneath the blankets and told her she was his best girl. It had a life of its own, starting in her lower abdomen and spreading downwards to become a softening heat between her legs.

Mama sighed. 'This war – I hate it. I used to have such faith.'

'And the children?'

'Dorli's going to be married, God willing. It doesn't matter too much that we've only a few bits and bobs for her dowry – the man in question isn't short of money. So, she's a relief.' She paused as though thinking. 'Anton's grown up wild. You mightn't be surprised. But I don't understand him. Ursula follows his every example – you remember how she always doted on him, even as a toddler. I do worry about her. It seems nothing can correct her.'

Ursula flinched at the hopeless tone in her mother's voice. Was she really so bad?

'I'm sure we were the same,' said Siegfried. 'I spent all my time playing in ditches and refusing to be told. My mother wrung her hands till they were creased.'

Mama made a quiet sound, like 'Hmm', mixed with a small laugh. 'And now look,' she said. 'Quite a success.'

'Oh, hardly.'

'You're better off than any person around here. And that car. I'm sure the heads are really turning.'

'Perhaps.'

There was a long silence. Ursula breathed softly for fear of being heard; she was ravenous and her stomach threatened to emit a loud, demanding wail at any moment. The night air came coldly through the shutters and the thin pane of the window, and an icy draught trickled from the join in the sash. Her knees ached, locked in their bent position, and she longed to straighten them.

'You should've visited,' said Mama.

'It wasn't easy.'

'Leo used to talk of you all the time. Then nothing, as though you'd never been known here.' Mama had adopted an unnervingly personal tone. 'And you were just as bad,' she added. 'Throwing it all away without so much as another word.'

'I couldn't stand it, Mali,' Siegfried said. Ursula cringed even more at the use of her mother's forename. 'A man should respect his wife and that's the end of it. I couldn't pretend not to care.'

What were they talking of? Who was this person who seemed to know Mama so well, spoke to her as if they had an understanding, a bond that'd been formed years before Ursula's memory began? After a moment she heard the clink of Siegfried's glass being placed on the coffee table.

'I'd do the same – I'd say the same, even now. I saw too much of it from my father. And you – I'm upsetting you,' said Siegfried. 'Of course.' His voice was brusque. 'I'm sorry.'

59

Mama seemed to have turned mute.

The silence lengthened, and Ursula waited. She felt a cough tickling her chest, but she willed it away, screwed her eyes tightly shut. Her legs were beginning to hurt in earnest. There were a few sighs from the grown-ups and she used their cover to move just a little before the cramp became too acute. She slowly stretched her legs and placed her feet against the wall. Blood fizzed into her veins. She winced.

'Mali,' said Siegfried. The settle made little cracking sounds as somebody shifted their weight along it. 'I thought of you.'

There was silence again. Ursula was close to despair: the adults didn't appear to be about to leave and she'd soon have to come out of her hiding place and face the consequences; her bladder was full, her knees throbbed, and she was perishing from cold. Mama would demand to know what she was playing at, spying in her own home, and she'd be mortified in front of the stranger. But just as she was truly starting to panic, her prayers were answered and Siegfried stood up.

'I should go,' he said. His shoes were audible again on the floorboards.

Mama and he came very close to the curtains behind which Ursula was hiding. She heard them clearing their throats. Ursula stopped breathing; her heart pumped hard in her chest.

'So, you'll call again?' said Mama. She sounded gloomy.

'Of course,' said Siegfried. 'I'll come in a few weeks.' The hinge on the door creaked. 'I can work on the papers right away.'

'Thank you.'

'It's nothing,' said Siegfried. 'For an old friend.'

The two of them went out into the hallway and the living-room door closed behind them. There was an awkward muffled goodbye.

After a moment Ursula heard the engine splutter outside and a soft toot of the horn. She peeped through the shutters to see the car pull out of the yard and retreat into the night, its rear lights bobbing on the bumpy track. A yellow electric glow fell on to the doorstep from inside the house. After a moment Mama closed the front door and the light disappeared. Ursula dropped softly from the windowsill and made her escape up the stairs.

5

The hunt continued over the following weeks – several prisoners remained uncaptured having taken small valueless items necessary for their escape, such as clothing to disguise their identity, and food. This hat or those boots were discovered to be missing, and reported to the police, presumed stolen. It was rumoured that someone locally may have hidden one of the dangerous men, aiding the getaway and risking all of their lives. House inspections were more regular and thorough. Searches were made further afield. Ursula's house was visited twice more by SS and local farmers, and the loudspeaker still blared its warning through the village. However, most of the Russians had been killed or returned to the camp and killed there. Ursula began to tire of the topic; it had been interesting to hear of it for a while but it was all anybody talked about, a veritable babble coming from the queue at the grocer's when she passed on her way to school, or when she ran errands to collect rations. It seemed that the Russians had done little real damage to property or people; only Anton had received a cut in Frau Hillier's yard – no one else had been attacked. But the stories were told again and again; captures and killings and sightings in gardens, complete with grisly details, the drama increasing with each repetition. Herr Siedler, the richest of the Felddorf farmers, had shot a Russian who knelt pleading before him. His hand hadn't trembled and the inmate had crumpled like an empty sack. The local butcher had beaten a prisoner senseless inside his shop with a leg of pork, before hailing the SS to finish the job. The butcher's daughter had been heard to say, 'Carve him up on our block, it would be a fitting end.' Herr Adler had blown a hole the size of a dinner plate in a man's stomach using a shotgun from not a foot away and Herr Esterbauer, with steady hand and eye, had taken down two men running in the near dark, a testament to his excellent abilities with a gun. Frau Hillier had made her outrage known to Herr Esterbauer by storming up to his farmhouse and hammering on the door, much to the consternation of Mama who'd been working near by. 'What kind of man are you?' she demanded. She was ushered inside. Frau Hillier was no less audible once the door was closed. 'How could you finish them like dogs? They were helpless. Have you forgotten your God? Can this Party mean so much to you? Erich, I am horrified, just horrified!' Herr Esterbauer's reply was too deep and too quiet for Mama to hear but Frau Hillier tore from the house, cheeks blotched white with rage and grief, and didn't stop when Herr Esterbauer bellowed after her from the door.

Even Frau Gerg, the head of the League of German Girls, was praised, despite her unpopularity, for her pluck with riding whip and pistol, preventing a cowardly prisoner from scaling the fence to re-enter the camp and evade his punishment.

Anton had his picture taken and was celebrated in his Hitler Youth brigade. His photo was displayed in the glass-fronted cabinet in the Hitler Youth meeting hall, and he received an early promotion to section leader. He was presented with a lavishly decorated ceremonial dagger that symbolised his new rank. He showed the dagger to Ursula when he got home, angling the blade to catch the light, eyes shining with pride.

'It's a good job that Hillier boy stays away these days,' he said. 'I can't have my sister hanging around with someone like that – I have to set a good example.'

It was a quiet Saturday with an unusual air of contentment. Ursula and Anton had finished their chores and lounged on the rug in the living room throwing dice and thinking up forfeits, a rare moment when Anton wasn't busy with his Hitler Youth duties or playing football with his friends. Mama was on the settle with her sewing spread out, Dorli was at a League social and wasn't around to pester or nag them. Mama had even plaited Ursula's hair, the firm tug and shivery scrape of her fingernails sending Ursula into a blissful stupor. Mama hadn't yet tutted or told them to grow up or to do something worthwhile.

Just after midday the spell was broken. Siegfried arrived in his car and as soon as Mama heard the distinctive engine she put her sewing to one side and hurried to the door. A blast of cold air blew into the house and kept on blowing, lifting Ursula's skirt into the shape of a bell, and wafting Mama's half-mended petticoat to the floor. Ursula leaned to one side until she glimpsed the long black bonnet nosing into its parking place. A moment later Siegfried was in the hall.

'Hello!' he called. 'Hello!'

Whenever he arrived, which was often, he always sounded like a hooting owl – too cheerful somehow, too keen. He kissed Mama on each cheek, making extravagant lip-smacking sounds.

'What a surprise!' said Mama.

'I hope you don't mind,' said Siegfried.

'Not at all.'

He popped his head around the doorframe, gave the children a salute. His teeth appeared. The adults went off towards the kitchen, Siegfried complaining about the roads and the potholes that were getting worse and worse.

'Brilliant,' said Anton. 'Him again.'

Anton's almost instant aversion to the man had grown stronger and Ursula wondered what he'd found that annoyed him so much. Siegfried had only brief encounters with the children; his appearance always heralded unceremonious expulsion for Ursula and Anton, no matter what the weather, giving them little chance to get an impression of him. Perhaps it was the fact of being chucked out that bothered Anton? She studied him for a moment; he stared ferociously at the carpet and then glanced out of the window. The trees were flecked with stubborn snow – a cold day to be outdoors, but nothing out of the ordinary. She decided she'd find her coat and scarf in readiness. She got up and went into the hall. Muffled voices came from behind the kitchen door and snatches of laughter. She lingered for a moment – it was good to hear her mother happy.

'I shouldn't bother if I were you,' called Anton from the living room. 'They don't want you in there.'

She moved away, humiliated, and searched for her scarf on the row of coat hooks. She found it hidden beneath Siegfried's black trench coat and hat and lifted them out of the way to an adjacent peg. They were very heavy; the hat was particularly fine. She loved the red lining of the coat, silken and cool, like dipping her hand into a pool in summertime. She pulled his wallet from the inner pocket, took a note and several coins and crushed them in her palm. Guilt and thrill heated her body and kicked her heartbeat into a fast canter. She retrieved her scarf. Mama laughed in the kitchen.

It wasn't long until they were ejected.

'All right, children,' said Mama, clapping her hands briskly. 'Out with you.'

'But why?' Anton groaned.

'No arguing,' said Mama. 'Off you go! Be sure to be back by dark or you'll miss dinner.'

Out in the yard the bolt slid secretively into place behind them. Anton cursed and strode at a frightful pace away from the house. Ursula trotted to keep up. They collected short skis from the shed, and ski poles, and set out across the field towards the pool.

'Damn her!' Anton shouted over his shoulder as they swished noisily along, fine snowflakes swirling across the hill to sting their faces. 'I'm not going back.'

'What do you mean?' called Ursula above the rushing air. She was hungry already and dinner would be a good one. Last time Siegfried had brought all sorts of expensive things like butter and high quality smoked ham, and a bar of perfumed soap (though of course you couldn't eat that). She'd never smelled anything so lovely.

At a gap in the trees they pitched themselves down the snow-covered bank, reached the bottom without encountering any devious loops of bramble, and stopped beside the river. Ursula propped her skis against a tree trunk and went to the edge of the bank where she squatted and leaned over, feeling for one of the icicles. At this time of year an army of them plunged from the frozen mud of the overhang. She chose a large one and snapped it off at the base, held it in her mittened hand like the long tooth of an enormous creature and crunched a mouthful. It tasted of rain and grit. She and Anton climbed down to the beach that edged the pool, a crescent of detritus and small stones overshadowed by flat, oval rocks. Ice bulged and furled where it collected over roots.

Tobias Messer had drowned in the river pool the previous year. He was the son of a neighbour, slightly older than Anton, and had got stuck under the ice and then trapped beneath a shelf of rock. A case of stupidity more than bad luck. He'd crossed the ice in early spring and everyone knew that was dangerous. When Tobias was pulled from the water his body was partially frozen and Mama made a point of recounting the details to her children, even though she'd not seen the boy herself. She said his lips were black and his cheeks were blue and that he'd had no chance at all once he was in the bone-numbing water.

'Why must you always play at the river anyway,' she asked them continually, 'when you have so much space?'

But the river was their favourite haunt, nestled amongst the trees, accessible only by narrow deer tracks that wended downwards. Once at water level, the muddy banks formed protective walls and the firs bowed overhead like a scratchy ceiling. It used to be the perfect retreat when the house was awful with anger, with Mama and Papa's frantic shouting that rebounded from the hard floors and the beams, the crash and thud and scuffle that inevitably followed, and then silence. The pine forest was always damp and chill, full of mushroomy smells, the trees unassailable, tall and straight as ship's masts with shaggy black hair and cloaks of ivy or vine – even Anton couldn't get to their tops despite his feats of daring, ending in tumbles, cuts, bruises, a sprained ankle. Dead trunks became bridges and a piece of twine from one side of the stream to the other served as a line for a small red bucket. They loved to sit on opposite banks and send things back and forth.

The river was best in summer when water muttered over the rocks, the shallow flow easily dammed or diverted into narrow runs along which you could race a leaf-boat; such a tranquil, welcoming place. The oval rocks that overhung the pool where Tobias had died were especially wonderful; level platforms covered in ferns like tousled green hair. When the sun was high and unremitting, and Ursula and Anton had baked themselves in the fields gathering hay with the adults, stamping on top of the hay carts to compress the load – sweaty, dusty work – they slipped away as soon as they could for a swim. The rocks were ideal as diving boards or for sunbathing. The river gabbled, never quiet, but peaceful beyond anything, beyond anywhere. Ursula liked to daydream, clothes stiffening in the heat after a swim, drowsily watching the flies that dithered above the water, their wings catching sunlight so that they shone like gold. She often woke to a yell and the crash of Anton's body as it hit the water; naked, long-limbed, his young muscles prominent, the unmarked clarity of his skin stretched tight against his veins. She enjoyed watching him surface, hair sleek to his skull like an otter's, eyes bleary and with water dribbling down his chin. He'd look up at her, surrounded by ripples, each carrying a glaze of creamy light towards the edge of the pool, his nakedness a green-white shape in the deep, and she'd think that no one was as perfect as her brother; no one was quite like him.

'Help me with this,' said Anton. He crouched above a rock, unable to lift it. Ursula took hold of the other side; the rock was large and frozen in quite hard. They wobbled and kicked it until it came free. They swung it between them then threw it as far as they could into the white circle of the frozen pool – it landed with a sharp crack. The river swallowed the stone and the hole in the ice was a black scar.

'At least the fish can breathe now,' said Anton. Ursula smacked him on the arm but he caught her wrist and twisted it until she submitted.

They stayed a while beside the pool breaking off more icicles and aiming pebbles into the hole. Ursula tried to persuade Anton to come back for dinner. He was obstinate; he shook his head.

'You go on,' he said. 'If you want to.'

'Oh, come on. Don't be a bore.'

'I'm not going. I don't want to see Mr City Slicker.'

Ursula had never heard the term 'city slicker' before. She thought it suited Siegfried with his Brylcreemed hair and polished shoes. 'He might be gone.'

'He'll stay for dinner. He'll probably eat as much as he can.'

'That's hardly fair – he gives Mama things. He always brings things.'

'And where does he get it?' Anton said. 'He's crooked.'

'I think he's all right.'

'Do you?' Anton was scornful.

'Yes. It's nice Mama has a friend.'

'Friend? You don't know the half of it.'

'What do you mean?'

'I'm just saying that you don't know what's going on.'

'What do you mean?' said Ursula again, frustrated.

'I've noticed things.'

'What things?'

Anton shrugged.

Ursula battled a sudden urge to cry. He never used to keep his thoughts from her but he did so increasingly. They sat in silence – he added no more to his cryptic accusations against Siegfried and she stubbornly refused to ask.

A doe appeared on the opposite bank, grazing cautiously through the snow. It stepped delicately, noiselessly. After a moment, it turned and showed its pale haunches; Anton aimed at it with an imaginary gun, screwing up one of his eyes. For a second Ursula wished she really did have a gun; she thought about venison and wanted to hear the shot, to pull the trigger herself.

'Bang!' she yelled.

The deer exploded into terrified flight and Anton clamped a hand to his chest. The animal sprang up the slope, shaking and rustling the undergrowth. It vanished over the top of the incline. Anton smiled one of his sly smiles. He pushed Ursula backwards into the dirt, still smiling, and then she knew that she'd pleased him.

It was beginning to get dark when they trudged homewards with their skis on their backs, the bare-twigged trees forming a net against the twilight. They walked across the field instead of skiing, because Anton didn't want to hurry. He was a hunched silhouette, breath steaming ahead of him. The shiny black car was still at the house, an eerie occupant of the yard; the plush interior of the vehicle was blanked by deep shadows; the unlit headlamps glinted. They went round to the back door, kicked off their boots and went into the kitchen. It was deserted, a pot bubbled on the hot plate, the lid jumping and releasing little belches of steam. They hung their coats and heard voices in the living room and a record playing – Ursula's spirits lifted as soon as she heard the music, it always meant that Mama was in a good mood and it made the place so much more pleasant. Anton went upstairs without a word and Ursula put her mittens and hat to dry in the scullery and smoothed her hair as best she could. She opened the door to the living room; the sound of violins swelled. Mama was seated on the floor alongside Siegfried and Dorli. They were playing cards. Mama had taken off her shoes, Dorli was flushed with excitement and Siegfried sat cross-legged with his tie undone, a cigar resting in the black Czechoslovakian glass ashtray on the floor, one of the only valuable things they owned. Tobacco smoke floated in a blue cloud near the ceiling. All three looked at Ursula and she felt suddenly shy, like an intruder, aware of her messy appearance and her socks that were falling down and trailing from her toes.

'Are you joining us?' said Siegfried in a friendly tone.

She came into the room and sat next to her sister. She tucked her dress over her knees. Siegfried had a glass of schnapps beside the ashtray. He took a swift mouthful then winked at her. On one of his fingers was a gold ring.

'Well, I suppose it's dinnertime now,' said Mama, reaching for her shoes.

'Let him have his turn,' begged Dorli.

Siegfried surveyed his hand then set down a pair of queens, which seemed to win him something because he grinned in triumph.

'We can carry on the game later?' said Dorli.

'I think not,' said Mama, looking at Siegfried. 'You're leaving, aren't you?'

Siegfried nodded. 'I must get back,' he said. 'The weather looks threatening. I wouldn't want to get stuck in the mud.' He stood with a sudden springing motion then executed a little bow. He was unlike any man Ursula had met before, smooth and charming, funny and peculiar, and he made Mama smile so that her dimples showed. In the hall, Siegfried prepared to say goodbye to Mama. Dorli appeared behind Ursula, yanked her by the arm and dragged her to the kitchen.

'Really, Uschi,' she scolded. 'There's no need to stare like a complete *Dummkopf*.'

Ursula grew red-faced because she supposed she had been staring without realising it and now Siegfried would think she was a simpleton, or an ill-bred country girl. She heard the guttural rev of his engine and felt ridiculous. Dorli promptly began her bustling, an irritating affectation she'd recently adopted, which Ursula assumed was preparation for being a good *Hausfrau* to Herr Oberndorfer. She took small, precise steps instead of loafing about like she used to do, lifted the plates from the cupboard, bending low from the waist like Mama did, except that her breasts didn't hang like Mama's, and her bottom wasn't so wide.

The next day was Sunday and when Ursula went outside Schosi appeared from behind the firs, nervous and wide-eyed, stuttering a hello. She went to greet him, a welcome diversion from cleaning the henhouse. He was very jittery and refused to shake her hand – it took him a while to be calm enough to speak and she wondered if he'd lost his cat for good this time. She tried to make him more comfortable. 'Are you looking for Simmy?' she asked.

Schosi didn't answer but twisted his comfort blanket around his finger with great concentration. After a while he replied with a question of his own. 'Are you going to church today?'

'No, we don't go very often.'

Schosi pulled his mouth tight across his teeth – his face vibrated. 'My mama's gone to church. She'll pray and sing and eat the body of Christ.'

'That's nice. Why don't you go with her?'

'Not allowed,' he said quickly. 'And not allowed here.'

Anton came out of the shed. He stopped and cursed when he saw Schosi.

'Oh, let him stay,' cajoled Ursula. 'Just for a little while.'

'For God's sake.' Anton scowled at her. 'What's wrong with you?'

They finished mucking out the henhouse, Schosi observing silent as a shadow. Ursula gave him the basket and told him to collect the eggs from the laying box. He did so with great care. Ursula and Anton hastily swilled and scrubbed the perches, wiped the wet away with rags and tossed down new straw without waiting for the coop to properly dry. Anton went to the shed and fetched his bag, which he slung over his back then they set off to the river with Schosi in tow.

Schosi had a long-legged, precarious walk and breathed like a pair of bellows so after a while Ursula took his arm and walked beside him. She felt sorry for him because he wasn't allowed to go to church and seemed very anxious. Perhaps he was lonely.

'Playing the good Samaritan?' said Anton.

'Oh, leave off!' said Ursula, retrieving her hand from the crook of Schosi's elbow. 'I was just making sure he didn't fall over.'

When they reached the pool the hole in the ice was still open, but less than half the size. It wasn't the great wound they'd made the day before. It looked now as though it was a natural occurrence, just a gap in the ice.

'It's like a squinty eye,' said Ursula.

'Squinty eye,' echoed Schosi.

Anton scrambled down the bank and went on to the ice. He edged towards the hole, the ice creaking and whistling beneath his weight, a sure sign that it was getting thinner.

'What are you doing?' said Ursula, horrified, thinking about the cold black death of Tobias Messer.

Anton stopped at intervals, watching for hairline cracks beneath his boots, and Schosi called to him every few seconds to take care. When Anton was close to the hole, he halted. He waited a moment, looking into the water. Then he took off his leather bag and put his hand inside it. Ursula tried to see what he was doing – his back was to her and all around him the snow glittered sharply in the morning light, so that she blinked and couldn't focus. Anton pulled something out of his bag and held it towards

the hole. After a second or so, Ursula saw the object
convulse in his grip. It was a young cat. Anton must have
carried it from the shed where the now teenage litter slept
heaped on top of each other in an old crate. He must have
reached his hand amongst the warm furry bodies, forced
the cat inside his thick leather bag. Had it not cried as
they went over the field? Had the wind blown its mewing
away? Anton shifted his hold on the slender body so that it
dangled from the loose skin of its neck. The cat's thin face
was stretched tight, its pale pink gums and teeth bared, its
tongue curled like a rose petal, its ginger fur smooth with
the newness of youth. It squirmed for a moment and then
contracted into an inert ball, surrendering to Anton's hold.
Without much hesitation he tossed the cat into the hole. It
fell with a small splash and disappeared from view. Ursula
stood immovable, not breathing. She felt suspended, stuck
in a fraction of a second as the cat sailed through the air.

Schosi lurched forward. 'You dropped it!' he yelled, his
voice high with panic. 'You dropped it! Get it! Get it!' He
stumbled and slid towards the edge of the ice, eyes wide.
Ursula grasped his sleeve. Meanwhile, Anton crouched
beside the hole, looking in.

'No!' she said to Schosi. 'It's gone. Leave it!'

'Can't leave it!' Schosi bellowed, tugging at her hand to
free his sleeve. She gripped harder but he wrested himself
away and hurtled on to the ice, sliding about and yelling,
'Get it! It's drowning! Quick! Get it!' The ice gave an
alarming crack and Ursula saw it bend and sag beneath
the weight of two people. There was another loud crack
and Anton, realising the danger, leapt towards Schosi,
collided with him and pushed him backwards towards the
edge of the pool. Schosi fell and Anton, heaving with all

his effort, dragged Schosi by his coat from the ice and on to solid ground. A stark black gap opened where they had stood, cutting the ice sheet almost in two.

'Stupid damn *imbecile*!' Anton glared down at Schosi where he lay then kicked him. 'What the hell do you think you're doing? Are you completely thick? Completely stupid?' Schosi covered his face with his hands, his breath wheezing torturously. He was crying.

Ursula shook her head at Anton because she couldn't speak. She ran up the bank towards the field.

'Uschi!' Anton yelled.

She kept running – she could hear Schosi wailing, 'The cat! The cat!'

'Stop right now!'

She stopped despite herself. Anton had borrowed Papa's voice, hollering a command that must be obeyed, or God help your backside. She started to cry and scrubbed her tears away so her brother wouldn't see them. He climbed towards her, arms out to steady himself, and she thought that if she threw something at him and he fell backwards into the pool it'd serve him right. 'Why?' she said when he reached her.

He shrugged. Behind him, Schosi was crouching beside the pool's edge.

'You know I love them,' she said.

'But they're always killed anyway,' said Anton. 'What's the difference if their heads are smashed, or if they're thrown in the stream?'

'I don't know,' said Ursula. She tried to formulate her thoughts. Schosi came slowly up the bank and into the field, watching Anton with wide, woeful eyes. 'Mama does it when I'm not around so I don't have to see. And . . .' She thought of Anton's face as he'd turned from the hole, his eyes narrower than usual, a small hard smile on his lips. 'Because you're not supposed to enjoy it.'

Anton watched her, mystified. After a while he put an arm over her shoulder in a comradely headlock. 'Don't tell anyone, will you?'

All three set off up the hill and Ursula didn't reply because she didn't want to, but she knew already that she wouldn't tell.

They arrived back in the yard after dark, even later than the previous night. Schosi had gone off home some hours before, still whimpering, and Anton had called after him to be quiet, he was lucky it hadn't been him in the hole. A dim light was on in the kitchen – the shutters hadn't yet been properly closed. Dorli was drying a plate and placing it on the dresser; Mama worked at the sink. They'd already had supper.

Anton and Ursula squatted beneath the window.

'What shall we say?' said Ursula. 'Shall we say we saw a wild boar? And we hid until it was gone?'

Anton shook his head, his face in deep shadow. The moon was up, a silver disc sunk in a sheet of small clouds that covered the whole sky like a lumpy feather quilt, high above everything. The wind blew mist from the trout stream and with it the smell of the cow – the sweet stench of slurry that pooled like green soup and froze. Ursula shivered. She imagined Mama gripping a wooden spoon so that her knuckles showed. 'Or, shall we say that I fell over? I can pretend to limp. I'm good at pretending to limp.'

'Uschi,' said Anton. 'You always think of lying.'

Ursula bridled at the criticism. Anton often lied to Mama, saying he'd been in lessons when in fact he'd been kicking a ball about with Rudi.

'I'm not going to lie. I don't feel I should have to,' said Anton. 'Not when she acts like a whore and lies to us all. She should be the one sneaking and feeling like a dog.' He stood and looked boldly in through the gap in the shutters.

'What do you mean?' Ursula looked at her brother's boots, caked with snow. 'Why are you saying that?'

'You don't want to hear it, Uschi. But I saw.'

'Saw what?'

'She'd lie if you asked her.' Anton looked at his sister. 'She knows she's doing wrong by us, and Papa too.'

'Did she kiss him?' Ursula imagined her mother kissing Siegfried and felt sick.

'Worse than that.'

'What do you mean, worse than that?'

6

In the morning, Siegfried's car was still there and Anton said they were probably fucking. Ursula didn't know exactly what this meant, not having heard the word before, but from the harsh and indecent sound, and the way it felt filthy in the mouth, she could make a good guess. Anton was furious – she asked no questions of him. They went early to school to avoid seeing the adults and as they left the house he kicked the boot scraper, which spun on the ice and clanged against the rain butt with a sound almost as impressive as the village church bell. Ursula ran after her brother – they'd done none of their chores and there'd be hell to pay.

—

They played tag along the track and then Anton began one of his HY songs:

We shall march on our way,
Even if all crashes in sorrow,
For Germany hears us today!
The whole world tomorrow!

They marched like soldiers side by side and Ursula gnawed her bread, nibbled off the mould and spat it out. They reached the village. The road was dotted with early-shift factory workers who tramped with heads down. Amongst them were prisoners in chains accompanied by guards.

'There's Frau Hillier,' said Anton. He pointed to Schosi's mama wrapped in a bulky coat, a bag over her shoulder. She walked slowly alongside the other workers as though she was very tired. Above them the sky was full of black clouds; soon it would snow. As they overtook Frau Hillier they hid their faces. The camp fence was adjacent to them on the right. A figure stood amongst the rows of wooden huts, an armed guard. Ursula looked quickly away. They descended the hill to the church, the white walls distinct in the dark dawn. Specks of snow fell. They ran across the graveyard and sat in the porch beside the holy water on a skinny stone ledge. A thin snowfall began and hissed on the grass and on the church roof. Flakes blew in near their feet and melted.

'There'll be a lot of gossip, if they find out, won't there?' said Ursula.

'What do you think? What happened to Frau Linser when she was caught with a Polish worker?'

'She was given stale bread and rotten meat and made unwelcome everywhere.'

Anton nodded.

'Siegfried's not a Pole though – and he's respectable-looking.'

'He's a crook.'

'Oh, come on. He's not really.'

'He damn well is!'

The parcels secreted into Mama's hand; Siegfried's significant smile; Mama's nervousness. Her whispered rebukes to Siegfried in the hall. Ursula knew, but didn't care and didn't want it spoiled, the small wealth he brought, this taste of a world beyond her own. If anything, the subterfuge appealed to her, the forbidden things concealed behind rows of preserve jars in the cellar – coffee and cigarettes, tinned sardines and chocolate. Ursula had been to rummage amongst them, pilfered morsels. She'd found the small wrap of plain brown paper containing chocolate, opened it carefully, trying not to tear or wrinkle it. Fragments of chocolate lay like dusty stones and she'd chosen a large piece, rewrapped the remainder and returned the package to its hiding place. Then she'd put the chocolate into her mouth and sucked and sucked. The sweet, heavy, exploding flavour coated her tongue and momentarily drugged her. She kept her mouth closed to stop the saliva drooling. It was unbelievably delicious. She'd stood for a long time trying to resist recklessly gobbling the rest, the preserve jars reflecting the liquid flame of her candle.

When the snow eased and they wandered into the graveyard, a woman was tending one of the graves, clearing leaves and weeds from amongst the shrubs. Her skirt trailed behind her in the wet. It was Frau Gerg. Ursula's steps faltered and she resisted the urge to turn and walk the other way. She hid behind her brother and hoped to go unnoticed. She'd missed the weekly League meeting, yet again. She hated going; she'd no idea if Marta had delivered her string of excuses and, if she had, whether she'd been believed. She dreaded even a glare from Frau Gerg, which was piercing, scouring and harsh, a feeling not unlike having a pumice stone applied violently to the face. Frau Gerg had once slapped Ursula across the cheek for being late, and it was common knowledge that she didn't bat an eyelid about sending people to the camps. Mama said Frau Gerg was just as terrifying for grown-ups and kept her high place in the village by informing on people – asocials and traitors – including her own neighbour, Herr Blumsberg, who'd run the ironmonger's and listened to Allied broadcasts on an illegal radio. Apparently, she'd heard him late in the evening when everything was quiet and his window wasn't properly closed. The British national anthem had floated out into the night and she'd known at once he was a traitor. She and Herr Adler were good chums.

Anton spoke as soon as they were out of earshot. 'Perhaps there's another way,' he said. He unearthed a fir cone from its nest of snow and kicked it. He looked sideways at Ursula. 'We could tell someone.'

'What do you mean?'

'Tell someone he's a thief. We could have him in prison before you know it.'

Ursula stared at her brother. 'No,' she said. The reality of what he was suggesting registered and she felt quite dizzy. 'We couldn't.'

'We could. We could go right now to the police.'

'But why? And anyway, Mama would know. She'd guess it was us.'

'No she wouldn't!' Anton scoffed. 'How on earth would she guess?

'Because we've seen him bringing the parcels.'

'Yes, but someone might've seen him in Vienna too – the Gestapo might follow him here.'

'It's wrong. He's a good person. I don't want him to go to prison.'

'You're soft on him.' Anton gave her a look of distaste. 'Use your loaf. It's wrong that he steals, and it's wrong that he fucks a woman who's not his wife. He must *have* a wife in the city, otherwise why wouldn't he marry Mama?' He glared at her and she daren't reply. 'It's also wrong that he isn't fighting in the war,' he continued. 'Why's he not fighting with the rest? Why's he allowed to live like this? Just doing what he likes when people like our papa have to die.'

Ursula couldn't answer him. She didn't know. She'd never thought about those things before. Why *was* Siegfried not at war with the other men? He was fit and healthy and not too old. How come he had a car just like the Party officials? What kind of a man had taken Papa's place?

'But can we wait a little while?' she said eventually, hoping to find a way to dissuade him. The plan was too cruel, too drastic. 'Can we please just wait?'

'Why?'

'Because I feel afraid.'

Marta Fingerlos was the person to talk to about fucking because she was from a very religious family. She often quoted her papa about the lusts of men, whores and harlots and Ursula supposed that if it was true about the mistress then he was well placed to know. Herr Fingerlos was devout and sat three rows back in church. He was also very dashing, according to Mama, and had a condition. Something to do with his heart. Everyone knew which was his place amongst the pews and wouldn't dream of sitting there. He'd spoken to his daughter about the facts of life, without many facts divulged, and emphasised the importance of saving her virtue for her husband. When she married, with God's blessing and her father's too, her husband would provide her with children – eight or nine, God willing, with a golden Mother's Cross awarded by the Führer himself. But anything other than this, any hanky-panky or disgraceful behaviour, and he'd disown her immediately. This did nothing to prevent Marta from trying to catch the eye of the boys; she knew just how to swirl the hem of her dress and give coy, inviting smiles.

The first few weeks of March came and went before Ursula broached the topic with Marta, during which time the visits from Siegfried continued. Anton hadn't gone to the police station – Ursula had pleaded with him to abandon the idea. His plan, she pointed out, would also incriminate Mama, who'd accepted the illegal parcels and kept them in her house. She implored Anton to spare her; she didn't want to be parentless and starving. Eventually he'd relented, if only temporarily.

She chose her moment with Marta on a day when rain rinsed the grass, drummed incessantly on the windows at school, and sluiced in a silver curtain from the eaves of the buildings. The girls ran homewards after lessons, dodged from doorway to doorway in the vain hope of staying dry. It was a pointless mission and they were now resigned to sogginess, seated on the wall of the village bridge looking down at the river, which flew mad with froth over the rocks. Marta could rest easy – it was too wet for anyone to wander by and see them together. They found pebbles and threw them into the rush.

'What does "fucking" mean?' said Ursula.

'Oh, rude!' squealed Marta. 'It means "fornicating".' She looked at Ursula, beady-eyed. 'Why? Who's been fornicating?'

Ursula had prepared an answer for this question. 'Anton's friend.'

'Scandalous!' Marta feigned disgust. 'Who was it?'

'I don't know,' said Ursula. 'Toni won't tell.'

'Well, who are his friends?'

'I'm not sure. I don't really know them. Someone at the HY.'

'And you don't know who the girl was?'

'No.'

The two friends were silent for a while. Ursula was almost disappointed to learn that fucking was no worse than fornication; it seemed a waste of a shocking word. But she supposed it was enough to know that Mama was a fornicator. Rain blew from the thick clouds, light but dense, a lull between the brutal showers. She was growing cold. A shiver convulsed her body.

'If a boy tried to do it to me, I'd scream till I was purple,' Marta said. 'Papa said only Jezebels let their knickers down.'

'Well she let them down all right,' said Ursula, suppressing the worry that Marta would ask Anton about the fictitious girl. 'I hear she's a loose type who'd go with anyone.' Marta tittered with delight. 'In fact,' continued Ursula, getting carried away, '"Jezebel" seems too nice a word for a girl like her. How about "slut"?' She threw another stone; it flew in an impressive arc and splashed near the water's edge, guzzled by the current. 'Jezebel'. It did sound nice, like the name of a flower or a jewel. There were so many names for a woman like Mama. What was Siegfried then? 'Philanderer'? 'Adulterer'? They seemed the nearest thing, but so formal, with nothing like the punch. Perhaps Ursula would tell Marta the truth; she was a friend after all. Perhaps she'd listen and keep the secret and sympathise because her papa was an adulterer.

But just then, Marta leaned in close and whispered, 'I saw a man in the forest yesterday with his peter in his hand. He opened his trousers and pulled it out. It was quite big. And hairy too.'

Ursula forgot her idea, enthralled. 'What did you do?'

'I went home a different way. He was Slav or something.'

Slavs rode on top of the cattle trucks that roared through the village on their way to Brauhausen market, their faces shiny with perspiration. They worked in the fields and factories, had *P* for Poland stitched on to their uniforms and weren't allowed into churches or on trains.

'Did you run?' Ursula's pulse rose and her imagination filled with shadows, fast movements in the dark, in the snow, a hot–cold feeling.

'Yes. You have to watch out. They aren't like us. They're more like beasts. Shame on him.' Marta flicked her bedraggled hair and managed to look prim even though the white of her underwear showed clearly through her rain-soaked dress.

Ursula tried to think of something to say but her body stirred in a way that made her anxious, a fast eddy in her blood, like the chaotic river below, swirling, pushing, rushing. She thought of the red spear of flesh protruding from the groin of the Fingerlos dog, the bull and the cow, the nanny goat bleating beneath the stud, and Siegfried astride Mama, his tongue licking her cheek like on the picture-postcards of Krampus and the maiden.

'It's your mama, isn't it?' said Marta.

'What?'

'It's your mama who's been fornicating.'

Ursula's face kindled a fire even in the bitter rain.

'Well?' insisted Marta. Droplets ran off the end of her nose and gathered on her lashes. She bent near to Ursula's face to see her expression, unavoidable, tenacious as a dog with a juicy bone.

'No,' said Ursula. The word dropped unconvincingly from her lips. She was too shocked to lie with conviction.

Marta smirked.

'I'm cold,' said Ursula. She scrambled from the wall on to the road.

'People've seen his car. He drives right by our window. It's not hard to work it out.' Marta's eyes became slits, full of malice. 'Stop fibbing, Uschi. No one can trust a person like you.'

Ursula began to walk away. Marta called after her, her voice sharp above the gush of water. 'My mama says she won't tell anyone. Frau Hildesheim's just a weak woman. A sinner led astray.' She raised her voice still further. 'But you'd better watch yourself. Like mother like daughter. I've seen the way you look at Sepp.'

Ursula broke into a run. She could hear Marta shouting something more about the church and godliness. She splattered through a puddle as she turned the corner, jumped the ditch at the side of the road into the field. Her chest thumped with a painful feeling; she felt the wrongness and dirt of her life surrounding her, a frightening confusion of trying and trying to be someone, someone better, to fit with this place, with these people, but never succeeding, and how could she when her mother did something like this? She burned with anger towards Marta but feared she was right; she *was* a liar. Her family weren't right, weren't as they should be, and everyone in Felddorf could see it. She must try not to care. None of them really knew her and she was glad. Mud squelched from the saturated ground and splashed her legs black. Her boots chafed her anklebones but she ignored the pain. She fell over several times before she reached her house.

7

It wasn't long before the judgement of the village fell like a gavel on to the Hildesheims. Perhaps Marta's mother had found it difficult to hold her tongue; perhaps she'd never intended to resist. News spread through the ranks at church and amongst the shopkeepers and their customers. Housewives worn out by endless days of wartime hardship feasted on the rumour like starving crows, met at their gates and fences to tear at the victuals – welcome relief from suffering, grief, fear and frustration. They could forget momentarily about lost sons, missing husbands and cousins, the hopeless atmosphere of near defeat, the threat of bombings, the uncertain future. The housewives conjectured viciously, happily, repeating well-worn condemnations – they'd often wondered about that woman, not from round here, not quite proper. She hadn't been to a church service for months – a sure sign of something gone bad.

'Empty seats again on Sunday.'

'It seems that she's not easy in the presence of the Lord.'

'Well, how could she sit there – before the eyes of God – I never could.'

'You never would though, would you?'

'It takes a certain type of woman.'

'Her husband will be turning in his grave.'

'She didn't grieve for long, they say.'

'Frau Fingerlos made it quite clear.'

'That black car coming and going.'

'Parked outside for days.'

'He's a no-good type – married of course.'

'And I always said she was trouble.'

'No scruples.'

'Her voice—'

'Her smile—'

'Saucy.'

'Bold.'

'Exactly.'

Ursula felt the ripple of hostility at school, no longer mere taunts but a whisper of enmity, faces closing like fists as she approached. Marta didn't wait for her any more in the mornings on the track but instead untied the Fingerlos dog, a vicious cur called Gabriel, so that he'd terrorise her as she passed. Marta spent her time with the fat girl in the dirndl and her younger cousins, all dumpy, blonde and ruddy, a good hearty Germanic-Austrian family, and good Catholics too. They shrieked together in the playground and grew quiet when Ursula was near, Marta looking over with hatred in her expression. Ursula hurried to escape them and thought how unfair it was that the rules were different for Marta. She wished she herself had only a philandering father, which was a much more normal, wholesome thing. Her shame was a heavy substance that lodged somewhere in the centre of her chest – it hurt and made it hard to breathe. She reminded herself that Anton was somewhere within the school grounds with his friends, that she wasn't only the daughter of a whore but also the favourite sister of Anton Hildesheim, Hitler Youth hero.

One afternoon when school was finished, Anton was waiting for her at the playground gate. Her heart leapt to see him there, an unusual treat, and she hurried over. When she reached him she saw that his mouth was smeared with blood and his collar torn on one side.

'Are you all right?' she asked.

He threaded his arm around her waist and pulled her to his side. They set off walking. 'Better than the other boy,' he said, baring his teeth; his lips were swollen and crimson. He switched his step so that their feet fell in time. 'You?'

'Fine,' she said.

'No, you're not. I can tell. Is it that Marta girl?' He watched her closely. 'That stuck-up bitch? Don't listen to her. She's a snake. She's nothing.' He squeezed her waist and kept close as they turned off the road and walked the length of the track. It made her feel stronger – more solid. Before they entered the yard he stopped and took hold of her chin, tilting her face to his. She was afraid for a moment that he was angry with her because he looked at her so fiercely. 'You're better than the lot of them,' he said with force. A couple of tears trickled from her eyes and ran uncomfortably into her ears. 'You don't need anyone because you've got me.'

On Tuesday, the baker's wife, Frau Arnold, closed the shop door in Mama's face saying that she didn't want her type of person coming in. Several other customers were queuing by the counter and watched saucer-eyed as Mama was turned away. No doubt Frau Arnold enlightened them, explained the ill repute that Mama would bring if she were to accept her custom. Mama returned to the house. She said that the baker and his wife had always been an idiotic pair and that she'd no idea what the woman was talking about. Dorli heard the news and covered her face with her hands. Ursula was certain that this was only the beginning. Mama tossed her cloth bag, empty of bread, on to the table.

Mama's stubbornness led them to church a few days later to face the crowds on the feast day of the Annunciation of Mary. She buttoned herself into her better dress, wore a string of pearls around her neck and smart black shoes. She insisted on baths for all the children and spent a long time braiding Dorli's hair and combing Ursula's into pigtails so neat and tight that her head ached. Anton was his usual surly self; Ursula saw him watching as Mama stood before the mirror in the hall and drew several determined breaths. He gave a sardonic smile and Ursula wished that just this once he wouldn't mock and make Mama seem ridiculous.

The people waiting outside the church squinted in the glare of the sun. One or two horses, harnessed into the shafts of traps, stood cropping the short grass at the edge of the road, their muscular lips wrapping and gripping like pairs of mittened hands. The farmers stood together and rocked back on the heels of their boots, Herr Esterbauer amongst them. Ursula scanned the crowd for familiar faces from her class. She saw one or two of the boys, and Marta standing with her parents. Marta's father rested his hands on his daughter's shoulders; every so often he smiled and ruffled her hair. Ursula turned her back.

Anton sauntered off to speak with Rudi. Rudi had obviously been fighting again or had received another beating from Herr Adler, the hog; one of his eyes was swollen like a *Zwetschken* plum. The boys talked intently and there was something secretive in their manner. Ursula watched them with trepidation. Anton sometimes mentioned how he longed to go off to join the fighting – he didn't have to wait till he was sixteen; the army would have him on air defence in Vienna. Perhaps he'd run away with Rudi and leave her. After all, everything was so hopeless in Felddorf. She looked elsewhere, not wanting to be caught staring. She spotted Sepp amongst the crowd. He stood politely with a woman Ursula recognised; she was always at church. It must be Frau Sontheimer, Sepp's aunt. She wore a respectable green jacket of a traditional style and had a pale face with a high forehead and sad mouth. Ursula had heard Mama talk of her, a spinster with strange ideas and a guarded look in her eyes, which the villagers mistook for conceit. She had no friends here, and it looked to be true; the surrounding parishioners ignored Frau Sontheimer as if she wasn't there and she did the same, keeping her gaze fixed on the middle distance.

The church bell gave its dull chime. Conversations petered out and the richer farmers withdrew their pocket watches to check the timing of the bell and to display the rare flash of gold. Mama joined the disorderly queue somewhere at the middle, Anton, Ursula and Dorli crowding behind. There was the hush and rustle of bodies; the church would be full. Even the farmers joined the press, their steel-plated boots clicking against the stones. Usually they remained outside, talking business, while their wives prayed on behalf of the family. When the wives emerged, sanctified and soothed for another week, the farmers would untie their horses and traps, wives perched on the back with chubby ankles crossed, and drive to the Gasthaus, where they'd drink for the rest of the afternoon. But today was a holy day of obligation and the men came in.

As the frame of the church door closed over Ursula's head she took a small fold of Mama's dress between finger and thumb and felt comforted. Suddenly, to her right, was Sepp, crammed against her by the pushing people, his shoulder touching hers. She felt the contact as an intense jolt. He glanced at her and smiled. His cheeks shone like two freckled apples and his eyes were so dark that light danced in them, mischievous and warm. Ursula tried to smile but her face was frozen. Her stomach grew sick and tight; the press of him against her seemed to burn, to set her trembling. She looked down at the floor, overcome with shyness; his fringe fell into his eyes in such a charming way. Why had Mama done her hairstyle in this ugly fashion, scraped tight and unforgiving? And it was much too short, chopped bluntly by her harassed scissors. Sepp was jolted forward and he disappeared into the church.

As soon as Ursula and her family were seated, people in front began to swivel and peer at Mama. They were alone in their pew because the people who normally shared it with them had chosen other places. Marta's father, Herr Fingerlos, gazed sternly and Marta made no pretence at subtlety as she turned fully on the pew, kneeling up to gawk. Frau Gerg stared at Mama with a cold ferociousness that made Ursula afraid and Frau Arnold, the baker's wife, pressed a grubby-gloved hand to her lips as though holding the laughter in. Perhaps it wasn't too late to escape, thought Ursula. Couldn't they just leave now, before the service began? Dorli's hands were knotted in her lap; across the aisle with the boys and men Anton slumped low. Ursula wanted to crawl beneath her bench and curl up on the kneeling cushions. There could surely be no sense in staying? But Mama sat rigid, eyes fixed on something just above the altar; perhaps she was praying. Just then Frau Hillier rose abruptly and noisily from a pew a few rows behind them, saying 'Excuse me' and squeezing past everyone with a lot of rustling and palaver. She approached Ursula and her family. The choirboys were in position and the priest was about to ascend the pulpit, but hesitated when he saw Frau Hillier. She stopped beside the Hildesheim pew and cleared her throat. Her hat, which was a brown globe-like thing with moth holes along the brim, perched with old-fashioned severity atop her head. Ursula readied herself for a tirade. Frau Hillier would lambast them in front of the whole church; she'd have Mama thrown out. Ursula pleaded with God, hopelessly, that they'd be spared.

'May I sit beside you, Frau Hildesheim?' said Frau Hillier. 'It seems,' she announced, 'that some here are intent on making you feel uncomfortable.'

Mama looked bewildered but nodded and indicated that the children should stand to let Frau Hillier get in. As she passed, Ursula caught a strong whiff of wood smoke, then Frau Hillier trod heavily on Ursula's foot. She bit her lip in agony. Frau Hillier plumped down next to Mama and focused serenely on the priest, her hands neatly folded on top of her handbag. The priest began and Ursula tried to be calm as the Latin flowed over her, a lulling stream of sound; a boat slowly rocking at a river's edge.

'Come with me,' said Frau Hillier once the service was over and they were outside. She took Mama's arm and started towards the graveyard, which was filled with people talking, wandering and visiting buried relations. 'Let's have a walk.'

'I really think we ought to leave,' said Mama. Dorli nodded emphatically.

'If I may say so,' said Frau Hillier, 'don't be a coward. You've every right to be here. Don't let small-minded people shoo you away. It's your place too. Come!'

Their neighbour's words must have pricked Mama's pride because after a pause she said, 'Children,' and allowed Frau Hillier to lead her. Ursula and Dorli followed. Anton dawdled as far behind as possible and kept glancing around and up at the hill. The family walked along the rows of neat graves, resplendent with curling metalwork, ornaments and candles. The day had turned humid, the horizon slate-dark – a downpour was due. They reached the plot where Frau Hillier's husband was buried and she lit a candle and refilled the holy water dish.

Sepp was near by – he picked dead leaves from amongst the flowers on a grave while his aunt directed him. Ursula left her family and wandered closer, meandering as though daydreaming; she looked up at the trees and then down at the trodden grass, aware all the while of Sepp's stooping shape. With fists full of dead leaves and flower stalks he set off for the compost heap. Ursula was directly in his path.

'Hello,' he said, stopping in front of her.

Her heart jumped with panic; she hadn't expected him to speak to her. 'Oh, hello,' she said, flustered.

'I've seen you at school, haven't I?' He had a smudge of dirt on his upper lip that looked like a lopsided moustache.

She shrugged, trying to prevent a blush from developing. 'Probably.' She steeled herself for nosy questions.

'What's your name?' he asked.

'Ursula.'

'I'm Sepp,' he said. 'I can't shake your hand.' He indicated the leaves he held. 'Sorry.'

'It's all right.' She smiled and the blush arrived, pulsing in her cheeks – he couldn't fail to notice. He really did have such nice, wide-open eyes. They looked directly at her, closely at her, which was not something she was used to. His fringe curved to brush his eyelids, which was somehow the most beautiful thing she'd ever seen, and she allowed herself to bask for a moment. Being near to him felt nerve-rackingly splendid, like being at the top of a great cliff with a sun-blinded lake stretched out beneath, the feeling that she might just jump – exhilarating, frightening.

A hand gripped her elbow. 'Hey,' said Anton. 'Come here!' He tugged her arm until she went with him. He took her back towards their family.

'Goodbye!' called Sepp.

Anton swivelled and Ursula saw the filthy scowl he levelled.

'What's the matter?' she hissed. But just then a shrill voice rang out.

'Intolerable!' It rose above the wind that now stirred the leaves, a cry meant to stun and deafen, like the piercing blast emitted by an owl as it swoops to snatch the harvest mouse. Frau Gerg stood stock-still and glared from beneath her thin brows at Ursula's family and Frau Hillier. Beyond her a cluster of women forgot their conversation and watched, their dresses billowing.

'Emmalina!' Frau Gerg yelled. A thin woman with strenuous grey hair controlled by her headscarf, broke away from the group and hurried over to stand restlessly beside her friend. 'There's something in the vicinity', said Frau Gerg, 'that smells unpleasant.' Emmalina said nothing. 'I can't believe the nerve,' Frau Gerg continued, as if to Emmalina, but in fact addressing Mama and Frau Hillier. She drew herself up, and began to quote from the Bible. '"Now the works of the flesh are manifest"' – her index finger was stiffly extended – '"which are these, adultery, fornication, uncleanness, lasciviousness . . . They which do such things shall not inherit the kingdom of God."' Her tone was strident and Ursula was reminded of the crowds she'd heard on the wireless; a thousand voices chanting and booming, '*Sieg Heil! Sieg Heil!*'

Frau Arnold hurried to join them. 'What's going on?' she panted.

Frau Gerg stared at Mama. 'There are some who flout the will of God and think themselves above His law.'

'One deviance leads to another,' said Frau Arnold, perspiring in the humid air and dabbing a handkerchief to her shining cheeks and forehead. 'That's what I believe.'

Emmalina threw Frau Arnold an irritated look. She wasn't of the same vindictive nature as her friends and she was ill at ease.

'Indeed,' said Frau Gerg. 'It makes a mockery of our feast day to see that family here. And sets a bad example to all the children.' The two women agreed with one another over this. 'I'll be speaking to Father Jordan,' finished Frau

Gerg. 'You'll not be permitted again!' She began to turn away as if the matter was settled.

'Excuse me,' said Frau Hillier sharply. 'May I stop you?' Ursula looked at Frau Hillier in fright and Dorli took tight hold of Ursula's arm. Frau Gerg turned back to face Frau Hillier, eyebrows arched. 'It's not up to you who comes to this church, whether they flout God's will or not. You can't just bar whoever you choose.' Frau Hillier took a step forward and pointed directly at Frau Gerg. 'Or else we'd all be subject to your latest grudge or prejudice.' Next she jabbed her finger in the direction of Frau Arnold who recoiled, like a snail retreating into its shell. 'You're nothing but a rotten gossip. Leave judging to the Lord and get on with your own petty lives. Both of you.'

In the awful silence that followed, Ursula was filled with admiring dread – no one insulted Frau Gerg, no one dared. What had possessed Frau Hillier? Did she have no care for her safety? Wind barged through the graveyard now, bending the bushes and extinguishing candles, the air full of lightning, the kind that signalled a cloudburst, flickering constantly above the treetops. People were hastily clearing out so that the little group was soon left stranded. Frau Gerg's top lip curled upwards, showing her teeth, dainty as daisy petals, crowded closely into her gums; her gaze travelled up and down Frau Hillier's shabby attire then came to rest on her face, which appeared very lovely to Ursula just then. Beside her, Mama fiddled with the sash of her dress, folding and unfolding it.

'Frau Hillier,' said Frau Gerg with measured hostility. 'There's something you don't understand – and your friend here' – she looked at Mama – 'with her lustful appetite and that man of hers. You're both mothers. You should look at the state of your children and know that God is not pleased. Especially your son, Frau Hillier.' She tilted her head and gave a tight smile. 'That unfortunate, afflicted child.'

Ursula looked at Mama. What did Frau Gerg mean, the state of the children? Was she suggesting they were idiots, like Schosi? Was it about the League meetings, her absence, lateness, or scruffy uniform? Frau Gerg's eyes rested briefly on her, bright, exposing lamps; they saw every disobedient thing she'd done, every dirty thought and action, every time she'd cheated or sneaked or been untrue, the elaborate excuses that came so easily to her lips, dishonest boasts and made-up anecdotes, the urge to exaggerate that swelled inside her and came spilling out with a will of its own, her stealing, truanting, and secrets, the wickedness in her heart. Mama's mouth had fallen open as if she was going to defend herself but no words arrived. Ursula heard only a rasping sound; Dorli, gripping her with clawed hand, was taking great heaving breaths as if she was trying not to suffocate.

'Let's go now,' said Mama. She turned and began across the grass. She looked almost drunk, the way she walked with her head bowed and nearly tripped over the foot of a grave as she passed it. Frau Arnold and Emmalina had melted away. Frau Hillier was locked in a potent staring contest with Frau Gerg. Ursula ran after Mama who was nearly out of the churchyard heading towards the hill, and Dorli came bleating and crying behind.

The storm broke when they were on the track, a warm deluge battering Ursula's skull. She undid her plaits and let her hair hang sodden down her back. Wet grasses bowed in silver cushions along the verge and Anton squelched through puddles beside her.

'We're ruined,' she said. 'Aren't we?'

He didn't reply. Their good name was muck, if they'd ever had one. It ran away in dirty rivulets like the brown water that now splashed under their feet. And things at school would only worsen.

'Why didn't you want me to speak to Sepp?' she asked after a while.

'Because he's a bad type, Uschi,' Anton answered immediately. 'He and I fought only recently after some low-down things he said. He's a Commie, you know, and a traitor.' He shook his head. 'While I was trying to protect us.' He wrinkled his nose. 'From the Russians, I mean, those Sontheimers hid one in their cellar.'

'Really?' Ursula was astounded. 'I heard people saying that someone did. Gosh!' She struggled to imagine how somebody could do such a thing. Especially a quiet, godly person like Frau Sontheimer. And Sepp – so cheerful and nice. They risked the guillotine. 'How do you know?'

'I just know.' He sniffed. 'And he's jealous of me, that's clear enough, because of my rank, because of the dagger and all that. He isn't on board, you know?' Anton wiped rain from his face then put his arm around her. 'He's the wrong type of boy. Don't speak to him again.'

Ursula was silent for a while; her breath came shallow through lungs cramped with disappointment. She hadn't thought Sepp was the fighting type or a traitor. He seemed so decent. She felt a twinge of sullen defiance. Anton had bossed her as usual. He told her what to do without any hesitation as if she were a child.

'You'll hurt me if you do, Uschi,' he said and looked at her, his fringe plastered to his forehead. 'It really would let me down.'

8

By harvest time, not long after Ursula's fourteenth birthday, Mama's pregnancy was an open fact in the household. For the first week or so it was a favourite topic of debate between Anton and Ursula. Anton said that the baby was Siegfried's bastard while Ursula held fast in her conviction that it was in fact Papa's, until she asked Dorli's opinion on the matter.

'There are some things you shouldn't talk about, Uschi,' she said. 'You never seem to understand that. But to answer your question – the child has nothing to do with Papa.' She paused and a tragic look passed over her face. 'I don't know what will become of me now. I don't know *what* Herr Oberndorfer will think of me.' She went out to milk the cow looking miserable but Ursula couldn't feel sorry for her; she always behaved as though she was the only one who suffered.

Anton was exultant. 'She can't lie after this. She's got herself a bastard. A bloody bastard kid.'

Siegfried's visits became more frequent, as did Frau Hillier's. Frau Hillier often called by on her way home from work or came to help in the garden at the weekend; she said her own garden was so small and shaded that it was virtually useless and it was a joy to tend vegetables that would actually grow. She seemed not to look down on Mama for the bulge that nestled beneath her apron. On these visits Schosi came with her.

'I can't stop him,' she said. 'Nothing I do makes a difference. So I may as well bring him myself. Meeting your Ursula has really gone to his head.'

Ursula was pleased that Schosi liked her so much; it warmed her more than she'd care to admit. She found herself glad to see him and eager for his company. She was glad also that he was allowed more freedom. It was wrong to keep him shut away – surely there was no need for it. It made him happy to wander further afield. Ursula sometimes saw him on the track picking wild strawberries as he slowly made his way to call on her, while trying to shoo his beloved Simmy back towards home. Simmy, a stocky ginger tom, who seemed more like a dog in his propensity to follow Schosi about, was placidly unresponsive. Ursula began to understand why Schosi had screamed so tragically and run on to the ice that day. He exuded love for the cat, as attentive as if it were another human being.

On one of Frau Hillier's visits, she, Mama, Ursula and Schosi were weeding the vegetable beds that edged the field, and it was Ursula's job to take the weed-filled buckets to the animals. On the third occasion, when she returned, Schosi had gone to the outhouse and the women had paused in their work and were talking in hushed tones.

'She can ask all she likes,' said Frau Hillier. 'They'll have nothing to tell.'

'So she's digging about then?' said Mama. 'Oh God! I'm afraid for you! That woman is poisonous, Gita.'

Ursula squatted beside them. 'Who is?'

'That woman is bitter,' said Frau Hillier with a vicious stab of her trowel into the soil. 'She had one of her own, a few years back. Did you know?' Mama shook her head and Frau Hillier glanced to check whether Schosi was still out of earshot. 'A late baby, not entirely right. She wrote to them herself – gave him up willingly.'

'How vile! How heartless!'

'Are you talking about Frau Gerg?' asked Ursula.

'But then not everyone's got a heart.'

'What happened?' said Ursula more loudly. 'What did she do?'

'Nothing, dear,' said Mama, placating her with a pat to the knee.

Ursula was offended – she was old enough to understand; they were rude to exclude her. She stood and snatched up the bucket. Just then, Schosi reappeared, and Frau Hillier called, 'Schatzi, come!' She went and hugged him and tickled under his arms until he doubled over, gasping. 'Come, my little mouse, my little rabbit.' She chuckled. 'What have you been doing?'

Ursula wandered off, irritated. Let them gossip, talk in half-sentences, make a drama. She didn't care what Frau Gerg had done, though she could well imagine her as heartless, hollow-chested, a dark space beneath her ribs filled only with bubbling bile. Frau Hillier was probably making a fuss about nothing; she just liked to bundle Schosi about and keep him close like a baby; that was all. He was quite safe.

Schosi disentangled himself from his mother and followed Ursula across the yard. She waited for him, somewhat cheered. She no longer believed what Anton had said about him being mad or perverted. He lost his stutter as long as he was at ease and spoke in a hushed monotone; he didn't fidget so much any more with his piece of cloth.

'Play with Uschi?' he said once he reached her. 'Little bear,' he added, putting his hands up to make a pair of ears.

Startled that he knew the meaning of her name, she cuffed him on the arm then led him to the cowshed. There, she tossed hay down from the loft while he put it in the mangers. Afterwards, he leaned against the nail-bitten frame of the door to watch the cow and goats and caged rabbits. He seemed to love the warm, dust-moted shed, strung with sunbeams that threaded through the ageing planks, sweet-smelling of the animals' bodies and buttery straw. It was a safe place, thought Ursula, a slow place. And he brought an even deeper calm. She stood next to him, not speaking, and his air of quiet contentment stilled the flutter in her mind, turned her limbs soft and heavy, drove away the dark things just out of view.

Siegfried arrived in his car at odd times of the night, the vehicle much scruffier these days, the paintwork scratched by flying debris, an awful dent in the bonnet where Siegfried said a large chunk of masonry had fallen from a parapet as he drove beneath. He held Mama's arm whenever she rose from the settle and ran around the table to pull a chair out for her, and generally behaved very oddly. He rebuked the children once or twice when they were unhelpful or lazy.

'Your mother's in no state to be dealing with disobedience. Do as you're told!'

The children took these remonstrations with a silent malevolence. Ursula tried to remember Papa's face, but it was fading. The nut-brown skin and crooked nose blended with the plump cheeks and dark moustache of Siegfried. Siegfried was the man who sat in the armchair in the living room and stayed sitting up with Mama long after the children went to bed. He carved the meat at mealtimes and was served first by Mama. He leaned on the edge of the kitchen work surface as Mama hurried through her tasks, talking to her about things happening in the capital. He made comments about the Russians and the political situation. They talked about the state of Austria, about the future of Austria, about Stalin. They shook their heads. He joined in with the cleaning; the house hadn't received a thorough clean since Papa died. He helped Ursula to beat the rugs, which were thrown over the washing line. Grey clouds enveloped them and they coughed and spluttered, the dull thwack of their woven cane paddles finding a rhythm. He called out 'One and two and three and four' and they kept on until the rugs were bright and the dirt gone. Ursula enjoyed the sport of it but felt disloyal. She wondered whether amongst the dust there was something of Papa floating away on the breeze. When Siegfried interfered with the feeding of the animals, using dandelion leaves to play tug of war with the rabbits through the wire, brought her gifts and repaired her rickety bed, when he sang while shaving and filled the house with good cheer, when he was kinder to Mama than Papa had ever been, Ursula made an effort to despise him.

'Why's your Mama so fat?' the kids chanted at school. 'What's she keeping in the oven?'

They threw dirt in Ursula's hair and stuck their feet out to trip her in the corridor. She kept close to Anton as much as she could. He often reminded her about their plan to report Siegfried. He'd investigated Siegfried's car one night and found a secret compartment beneath the carpeted lining of the boot, a flap that revealed a space below in which to hide things. It'd be so easy, he cajoled when they met on the balcony. 'Or are we just going to let them play happy families? Like we never existed. Like Papa never existed. You changed your mind yet?'

She deliberated, torn. It seemed more tempting now, more necessary. This man was ruining everything: who knew what he'd do next? Would she and Anton and Dorli be turned out? Anton said it was possible. Mama seemed delirious whenever Siegfried was around; whenever he came or went she was on the doorstep, arms waving madly above her head like a conductor. Ursula had seen them kissing in the house when they thought they were unobserved, faces squashed together in a way that looked painful, jaws working. She didn't like to see her mother behave so unguardedly and her dreams were filled with anxiety about a home that wasn't home but full of strangers. But it would be too cruel – unforgivable. It would hurt Mama terribly. And how could she condemn a man for stealing when her own hands twitched in every shop and she often took what wasn't hers?

'What about Mama?' She tried the same tack.

'She'd be all right. He's the one they want. He's the thief. We'll just mention the car. Give the registration.'

'Someone will see us if we go to the police station.'

'We go in the night, after the station's shut, you dummy.'
A sweat broke out on Ursula's skin – it would be terribly
frightening sneaking out after curfew to do such a thing.
But most of all she fretted because it would be wrong.

The following evening the house was blind and dark by
dinnertime and the apple tree whipped against the cladding
in disjointed rhythms. The wind was so strong it sounded
as though an army shook the doors till the latches jumped,
boomed the shutters and threw whistling grenades down
the flue pipe. Ursula huddled close to the Tirolia – Anton
hadn't come home after school. He was more than likely
with Rudi and this made her skittish. At around six o'clock
planes went over, their engines guttural and menacing,
just audible above the wind. Ursula ran to the upstairs
balcony. All that was visible was the thick, fast-flying
clouds, but hidden above was the enemy. Mama prayed
for Siegfried who was in the city overnight – the wireless
reported terrible destruction in Vienna, Graz, Salzburg,
Linz; smoking holes in buildings, civilians masked against
gases.

Not long after seven, Frau Hillier arrived with Schosi
in tow – Ursula's mood sank further to find it was not
Anton. They'd brought candles in case there was another
power cut, of which there'd been plenty of late, and some
of Herr Esterbauer's home-made schnapps. Frau Hillier
was soon talking with Mama, both ensconced in easy
chairs with drinks in hand, and Schosi watched Ursula
finish her homework, which was to stitch a sampler with
the word 'Deutschland'. He sat very close and dug his
fingers into the coloured balls of thread. Mama launched
into a diatribe about Anton's worsening behaviour, his

selfishness and disrespect, while Frau Hillier grunted her agreement. Ursula sensed the influence of Siegfried in Mama's galvanised air. She and Anton fought continually these days; the air crackled between them.

'Tonight, he can go hungry!' she retorted. 'I didn't save his portion, and why should I?'

'Quite,' said Frau Hillier.

When Anton arrived close to eight, he merely walked into the kitchen, swiped bread from the pantry, stuffed it into his mouth then dropped into a chair, chewing.

'That's rationed, you know!' Mama uncrossed her legs as if to stand.

Anton eyed her, malignant.

Schosi began to stammer, fumbled for Ursula's hand and drew his chair close. Mama glowered at Anton then reached for the schnapps bottle, stretching to where it stood on the table with some difficulty due to her boulder-like belly. She poured herself a second glassful.

'Fat pig,' said Anton loudly. 'Fat bitch.'

There was a sharp silence. Anton's eyelids lowered; languorous, satisfied.

Schosi clung to Ursula as though he hoped to be cradled, his hand almost crushing hers. Frau Hillier gaped in outrage. Mama heaved herself upright, strode across the kitchen and hit Anton across the cheek, a resounding whack right from the shoulder. He leapt from his seat, chest puffed like a swan. He glared at Mama for a few seconds then stalked from the room.

Mama buckled into her chair, weeping. She pressed her fingers to the creases in her forehead. She wailed, 'I don't know what's wrong with him! I can't fight him any more!'

'Have strength. You did the right thing.' Frau Hillier spoke tersely, her fists balled. 'He's got a nasty streak, that's for sure.'

'No, he hasn't!' said Ursula hotly. 'You don't understand! You shouldn't speak of him that way. It isn't fair.' She stood and wriggled her hand free of Schosi's. 'Mama, you're hurting him!' Mama looked at her, tear-streaked and baffled. 'He's just unhappy. And ashamed, and misses Papa.' But perhaps, she thought as she walked to the kitchen door, there *was* something wrong with him. Something underneath. He was always angry, always ready with venom. Dorli appeared, barging Ursula aside as she entered. She went immediately to Mama and took her hand, saying that Anton was an ungrateful hoodlum with the kind of manners one found everywhere nowadays amongst boys. They had no respect for their elders and believed themselves superior. Ursula thought her sister sounded like an old grandmother; she couldn't abide the sickly, consoling expression that she always used at times like this.

'He'll be back with his tail between his legs, you'll see.'

But Ursula couldn't imagine that – Dorli didn't seem to know Anton at all.

She slipped upstairs and into Anton's room and closed the door behind her. He was hunched over the windowsill, the glass opaque with his breath, looking out at the dark of the yard where the fir cones and seeds lay wet and mushy at the feet of the tall trees.

'Mama's so upset,' she said.

'I don't care,' came the abrupt reply. 'I'm sick of this place. I'll not be here much longer.'

'Not here?' Fear lurched in her – those words 'not here' unthinkable. 'You're not going? Are you?' She moved closer. The ceremonial dagger was on the sill beside him, a tapered, elegant shape. His arm rested next to it in an awkward fashion, so that the inner forearm was upwards and exposed. The skin was dark, wet, glistening; between the wrist and elbow of his left arm were a dozen furious cuts, criss-crossed, raised and bleeding.

She halted, aghast; a small pool of blood gathered on the painted wooden sill. 'Toni!' she croaked. She took a step towards him, heart thumping. He clamped his arm possessively against his front; the other side was red too, where he'd been leaning. He angled his body away.

'If he stays, I go,' he said.

She edged nearer, eyeing the dagger. Could she get to it? Her heartbeat thudded impossibly fast in her chest. Should she call Mama? A doctor? How deep were the cuts? She struggled to calm her breath.

Anton glanced at her, sly, watchful. 'If you won't . . . if you're with *them* now.' He reached for the dagger, picked it up.

'Don't, Toni!' She held out her hands.

He pushed the point against his arm near the elbow where the skin was still white and clean. 'I want rid of him.'

'Me too.'

He dug the blade and dragged, a stiff movement, blood beading then spilling in a dark, deliberate trickle.

'Ursula!' Mama called from downstairs.

She jumped hard; her throat constricted so that no words would come. It was agony to see him do it. Terror strangled her momentarily.

He stopped.

'You're stupid,' she whispered. 'Stupid!'

After a while he let her come and dab the blood away. She used her skirt, gently wiping, bending close to look. The cuts were long and ragged-edged, slashing messily one over the other, like the efforts of a drunken ploughman. But they weren't as severe as all the blood would suggest – with tight binding they'd be staunched and would heal. But still her fingers shook violently and a deep ache squeezed in her chest. It was as if he'd cut her too. She bent to kiss where she tended; the flesh burned beneath her lips. 'You have to wash this. I'll bring water.' Tears stung her nose and filled her vision.

'I could be useful,' he continued. 'I could do well.'

She blinked rapidly to dry her eyes. 'At the Front?' She imagined the house without him, vacant. No one to comfort her or understand about the shadows and anxious dreams. If he left – she daren't think it – alone he might push the knife too deep. The tears came properly then. She pressed her cuffs to her eyes, which were quickly sodden. 'And what would *I* do?'

'You'd be all right.'

'I wouldn't.'

'You've got your new friends.'

'Schosi?'

'And that Commie, Sontheimer.'

'Ursula!' Mama called again, impatient.

'He's not my friend.'

'More than,' he said. 'Well, go to her then. She probably can't stand us talking. '

Ursula removed her skirt – she'd wash the blood out and put on another. She crossed the room to the door. 'It's not more than.' She held the latch as if it were important, hand still shaking; she felt helpless – a gasping fish pulled on to the stones. What could she say to please him? To keep him? 'I don't like her either.' But the statement was limp and forced. She didn't hate Mama like Anton did; she didn't even hate Siegfried. But he had to go; that was clear now. 'Write the note,' she said. 'Let's do it tonight.'

In the hall she put on her coat and buttoned it high, then wrapped her scarf around tightly. It made her feel protected, less visible. She went outside to lock the chickens in their coop. Just as she did so Siegfried's car came along the track, exhaust snarling in a grey cloud from its damaged pipe, sending roosting crows flapping from the treetops. She hurried around the corner to the henhouse so that she was out of view. After shutting the hatches against the fox, she waited till Siegfried had gone inside. She prayed that Anton wouldn't bolt at the first glimpse of him, that he'd keep his temper and hold to their plan. When she went back to the front of the house she saw his outline in the upstairs window and was reassured. She entered the porch, quietly removed her boots; her mind strayed constantly to the terrifying task that awaited her. As she passed the framed world map in the hallway, she caught sight of her own reflection. Her face was a white triangle, hovering vaporous over the red expanse that was Russia. She tried to smooth the tangles of her hair but her fingers got stuck in the knots.

Just then she heard a sharp creak. She turned and there was Siegfried, coming down the stairs. He'd probably gone to put his bag and luxurious coat in Mama's bedroom. He no longer hung the coat in the hallway. She supposed he'd noticed how often his wallet was returned to a different pocket, minus a few Reichsmarks.

'Ursula,' he said, in his pleasant, well-bred voice. 'I didn't see you there. Are you all right?'

She nodded. She didn't often answer Siegfried when he addressed her though he was persistently attentive. He always asked her if she'd enjoyed her day at school and she responded with a monosyllable, unused to such consideration from an adult or to the concept that school could ever be enjoyable, convinced he merely courted her in order to more comfortably exploit them, exploit Mama.

'You look pale.' He came down with a dry swish of his hand along the banister. 'Are you sure you're well?' He bent to look into her face, frowning. She nodded again, feeling treacherous. A few flecks of cotton wool adhered to his cheeks where he'd cut himself shaving; the skin looked pink, too tender. 'You seem under the weather. You should get some sleep.' He touched her lightly on the arm. 'Do you want something hot to drink?'

She shook her head vehemently and ran up the stairs.

After dark, once Mama, Siegfried and Dorli had retired, Ursula moved like a breath along the balcony to Anton's room, the clouds gone, the wind calmed so that she had to tread with extra care. Anton opened the window. She climbed in and sat beside him on his eiderdown. Between them was the envelope ready for the station mailbox, addressed to *Felddorf Police*. Anton held the note itself and unfolded it for her inspection. He'd written in his splodgy hand all their accusations. From somewhere – the bureau probably – he'd found Siegfried's Vienna address and included that also. She nibbled her nails as she read; Siegfried's kindness lingered like an accusation. They were doing a bad thing; she'd regret it. And what if they were caught? The Hitler Youth patrolled the streets at night and punishments were harsh for youngsters breaking curfew. But Anton risked all, including his precious dagger. She daren't show cowardice now.

They skulked on the pavement opposite the station. The sky was cumbersome with stars, a glimmering lid over the village. A still night, thought Ursula, to help her be still. But her whole body shook. Anton was more composed, the note in his pocket. The street was deadly quiet with no patrol in sight.

'Let's do it.' He took her hand, pulled her towards the station.

'I can't.'

'Why not?' He gave her an assessing look. 'What you scared of?'

'I'm not scared.'

'Well, what then?'

She didn't answer and after a moment he sort of hissed at her then set off across the road. She knew she should follow but instead drew back into the thick fir hedge. What a gutless creative she was. Anton walked briskly up to the station, opened the mailbox and put the letter inside as confidently as if he delivered post to the police every day. The lid of the box shrieked rustily. Ursula shrank further into the hedge so that the fir fronds meshed together in front of her face and cloaked her. She peered in each direction along the road, afraid to see a lantern or torch beam, but the street was dark. Anton recrossed the road and together they ran home. Her heart pounded with fear, guilt, dread, relief, her steps lifted by a heady, hysterical feeling, tears almost springing free but not quite. It was done – there was no undoing it now. She closed her mind to thoughts of Siegfried. He was a cuckoo in the nest, a leech. He didn't mean anything to them.

9

Schosi sat in the attic on the edge of his bed. He was restless and wanted to go outside. It was nearly time to feed the cats and then it would be a while longer before his mama came home from the factory. He got up and went to the window, which overlooked the garden as small as a postage stamp. Below, Simmy jumped the fence and set off across the meadow. He always chose to go in the same direction, parting the grass with his thick body, and Schosi was comforted watching him strike out on his journey. He often wondered where the cat went and had once followed, the evening sun catching the red of Simmy's coat so that it flamed, until they reached the edge of the woods. The trees swallowed the cat but Schosi dared not go where the sunlight couldn't reach.

The girl – little bear – was daring and comforting too, he thought. It had been good to sit with her at the table playing with the wool. She'd helped him not to grow wild when Anton had flown through the Hildesheim kitchen black with anger. He was pleased that now he was allowed to see her and that his mama would sometimes go with him. She said that there were still rules – he mustn't forget, he was only allowed to the Hildesheim house in the evenings or at the weekend, not any time, not wandering after Simmy.

As Schosi looked out, a woman appeared on the track. For a second he mistook her for his mama but this woman lifted her feet high over the grasses and patches of mud like the fine horse in the painting on Herr Esterbauer's wall. She had a thin face quite unlike his mama's. Her gloved hands waved as she tried to keep her balance on the rough ground. Schosi drew back from the glass and hid behind the curtain; she was a stranger. She stopped directly in front of his fence. She looked at the house, peered into the downstairs windows for a few moments, then raised her face and looked up at the attic window, shielding her eyes against the low sun. He kept still – he didn't like the way she looked. Her mouth was small and her eyebrows were two thin lines. It reminded him somehow of the Führer's face. She might be the type of person his mama warned him about – unkind, someone who didn't understand about him and meant him harm. He moved away from the window and sat once more on the edge of his bed, took out his comfort blanket and twisted it round his finger. He let it unravel and watched it spin.

When he heard the scrape of the gate against the path he knew that the woman was now in the garden. She would be looking in at the windows. He felt scared in case she could get inside but the door was locked, he reminded himself, the bolts drawn tight. He pressed the face of his wristwatch to his ear and listened to the small, tight tick. He remained in this position until he heard the gate scrape once more. He wanted to creep to the glass to check, to be sure she was gone, but she might be out there, waiting.

He dragged the covers off the bed and wrapped them around his shoulders. The chill of evening had begun to fill the house and darkness too, blanking out the corners of the attic room. He didn't light a lamp even though he was scared of the dark. He lay down, the blanket tucked protectively around his neck, and prayed his mama would soon come.

10

Schosi had begged and begged and pestered and pestered to go to his papa's grave until Ursula had thumped him on the arm and told him that she'd take him, but to keep his mouth shut about it. She went when she knew the church would be quiet and took him along a footpath behind the houses rather than along the main street. She knew she oughtn't to break Frau Hillier's regulations but he'd rot away from boredom at this rate, always having to be accounted for and never allowed to try anything new. He would come to no bother on a short walk like this. She hoped he felt a kick of life in his veins as they went through the fields dotted with rye stooks – a secret, an adventure, a scheme; that he enjoyed the soft breeze and the birds above zigzagging against the sky. To their left, gaps in the hedges and fences showed portions of the village. Schosi pointed excitedly when he saw the Gasthaus, its name painted on the front wall in fine scrolling letters and soldiers standing by the fountain smoking, a motorcycle parked amongst them. A group of Hitler Youth were going door to door for scrap metal, dragging a handcart full of dented pans and piping and a rust-ravaged bath. Ursula was in a nervous mood, not only because of their forbidden excursion but because Siegfried hadn't been to visit for almost two weeks. This had put Mama in a vengeful temper, careering from tears to silence to snappishness. But at least, she thought, it had prevented Anton from leaving. As the days passed she became less and less certain whether she'd be regretful or glad if a letter arrived with news of Siegfried's arrest. She didn't want to be the reason for Mama's alarming, fragile pallor, the red-eyed gloom she brought downstairs each morning, which clung to everything like low-lying fog. She hadn't truly understood the depth of her mother's attachment until now. Mama was no longer full of energy and alight with hope; there was only the belly, taut and huge, pushing everything else aside. She offered Ursula barely a smile and a thousand criticisms: lazy, useless, stupid girl, why can't you be more like your sister?

After a while they came to where the camp fence ran adjacent to the footpath. Structures much like sturdy hunting towers stood at each corner. If Siegfried were thrown into a place like that he might be beaten or starved. He'd certainly suffer. She pictured him as thin as those escaped Bolsheviks had been, as frantic. In one of the towers a guard stood with his back to the outside world. His shoulders were sharp and Ursula saw the butt of a gun. They trod quickly and quietly until the camp was behind them, Schosi seeming to understand the menace of that place, that watchful figure.

They joined the road near the church; fallen berries popped beneath their boots with a satisfying sound. This would be the first time she'd visited the church since the day Frau Gerg had shamed them in the churchyard and Anton had warned her away from 'the wrong type of boy'. She'd seen Sepp since, once or twice at school, but hadn't spoken to him. It was hard to resist; he often waved and seemed so wholesome. Only the other day at school she'd observed as he played marbles alone; he often seemed to be without companions, as she was. He'd squatted and taken a careful shot, his long legs doubled at either side like a grasshopper's. She'd liked his grey shorts and the polished tan of his knees. The smooth healthiness of his skin reminded her of a conker, or a walnut bowl rubbed with oil.

She sighed while she walked, preoccupied, squeezed Schosi's arm as warm feelings filled her body – longing, admiration. How would it feel to be kissed? What would she do? She remembered the way Sepp had stood in the graveyard with his fists full of leaves, how wondrous he'd looked, as though all the brilliance of summer was in that single face. She imagined kissing him: he was unable to hold her because his hands were full; she lifted her arms to his shoulders – their lips softly touched.

Schosi looked at her and put his hand on hers.

She waited at the top of the slope while Schosi visited the church. He loved to show her what he could do without help, so she let him. It was good for him to try. She sat cross-legged at the edge of the road as he went down the hill and stepped inside the church porch. He re-emerged after a few minutes holding the tin cup from the font. She smiled, watching him; he progressed gingerly over the grass to his papa's grave and was soon out of sight.

After a while she grew cold and damp. She tried to shin up the wall that overlooked the graveyard so that she could see what Schosi was doing, but the wall was too sheer and she grazed her knee on the stones. She wandered a little along the lane, which had a few houses on it. She found an apple tree overhanging a garden fence. The lowest bough was just within reach and she deftly plucked several apples, glancing over her shoulder to check she wasn't being observed; another few fell to the ground as she did so, ready and ripe. She hid the stolen fruit under her coat and returned to her waiting place, put them in the long grass and resumed her pacing. Eventually Schosi appeared, a boy with him; the boy opened the gate for Schosi so that he could walk out and Schosi came over the grass and up the road towards Ursula while the boy looked on. It was Sepp.

'There were dead bugs,' Schosi said, out of breath when he reached Ursula. He pointed back at the churchyard. 'In the dish.'

He meant the dish of holy water on his papa's grave.

'Did you tip them out?' she asked absently.

He nodded. Sepp began up the hill towards them. Ursula raked her fingers through the ends of her hair, smoothed her skirts and pulled her socks up to where they ought to be. 'Slattern' was the latest insult launched her way in school and she was afraid it was true; her sloppiness was undeniable. It also occurred to her that if Sepp hadn't known about her mother's disgrace last time they met, he surely would now. From the size of Mama's bump he'd probably wagered on bastard twins.

'Hello!' he called when he'd almost reached them. He stopped beside Schosi. Ursula smiled and put her hands inside her cardigan sleeves, which she'd hastily rolled to hide the fray. She thought he seemed slightly taller than before and he was dressed very smartly. He wore a good suit and his hair was combed treacle-smooth. 'I've just been talking to your friend.'

Schosi tried to speak; his stutter forced his arm to flop up and down, an involuntary spasm, as though to whip the stuck words out into the open. Sepp waited. After a while Schosi gave up, red-faced from effort.

'How are you?' Sepp asked Ursula. He glanced at her shyly.

'Fine, thanks,' she said stiffly, reminding herself of what her brother had said about Sepp and his aunt siding with the enemy and Sepp being unpleasant to Anton at the Hitler Youth. She should walk away now, she thought, if she was going to be loyal. She hesitated. She tried to imagine Sepp swinging for her brother, saying low-down things.

'I like your ribbons,' said Sepp. 'I mean I like their colour.'

The ribbons were of a smooth lemon yellow material, pilfered last week from another girl's bag at school. The inevitable blush began to heat her face. 'Thanks. They're only cheap.'

'They're nice.'

Schosi tried again to speak. 'My p-p-papa,' he managed.

Sepp looked stumped. Then after a second he said, 'Oh, your papa! I was asking your friend if he was looking for someone because he seemed lost.' Beads of sweat had appeared on Sepp's nose and upper lip. Ursula had the urge to reach out and touch the damp skin with her finger. It had a thirsty look, like petals or leaves after rain. She forced herself to stare at her shoes. But Anton was so difficult, she thought. There were so many things that made him cross. She could far more easily picture him hitting Sepp than the other way round. She bet it had been Anton who'd landed the first punch. But then, he'd had reason to.

'I was wondering if you—' Sepp began. He shuffled about.

'Josef!' A high voice called from the base of the hill; a slender arm waved from the church doorway and a head poked around the doorframe. The head was plaited prettily and at the end of each pigtail was a large bow. It was Marta.

Sepp waved back to her. He turned to Ursula with an apologetic expression. 'We're Confirmation partners, Marta and I,' he explained. 'It's our rehearsal today.' A woman emerged from the doorway and stood beside Marta; both stared up the hill. The woman beckoned briskly. 'That's our mentor. She's a frightful bore.'

Ursula smiled and nodded, jealousy igniting in the hollow of her belly, a sour pain that burned like Mama's black stomach ointment. Marta and Sepp Confirmation partners; of course, she'd been right all those months ago. The two would share a ceremony. Marta would walk with him up the aisle to be blessed and taken into the church – she'd wear her glorious dress encrusted in lace so fine that everyone would marvel. They'd look for all the world like a couple being married. She imagined the preparation classes they'd been attending together each week. Sepp must love her by now; how could he not? She was pretty and rich and wore ribbons far more lavish than Ursula's. She had the kind of family that everyone spoke well of. And now she was spending time with him after school, and every Saturday, getting to know him, casting her spell.

'Well, hadn't you better go?' said Ursula. The words emerged clipped and cool. She hadn't meant them to; it was just that she couldn't quite talk normally.

'Yes, I suppose,' said Sepp. He held out his hand to Schosi. Schosi hesitated then shook it. Sepp seized Ursula's hand next. She was unable to meet his eye, the grip of his fingers around hers almost more than she could tolerate. She pulled sharply away.

'Bye,' she said.

'Nice to see you.' He tried to smile at her but she didn't allow it. He went off down the hill.

Ursula watched him go then picked up the stolen apples, handed four of them to Schosi and put the rest in her pocket. Schosi was delighted and thanked her. He bit into one of them and put the others into his voluminous coat. What awful luck, she thought glumly as they set off, dragging her feet through the mulch of pine needles and soil at the roadside, not caring that it dirtied her boots. What a horrible thing to happen. She wished she'd never come so she'd not found out. She was surprised Marta hadn't already made a point of announcing it to her at school. What a liar Marta was; she'd warned Ursula not to encourage Sepp but all the while was planning to make eyes at him herself. Well, Marta wouldn't want him half as much if Ursula told her about what Sepp and his aunt had done. Marta couldn't abide Russians or Communists or anyone like that.

'Uschi.' Anton was sitting on the wall overlooking the road and church.

She stopped, startled. She hadn't seen or heard him arrive.

'Having a good time?' He sprang from the wall with alarming energy. Ursula's sour ointment instantly mixed with the dull churn of guilt. 'Having a friendly chat with that no-good piece of shit?'

She shook her head as Anton came towards her, an intense flush leaping into his face. He grabbed a handful of her cardigan. She flinched, certain he'd strike her. 'I could hear you. I saw you smiling and shaking his hand.' He shoved her. 'You've got the hots for him. It's ridiculous. I bet he's laughing.' He adopted a silly girlish voice. 'All pink and lovestruck – what a treat for him.' He began to walk away. 'I asked you to do one thing, which was to stay away from him. But you don't give a damn how it makes me feel.'

Ursula went after him and Schosi followed. 'I didn't want to speak to him. He came up to me.'

'Oh, don't bother.' Anton walked faster.

'Toni, please!'

He turned and sneered. 'If he knew you like I do, do you think he'd smile at you then?'

She stopped dead. 'Don't say that!' The shadow loomed and clutched, sent her heart into an anxious muddling beat. He knew all her secrets, the worst of them. She hurried after him again. Soon they neared the centre of the village, the camp to their left, Ursula jogging to keep up, Schosi at her side, panting, his shoes slapping loudly on the road.

'He was talking to Schosi, not me,' she exclaimed breathlessly as she caught up with her brother. She couldn't stand it if he thought her so faithless, even if she had been tempted.

Anton lunged towards Schosi and pushed him; Schosi's half-eaten apple flew and he fell heavily to the ground, the other apples rolling free from his coat. He sat, pressing his chest and gulping air, then scrambled to retrieve the fruit from the gutter. He was tearful, trying without success to wipe clean the apple he'd been eating, which was covered in grit. His leg was grazed and bleeding.

'Don't use the idiot as an excuse,' said Anton. 'You shouldn't have brought him here. He'll be taken off on the murder bus.' He pretended to snatch Schosi, hands outstretched. 'And it'd be good riddance!'

Just then, the gates to the camp opened with a jangle of wire. A guard appeared. Beyond him, prisoners carried tools and pushed barrows, exiting the camp; another guard herded them at the rear. They lined up on the verge. Ursula took Schosi's arm. She walked fast but didn't run, not wanting to draw attention, all Frau Hillier's worried comments springing to her mind. She should have gone back on the footpath, not on the road. Anton followed, kicking at Schosi's feet like a hound worrying a sheep.

'Stop it!' said Ursula. 'Just lay off him!'

'Or what?'

They reached Frau Gerg's grand house. Vines tumbled from the balcony, the red of autumn bleeding through the leaves, matching the swastika flags that poked from amongst them.

'Hey, Frau Gerg!' Anton cupped his hands around his mouth. 'Here's your Hillier boy. Here's the one you've been looking for. He's subnormal all right!' He grabbed a corner of Schosi's coat and delved into the pockets. He tossed the apples out on to the road. 'And a thief too!' A shadow moved behind the net curtain at the downstairs window. 'He stole these just now from someone's garden. He should be dealt with.'

'Anton!' Ursula wrenched Schosi free of her brother. 'They're my apples. Stop it!'

'You should keep an eye on those Sontheimers too,' Anton continued, his voice growing louder. 'They're traitors and Russian-lovers. They hid one of those criminals. I saw them do it!'

The door to the grand house opened and Frau Gerg appeared, her narrow face blotchy as if it had been scrubbed raw and the thin brows unpainted, faint curves above her unblinking eyes. She stepped outside a little way amongst the crowds of ornaments that cluttered her steps; she stared at Schosi much as someone would stare at any repulsive and alien thing – a centipede or a wriggling creature from the bottom of a pond. Ursula ran, dragging Schosi with her. Anton gave chase, laughing. An apple pounded into the road near Schosi's feet and the white flesh exploded. Another apple thumped Schosi's back with a hollow sound.

'You're for the oven!' called Anton. 'You're for the chop!'

Ursula ran as fast as she could, crying, hating her brother, shocked because she hadn't known he could be so cruel. Why had she brought Schosi here, into this danger? What a stupid thing to have done. She looked behind but Anton no longer followed. He sauntered towards Frau Gerg, whose sharp face still poked from the doorway, intent, dog-like, sniffing the wind.

That night Ursula woke several times from dreams of suffocation and her brother's face above hers, pushing her down into the stifling bedclothes. A tall shape stood near by in the shadows, watching, a thing she couldn't quite see, a wrong thing, a dirty thing. She was to blame; it was her fault. She'd let everybody down. She'd never be good, not ever. She was guilty and full of sin.

In the morning a telegram arrived. Mama read it then buckled forward; a long, straining cry wrung from her like the hopeless bray of a lonely donkey beaten till it bled. Ursula caught the few words she gasped amidst the tears: 'The People's Army. Oh, Sigi – my love.'

Ursula wanted to run to her, to hug her and tell her it would be all right, but she couldn't because she'd brought this grief, she'd made this happen. A summons to the People's Army – it was as good as a death sentence; everyone knew that. Wretched, she stood by and wished all her actions undone.

Part Two

11

Schosi and his mama ate dinner in the kitchen of their house. Her face glowed like a yellow apricot, soft and pleasant-looking in the pool of candlelight. Beyond her, darkness stood in the living-room doorway and outside the trees were loud. There was no talk between Schosi and his mother – the groans and cracks and squeals of the branches were enough to fill the air, and the whispering rustle of the leaf drifts moving against the base of the house. One of the flowerpots toppled on the front step, the small shrub in the pot caught by a strong gust. The pot rolled about on the stone and Schosi's mama got up and opened the door to set it right.

'It's cracked,' she shouted and a gale blew down the hallway and into the kitchen. The tea towels fell from above the stove.

Bedtime would soon arrive and then Schosi would be alone in the loft listening to the woods and the rattle of glass. He licked his plate while his mother wasn't looking and put it in the sink.

Silvery morning came through the loft window. The birds peep-peeped to each other. Schosi turned in his bed – his hot-water bottle, now cold, sloshed against his feet. Today he was to stay at home and get the wood in the basket. His mother was awake downstairs, so he got out of bed and wrapped the blanket around his body. He went to the trapdoor. 'Mama!' he called.

She came to the bottom of the ladder. 'Come on down, my mouse,' she said. 'So I can say goodbye.'

He dropped the blanket and climbed down the ladder, shivering in his long johns, his bare feet already numb with cold. She put her hands on his shoulders and kissed the top of his head.

'Be good,' she said. 'Get the wood in. No wandering.' She embraced him and he breathed the smoky smell of her hair.

She went out of the front door and closed the screen but not the door itself, so that they could speak through the mesh. 'Your breakfast's on the table under the basket,' she said. 'Promise me, my love – no wandering. Do you promise?'

'I promise,' he said.

Schosi watched his mother with her slow limp go off along the track. She walked with her head down in the sifting rain. She went round the corner out of sight. Schosi climbed back up the ladder and got dressed. His long johns showed below his trousers so he pulled his socks over the top to cover them. He put on his coat because it was cold, and his favourite hat. He made his bed – the blue material rippled when he tried to smooth it – he liked the way it looked, like wavelets on a pond. He twirled his comfort blanket before laying it on the pillow, then put on his boots.

Downstairs he ladled warm water from the water chamber into a mug and also washed his face. He sat down to his breakfast, lifted the basket, which was upturned over the meal to keep the bugs and mice away. It was bread with pickled gherkin and kohlrabi, all cut in pieces for him. There was a slice of Herr Esterbauer's bacon, also cut up, which the farmer gave to them even though it was breaking the rules. Schosi's mama had dusted the food with salt, which was a special treat because salt was for stews and preserving. After eating, he said his prayers in the living room. He thought of his mother at the factory and prayed she wouldn't be too tired. He thought about little bear and wished her good things. He finished his prayers and went to feed the cats in the woodshed. They coiled around his ankles, tails vibrating, poker-straight. He leaned against the woodstack to watch them. Simmy hunched over his bowl, his muscular ginger shoulders in two peaks, his stubby tail swishing. Schosi brushed his fingertips between the tattered, mite-encrusted ears and Simmy spoke to him, a soft, questioning greeting.

Inside, Schosi settled on the armchair in the kitchen with his wristwatch. He wound it and put it to his ear. He focused on the comforting noise, regular, gentle and pleasing. He enjoyed doing this more than most things; he liked to guess when the big hand would get to one of the markers, though he lost track when he tried to count around the face in the correct order.

A loud knock shook the front door and he jumped violently. He stuffed the wristwatch in his pocket. A visitor had come once before when his mother was at work. It'd been Herr Esterbauer delivering a tin whistle, which was a gift Schosi had barely touched because it made a terrible shrieking sound. The knock came again. He knew what he must do – he must hide. Even if he thought it might be Herr Esterbauer or another friend, his mother had strictly told him not to open the door. The best hiding place was the cellar, which had only enough space for a few bags of potatoes. He hated it down there. It was dark and smelled disgusting.

He got out of his chair very carefully. He knew he was clumsy and heavy-footed, and the people outside – he could hear them talking – mustn't know he was here. He crept from the stove to the cellar hatch and lifted it quietly. The whiff of damp and rat urine and droppings reached him. He stepped on to the first of the stairs, held the hatch open with one hand and allowed it to lower over his head as he climbed slowly down. Darkness closed over him and he could hardly see; his foot bumped against an object; he stumbled and let go of the hatch and put his hand on to the wall to steady himself. The hatch dropped with a bang just missing his head. He felt his way forward; his foot struck the object again – it was a sack, he could feel the rough material. A loud clattering and then a splintering sound came from the front door. His heart galloped, galumphing with its unequal gait, hurting him. He navigated the last low step and then squatted on the floor and held on to the sack, the only familiar thing, the only other presence he could sense in the darkness. His eyes were met with pure blackness. He heard feet on the floor above. Someone was in the house – people walked above him. He pulled out his wristwatch and pressed it to his ear. This calmed him a little. He wished his mama would come. She'd greet the visitors and ask them what they wanted then send them off. And once they were gone, she'd let him come out. She'd give him an apple for being brave and a cup of hot *Malzkaffee*.

The people stopped directly above. 'In here,' came a voice.

The hatch rattled and lifted; light flooded in. Schosi hid his face behind the sack and hoped he wasn't visible; he held the wristwatch against his ear as hard as he could.

'Ah!' said the voice.

A small pair of feet on the end of a fat pair of legs came down the stone stairs and a hand grasped Schosi's collar and pulled him upright. He struck his head on the low ceiling. He was hauled upwards. A second man waited at the top of the steps. He was a policeman, short and thin, his belt fastened neatly around his small waist, his face pointed and beady-eyed. Like a weasel, thought Schosi.

'Are you Hillier Schosi?' asked the weasel. Schosi didn't reply, his mother having told him never to speak to a man in uniform. Schosi looked at the other man, who was much larger. When he realised who it was he became weak with fright. It was Herr Adler, the Party inspector. This was the person his mama warned him of more than anyone – when Herr Adler came Schosi must leave the house entirely, hurry out of the back door and scramble up the steep, weed-clogged bank to wait in the copse till the inspector was gone. Herr Adler shifted his grasp on Schosi's forearm; his pudgy hands squeezed too tightly so that Schosi's wrist began to ache.

'Answer him!' he snapped.

Schosi looked at each of the men then nodded.

'You have been reported as being unruly in the village of Felddorf. You have been seen stealing fruit from a garden.'

'N-n-no!' exclaimed Schosi, despite himself.

'Where's your mother?' asked the weasel-faced officer.

'Disgraceful,' muttered Herr Adler. 'The state of him. The whole house is a tip as usual. She clearly can't care for this boy – Frau Gerg was not wrong in her assessment. And he certainly can't care for himself. He can barely understand what we're saying.'

'Let's go,' said the weasel. 'Let's get him to the surgery.'

Herr Adler nodded and moved Schosi down the hallway. Schosi looked up at the inspector's bulky cheeks that bristled like pork flesh, the small red mouth – he was much more terrible up close than when Schosi had peeped through foliage to watch him searching the woodshed and yard. Schosi tried to resist briefly as they went through the front door but Herr Adler hit him hard across the head so that his neck jerked in agony and he felt dizzy. He was pushed over the threshold.

The men talked as they went along the track towards the village, mostly about what they would eat for lunch. Herr Adler planned to have rye bread and sausage and a beer at the Gasthaus. The weasel described the meal of *Knödl* and cheese that his wife would be preparing. He too liked a beer with his lunch and suggested he could meet Herr Adler at the Gasthaus before the station reopened.

Schosi was less frightened now that the men were ignoring him and talking about normal things. He trotted to keep up with Herr Adler – maybe his mama would come and get him once he was in the village. She always knew what to do. He hadn't stolen any fruit. He'd tell her that and she'd believe him. He watched the crows with grey beaks in the treetops – they flapped from branch to branch, following him.

It started to rain just as they reached Felddorf, the same fine rain as when his mama had left for work, so that even the cheeriest houses looked blurry and colourless. A woman watched from a window, her face framed by net curtains, her gaze tracking them as they passed. Schosi realised that it was the same woman with the bony face and the thin brows who'd come to his house, and who he'd also seen here once before with Ursula and Anton. He craned his neck to look back but Herr Adler shook him until he faced forward again.

They reached the doctor's surgery. Schosi became very anxious the moment they went inside. He remembered the hallway from a long time ago, the smell of leather and dust and the wide passageway with doors along it. The weasel stopped outside one of the doors, which had a gold square of metal on it with some writing. He knocked. After a couple of seconds a voice called, 'Come!' and the weasel opened the door. They went into the room where a man sat behind a desk in front of a small window. Schosi knew that the man was a doctor – he wore a white coat and had black-framed glasses. He gestured to a chair but Herr Adler shook his head.

'No, thank you, we're in a hurry. We just want to bring this boy to your attention.'

The doctor looked at Schosi. His eyes were large behind his spectacles and they moved slowly, like fish underwater.

'It's been reported to us that he's cretinous, and neglected by his mother. He's been stealing fruit and causing trouble in general. We have reliable witnesses.'

Schosi became upset again. He wasn't a thief. Where was his mother? He must get away. They were telling lies about him. He struggled to free his arm from Herr Adler's solid grip; he wrenched back and forth, but Herr Adler only strengthened his hold until Schosi gave up and stopped struggling. His breath gasped loudly in and out.

Herr Adler watched Schosi's attempt to disentangle himself with amusement, then, after a moment, continued speaking.

'He's very troublesome, as you can see. And he's living in squalid conditions. His mother can't care for him – she's rather unconventional, a dubious character, I can assure you. We thought it best that you assess his case and consider other options for him. Things can't go on as they are.'

'Does he have a name?' said the doctor.

'Hillier Schosi.'

The doctor scribbled on a notepad. Once he'd finished he nodded. 'Leave him with me, gentlemen. Thank you.'

Herr Adler and the policeman left the room and closed the door.

12

Mama didn't go to work that day. She stayed in bed. When Ursula got home from school in the afternoon Mama was still in the bedroom and nothing had moved in the kitchen – the bread hadn't been touched and Edi was calling in pain from the cowshed, her udder full to bursting. Ursula went up to the bedroom door and listened. Silence. She went inside and Mama was a lump under the covers. She crossed to the bedside, touched Mama's hip and shook it. Mama raised her head.

'Edi needs milking.'

Mama let her head drop on to the pillow and sighed.

Ursula went downstairs, put on her headscarf, collected the milking pail, and went out to the cowshed. Her thoughts were crowded with worry. She'd not been able to concentrate in school and had been told off by Herr

Gruber, but she hadn't cared; her mind was elsewhere; there were too many things; she couldn't clearly see or understand. Her feelings – anger, sadness, guilt, fear – were meshed together in a tangle so that she felt she was snagged in the centre of a thicket of thorns.

Edi was shifting her feet and the veins on her udder bulged, the whole thing terribly swollen. Ursula milked her and it took a long time – she wasn't as quick as Mama and had to concentrate; between the regular movements of her hands she tried not to think. But the behaviour of Anton in the village kept replaying in her memory. This made her own veins thump; it physically hurt to be angry with him, an aching throb. She went over in her mind the spite and fury of his outburst in the village. The shock of it still made her fingers shake. He was vengeful, but for what? Just because she spoke to others, had made a friend he didn't like? Schosi didn't deserve that. He could have got into real trouble. And Sepp too – his aunt. She began to fret then about what Anton had said of Sepp. Had they really hidden a Russian? Was that why Sepp had made comments in the playground about the prisoners being murdered? A Russian-lover. A Commie. Some would think he deserved to be punished. She prayed that nothing would come of it but her nerves said otherwise. An echo of her stifling dream crouched at the edge of her thoughts, accusatory. She'd taken Schosi where she shouldn't have. She'd ignored all his mother's warnings in a fit of pique.

The cats came and sat near her stool, waiting for a game that she always played with them whenever she milked the cow or goat. Once she'd got a good amount of milk out and Edi was more comfortable, she turned one of the teats towards the cats. They rose on to their haunches, then she

142

squirted milk into the air and the cats opened their mouths. Once Ursula had tired of the game, the cats sat and licked their faces, cleaned their legs and paws and settled in the straw in case there was a second round. She was glad to have the animals all to herself again, without having to share them with Siegfried. But conscription to the People's Army – the poor man. A wave of near panic washed over her. He'd die for certain and Mama would lose her mind entirely. The locals often muttered about the pointless slaughter of their men, as grandfathers and young sons were dragged from families and deployed to the front line. It was Hitler's blind pride, they said. Only fanatics like Herr Adler and Frau Gerg still believed in the final victory. How could Siegfried survive, when it was said that the bullets supplied were often the wrong type for the guns, or else the guns themselves were factory rejects that misfired, or relics from the Great War? Ursula thought of how patient he'd been with her and of the gifts he'd brought. She was ungrateful, spiteful, selfish. No matter if he was a philanderer and a cheat, he was a person and Mama loved him and he'd still be here if it wasn't for her. She dried her tears. She'd take a walk to calm herself – she'd go to Schosi's house, check he was all right, spend an hour in his ordered world of few words, of watches and comfort blankets, of firewood placed carefully and precisely in the basket, of prayer in front of the Holy Mary. She'd read to him or invent a story while he dozed in her lap. He always made her feel better and asked no questions – he liked her no matter what.

She rapped on the side window of Schosi's house using four short knocks, their signal. She tried a second time before going to the door. Instead of being locked, it wasn't quite closed and swung inwards at her touch. She noticed a splintered indentation on the doorframe, wood showing bright through the paint. She stepped inside; the house was silent. The cellar hatch spiked up from the floor throwing a wedge of shadow; she went and looked down into the cramped space but there were only sacks. She found herself treading softly, holding her breath, dry-mouthed. She climbed slowly to the loft, peered into the room, hopeful that Schosi would be asleep on his bed. The bed was empty, his comfort blanket crumpled on the pillow. After descending, she ventured out into the back yard. She half expected to see the Russian inmate there, even though the body had been dragged away months before. The yard was quiet and ordinary in daylight. Cats sat in the entrance of the woodshed but Schosi was nowhere to be seen. She was certain he was supposed to be at home today rather than at the farm. But then maybe he'd been called in to cover for Mama's absence. That would be a sensible explanation. She returned to the front of the house and wandered in the garden not knowing what to do, rubbing her hands together distractedly, kicking at the heads of weeds. She inspected the splintered mark again, the flakes of dislodged paint crunching beneath her shoes, and then walked into the adjacent field and called his name. Perhaps she should just go home. He was probably fine. She wandered for a while, picking grasses as she went and trying to make them whistle. They were all the wrong thickness and ripped between her fingers. She found herself near the top of the sloping field, and realised that she was already part-way towards Herr Esterbauer's place; she may as well go and see whether Schosi was there. Herr Esterbauer would probably

144

be pleased that she was keeping an eye on him. She struck off and felt better for having made a decision. The fields were damp from rain, the hills and forest dull green and autumn brown, dreary but somehow refreshing too. She remembered Papa commenting on the fine Austrian air. She breathed a lungful.

At the farm the Polish women were sweeping; their stiff brushes hissed on the concrete and the whole yard was awash with muddy water. Herr Esterbauer was in the house eating a late lunch. He came to the door with a bread roll in his hand and flour on his face.

'Is Schosi at work today?' Ursula asked.

He shook his head, swallowed and then wiped the flour away. 'No, no, never on Wednesdays. He's at home.'

Her stomach lurched with horrible dread and she stared at him. 'But he isn't at home. I just called on him.'

Herr Esterbauer frowned. 'Frau Hillier said you aren't to go there.'

'I know, but I was alone and Mama isn't well and I thought I'd just walk by.'

'That's no excuse,' he said. But he wasn't really angry; his brow was furrowed with concern.

'Let's go searching,' he said. He went into the house and came back a moment later with his coat. He put on his boots, which stood outside the door.

'Lidia,' Herr Esterbauer called to one of the Polish women as he crossed the farmyard. 'I have to go out. Please take care of my mother. Just make sure she doesn't get out of the house.'

The woman called Lidia nodded. She carried her broom to the shed. Herr Esterbauer led Ursula over the fields towards Schosi's house, and then onwards to the village.

13

Schosi sat beside a small boy on the bus. The boy had arrived at the doctor's surgery from another town and had been examined in the same room. The rest of the bus was full of strangers. The man from the surgery, not the doctor but the one who'd taken notes while the doctor examined Schosi, covering a piece of paper with spidery handwriting, sat behind the boys. Schosi didn't know where they were going. He was sure his mother wouldn't know where he was, even though the man had told him she would. He stared out of the window as the bus lurched and bounced along the pitted road. Dirty puddles filled the potholes and when the wheel of the bus hit one of them, brown water leapt up to the window near his face. The boy beside him had knees that were red and grazed and was sniffling into a large yellow handkerchief. Schosi wondered what was wrong with him. Was he missing his mama? Was he worried because he was in trouble and was unexpectedly going on a journey? He watched the boy for a while. After a bit, the little boy put his hand into his pocket and took out a pale object, small and round; it shone like a polished stone, but it wasn't a stone, and there were striped patterns on its surface.

'What is that?' said Schosi.

The boy jumped and stared at Schosi. His mud-coloured eyes stretched wide and his handkerchief fell away from his nose. His lip was covered in snot.

'What is that?' repeated Schosi.

The boy glanced down at the object in his palm. He turned it over and there was a hole on its underside.

'A shell,' he said. He turned it again and the shell gleamed, faintly pink, but mostly cream in colour. Schosi thought it was beautiful. 'From my Oma,' added the boy.

He put the shell back in his pocket. Schosi was disappointed. He'd wanted to hold the shell and look at it properly. He'd never seen one before. He gazed out of the window again, but kept thinking about the shell and checking to see if the boy had taken it out again. The boy just stared ahead, legs swinging, hands by his sides.

Buildings appeared as they reached the edge of a town. Some of them were broken and falling down, one had no roof. Schosi saw a dog trotting on the pavement alongside the bus. The dog had a bushy tail, sharp ribs and thin legs. The houses were more and more ruined as the bus carried on through the streets; there were piles of stones and people wearing striped clothes digging, and some boys in Hitler Youth uniforms pushing wheelbarrows full of stones and mud. A large colourful building appeared. Schosi vaguely remembered it; he'd seen it before. He recognised the yellow paint with red-and-black patterns. It looked like a Rathaus. It was much bigger than the Rathaus in Felddorf, but it had the same red flags on the front with the black-and-white symbol. Beside the Rathaus one of the buildings was gone and he could see through the gap to the houses behind. Smoke came from somewhere and he could smell it. One or two cars drove slowly by.

Eventually they stopped. There were women in nurse uniforms waiting on the pavement. The man from the surgery prodded the boys.

'Up you get!'

The man ushered the boys along the aisle of the bus. Other people began to rise and file out on to the pavement. One of the nurses grabbed Schosi as he climbed down from the high step. She turned him round and held both his arms from behind, so that he couldn't see her. The other people walked away down the pavement, some went right, some left. The man from the surgery and the small boy stayed near to Schosi as they set off walking. Soon, they passed through high black gates and along a narrow road that had trees at the sides. The trees had big shiny leaves and tangled vines wrapped round them. Schosi saw a large grey building. He knew straight away that it was Brauhausen Hospital; he remembered the square grey shape and the many windows from long ago. His mama had brought him to the health centre here and the man had stabbed him with needles. He'd felt ill afterwards and his mama had cried. She'd said it was wrong to do that to her boy, to take that from her boy. He didn't want to be here at this place but the woman holding his arms was marching him forwards. He began to panic, remembering how they'd hurt him and made his stomach ache for days and days. This time his mother wasn't with him, and he was accused of stealing. He hadn't stolen anything! Nothing at all!

He tried to twist to look at his captor. The nurse only tightened her hold and shoved him till he turned forward again. He felt more and more afraid as the grey hospital grew larger and higher above him. They passed a statue standing in the shallow dish of a fountain; a dark lumpy column with green slime coating it, like the green slime on Schosi's house. As they reached the entrance, the high wooden doors opened and swung inwards, so that he could see into the lobby; above the doorway was some writing that he couldn't read. Their footsteps echoed loudly on the polished floor and bounced off the high ceiling. Schosi was guided along many corridors with doors set into the walls at regular intervals. The nurse was pushing and forcing him to go fast.

'Mama!' he called. But he knew she was nowhere near and couldn't hear him.

He glimpsed the small boy to his left – another nurse held him by the hand. They went through some thick double doors that were unbolted and then bolted again behind. Beyond was an identical corridor. The smell became even stronger, the stench, like an outhouse, made Schosi retch. They stopped. The nurse gripped Schosi by his shoulders and moved him so that he faced the brown wall, the small boy placed beside him. The man from the surgery spoke to the nurse who'd held Schosi.

'He's had an initial assessment. Here's the report.' He handed the piece of paper to the nurse. 'He's fifteen years of age, severely maladjusted, congenitally inferior and unfit for education or work. He's also socially abnormal.'

The nurse murmured agreement. Papers rustled. The man spoke again.

'See here – prominent frontal bulges and flat back of head – there's more detail on page two. It's pretty conclusive.'

'Yes,' said the nurse decisively. 'Quite.'

The man bade her good day and went to speak with the other nurse concerning the little boy. Schosi caught the words 'idiocy' and 'retardation'. The man had a bossy tone and the nurse replied very obediently.

'He's underdeveloped and feeble-minded. One foot is deformed.'

As the adults spoke Schosi glanced at the little boy. The boy was resting his forehead on the wall, and his hand was in his shorts pocket, fiddling with something inside. Schosi knew that he was holding the shell. Schosi felt for his wristwatch in his own pocket but he daren't take it out. He wished fervently that he'd brought his comfort blanket. He pictured where he'd left it, on the topside of his pillow. After a while the man went away and the nurses spoke to one another, then one of them came towards them.

'Stay here. Do not move. We will be back in a moment.'

Schosi was frightened by the woman's hard voice and he stayed still and copied the small boy by placing his forehead against the wall. It was cold and smelled of oil paint.

'What's happening?' said the boy to Schosi.

Schosi shrugged.

The little boy began to sniffle again and took out the yellow handkerchief.

'Can I see the shell?' asked Schosi.

The little boy shook his head. 'It's mine.'

'Show me,' Schosi persevered. 'Please?'

The boy hesitated for a moment and then he took the shell out of his pocket. He held it so that Schosi could look at it. Schosi reached over very carefully and touched it with the tip of his finger. He stroked the brown striped pattern. It was very smooth and the inside shone with a lovely light. He stroked it for a little while longer. It was one of the most wonderful things he'd ever seen.

'It's from my Oma,' the boy said again. 'It's mine.'

The shell went back in his pocket just as the nurses appeared some distance down the corridor. Their skirts flapped as they strode along. They carried blankets.

'Come,' said one of the nurses as soon as she arrived. She seemed to be the boss and the other nurse took direction from her. The one who had spoken was very ugly, like a bulldog, with curly hair and a thick jaw. 'This way.'

Schosi and the little boy were led down the corridor. The nurses stopped outside one of the doorways and indicated that they should go through it. Schosi peered inside. It was a large room full of beds with a black-and-white-tiled floor and brown walls. Pale daylight was coming in. The beds were very close together in rows and sitting on the beds were many boys.

'Go on!' commanded the nurse. 'Get on with it!' She pushed Schosi into the room and over to one of the beds. She threw one of the thin blankets on top of the bare mattress. 'If you wet this blanket, you wash it yourself,' she said. Schosi looked at her dumbly, not able to understand her rapid speech. 'Turn out your pockets.' Schosi tried to work out what she meant but couldn't. The nurse tutted, shoved her hands into his trouser pockets and yanked them inside out. She found his wristwatch and put it in her apron. He wanted to protest but instinct told him to stay quiet though a painful feeling filled his chest like hot liquid. The other nurse checked the pockets of the little boy, who'd been placed in the bed next to Schosi. She discovered the shell.

'No!' said the boy in desperation as the shell was taken from him.

'What do you mean, no?' snapped the boss nurse with the bulldog face. 'We'll have no silly trinkets here.' And with that she threw the shell on to the floor and crushed it beneath her heavy shoe until it was in fragments. The boy wailed loudly in the echoing dormitory, tears flooding his cheeks.

'Be quiet!' said the nurse and lifted him roughly on to the edge of his bed. He immediately struggled back off the bed and on to his feet and continued to cry. The nurse slapped him smartly across the cheek. The boy cried and cried. The nurse shook her head. 'Dinner in one hour,' she said. Both women walked out, throwing a warning glance at the room as they exited.

'You won't last long in here', came a voice from a bed across the room, 'if you carry on like that.'

The boy who'd spoken had raised himself on to his elbow and was frowning crossly. Schosi's companion stared at the older boy who soon lay down again. His crying subsided gradually. Then he came and stood beside Schosi. Some of the children, who were lounging or sitting on their beds, watched them. They reminded Schosi of owls, wide-eyed with dark circles beneath, staring and malevolent. No one talked, though some of them sighed and one of them began crying softly, but Schosi couldn't tell which boy it was. Every now and then a nurse came by and looked into the room, always with a frown, and said, 'No talking!' then walked away. Schosi looked at the narrow windows. It was wet outside. Trees crowded close against the glass; the leaves were yellow. Some of the leaves had come off and were stuck to the glass. What had he done to be put here? he wondered. What had he done wrong?

'My name's Aldo,' said the little boy. He looked at Schosi with his mud-brown eyes. 'What's yours?'

'Hillier Schosi,' said Schosi.

'Trommler Aldo,' said Aldo. 'I'm from Lichtenfeld.'

Schosi didn't know where Lichtenfeld was. Aldo told him it was in Germany. They lapsed back into silence. Schosi noticed that Aldo was putting his hand again and again into his pocket, looking for his shell.

14

Ursula and Herr Esterbauer made their way as fast as they could along the track. They soon reached Ursula's house.

'You stay here,' Herr Esterbauer told her. 'I'll be quicker on my own. And send your mother up to the farm. I know she's not well but I don't trust the Poles without supervision.' He lowered his voice. 'She'll have to make up some lie about where I've gone.'

Ursula had assumed she'd be going along to help look for Schosi – he was her friend and she was the one who'd discovered he was gone. She didn't want to be left behind – she was scared for him. She had an awful feeling about it being her fault and that something bad had happened. She hated waiting, and then the adults always told her only what she ought to know, never what really happened. She watched Herr Esterbauer clomping along the track away from the house, not even saying goodbye to her, and felt angry. She ran after him.

'Wait!' Her voice came out louder than she'd intended. 'Let me come.' Herr Esterbauer stopped and turned to look at her. She clenched her fists inside her coat pockets and hoped the farmer wouldn't shout or send her away. 'Please. I want to help.'

Herr Esterbauer considered for a moment, his face serious.

'All right, you can come. But at least run inside and tell your mother that I need her to go up to the farm.' She began to dash towards the front door. 'Be quick! And if you can't keep up with me then you'll have to forget it.'

She hurried into the house and up to Mama's bedroom. Mama was seated in a chair beside the window staring at her hands, which lay in her lap; she wasn't looking out.

'Mama,' said Ursula, breathless. 'Herr Esterbauer needs you to go up to the farm. We've got to look for Schosi. He's lost.'

Mama didn't answer at first then blinked as though waking from a dream. 'Lost?' she echoed. 'How?'

'I don't know. He's not at the farm and he's not at home. He's gone missing. Herr Esterbauer needs you to look after the farm while he's searching the village and to lie if anyone asks you what he's doing.' Ursula wasn't sure Mama had heard her. She took a step forward, impatient. 'Can you do it?'

Mama frowned then stood. She stretched, her body thinner than it had been a few months before, apart from her belly, which stuck out disturbingly. She walked over to her set of drawers. 'Tell him I can take care of things for as long as he needs me to.'

Ursula sped down the stairs and out of the house – the farmer was still there, pacing beside the firs. She ran to the shed, shouting the news as she went that Mama had agreed to oversee at the farm. She flung open the shed door and went inside.

'Hey!' called Herr Esterbauer. 'Where are you going?'

She didn't answer; she was too busy disentangling the bicycle and dragging it into the yard. She climbed on, unable to reach the saddle – it had belonged to Papa and was much too large – and rode towards Herr Esterbauer. He threw his arms in the air in exasperation. 'Come on then,' he said. 'I'll run.'

They set off along the track. The bike squeaked like a greedy chick – the rod brakes didn't work, they were old and stiff and Ursula's hands too weak to squeeze them. She pedalled as hard as she could to build up speed. She steered frantically to avoid crashing into the deep cart tracks. Herr Esterbauer ran alongside, leaping like a young man, coat sailing, white hair fluttering beneath the rim of his hat. He caught her handlebars when she hit a deep pothole and almost toppled sideways.

They reached the village and Ursula put one foot in the dirt to slow herself. The road was quiet, only one or two women talking on the pavement. They surveyed the road for a sign of Schosi.

'The church,' said Herr Esterbauer.

Ursula nodded. Herr Esterbauer jogged, keys or coins jingled in his pocket; sweat glistened on his wrinkled forehead. They looked around for Schosi as they went, in case he might be hiding somewhere, or might have passed by and left some clue. Ursula looked between the houses, into the little gaps and lanes and tracks; she scanned the ground for items belonging to him – a glove, a hat or a wristwatch. They reached the bakery and the grocer's. People were going in and out and there was a delivery of ice for the meat counter at the butcher's. Herr Esterbauer tipped his hat to one or two of the ladies. They smiled and nodded in reply. He was a popular man and Ursula was glad to be seen with him. After a few minutes they reached Frau Gerg's house with its two balconies and many flowerpots and ornaments. The door opened and Frau Gerg appeared. She waved.

'Herr Esterbauer,' she called. 'Whatever is the matter?'

Ursula had never heard her so sweet, so conniving. She glided down the steps.

Herr Esterbauer slowed but didn't stop. 'Nothing's the matter,' he said.

'Are you looking for someone?'

'No, no,' said Herr Esterbauer.

'Has it anything to do with what I saw this morning? The Hillier boy that works on your farm being dragged along by Herr Adler and a constable?'

Herr Esterbauer halted. 'Herr Adler?' he said. 'Are you sure it was the Hillier boy?'

'Oh, quite sure. I recognised him though I haven't seen him for years. The officer and Herr Adler were being rather rough.' Frau Gerg smiled in a way that was most unpleasant.

Ursula swallowed on a throat that was suddenly as dry as parchment; she remembered the day in the village when Frau Gerg had stared after Schosi with that hungry look. The police, the Party, had taken him. Surely not for the fruit. Surely that couldn't be enough reason. But it must be. It was her fault – her fault entirely.

'Come on,' said Herr Esterbauer to Ursula, setting off at a pace towards the police station. She shot a look of pure loathing at Frau Gerg before cycling after him, trying not to collide with people on the road, shoppers with shopping baskets, a delivery man with a cart. She wrestled with the heavy bicycle, difficult to ride on a slight incline, and imagined how frightened Schosi must be – he hated to be in trouble, even over the smallest thing. He'd be distraught if he was thrown in jail or locked in handcuffs. An unsettling awareness was in her mind. She tried to push it aside but it was persistent: Anton. It was Anton who'd done this. Just as much as Frau Gerg and Herr Adler – he'd deliberately shouted outside Frau Gerg's house and called Schosi a thief. He'd gone back to speak with Frau Gerg. About what? About Schosi. Perhaps about Sepp, too.

The police station was off the main road, around the corner from the Rathaus and the Gasthaus. They stopped outside the entrance; Ursula dropped her bicycle on to the verge. Herr Esterbauer wasted no time in striding into the station, forgetting to hold the door for Ursula. She hopped inside just behind him.

It was warm in the station; a policeman was seated at a wide desk, smoking and filling out paperwork. He looked up without raising his head, his forehead corrugated. His eyes were marbled pink.

'*Grüss Gott*,' he greeted them. 'How can I help you?' He placed his cigarette in the ashtray on the desk and eyed Herr Esterbauer.

'I'm looking for my employee,' said Herr Esterbauer. 'Missing from work, and from his home. A boy called Hillier Schosi.' Herr Esterbauer towered over the policeman, seeming enormous in the narrow reception room. The policeman was small-framed and thin – a runt in comparison to the broad farmer. From his position at the desk he was forced to crane his neck to see Herr Esterbauer's face properly, like a child seated before a teacher. Herr Esterbauer continued. 'A woman in the village said she saw him this morning being taken along the road by Herr Adler and one of your officers.'

Recognition dawned in the policeman's expression. 'Yes,' he said, taking another drag from his cigarette then stubbing it out. 'You must be Herr Esterbauer, the farmer.'

'That's me.' Herr Esterbauer tapped the edge of the desk with one of his thick fingers. 'I'm most put out that the boy hasn't turned up to work. Where is he?'

'He was caught stealing and behaving improperly in the village, according to our witnesses.'

Ursula drew in a breath, her cheeks and ears flamed. Should she speak out? Tell the policeman it was she who was the thief? But he'd not listen, she told herself; it was too late. Her heartbeat grew rapid as she tried to quieten the inner voice that whispered 'Coward'. She wished even more passionately that she'd never brought Schosi to the village. Stupid, careless, pig-headed girl. The policeman shrugged. 'So . . .' He spread his hands as if to say, 'What can I do?' Then he glanced to the side through a partially open door, from behind which came the sound of voices. He seemed uncomfortable.

'But where is he?' said Herr Esterbauer again. His tone was gruff and laced with threat.

'That will be up to the doctor, mein Herr,' said the policeman. 'I imagine they'll have found a suitable place for him.'

'What do you mean?' said Herr Esterbauer. 'Talk straight, man!' He slammed his palm on to the desktop and leaned

159

close to the policeman. The policeman shrank back in his chair. Ursula didn't know quite what the farmer would do next, whether he'd entirely lose his temper, whether he'd make everything worse.

The policeman shuffled his papers to one side. 'He was taken to the surgery for assessment. He's clearly not right in the head. And with no one to supervise him. The boy lives like an animal.'

Herr Esterbauer's hand bashed even more loudly on to the tabletop. The policeman jumped, eyes widening. 'He works for me!' he shouted. 'I'm losing money and valuable time because of your meddling.'

'Well, I suppose the fault is your own,' snapped the policeman. 'You should choose appropriate employees, rather than idiots and reprobates.'

Herr Esterbauer glared, his chest heaved and his cheeks were ruddy with rage. He said nothing but stood for a while, his whole body tense with fury. Then he swiped his hand through the air dismissively. 'Bah!' he said. 'You're not worth the breath. Come on, Ursula.' He turned.

Ursula trotted after him out of the station.

'Some people', said Herr Esterbauer as she hastily grabbed her bicycle, 'are rotten.'

Hurrying back through the village they drew curious glances from onlookers. Herr Esterbauer did look rather wild, his expression grim and determined, his strides long. Frau Gerg again watched them as they passed but Herr Esterbauer didn't even glance her way, so fixed was he on their destination, which was the surgery at the other end of the street.

When they arrived he said he'd better go in alone: doctors had no patience with children. He promised he'd tell her everything. Ursula accepted his decision reluctantly and waited beside the surgery's ochre-painted wall. It seemed a long time until he emerged, replacing his hat.

'What happened?'

Herr Esterbauer shook his head; he was sweating and grey-faced. 'Bad news.' He held out his hand. 'Come. Walk with me to the factory. I have to tell Frau Hillier.'

'What is it? Tell me!' Ursula was horror-struck. She took the farmer's hand, which was rough and dry and hard as wood. Herr Esterbauer pushed her bicycle one-handed and Ursula was like a child again, led firmly along as she had been by her papa long ago.

'He's been sent off,' said the farmer. 'To the mental hospital in Brauhausen.' He cursed. 'I suspected as much.'

'The mental hospital?' said Ursula. 'But why? He's innocent – he's not – he'd never hurt anyone.' She'd almost said, 'He's not the kind of boy to be a thief,' but then she didn't want to admit her part, or admit that she'd said nothing.

'You don't have to be causing harm to go there,' said Herr Esterbauer. 'My mother would be a perfect candidate. For all the complaining I do, I'd hate to see them take her. A bad place to be, a very bad place indeed.'

'Why so bad?' said Ursula. But she thought she'd already guessed as she remembered Frau Hillier's whispers to Mama, the story of a boy snatched from Lillienfeld, his parents receiving ashes in the post two weeks later with only a name tag to identify that this was their son, about chimneys raining human hair on to towns, the smell of meat, buses going in full, coming out empty – the murder box, the oven.

The farmer squeezed her hand. 'Boys like Schosi don't tend to come back.'

Frau Hillier was fetched from the production line and brought into the foyer. The foreman lingered by the door. 'She'll drop below her quota,' the man kept saying. 'She'll fall behind.'

Frau Hillier wiped her oily hands on a rag. Her stockings were torn, her arms black. She had smudges on her face that looked like deep bruises. She eyed Herr Esterbauer with apprehension, sensing at once that something was wrong.

'Frau Hillier, your Schosi's been arrested and sent away.' Herr Esterbauer blurted the news in a rush of words, as though he couldn't bear to hesitate. There was no way to say it more gently. 'He's gone to Brauhausen, to the mental institution. I'm going to get him out. I'm going today to get him out of there.'

Frau Hillier clapped a hand to her mouth. She turned ghastly white – her eyes rolled, loose and ugly. Herr Esterbauer caught her arm just in time to slow her fall as she crumpled to the dirty tiles, head lolling, her face waxen beneath the muck. Herr Esterbauer squatted and cradled her head in his hands. He stroked the hair away from her forehead.

Ursula wandered by the exit while Herr Esterbauer held Frau Hillier on the floor. She felt uncomfortable being near to them just as sometimes she'd felt uncomfortable being near to Mama and Siegfried when they were being affectionate or sharing long meaningful looks. It was clear to Ursula that Herr Esterbauer loved Frau Hillier very much, and it was probably clear to the horrid snooping foreman too, who still stood in the corner, arms officiously crossed.

Herr Esterbauer waited for Frau Hillier to come back to consciousness, watching her face intently – he knelt perfectly still, his large mud-caked boots braced against the floor.

15

The door of the dormitory flew wide. The metal handle struck the wall and there was a deafening, shrill whistle. Schosi woke with a shock. He stared at the grey paintwork alongside his bed and the ceiling high above. Morning light shone with a flat glare on to everything. He tried to remember where he was, mind fogged and cluttered with anxious repetitions, an extension of his dreams, something about being stuck in the horse chestnut tree near Herr Esterbauer's farm, amongst the pungent cream-white flowers, drunk on their scent, almost falling. A blue bulb glowed on the ceiling, attached to a small box – it'd been the only thing he'd been able to see in the darkness when he'd woken in the night. He wasn't at home. He was somewhere strange – somewhere bad. He couldn't yet recall the fact that he and Aldo had been transferred in the middle of the night from Brauhausen Hospital to a second hospital, the Hartburg in Vienna. After a while lying in the bed in the harsh morning light some bits of memory returned of the confusing events of yesterday and of the night, the nurses coming in darkness to the Brauhausen dormitory, shaking them from sleep, bringing them out into the bitter air in only their underwear. Schosi had worried about his clothes – they'd left them behind. The two boys had been put on to another bus. Schosi hadn't been able to see out of the windows because there were thick curtains screening the glass, and when he'd tried to part them a nurse had hit him across the head with a rolled-up magazine. They'd driven for a long time and he and Aldo had eventually slept in their queasy, swaying cradle. Then they were woken and told to get out on to tarmac wet with rain. They'd stood and shivered and looked up at another hospital building, even larger, unlit and crowded by many trees. Nurses had led them inside, smothered their mouths and hurried them through a small door where they were received like parcels being delivered. More hands, gloved, pressed over their mouths and they were marched up a flight of stairs and along corridors to a small office. They were weighed on tall clanking scales and given an injection. Then put inside a black room full of sleeping people. Schosi was lifted, drowsy and weak, and tucked tightly into a bed; the blanket clamped unpleasantly across his neck so that if he'd had the strength he would have wrenched it away as soon as the nurse closed the door.

By daylight, the new dormitory was tall, echoing, with high windows covered on the outside by pale green bars, the walls grey now rather than brown but still the same oil-paint smell and the same greased shine. There were even more boys here than there had been at Brauhausen, the beds just as tightly arranged and the room much larger. Schosi searched for Aldo. He was in the bed that abutted the end of his own. Schosi sat – Aldo was so small that it looked as though there was no one lying under the blanket, but there was his face on the pillow, his lavender eyelids flickering with sleep.

Just at that moment another shrill whistle pierced the air. Schosi clamped his hands over his ears to block out the noise – the horrible, painful, disorientating blast reverberated in the echoing dormitory, worse than the tin whistle Herr Esterbauer had given to him – far, far worse. Everywhere was a sudden rustling and creaking; the other boys were sitting upright, throwing covers aside. The whistle stopped. A nurse stood inside the doorway, one hand on her hip. She had a tiny upturned nose, glasses and a cap like a handkerchief. She looked around then blew on the whistle again, a short hard blast. She let it fall on a string around her neck.

'Up!' she said, clapping.

Across the room boys scrambled from their beds and stood to attention. The nurse clapped again, entering the room. In the bed adjacent to Schosi, Aldo lay immobile.

'Quickly!' shouted the nurse. 'How long are you lazy bastards going to lie here?' She whipped the blanket away from one of the boys who hadn't risen, moved to Aldo's bed and did the same. She threw Aldo's blanket on to the floor – he sat up slowly.

'Get out of bed!' said the nurse. 'I shouldn't have to tell you twice.' She turned to Schosi. He hastily stood. 'Stand straight!' said the nurse to him. 'Hands by your sides.' He obeyed. She tossed some clothes at Schosi and

Aldo – clothes that didn't belong to them – then she pointed at Schosi. 'One,' she said. She turned to Aldo. 'Two.' She went off around the room and counted each boy – thirty in total. 'Get dressed,' she said. 'No dilly-dallying.' She walked to the doorway. 'Washroom in five minutes.' She raised a warning finger. 'I'll be timing you.'

Hullabaloo descended as the entire dormitory rushed to dress. Boys pushed each other out of the way, threw pyjamas (if they had any) on to the floor, writhed on the edge of their beds to pull shorts into place. Aldo hopped on one leg, struggling to get his foot into his shoe. His foot was an awkward twisted shape and wouldn't easily fit. He lost his balance and fell back on to his bed, coughing. Eventually he recovered and managed to get his shoe on. Schosi watched as he tied the lace in a trailing knot rather than a proper bow. Aldo began to button his shirt, a ragged thing with holes at the elbows. When he'd finished it was all askew. Schosi knew that he'd done them wrongly and would be told off. He finished fastening his own buttons, taking care to do it right. Some of the other boys were already leaving the dormitory. The boy leading the line seemed to be in charge of the other boys and was quite a bit taller than the rest. He had fair hair that flicked at his temples and the nape of his neck.

'Your buttons are wrong.'

Aldo glanced down at his shirtfront and then back up at Schosi, his expression helpless. Schosi reached out to fix them but Aldo shrank back and shook his head.

They left the dormitory, hurrying to catch the tail end of the line. All the children moved quickly, subdued and quiet. Bare feet pattered. The floor was cold. The washroom swallowed them up, a large tiled room full of toilets and urinals and sinks. They formed a queue and took it in turns in sets of three to pee at the urinals and wash their hands and faces at the taps. Schosi shivered uncontrollably. The water was like ice and there was no heater; the windows were the same as in the dormitory, tall and green-barred, admitting frigid November air through minute gaps. The glass was warped and the trees outside looked buckled and distorted.

Aldo cried as they left the washroom because he searched for his shell and remembered that it had been destroyed. 'My Oma said to keep it,' he said. 'She said never to lose it.'

Schosi wanted to reassure Aldo but he didn't know how.

The next room was a long hall full of tables and wooden benches, where they had to stand in the doorway and wait. There were some girls queuing at the other entrance, all in scruffy dresses and with plaited or cropped hair. They were whey-faced, ghostly girls, and Schosi compared them to little bear, who was always golden or rosy or laughing at him. The walls of the cavernous room were red, with deep chips where chunks of plaster had fallen off. A tall clock stood against the near wall; a picture of the Führer hung above a broad archway through which nurses wheeled trolleys of food. There was a tureen on each trolley and stacks of bowls. One of the nurses indicated that the children should take their seats, and the boys and girls filed in and sat at separate tables, all quiet, all seeming to know their place. Schosi and Aldo sat next to one another. On Schosi's other side was the boy who'd led the line, the tall one with the light feathery hair. Schosi was in awe of him and took care that neither his leg nor elbow touched him. The nurses began to push the trolleys to the tables, keeping pace with one another. The wheels squeaked and the bowls chattered. They progressed along the rows of children and doled out breakfast to each. When one of the nurses reached Schosi she stood behind, so that his neck tingled, dished up a ladleful of whatever was in the tureen, and then bashed the bowl down in front of him. The food was pale in colour, and lumpy. Steam rolled faintly from its surface. It didn't look like much, but it was warm and had a sweet scent. Schosi salivated, gripping his spoon.

'I hate semolina,' whispered Aldo once the nurse had moved on.

'What's semolina?' said Schosi.

'This is,' said Aldo, pointing to his own bowl, lined with the same pale mess.

Schosi had never heard of semolina. Perhaps he should hate it too, but he was too hungry for that. As soon as the nurse gave permission to begin, he shovelled the sticky mixture into his mouth, devoured the lot in less than a minute, and then wiped up some of the remnants with his finger. He looked hopefully around for a second helping, but the trolleys were gone and only one nurse remained, watching them as they ate.

The leader boy beside Schosi ate with deliberate slowness, as though he was forcing his food down, or else it was the opposite and he didn't want the meal to be over. He slid the spoon into his mouth, pinching his lips tight and drawing the spoon out completely clean. Schosi watched from the sides of his eyes, fascinated by the calmness that surrounded him. He slowly turned his head to study him more openly. The boy was clear-skinned and very fair, blue smudges showing below his eyes, and his lips were almost the same colour as his face. His eyelashes were long and curved, like a cow's, thought Schosi, and his hair pretty like a girl's. After a moment the boy turned to look at him. He pulled the spotless spoon from his mouth.

'What?' he said, so quietly that Schosi almost didn't hear.

Schosi blushed and looked back at his empty bowl. The boy stared at him for a while and then went back to his methodical breakfast. Schosi could feel the unfriendly gaze of several boys who were seated opposite. He kept his eyes on the table.

When breakfast was finished, the children stood and filed over to the archway where the Führer's portrait hung to deliver their empty bowls to the trolley. Everything at the hospital seemed to be about walking or standing in lines, in the right place, in the right way. When Schosi was nearly at the trolley, the boy directly behind hit him on the elbow so that his bowl flew from his grasp and landed on the floor. It cracked like a great egg and a thin spray of semolina flicked across the wooden floor.

'Who was that?' A nurse came down the line.

The boys retreated like a tide so that Schosi was left stranded. He saw Aldo ahead, leaning to look at him, a scum of semolina around his mouth. The nurse stopped in front of Schosi. It was the same woman who'd blasted on the whistle that morning. She thrust forwards her miniature nose.

'Was it you?'

Schosi glanced around. The boy who'd pushed him – a knock-kneed lad with a bulbous forehead and dark skin –

slid a look at Schosi then returned to the mute scrutiny of his own toes. Schosi looked again at the nurse.

'Clumsy child! Go and fetch a cloth! Take those pieces to the rubbish bin immediately!'

That was too many instructions for Schosi, and delivered too fast. He stared at her in confusion, felt a sudden need for the toilet and grasped at his groin to prevent pee from escaping.

'Hands!' yelped the nurse. 'Hands!' Schosi returned his hands to his sides. Warmth spread between his legs, and relief. The nurse turned away. 'Ugh. Revolting. Nurse!' She called for a colleague, who trotted pony-like through the arch to join them. 'Take this one to the washroom. He's made a complete mess of himself. He'll require a nappy.'

The second nurse, a pale-haired girl, nodded and took him by the elbow and walked with him across the hall – she didn't look at him but as she went she slowed her pace so he didn't have to hurry so much. 'Don't worry,' she said.

Schosi wondered where she was taking him, to the toilet, he hoped, because he still needed to pee some more. His mama said he should learn to make it on time, and today he'd failed, in front of everyone. The shame of it brought him close to tears. Nappies were for babies. The boys and girls turned in their queues to watch him and a cautious whisper began amongst them. They were silenced immediately by a remark from the small-nosed nurse.

The young nurse's black shoes oink-oinked on the polished floor as she escorted Schosi along the corridor. Her delicate fingers gripped his arm. She took a turning, away from his dormitory, down a shaded corridor. As they passed along it, Schosi saw a patch of wall that was covered in scribbles – pencil or charcoal – lines that criss-crossed and looped. It wasn't a picture – perhaps it was words. Schosi couldn't read them, but then he couldn't even read his name. His mama had tried to teach him, but he'd disappointed her.

The nurse spoke when they reached a door. 'Wait here a moment.'

She went into the room, leaving Schosi in the corridor. A covered cart with tall wheels crouched against the wall near by, the blue canvas unfastened and trailing. It was different to the farm carts at harvest time or his mama's handcart – it had no dirt or straw on the wheel spokes. But perhaps a cat lived there, asleep amongst offcuts of wood and scraps of hay, a favourite place for the cats at the farm. A pang of intense homesickness struck him in the stomach. His shorts were uncomfortable, the pee had turned chilly and the wet material stuck to his skin. Cold air blew out from the doorway – he looked inside and saw a couple of beds, and windows covered by the same cage of pale green bars, except that these windows were propped wide so that the bars were exposed. Schosi could hear a breeze in the branches of the trees outside. He wondered if a bird might fly in by mistake. There was some banging and shuffling from somewhere in the room and he guessed it was the nurse, though he couldn't see her. He edged inside a little. A boy in the nearest bed lay with his back to Schosi. He was small and Schosi was surprised he wasn't frozen solid because he had no blankets. He went a step further so he could peer around the edge of the door. Rows of beds filled the room just like his dormitory, but this was a smaller space. Each bed had a child asleep even though it was after breakfast time. None had blankets. There was a girl lying a few metres away, her hair in rags across her face, a long trail of drool joining her mouth to the mattress. Her feet were greyish-blue. There was vomit on the floor beside her bed. He began to notice the smell. Perhaps it was his own shorts, but the stink of pee was very strong and the medicine smell was even worse, stronger than anywhere else, as if this was the place where it began, spreading from here to the rest of the ward. A strong gust of air came in through the windows and lifted the nightgown of the drooling girl so that her legs were exposed. She didn't stir. He began to feel afraid. There was a feeling in the room, something he recognised – it felt like when the cats got old and went off to lie somewhere alone, not moving any more, not seeing through their eyes, not breathing at all in the end – that sour smell, the stiffness, the eerie quiet. He heard another bang and craned his head round to see the nurse. She was closing a tall cupboard with plain wooden doors. Schosi dodged from sight.

16

'The sheets must match exactly,' said the nurse instructing Schosi and Aldo. She stooped and squinted along the regimental dormitory beds, checking that each folded sheet was level with the rest. 'When the inspecting officer comes, he should be able to see a precise line from here to the end of the room, like this.' The blanket was to be arranged in a square with the second sheet turned over. The square of blanket should be positioned at the foot of the bed, the pillow at the head, plumped and smoothed. The sheet overlapping must be the exact length of two toothbrushes; the nurse demonstrated using a toothbrush belonging to one of the other boys.

They were ordered to practise and the nurse slapped them sharply every time they paused or got it wrong.

After their third or fourth failure the nurse grew angry. She tore the bedding off.

'No! That is wrong. Start from scratch! You will make your bed one hundred times until you have learned. Here at Hartburg we value discipline and order. We will not tolerate sloppiness.'

And so they spent long hours on this strange ritual, confused and frightened, hopelessly inept. Later, the angry nurse was replaced by a younger nurse with soft loops of pale hair pinned over her ears. She was less fierce – Schosi realised it was the same nurse who had accompanied him to get his nappy. She showed Schosi and Aldo what to do once more, but at a slower pace. Eventually, they were able to produce something close to the military precision that was expected, their beds tamed and geometric, mirroring the others in the dormitory. Schosi was tired and his arms ached. His stomach growled with hunger. They'd been allowed no food or drink while they worked.

The pale-haired nurse gave them each a piece of bread and then put them out in the side garden to play. There was another nurse in the garden, this one with a chalk-white face and heavy coat pulled tightly around her body. It was very cold, the sky full of yellow snow clouds. Some of the other children were already there, but they ignored Schosi and Aldo who stood against the hospital wall. Schosi's nappy scratched between his legs and embarrassed him. He'd been given another pair of shorts, tatty and too loose. The side garden was a narrow strip of grass with bald patches of mud. A sign stuck out from the brickwork with a white number on a blue background. Aldo told Schosi what it was. It was the number fifteen. Schosi remembered that that was his age and also the age of Ursula's brother.

He was reminded of Anton a second time when he saw the tall leader boy walking near the garden fence. Schosi thought the boy moved in a similar way to Anton, though more slowly. It seemed that the boy didn't want to play while they were in the garden. Instead he broke things. He snapped twig after twig that he found on the floor, and he broke stones (using other stones – banging, banging until they split), he kicked holes in the dirt with his elegant feet, peeled shreds of bark from the tree trunk, tearing deeper and deeper until the wood was raw orange and bled clear juice, curls of skin strewn on the tree roots. After a while the black-coated nurse came hollering over, cuffed him around the head so that he cowered momentarily. But he shot upright as soon as the nurse stepped away, rigid, rebellious, staring darkly.

Later on, when they'd come inside and were passing the dining-hall doors, they met other children in the corridor who were going in to eat. They weren't the ones from the freezing room but they looked ill – some were deformed. Schosi was unnerved by the sounds they made, groans and strange shouts; some had heads like lumpy rocks and mismatched faces. One child was so small she couldn't walk properly. A girl with hanging breasts clutched the toddler's arm, helped her not to fall.

'Poor bastards,' muttered one of the boys from Schosi's dormitory. 'You don't want to eat what they get fed.'

17

err Esterbauer took Frau Hillier home after the foreman eventually agreed to release her for the remainder of the day. They left the factory to the sound of his complaints, Frau Hillier leaning heavily on Herr Esterbauer and not seeming to hear the grumbling of her boss. Outside it was pleasant sunshine and Ursula trailed behind the grown-ups; she was worried that Frau Hillier knew, or would find out, that she'd taken Schosi through the village, or would somehow learn it was she who'd taken the apples. The regret she felt was becoming intolerable and she was tempted to confess just so that she could be punished in the way she felt she ought to be. Every few minutes Frau Hillier sobbed audibly, then calmed and became quiet, only to break into tears again. She spoke as soon as they'd left the village and had reached the secluded track.

'I can't simply go home,' she said amid fresh sobs. 'I can't sit there. I'll go mad.'

Herr Esterbauer nodded.

'I have to go to him.' Her voice grew high-pitched. 'I can't bear to think of it – he'll be frantic.'

'Yes,' said Herr Esterbauer. 'Of course you want to. But I don't think you should. It'll be easier for me, as his employer, a Party member too.' He looked at her. 'I know it'll be torture waiting here without knowing. But it might make the situation worse if you come – they've said things about you, invented reasons to call you an unfit mother. They'll be more likely to listen to me. A more professional angle, you see?' He was stroking her elbow. 'I'll explain he's of vital importance to the running of my farm, a trusted farmhand. I can vouch for his never having stolen from me.'

She sighed but didn't disagree. 'It was Frau Gerg,' she said with grim certainty. 'She couldn't stand to let me keep him.' She broke off and was silent.

When they reached the entrance to Ursula's yard Herr Esterbauer ruffled Ursula's hair. 'I'll be off on the bus this afternoon. I'll have him back safe in no time, with God's help.'

But he was a little too jovial; he could never be as sure as he sounded. She supposed he still thought her a child, who'd believe whatever a grown-up said, but she wasn't; she was old enough to leave school. 'I want to do something,' she said. 'I'll come to the hospital and help find him.'

'Don't be daft. You can't do that. It wouldn't make any difference if you did. You stay here.'

She tried to think of something useful she could contribute, other than to say it *should* be her; she should make amends. After a moment they said goodbye. She went across the yard, despondent, to put her bicycle away.

Anton was inside the shed. He was oiling his gun. He barely acknowledged her as she parked the bike against the shed wall then stood watching him. His hands were dirty and he tossed his hair back every so often to get it out of his eyes. His long legs, made for running, were smutted with oil below the turn-ups of his shorts; his sleeves, rolled to the elbow, showed his slim arms, the muscles flickering as he worked. He continued to ignore her and she felt a stab of anger. He didn't care at all that her friend was forced from home, from his mama, from her, that he might never return.

'He's been arrested and sent away like you wanted.' Her voice was hard.

Anton carried on polishing, looking at her from between his lashes, as though assessing whether he needed to bother with her or not.

She leaned towards him, fists balled. 'You meant this to happen. I bet you even went to the police station with that horrible woman.' Fury made her light, replaced her guilt for a moment. 'That was low, if you did. To team up with her. Well, he's my friend and he'll very likely die and it'll be on your conscience!'

'Not your friend,' said Anton. 'More like a dog.'

'No! I like being with him. He's nice to me.'

'Calm down!' He placed his hand over his ear. 'Stop yelling.'

'I won't!' she shouted more loudly. 'I thought you were supposed to be on my side. I thought you were supposed to look out for me. Well, you're not, and I—' She couldn't say she hated him: it wasn't true.

Anton stood and wiped his fingers on a rag. 'He wasn't good for you.' His tone was flat.

'You're wrong. He *is* good for me. You've got your gang at the HY. What have I got?'

'You're being ridiculous.'

'I'm not!' She walked towards the exit. 'You didn't want anyone knowing, that's the only reason. It's all about you and that stupid dagger. You didn't do it for me. Well, I'm going to find him.'

She'd fetch her things right now and go, she thought. She didn't care what he said.

'You won't be able to.'

'Yes, I will!' She left the shed, shoving the door so it crashed against the wall. She walked rapidly towards the house.

He stepped out behind her. 'If you go after him I'll leave!' he called. 'I'll be gone when you get back.'

'Fine!' She turned to aim her words more forcefully at him. 'See if I care.'

She packed her knapsack in a frenzy, grabbed spare clothes, a toothbrush and flannel, a few pieces of bread from the kitchen, and a small amount of money filched from the change jar. She expected Anton to appear at any moment to try to prevent her but he didn't and she supposed he'd gone back into the shed to prove a point. She thought about leaving a note for Mama but there was no time and she ran straight out of the house, across the yard and away down the track before Anton had a chance to reappear. He'd have a shock when he discovered that she'd really done it. Her bag bumped awkwardly at the base of her spine and she began to gasp with exertion; she didn't know what she planned other than to be there when the bus arrived and to go to Brauhausen Hospital – to find Schosi and bring him back to Felddorf.

At the bus stop Herr Esterbauer waited wearing a thick coat with collar upturned and a heavy, wide-brimmed hat. He had changed into smarter clothing and his boots were clean.

'Absolutely not!' he said as soon as he saw Ursula with her bulging knapsack. He gestured for her to go back the way she'd come, making a sweeping motion as though she was an intrusive leaf blowing into his hallway. 'Get away with you!'

'I'm catching the bus, Herr Esterbauer. I want to help.'

'Absolutely not!' he said again.

She turned away from him. He couldn't stop her.

'You're not listening. I'll tell your mama. You ought to be ashamed, disrespecting your elders like this.'

She ignored him, face flushed. She had to go, she just had to.

The bus appeared, wallowing over potholes, slow and mud-splashed. With a discordant squeal of brakes it stopped beside the waiting villagers. She wriggled towards the front of the queue.

'No you don't, young lady!' Herr Esterbauer came up behind her, took her arm and tried to pull her back. She wrenched herself free. He attempted a gentler tone. 'You mustn't come with me. I don't want you to. It's not safe and your mama will be upset.'

She shook her head, dodged him and shoved through tutting people until she was out of reach of the farmer.

'Fräulein Hildesheim!' People paused in fishing for coins and turned to see who was making such a din. 'Come back here!'

The elderly lady in front of Ursula climbed aboard and Ursula followed suit as quickly as she could, clutching the handrail, not looking at the other passengers, heart hammering against her ribcage, breath ragged, determined. She wouldn't listen; she wouldn't listen to anyone.

18

Steam enveloped the lingerers on the platform and billowed against the windowpane of Ursula's carriage as the train exited Brauhausen station. She rested her face against the glass and beside her the farmer settled in his seat, his leather bag across his knees, his cleaned and polished boots crossed. She avoided his eye and didn't speak; the least she could do was not bother him. The visit to Brauhausen Hospital had been unsuccessful. Ursula had known somehow, even as she walked behind the farmer along the leafy path that led to the hospital lobby, that Schosi was no longer there.

'I promised to send word to Frau Hillier if there was any news,' Herr Esterbauer had said curtly as they exited the hospital grounds and made their way to the train station. 'But the most urgent thing is to press onwards. You know the risk? You know his life is in danger?'

Ursula had nodded. She was glad that the farmer spoke to her frankly, albeit brusquely – he made no more mention of her behaviour earlier that day and she was thankful he involved her.

'Your mother will be wondering where you are,' he continued. 'You'd better write to her.'

At Brauhausen train station she'd stood a little way off on the platform, leaving him to smoke and check his watch repeatedly. He'd allowed her to hop on to the train ahead of him and hadn't tried to send her home this time. Perhaps he knew she'd only defy him. They'd settled in the same compartment with a terse, unspoken truce between them, she fidgety with defensive shame and gratitude, he irritated, resigned, worried.

As she gazed out, the train picked up speed. It emitted a high whistle, took a bend in the track and crossed a tributary of the Danube. They headed outwards through the bombed edges of Brauhausen town. They passed the demolished factory and oil refinery, debris scattered here and there as yet unattended to, the train windows framing the stricken scene. It was her first sighting of bombing on this scale, though she'd seen plenty of footage on the Weekly Update at the cinema, shots of explosions and blast craters at the Front. But this was different – it was so vast and there was not the grainy distance of celluloid between her and the ruins. Flakes of ash drifted and smutted the snow. Blackened sheds and unrecognisable buildings stood with no walls remaining, only charred timbers or metal girders poking out like broken bones from a carcass. The windows on the train were closed but a smell of sulphur and smoke entered the carriage. The fires hadn't long been extinguished and still smouldered. The train shuttled by, not fast but steadfast. The destroyed factory was soon left behind and they were amongst suburbs. Large houses lined the track, peeped like coquettes from behind high fences. Wide eaves, generous balconies, gardens blanketed with drifts, and paths carved clear with snow shovels. Ursula noted all the things she saw that were different to Felddorf, her worry for Schosi eddying beneath. She replayed the row with Anton; tightness sat high in her chest, restricting her breath. Would he really go? Surely he'd not meant it; surely he'd wait for her. She thought again of his cruelty, his snarling, mocking face. She hoped again that nothing would happen to Sepp or to his aunt. They seemed like good people, even if they had done a traitorous thing. Would there be anything definite to denounce them with? Anything more than rumour and Anton's loathing? It might be enough, she didn't know. Snow had been cleared from the track and heaped at the edges to form a jagged ridge. She'd never been this far from home – there were so many new places and unknown people. And then the capital – it wouldn't be long until the train reached its destination. She prayed for a swift journey. For Schosi, she thought.

Brauhausen town fell away and for a while the track was shielded by trees; mountain ash and untamed hazels with a hundred broom-handle offshoots. Beside Ursula, Herr Esterbauer was silent and stiff-backed, the shadows of the hazel brooms flickering across his countenance. Fields emerged, which swooped up to join the rim of the monochrome forest, snow-laden, and above bald peaks capped in ice. Tiny villages similar to Felddorf appeared and disappeared, no more than a few houses and farms, a Gasthaus and a painted church. The train stopped at many of them so that one or two people could get out or climb aboard. Every time the train halted Ursula found herself clenching her hands in her lap and Herr Esterbauer tapped his fingers on his leather bag with an incessant pattering. On the ground near one village was a row of dead wild boars, with straggling bloody coats, twenty or more resting on their broad sides, hooves curled as though in flight. The breathless sound of the pistons and the rattle of wheels filled the compartment – the panelling trembled, the luggage vibrated in the overhead rack.

The staff at Brauhausen Hospital had acted as shiftily as criminals. When Ursula and Herr Esterbauer had arrived and asked them for the release of Schosi, it was clear that they weren't going to be helpful. First the receptionist, a woman with dark bobbed hair and glasses, spent an age sorting through files, pretending that she couldn't find any record of Schosi Hillier until Ursula was on the verge of losing her temper. She forced herself to be calm; she mustn't give Herr Esterbauer reason to send her home. Once the receptionist finally found the name, she told them that Schosi was no longer under their care and that there was no record of his current whereabouts. Herr Esterbauer threatened to involve her manager if necessary, until she said that all she knew was that Schosi had been transferred by military decree to another institution, the whereabouts of which they'd be informed of at a later date. Herr Esterbauer at this point demanded to speak with her superior and a doctor was called into the room, a pallid, unhealthy individual who barely made eye contact with Herr Esterbauer and totally ignored the existence of Ursula. He ushered them into an office with a varnished door.

'Can I help you?' he said, moving about the room then stopping at his desk to absentmindedly organise papers.

'I need to find my employee – Hillier Schosi – who was brought here two days ago,' said Herr Esterbauer. 'But he's been transferred. I need to know where he is. His admission was a mistake – he's a capable worker.'

The doctor mused on this and pressed his fingers to his lips. He looked at the farmer. Ursula waited at the edge of the room, gripping the shoulder straps of her knapsack to keep her hands from fiddling.

'Hillier Schosi,' he mumbled. He walked to the centre of the room. 'We're not generally informed about the details of transfers of this kind.' He paused and eyed the farmer again. 'Often the patients are collected in the middle of the night. It's very normal for this to happen. I don't question the procedure – I may get wind of it the following morning, you understand.'

'You know where he's gone, then?' said Ursula.

The doctor raised his eyebrows, evidently not expecting her to speak. 'I wouldn't necessarily wish to disclose information that's guarded by the military.'

'I don't mind paying,' said Herr Esterbauer. 'If that's what you're after.'

The doctor made a pretence at recoiling from this reference to money, but he sharpened his attention like a dog that smells its dinner, and moved closer to Herr Esterbauer. He gave an oily smile. 'Well, I may have need of a bit of extra cash just now, as it happens.'

Herr Esterbauer withdrew his wallet and pulled out a roll of Reichsmarks. He counted off a generous sum, which made Ursula feel rather weak. It wasn't right that this beastly man should get so much. Herr Esterbauer handed the notes to the doctor, who glanced at them quickly in order to count them then stowed them in his pocket.

'He was taken on a bus to the Vienna Hartburg Mental Hospital,' said the doctor. 'Along with a group of other patients.'

'What kind of patients?' said Herr Esterbauer carefully.

'Mentally deficient – they'll be put in the children's ward.'

They left without saying another word. Within an hour they were on a train to Vienna.

The train passed through Wiener Neustadt, another town bombed, and then reached the low, tree-covered Wienerwald Hills and the town of Baden, where the train stopped. Passengers boarded, amongst them two women who came into Ursula and Herr Esterbauer's compartment. They were nurses in long black dresses, white pinafores, black shoes, pointed white collars and pointed white caps. They sat opposite Ursula and she watched them talking as the train lurched away from the platform. They spoke under their breath, as though exchanging secrets, leaning close, white caps touching. She noticed the way they grasped their handbags against their knees, the redness and roughness of their hands, similar to farmers' hands, or labourers' hands, made for rough work.

They soon reached the edge of Vienna. Like the surrounding towns, the city had been bombed. The industrial periphery was tattered and flattened, and the suburbs hung around the city like ragged underskirts. Apartment buildings crumbled here and there in ruins, others were untouched and splendid, some with golden paint or flowers scrolling across the plaster, a stark contrast to the simple houses of Felddorf. Herr Esterbauer watched the passing cityscape with dislike.

'I've never had occasion to come here,' he muttered. 'And no inclination either.'

Ursula looked at him, perplexed. How could he have never wished to see the capital? The place where the emperors had lived and where everything was grand and full of charm, where the Viennese Philharmonic Orchestra played in the glorious Opera House and where Manner Schnitten wafer biscuits were made? People dressed in long, heavy coats with crimson linings, like Siegfried, and drank coffee from tall glasses. What could he find objectionable about that? 'Why?' she asked.

Herr Esterbauer huffed. 'Because city people are a different breed. They have names like Turnicek, Kremicek, Karicek – always ending in "cek".'

Ursula pondered on this but couldn't quite comprehend him. Mama had once told her that Herr Esterbauer's own father had been Czechoslovakian and had changed his name to sound more Germanic when he'd moved here with his family. It seemed nonsensical then for Herr Esterbauer to hate all Easterners so much, though she was glad to have no Eastern heritage herself. She viewed Vienna with great curiosity as the train swayed onwards. The place seemed gargantuan. The streets she glimpsed were labyrinthine. Walls of cream and beige, with green or black railings for balconies, small parks crammed between them with regimented hedges and classical statues.

'My farm in summer,' said Herr Esterbauer, 'with green grass and good soil and cows in the shed. That's all I need.'

He uncrossed his feet and recrossed them in the other direction. 'That's where I belong.'

'Then it's even more kind that you've come,' said Ursula. 'And all for Frau Hillier.'

He looked at her. 'For the boy,' he corrected.

'And for her.'

He cleared his throat. 'Yes, for her too, I suppose.'

She realised then that he didn't think anyone knew. Mama and Dorli's speculations filled idle moments but of course no one spoke of it in front of him; his romantic feelings were a private thing.

Closer to the centre were domed churches and many-windowed buildings with gilt eagles spread-winged at their apex. The glass was gone from a lot of the frames. The train pulled in at the station and they alighted, the nurses from their compartment following along the platform and towards the exit. Members of the League of German Girls stood in pairs and handed out leaflets with rosy smiles. Ursula refused the pamphlets and passed them by. There were soldiers resting on benches in the concourse of the station and others milling in the main entrance hall. Many panes of glass were missing here, but the grandeur of the place was still staggering, and Ursula gazed up at the beams and struts of the mighty roof.

But they had little time to dawdle and hurried onwards, out of the station and across a busy street. Ursula immediately smelled the city – smoke, dust, exhaust, refuse, sewage – a pungent, choking mixture. It was noisy – there was construction work or road work near by, the sound of hammers and the throb of a large vehicle. The buildings soared far above her, many of them smudged with soot, scorched by fire. Some had no windows at all and here and there the plaster had fallen away in chunks on to the pavements. Everywhere rubble was heaped high against walls to clear the streets. Cars trundled along the adjacent road, and people – city people – walked or cycled, cautiously progressing in the icy conditions, wrapped from head to toe in shawls and overcoats, a hurrying multitude compared to the slow few who trod the narrow roads and tracks of Felddorf, every face recognisable. She stared around, stumbled on uneven paving slabs, and sweat beaded her forehead and lip despite the cold – here was the war, the bombing, the death she'd heard about on the radio, the wide streets a foreign place with signs and telephone poles and wires confusing the eye, a spider's web of tram lines overhead and tracks shining like rivers, dividing, merging and curving off around corners in the road. She followed the farmer closely; he kept his head down and made a beeline for a tram stop near by. A red-and-white tram waited, taking on passengers.

Herr Esterbauer hailed a passer-by, a dark-clothed man with smart hat and gloves, to ask the way to Hartburg. The man swivelled and pointed at another tram stop on the opposite side of the road and advised taking a certain tram then changing lines. He smiled tightly, not unfriendly, his dense moustache trimmed to a short rectangle like a wire brush.

'Thank you very much,' said Herr Esterbauer, touching the brim of his hat. They crossed the road through sparse traffic and whirring bicycles, Ursula stepping around mounds of dirty slush left over from the recent snow. They joined the queue at the tram stop and Herr Esterbauer readied his money. She untied her knapsack and retrieved her few coins but he waved her to put them away just as he had done on the train. A tram soon pulled up with a quiet moan of brakes and they hopped aboard. Shoppers and workers sat in rows along the wooden seats or held leather straps that dangled from the ceiling – the people here all looked dreadfully thin and worn out, not a sign of the glamour she'd imagined. Herr Esterbauer proffered his marks to the driver, but the man shook his head. He explained that tickets must be bought in advance at the adjacent tobacconist's shop – he pointed along the street.

'You'll have to get the next tram now, my friend!' called the driver as they stepped off on to the pavement. The driver had the distinctive seesawing vowels of the Viennese accent. Herr Esterbauer waved his acceptance but cursed under his breath as they made for the yellow-lit door of the tobacconist's.

Ursula thought of Schosi, lost in the city. Every delay was a calamity. Herr Esterbauer withdrew his pocket-watch and checked it; she pictured the hands moving busily around the face. She could almost hear the whirr – impatient, anxious.

The lights on the trams were switched off as evening began and they groaned and breathed along their tracks, concealed from enemy planes just as the houses were. She sat in the dark interior alongside the farmer and gaunt strangers, women wearing darned gloves and tattered hats, old men coughing as if they'd any moment die. She and Herr Esterbauer didn't converse – what could she say to him? He was so old and so taciturn, his usual jollity gone. She fingered the coins in her pockets and wondered if she should apologise now for pushing aboard the bus and then the train, for not answering him when he'd spoken to her, for imposing herself. But he didn't seem to expect anything and she was too awkward to blurt it into the taut silence. Her stomach squealed loudly and she gripped her middle, embarrassed.

'You're hungry?' he said. He took slices of cheese from his bag and offered them to her. She thanked him and ate them with some of the bread from her knapsack, enjoying the tasty cheese, aware that it was a generous gift and that she didn't deserve it. She smiled at him, watching him, unsure if he was still cross; he must be thawing, forgiving her. The silence seemed a little less heavy. Outside, churches sailed by, gloomy and magnificent, and statues stood in silhouette along the rims of roofs. Once, she saw the ominous hulk of a flak tower, which loomed huge and brutal above the other buildings, its concrete walls pitted, the angular ramparts supporting air defence guns visible on the protruding platforms. She pressed her eye close to the glass, heart kicking, breath clouding the window, desperately trying to see before the tower was lost to view. This was the type of place where Anton hoped to be stationed, manning those lofty guns. She scanned the tower for figures and the pedestrians on the adjacent pavement for a glimpse of his face.

'Built to last a thousand years,' murmured Herr Esterbauer close to her ear. 'To be plated in gold when the victory comes.'

No matter how you dressed those towers, she thought, they'd always be dreadful and warlike, but then perhaps that was what the Führer wanted. And her brother too – this hardness and death. She shivered and dreaded him just then. Why was he drawn to ugly things? She supposed in some way he'd always been like that, chopping the eyes and hearts of animals caught in his traps, pulling blue and stinking insides into a pail with delight. But she'd seen his gentleness too – once had anyway – his need for consolation. He'd nuzzled in, eyes closed, and asked for songs and stories, kissed her fingertips.

A little while later, the tram passed the twilit extravagance of the Schönbrunn Palace, twin columns topped with more eagles and the famous Gloriette, a symmetrical skeleton on the horizon above. Ursula had seen many pictures and it was strange to see with her own eyes where the emperors had lived, both more and less impressive than she'd expected it to be. The palace retreated as the tram made its way up the hill. She wished there was some way of letting Schosi know that they were close. She focused on the dark lobbies of the passing buildings and the ten-foot painted doors, her fear and confusion making all she saw unsettling and unfriendly; the dirty corners and rubble and scuffed, peeling paint seemed squalid and alien. Through a partly opened shutter she glimpsed a red-scarfed woman inside a wash house working alone at the row of sinks. A strange, soulless place. Perhaps Herr Esterbauer was right. She longed for home, not home as it was now but home as it used to be when she and Anton lived in a world that included no one but them, had escaped into one another, into intense games and caresses like slipping below the surface of a pool, no longer able to hear doors crash, the bellow of Papa's voice, the threats and tears and blows; they floated beneath and there was never a question of leaving each other, never this distance. She berated herself; her anger flared as she remembered his viciousness, his ill will towards Schosi, his disdain for her. A ripple of something stirred in her mind, of being unable to breathe, frozen but burning. It frightened her; she had the sense that if the feeling were allowed to grow it would gape wider and wider like a great mouth and swallow her. She pushed the jumbled thought away.

The tram stopped. Once they were on the pavement Herr Esterbauer took directions from a fellow passenger.

'You'll see it soon enough,' said the man. He was elderly and had swollen cheeks like two dumplings. 'The gateway is obvious. You can recognise all the brick and the church in the centre. A great maze of a place.' He began to shuffle away along the pavement. Then he stopped, turned and addressed Ursula. 'You got someone in there?'

'Yes,' she said. 'Our neighbour.'

'I'm sorry for you.'

They followed the route suggested, walking along streets lined with apartment blocks. Small shops were just closing, shutters fastened across the outside of windows; signs and produce were being taken in from the pavement. They found a post office still open and took the chance to send telegrams home. Herr Esterbauer wrote a short note to Frau Hillier:

Discovered his whereabouts. Vienna Hartburg Hosp. Must overnight here. Will send news tomorrow. Have strength.

Ursula wrote to Mama explaining that she'd gone with Herr Esterbauer and was sorry for any worry. She almost included a note to Anton but thought better of it. She'd nothing to say to him, except to lose face by begging him not to go anywhere, or to promise that she'd be back soon to make amends.

By the time they arrived at Hartburg Hospital it was completely dark. Ursula could see the tall gateposts only very faintly against the sky as she passed between them, thick pillars supporting cast-iron gates; the gates themselves stood open amongst the bushes. There was very little moonlight and the edges of the path were barely discernible. She strayed into the flower borders once or twice, her boots striking the frozen soil. Herr Esterbauer damned the darkness and after a while took her arm, as much for himself as anything. He cleared his throat often and took deep huffing breaths.

They followed the narrow road for quite some time – she wondered whether they were in the right place; there were no buildings, no sign that this was a hospital. Perhaps they'd strayed into a park, mistaking the gates for those of Hartburg. To the sides and ahead were leaning trees and areas of grass surrounded by miniature fences and evergreen shrubs. There were smaller paths branching off left and right and, far off in the gloom, the perimeter hedge, taller than two men. After a while they saw a shape, large and square and unlit. They walked towards it; the path curved to the right and she could soon see other buildings, blacked out and obscure, one with a high broad dome, which she guessed was the church that the old man had mentioned. One of the structures was much bigger than the rest.

'I expect that's the main building,' said Herr Esterbauer, looking ahead with a pinched expression and knitted brows. His rubbed his hands together restlessly. 'That'll be the place to begin our enquiries.'

Close to the buildings the trees grew very dense, firs with thick foliage near their tops. They produced a deepening blackness, enclosing Ursula and Herr Esterbauer in a tunnel, and there was a hush beneath the branches, an eerie quiet. It didn't seem right to chatter here and Ursula was glad of the sound of Herr Esterbauer's heavy boots to keep her company. One or two figures passed, stepping noiselessly on the thin carpet of pine needles. She supposed these were staff going off shift, or visitors returning home. Ursula and Herr Esterbauer spoke to none of them, even though some murmured a greeting.

The main building when they reached it showed no sign of activity, the façade lifeless, all the windows shuttered and the grand double doors closed. At the entranceway steps, Ursula looked upwards at the dark expanse of brick, tier upon tier of windows, the roof seeming to swing against the sky – a formidable place. Herr Esterbauer blew air through his lips, cleared his throat several more times, adjusted his hat, and looked up also.

'I'll go inside and ask a few questions,' he said. 'At least to find out where he is.'

Ursula felt sudden terror at the thought of waiting alone in the muffled air. 'I'll come too,' she said hastily.

'Better not. We don't know what you might see in there.' The farmer patted her shoulder. He adjusted his hat again before approaching the doors and turning one of the enormous handles. It moved stiffly then stopped. Herr Esterbauer rapped on the thick panels, the wood absorbing the knock so that Ursula wasn't sure whether anybody would hear him. After a few moments there were footsteps within and locks, bolts and chains clattered and banged. A crack of light appeared and the head and shoulders of a man wearing a cap. A hospital porter or night watchman.

'Good evening,' he said. 'Can I help you?'

'Good evening,' said Herr Esterbauer, straightening and using a businesslike voice. Ursula stepped up close beside the farmer. She tried to peer beyond the porter. 'I need to find out about a patient – he's been brought here by mistake. We're here to collect him.'

'Stop!' The man held up a supercilious gloved hand. 'You realise of course it's beyond curfew? Visiting hours are from ten in the morning until twelve, resuming at one until three thirty. Please come back during those times.'

The man began to close the door.

'Wait!' said Ursula. The watchman paused. 'It's just that we've come a long way and we need to know whether he's here.' The man's face was indistinguishable. 'Can you at least ask the receptionist to check the files for his name?'

'No. I cannot. The receptionist went home hours ago. What makes you think she'd be here at this time? Come back in the morning.'

The door was unceremoniously slammed and relocked from the inside.

Ursula stung with humiliation. Herr Esterbauer scowled as though he was considering wilder options, such as breaking in, or threatening the porter with a beating.

'We have to be patient,' he said after a moment. 'And above all respectable, if we're going to succeed.' He walked down the steps on to the gravel. 'We'll have to get a hotel for the night.'

They began the murky walk, retracing their route across the grounds, the vast lawns and immense buildings stretching out dimly on either side of them, the thick boundary hedges concealed by the deepening night so the place seemed limitless, the soft rustling of the trees the only sound. They continued in silence, two specks amongst edgeless shadow, beneath a blank, starless sky, and they registered for the first time the reality and magnitude of their task.

19

'You.' The chalk-faced nurse stood beside a bed containing a boy, the same one who'd not risen quickly the morning before. 'Get up!'

The boy moved but didn't rise. The nurse pulled him to a sitting position. His head lolled, eyes open but unseeing.

'Right,' she said. 'You're coming with me.' She dragged him to his feet, supporting him heavily because he swayed like a drunk, then led him out of the room. 'Washroom!' came a distracted call from the corridor. 'Five minutes.'

Schosi, Aldo and the others in the dormitory had watched the boy's removal in silence. As soon as the nurse was gone they began their usual scurry to find clothes, but this time a hum filled the room. Schosi and Aldo listened to the voices – it was strange to hear the boys come suddenly to life. A low urgent buzz like bees waking after a long winter. The two boys nearest to Schosi and Aldo were looking over at them, as if they wanted to tell them something. For the first time one of their neighbours addressed them.

'Poor bastard,' said one. He had a mouth full of gums with teeth that seemed to be struggling to emerge. He gestured with his thumb. 'We ain't going to see him again.'

'What d'you mean?' said Aldo. Aldo's pyjamas were on back to front, his hair in a wild cockscomb.

'He goes down the other corridor now. The sisters will put him on a different mealtime. Feeding up, ain't it? That's the end of him.'

Schosi couldn't understand what he was trying to tell them. Where was the poorly boy being taken? Why was everybody so excited? A feeling was growing between the boys in the dormitory, like before a storm breaks and there is pressure inside the skull. Their neighbour with the gums seemed unable to manage the fastenings on his shorts. His friend, whose fingers were just as shaky, tried to help him. Schosi realised he wasn't dressed himself. He rushed to throw on his shirt and shorts, yanked his collar straight, and his cuffs. Aldo followed suit. They forgot for a moment about anything else.

The tall leader boy didn't lead the line this time on the way to the washroom but walked at the back, a white blanket or coat wrapped around him, his arms trapped across his chest, tied with a white strap, a punishment for swearing at a nurse. Schosi washed at the sink, teeth chattering. Aldo cough-coughed like a dog. It echoed and made Schosi anxious and annoyed. Schosi went to the urinal to pee; another boy stood beside him and steam rose into their faces. When he turned round the tall boy was standing on the edge of the sink near the window. He raised his leg and balanced on one foot. Someone warned him to be careful, but the tall boy ignored it and kicked the window with all his might so his foot went through the glass. The pane fell, some of it outwards, some inwards, and smashed in pieces on the floor. Blood splashed all over the sink. One of the smaller boys screamed. Then the tall boy fell off the sink into the glass. The white coat trapped his arms so that he banged his head. Blood spread across the white tiles. Three nurses arrived; the small-nosed one pinned the tall boy to the floor. The other boys ran out of the washroom and Schosi followed, glad to be gone because the blood horrified him.

20

Ursula woke in a squeaking bed, springs sharp as knitting needles in her side, and the pillow soaked with drool. She wiped her face on her sleeve. She'd spent a restless night, her mind full of the hospital and of Schosi, of fears that they were already too late, her thoughts reeling in a never-ending loop of useless worry. She'd lain down exhausted, with most of her clothes still on because she hadn't remembered to bring a nightdress, but she'd not been able to settle. She was either too hot beneath the blankets, or too cold above them, and she soon grew uncomfortable in any position, turning and shifting, the bed springs jangling in protest. By morning, she was more exhausted than she'd been before she went to bed; her heart nudged uncomfortably and anxiety buzzed in her veins. She only knew that she must have slept eventually because the postal worker woke her at five o'clock with his cheerful whistle, floating up the spiralling stone stairwell from the letterboxes below.

The room Herr Esterbauer had taken for her was small, with space for a bed, a skinny wardrobe and a sink beside the window. The walls were white and the ceiling very high – dimensions exactly opposite to that of her own house, which had large broad rooms with low beams, and on every beam something hanging. The Viennese door was tall and fine, with bevelled panels and a golden handle and lock. Herr Esterbauer's room was beside hers and only slightly larger. The key that she'd been given by the landlady was huge, as long as her hand and heavy. The landlady lived in the adjacent apartment – Ursula had heard her wireless waltzing late into the night and the clinking of cutlery. She seemed a stolid and surly kind of person, none too friendly, but the price was a lot less than a hotel, Herr Esterbauer had said, and it was close to Hartburg, only a few streets away.

She rose and went to the small sink to wash her face. She needed daylight and opened the inner shutters and double window, then the outer shutters. She glanced down at the road below – she was high above the ground and the view made her dizzy, so she drew back. She concentrated instead on washing with the cracked sliver of soap then combed her hair. That morning they would walk to the hospital – she'd insisted Herr Esterbauer let her come, despite his protests. She dressed hastily, roughly, tugging her socks hard over her knees, her thumb tearing a hole in the wool. She struggled with her bootlaces and managed after much cursing to tie one of the smooth yellow ribbons around her hair. She took several deep breaths and commanded herself to be composed. She must remember Schosi. He needed her. She should keep a level head.

'I'm sorry, mein Herr,' said the Hartburg receptionist after they'd asked to see Schosi. 'We can't grant access to the patient at this time. He's undergoing treatment and won't be receiving visitors.'

'Treatment?' said Herr Esterbauer in a clipped tone. 'What kind of treatment?'

The woman raised her pencilled brows and looked at him coolly. Then she slid some papers into a slim cardboard file and wrote on it with a rapid hand – her voluminous curls vibrated on top of her head and her bosom shook beneath her thin blouse. 'I'm not at liberty to discuss the treatment of patients. That's for the doctor to do.'

'Well then, we wish to see the doctor!' retorted Ursula, gripping the edge of the counter.

Herr Esterbauer touched her arm, three fingers resting just lightly, cautioning her. She let her arm fall back to her side.

'None of the doctors are free today. You will need to make an appointment to see Dr Klein if you wish to discuss anything.'

Ursula watched Herr Esterbauer's fists clenching and unclenching and imagined another night in the rented room, not knowing whether Schosi was safe. Another telegram to Frau Hillier and to Mama. Another day when Anton might leave to join the fighting – and on and on and on. She couldn't stand it. She bit her lip then let out a short, loud breath.

'Well,' said Herr Esterbauer, his voice raising, 'please make an appointment with the doctor then. For as soon as possible.'

The woman retrieved a thick leather-bound book, opened it and leafed through at a leisurely pace. 'On Tuesday – at eleven in the morning. Shall I enter your name?'

'Tuesday?' exclaimed Ursula. 'That's too long!'

Herr Esterbauer stepped closer to the receptionist. 'Look, gnädige Frau. I have a business to take care of. I have employees. I can't spend days hanging about. This is unacceptable!'

The woman raised her face slowly and treated him to her blandest stare, her eyes seeming to grow duller, smaller, to shrink back into the recesses of her head. Herr Esterbauer opened his mouth then clamped it shut. His fists began their clenching and unclenching once more. His eyes darted here and there and his jaw muscles flickered and Ursula supposed he was worried about the farm as well as everything else. Both he and Ursula were silent for a moment as they contemplated five days of waiting, of not being able to do a single thing. Schosi would have no idea they were only blocks away. Perhaps somehow they could reassure him, thought Ursula. She stood on tiptoe and leaned on the counter so that her torso poked through the reception hatch.

'Please, at least give him a message.' She tried to catch the woman's gaze to implore her to take pity, but the small eyes slid left and right, impossible to pin, like trying to spear pickled onions on a greased plate. 'Can you just tell him that we're here in the city and that we'll be coming to see him very shortly? And that we'll take him home as soon as we can?'

'Patients are to receive no correspondence while undergoing treatment, not even from parents,' the receptionist recited mechanically.

'Can you at least tell us where the children's ward is?' demanded Ursula. The woman made no reply; her pen once again jerked across the page of a file. Ursula stared in anger at the placid face before her, the sliding eyes that refused to truly see them. Herr Esterbauer's hand appeared on her shoulder, pulled her gently back till she was standing normally again. She felt despair enter her heart and tried to banish it. This place was a prison and the staff were jailors, just as they had been at Brauhausen.

'I'm sorry for the inconvenience,' chirped the woman.

'Tuesday, at eleven,' said Herr Esterbauer; his grip on Ursula's shoulder tightened to the point of pain. 'May I please see the entry in the diary?'

The woman looked up sharply. Then an expression of genuine offence came on to her powdered face. She raised the ledger and turned its pages towards them so that they could read her entry. Beside Tuesday's date was written: *Herr Esterbauer, to see Dr Klein at eleven o'clock. Regarding the early discharge of Hillier Schosi, a recent patient.*

'Many heartfelt thanks – for all your help.' Herr Esterbauer tugged the brim of his hat, his expression stony, then they walked from the lobby, their footfalls resounding in the austere hall.

21

They kept their rooms on Gütteldorfer Strasse. Every morning they went to the green door of the landlady's apartment and rang the tarnished bell. Frau Petschka, usually in her housecoat and headscarf in the midst of some soapy or dusty task, took their Reichsmarks and enquired after their health.

'The rooms are OK?' she asked each time.

'Yes, thank you,' they invariably replied. 'Everything's in order.'

Herr Esterbauer sent a telegram every day to Frau Hillier and to Mama with instructions for the running of the farm, and about his mother's preferences so Mama could take care of her while he was away. The telegrams weren't cheap, charged per word, and Herr Esterbauer said he wasn't always as economical as he could be because he wanted to bring Frau Hillier some comfort. Sometimes Mama replied, berating Ursula, reminding her how indecorous it was to be in the city alone with a man, no matter who he was, and that she was fed up with pretending to the school that Ursula was ill. She said Frau Gerg had called at the house snooping, asking why Ursula wasn't at the League. This provoked another wrangling match between Ursula and Herr Esterbauer. She did feel bad about the worry she'd caused Mama, but she couldn't bear to give up and go home.

On the third morning, Mama ended her telegram with: *Anton has gone off with Rudi. Don't know where.* Ursula reread the words, trying to find something more, some clue, some hope. She gripped the paper, buckling it. Her face felt numb, her fingers icy – her lungs ached and her heart too. She sank on to the cold tiles. Her sobs echoed loudly in the peaceful post office. Herr Esterbauer, alarmed, stooped and stroked her shoulder, saying briskly, 'Come, come,' and, 'Hush now.' Anton was gone; she'd driven him off. He'd be killed. He'd be lost without her. He'd told her so many times he'd be lost without her. He'd go wherever was most dangerous and violent. He'd die. Herr Esterbauer propped her up and escorted her outside.

'All boys want to get stuck in, Ursula. Can't stop them, you know?' He rubbed her arm with firm, even strokes like when he soothed a horse and blotted her wet cheeks with his handkerchief, and she thought it would be all right if only it were that simple, but Anton had gone because she'd been unkind and had abandoned him. Now there was no one to keep him safe.

Herr Esterbauer arranged with the landlady that she cook them a meal every evening for an extra fee. She wasn't a good cook, and when she entered the room with another plate of steaming, wobbling meat, or a bowl of grey and undercooked stew, Ursula's heart sank. She missed Mama's cooking; even Dorli's efforts were better than this. There were few vegetables to garnish the meals, not an egg in sight.

In the evenings she was homesick; time dragged in the narrow room. She wished she'd remembered to bring a book, her thoughts without anything to divert them returning inexorably to the plights of Anton and Schosi. She and Herr Esterbauer played cards and dice and he tried to cheer her but she was poor company. He shared his newspaper with her sometimes but the articles were all about war and the approach of the Russians across Europe; they made no sense to her and only made her more afraid for Anton. Had he come here to the city or gone to the Front, to one of the places mentioned in the papers? Her mind was full of catastrophe, his bloodied face, eyes empty, tongue protruding, body torn and motionless on blackened ground. Should she search for him at the flak towers? Should she leave a notice there with her name and the Gütteldorfer address? She thought about Schosi, incarcerated somewhere in that grim, endless place, the terror he must feel. Did he know he was amongst murderers? Did he dread them every moment? Or was it already done? The stab of a needle into his frail arm, the fading of his patient, honest eyes? She choked on this thought. Sometimes she wept because it felt better than just sitting and thinking. For solace, she conjured pictures of Sepp, his liquorice hair, his elastic smile. But relief didn't last long; she wondered again if Anton had reported the Sontheimers. She suppressed a shudder of mortification.

She'd no idea what might happen – at the very least the boys would be real enemies now.

One evening Herr Esterbauer brought her pencil and paper and an envelope, having gone out especially to buy the things. 'So you can write to your mother,' he said. 'Or whoever you like.'

The kindness made her tearful and she thanked him in a quavering voice. But the only people she wanted to write to were Anton and Schosi and she didn't know where Anton was, and, even if a letter could miraculously bypass the spying hospital staff and reach Schosi, he couldn't read.

It wasn't long before Aldo was taken away. He coughed and coughed through every night and eventually became so tired that he couldn't stand. One morning he simply ignored the whistle and turned his back as the nurse came by, unable to open his eyes, unable to wake. The nurse lifted him easily in her burly arms. As Aldo was carried from the room Schosi wanted to call out to his friend but no words came.

'Poor bastard,' muttered Schosi's neighbour with the large gums.

'Poor bastard,' echoed his friend.

The dormitory once again filled with breathless chatter as everyone dressed. Boys glanced at Schosi, who was unable to hide his tears. He felt bad. He'd deserted Aldo on many occasions in the garden, or elsewhere, when Aldo had been slow and untalkative, or when his coughing had irritated him. Now he was sorry. The boy with the large gums patted Schosi on the back, rapidly as if he was beating dust from his clothing. He introduced himself as

209

Moritz then introduced his friend, who had yellowish skin and sore, blinking eyes.

'That's Paulin,' he said. 'He's all right.'

Paulin's grip, when he shook Schosi's hand, was damp and limp as a wilted lettuce leaf.

Later that day, Schosi, Moritz and Paulin dug in the sandpit in the garden. Moritz complained that it was goddamn freezing and that he hated playtime, but the sand was moist and formed easily into shapes and the three were soon building towers and smashing them and building them up again. It was the first time Schosi had enjoyed himself since arriving at the hospital and he even forgot for a moment where he was and about the perishing cold. Moritz dug a very deep hole in the sand that he said was nearly deep enough to get them beneath the fence and out of this damned place if only it wasn't right in the middle of the lawn.

The chalk-faced nurse came along the path behind them with keys jingling. She glanced at them then stopped. Moritz was using his hands to dig and spraying sand behind him like a dog, reaching far down into the crater he'd made, with backside raised, grunting with effort. The nurse's expression hardened. She stepped off the path and was suddenly moving fast, a black shape swooping towards them across the grass. Schosi's stomach lurched; he stuttered a high-pitched warning but Moritz didn't hear and didn't see until the nurse seized him by his jumper and hauled him up. With a powerful swing of her fist she crashed her bunch of keys into his face.

'What are you doing?' she shouted. 'You rat!' Blood ebbed from a puncture wound not far from Moritz's eye. The nurse knocked him into the sandpit. 'Fill that in!'

Cowering, he scrabbled, pushing sand back into the hole; blood dripped from his cheek.

'And you two!' She pointed at the lawn. 'Tidy that up!'

Schosi and Paulin hastily set to work, scooping spilled sand and throwing it into the pit. The nurse watched them, looming, frowning, the keys bristling from her fist.

When the garden looked neater she walked away without a word. They watched her retreating back. She entered the building through the nurses' entrance and was gone, her garden duty finished for the afternoon. Moritz wiped his hands on his jumper and gingerly touched the cut on his face. He winced. He looked frightening, blood smeared to his chin. The three squatted close together. They were all shaking. They rubbed their bare knees and blew into their cupped hands.

'She can't frighten me,' Moritz muttered after several silent minutes had passed, his brow sullen and his lower lip and jaw protruding. Every so often he snorted to clear the snot from his running nose. After a while he said abruptly, 'Wanna go and see Aldo?' He squinted at Schosi. 'I know where they've taken him.'

'Now?' said Schosi.

'Yeah, now.' Moritz spoke fiercely. 'While Sister ain't looking.' The nurse now on duty was the young pale-haired one, who Schosi had learned was called Sister Kuster. Moritz rose, rather unsteadily, and beckoned for them to follow. Paulin gave a fearful grimace and shook his head. Schosi too quailed at the thought. That nurse would surely kill them if they were caught. Why did Moritz want to go now? But he remembered Aldo and how sad and small he'd looked when he was taken away. He wanted to see him again, to be able to hug him, to pet his hair and make him better. He recalled little bear and her bravery, going into the woods alone, finding her way, taking Schosi to the village to visit his father's grave, and all the fearless games she played. She'd certainly go to see Aldo if she were here.

On the other side of the garden, Sister Kuster was involved in an activity with a little girl and was distracted. They were seated on miniature chairs beside a low, mildewed table. She offered the girl wooden blocks and helped her to set them in place. When the girl dropped the blocks or arranged them upside down Sister Kuster swatted her and hissed a rebuke. Then she patted the girl's sallow cheek to console her, glancing warily about as she did so. Moritz sauntered across the lawn and Schosi followed. Sister Kuster did not look up. They ducked around the corner of the building. Backs to the bricks, they were hidden from view and a few metres away was the door into the ward. At the base of a fir tree, a boy and a girl stopped their muddy game and stared.

'We got to get past the office,' said Moritz. 'I've done it before but there'll be some of those damn sisters around. They'll be on the phone probably. Or smoking away like hell.' He eyed Schosi appraisingly. 'You up to it?'

Schosi, heart somersaulting, tried to reply.

Moritz's eyes narrowed, a piercing, unblinking look. 'You want to see Aldo, or what? Or are you too chicken?'

'I want to go.' Schosi's stutter tripped his words.

Moritz peered briefly through the glass of the door. He pushed it open and led them inside.

They tiptoed swiftly along corridors. They came to a set of double doors, which were bolted. Moritz made a good job of sliding the bolts without making any noise.

He was trembling a lot and kept asking Schosi to look out for those bastard sisters. Schosi watched and listened but nobody came.

When they reached the nurses' office, the door was partly open and light fell out in a vivid wedge. There were low voices and shadows moving within. All Schosi could think of was the brutal bunch of keys, the shrieking whistles and foul mouths, quick-slapping hands and needles, the white jacket meant to strangle you, to imprison your arms. Somehow, with hand clutching his privates to prevent the pee from escaping, he managed to cross through the slice of lamplight. The phone rang, shockingly loud. He sprang into a run, shoes slapping heavily on the floor, only the din of the telephone disguising his reverberating steps. Just as he reached the end of the corridor and Moritz, the chiming of the phone ceased. A voice answered in a singsong tone – the chalk-faced nurse. 'Good afternoon, Hartburg Hospital, Sister Franz.'

Moritz dragged Schosi away down the deserted corridor. There were several broken bulbs overhead, throwing pockets of shadow on to the walls and floor. Schosi glimpsed the scribbled design on the plaster and he knew that they were nearing the freezing room. He didn't want Aldo to be in there but also he wanted to see him very much. The covered cart was parked against the wall as before and Moritz peered cautiously through the keyhole, listening for any telltale sound. He turned the handle slowly, smoothly. Schosi gripped the back of Moritz's jumper as they went inside. He suppressed a cough. The stench of pee and vomit was even worse than when he was here last.

The room wasn't staffed. The windows were open as normal and the temperature icy. The children were still sleeping, not a blanket amongst them, some lying only in pants and vest, their skin blotched pink and bluish purple. Schosi saw what he thought was his friend's hair against one of the pillows but realised the person was much too tall. He searched for a sign of the drooling girl he'd seen on his last visit, but couldn't see her. Perhaps she'd recovered and gone back to join the other girls in the dormitory. He walked around and looked into each face – they were all very thin and pale, their eyes sealed in the deepest sleep, crusts dried along their lashes, no flicker behind the delicate skin – some boys, some girls, some that were almost babies, some teenagers, some who were pretty and fair, others who were malformed and ugly, one with a lip that split and melted into the base of his nose. They wheezed and grunted as though struggling to draw air. Moritz was peering into a caged bed in the corner. The wire was so low over the occupant that there was no space to sit up.

'Hansi?' he whispered.

It was the tall boy from their dormitory. He lay on his side wearing only long johns, his graceful hands folded beneath his cheek. On his chin was a dark bruise and his arms and legs were scored with dreadful cuts. Moritz called him one more time but there was no response.

Schosi found Aldo asleep, just like the other children, and without any blanket. He didn't look like himself. His face when Schosi touched it was cold as snow. He remembered when he'd come here and the nurse had gone to the tall wooden cupboard. Perhaps there were more towels in there that he could use to cover his friend. He went to the cupboard and pulled the doors open while Moritz watched. Inside were piles of sheets and the white towels that had made Schosi's nappy. There were also grey blankets. Plenty of them – enough for all the children. He took one to Aldo, tucked it around him, doubled it beneath his chin. He looked a lot warmer, a lot better. Schosi stroked Aldo's hair then went to fetch another blanket – Moritz followed suit. They went to the nearest beds and spread them over the sleeping children; they returned to the wardrobe, grabbed more blankets and continued around the room. But there was no way of opening the cage to help the leader boy. Moritz began to cry bitterly, making tear tracks in the dried blood on his cheek. Schosi felt sick; he tried to catch his breath but the room was so silent and terrible that he couldn't and his chest wheezed and constricted.

The door handle turned and a hefty nurse strode into the room. She stopped in her tracks and stared at Schosi and Moritz as though they'd risen from the dead.

'What are you doing here?' Her eyes bulged and her thick neck flushed red.

Terror wakened in Schosi's bowels. He and Moritz stood with blankets draped across their arms, not moving.

'Don't you dare ignore me!' Her voice was shrill. 'Disobedient brats!' She dashed across the dormitory. 'Come here!'

She caught them easily, their legs having turned to water, and grasped each of them by the collar. She dragged them from the freezing room into the scribbled corridor. She marched along with the two boys stumbling at her sides, deliberately unbalancing them with shakes of her muscled arms. When they reached the office, she thrust the door open with her foot and flung them inside.

Sister Kuster and another nurse whom Schosi didn't recognise looked up. Chalk-faced Sister Franz was gone.

'Look what I found in dorm thirteen.'

'Oh Lord! There they are!' exclaimed Sister Kuster. 'We've been searching for them everywhere. The gardening staff have been looking in the grounds.' She lowered her voice slightly and spoke to the nurse seated beside her. 'He's an idiot.' She nodded towards Schosi. 'And the other most likely led him astray – he's in the asocial bracket.' She stood. Her eyes rested on Schosi and Moritz. 'Gracious, you two! What are you playing at? And what's the matter with your face?'

'We got lost, Sister,' said Moritz meekly. 'We went into the wrong dormitory.'

'Huh,' grunted the nurse who'd discovered them. 'They were getting blankets out of the cupboard.'

There was a moment of silence. Sister Kuster's eyes flickered from the boys to the floor and back to the older nurse who'd spoken. Then the hefty nurse clouted Schosi hard across the ear. 'You have broken the rules!' she rapped out, seeming even more furious than before. She hit Moritz next, a darting, accurate strike, her lips clamped fiercely inwards, her chin bunching. Moritz shielded his face with his arm.

'I'll take care of these,' said Sister Kuster. She quickly herded the boys towards the door. 'Back to the dormitory this instant!'

Do your job properly,' said the nurse. 'Don't lose them again. Remember you're on probation – you haven't passed yet.'

'Yes, Sister, of course.' Sister Kuster lowered her eyes. 'I'm sorry.'

'The quality of nurses these days,' the nurse muttered. 'They're not what they used to be.'

Sister Kuster chastised Schosi and Moritz all the way to the dormitory and pinched their ears, because, she said, she'd been made to look bad. Now she'd be forced to tell the Matron about their behaviour, who would tell Dr Heinrich Klein and it was his morning inspection tomorrow, so on your heads be it.

'Please don't tell the doctor,' cried Moritz. 'Please!' He tugged frantically on the sleeve of the young nurse. 'Please! Oh God! Please don't. Please!' His eyes shone wet and wide, and his face had drained of colour. Schosi watched his friend, alarmed.

'I've no choice,' she snapped. 'It's your own fault.'

When they reached the dormitory she instructed them to get ready for exercises in the big hall. They both looked so shaken and cheerless she appeared troubled herself for an instant – her mouth drooped at the corners. She hesitated before hurrying away.

22

Dr Heinrich Klein was standing close to the bottom of the bed. The man was tall and stooped, wearing the brown Nazi uniform that Schosi had been taught to fear above all things. On seeing the red armband Schosi recoiled and hid his face in the bedclothes. The man spoke.

'Good morning, children.' His voice was reedy and dry.

Schosi peeped over the edge of his blanket. The doctor was gazing around the room, a genial smile on his lips. He began to slowly patrol, moving away. Schosi sat up, along with the other boys. His body was sluggish and slow to respond. He was very hungry. He hadn't had enough to eat for many days and weakness was beginning to take hold, seeping into his muscles. Although he felt tired he daren't disobey the whistle, and the nurse kept her eye on everyone, commanding them silently to put on a good show for the visiting doctor. He climbed out of bed and stood at the foot of it. He raised his chin and screwed his eyes closed, hoping to be passed over. Dr Klein spoke to Moritz.

'I hear you've been breaking the rules. Again.'

Moritz kept his eyes to the front like a soldier. His hands were rigid and straight at his sides, as though being as neat as possible might avert his inevitable punishment. The cut on his face was now a dark scab.

'Well? Have you?'

Moritz stared speechlessly for a moment then nodded.

'And you?' said the doctor turning to Schosi. 'Hillier Schosi, yes? From Felddorf. You've also been naughty.' Schosi flushed. 'Hmm,' said Dr Klein. He turned to the nurse and said languidly, 'Take them out of here for a while – they can be of use – and teach them a lesson.'

The nurse nodded, thin-lipped. The doctor took a sweetie from his uniform pocket, which he placed in Schosi's palm. He gave one to Moritz also. Moritz stared at the treat and began to cry, though he wiped his tears away quickly. Schosi wondered why his friend had cried. He couldn't wait to eat the silver-wrapped treat and was full of relief.

'Try to behave,' said the doctor. A sudden cough racked him and his hand flew to cover his mouth. When he regained his breath, he unfolded a handkerchief from his breast pocket and smoothly deposited the contents of his mouth into the hanky, before returning it to his trouser pocket. Schosi thought of Herr Esterbauer who rather than using a hanky merely spat over his shoulder, or placed a stubby finger to his nostril and cleared the other with a hard blast of outward air. Schosi's mama always shook her head and said 'Only a farmer'. But Schosi thought the doctor was more revolting because he was secret and sly.

Dr Klein didn't stay long. He left after speaking with several of the other boys and giving sweets to them. The boys with sweets gobbled them immediately ('It's a toffee!' said one, his cheek bulging). The sweet, syrupy taste filled Schosi with pleasure. But Moritz didn't unwrap his. After a short while two nurses appeared in the doorway.

'Weber Moritz – Hillier Schosi,' said a hawk-faced woman with hair tightly scraped beneath her cap. 'Come.' She gestured with her clipboard. 'Doctor's orders.'

Schosi and Moritz were joined by the other boys who'd been given sweets and the whole group were then led from the room. Schosi's stomach growled and wrenched painfully; the mouthful of toffee had only made him more ravenous. He cast a look back at Paulin who watched them go, arms hanging, toes turned inwards, his expression grave.

The morning of the meeting with Dr Klein, Ursula woke early. She couldn't eat much of the breakfast brought by Frau Petschka. She dressed in her most presentable skirt, blouse and cardigan. She cleaned her shoes with a damp cloth. She decided against her ribbons. It would make her look too girlish. After brushing her teeth she went to wait on the landing. The door to Herr Esterbauer's room was ajar; she could see him standing at the sink wearing his long dark coat and leaning close to the mirror; he combed his moustache and stared at his reflection. When he emerged, his hat sharply creased and wearing a fine-looking scarf, he stopped and frowned at Ursula. Before he could speak she scampered downstairs, deliberate in her display of agile youth, calling, 'I'll be nothing but good!' She wouldn't stay behind at the apartment. It wouldn't do. She'd go mad.

'Impossible!' shouted the farmer, his voice ringing in the stone stairwell. 'Damn it all!'

Outside, she crossed the inner courtyard and went out of the main doors on to the street. He joined her on the pavement a moment later. He shook his head at her, scowling, hardly meeting her eye. He looked tired and drawn. She tried not to show her chagrin, readying herself to be sent back inside. The farmer sighed.

'If you come,' he said quietly, his energy gone, 'you must not say a word. Understand? With this kind of man you must tread like a mouse. He's extremely dangerous.'

She nodded, and her stomach grew even more unsettled now that she knew she'd meet the doctor. They might get answers; they might be allowed to take Schosi home. They set off walking, he sighing and retying his scarf, she humming – a cheery song from the League to distract herself. When they reached the main street it was busy with shoppers collecting rations, harassed and unsmiling, with sharp elbows and shoulders and clacking shoes. Herr Esterbauer tutted and swore, dodging baskets and prams; a butcher burst from his shop and booted a loitering dog in his doorway; his face was beetroot-coloured above his gore-splashed apron.

They headed onwards through residential roads, walking fast, until they reached Hartburg. At the gates they slowed before entering the grounds. Ursula wanted to take hold of Herr Esterbauer's arm but he was distant, speechless, gloved hands swinging briskly at his sides, eyes scanning the path ahead then glancing to the treetops, the leafless branches crowded with the hunched shapes of birds. Sometimes he released air from between his lips in a long, loud stream. Ursula's nose and forehead ached in the bitter temperature; the day was wan, the sky a washed-out, soap-water grey, and scraps of mist floated across the lawns. Ahead was the main building, adrift on the fog like an armoured ship.

They were shown into the doctor's spacious office; the nurse who'd led them there softly closed the door. The walls were lined with bookcases and filing cabinets – the desk at the far end spanned the width of the room. Dr Klein stood when they entered and raised his hand in the German greeting.

'*Heil Hitler!*'

'*Heil Hitler!*' responded Herr Esterbauer, drawing his heels together and lifting his arm very straight.

The doctor gestured towards the chairs in front of the magnificent desk, and resumed his place behind it. He reclined and surveyed the farmer. Herr Esterbauer sat with his gloves bunched in his fist, very upright and with his feet planted stolidly apart; he removed his hat and swiped his palm across his hair. Ursula took off her coat and arranged herself neatly on her seat. She was sweating already and watched the doctor warily. There was no mistaking the authority of the man. His brows were heavy and low, as if he never smiled, and his close-set eyes were at once penetrating and impenetrable. His movements were smooth with a refinement and poise that was somehow deceitful. Ursula loathed him instantly.

'So,' said Dr Klein, 'what is the problem?'

'I am a loyal Party member.' Herr Esterbauer's voice was overly strident in the plush room. 'I have been so for many years. I do well – my business does well – for which I heartily thank the Führer.' Herr Esterbauer spoke in High German, using the correct grammar Ursula had been taught in school, his vowels less drawling, less like the village. He tapped his gloves against his thigh. 'But my employee has been brought here under false pretences. He is indispensable to me. I am losing money every day that he is here.' He looked at the doctor, cleared his throat. 'I need him back.'

Dr Klein waited, swinging a pen between his fingers like a pendulum.

Herr Esterbauer continued, stressing the inconvenience of having to come to Vienna in person. He declared that Schosi was not feeble-minded – he could work like a horse and followed orders, he did his bit for the Reich. 'I would not allow some degenerate, some good-for-nothing to work for me!'

'He's an idiot,' interjected Dr Klein. His tone was flat. 'And our experience of him proves quite undeniably that he has a criminal nature. Abnormalities, socially speaking.'

Herr Esterbauer quickly dabbed his brow with his handkerchief. The office was warm and his cheeks were flushed. Ursula began to fidget; she willed him to persevere.

'Now . . .' Herr Esterbauer cleared his throat again. 'With respect, you're wrong. I'm in total support of these types being locked away.' He looked at the doctor squarely, gave a courteous nod. 'I applaud you wholeheartedly for the work you do. But this is a mistake. He is very capable.'

Ursula studied the farmer. Did he really support the doctor? He seemed in earnest. She knew he pitied none in the camps; he'd said so once. Perhaps he felt the same about the hospitals. But Schosi he loved. Schosi was different. She prayed that Dr Klein wouldn't detect how extravagantly Herr Esterbauer lied, or bent the truth at the very least. Dr Klein wasn't to know whether Schosi could be useful on the farm. He wasn't to know that in fact he required constant direction and wasn't much help at all, beyond his tool sharpening.

There was a lengthy pause. Ursula's pulse quickened in the silence; Dr Klein stared unblinkingly at Herr Esterbauer, and Herr Esterbauer tried to appear at ease but he shifted in his seat, dabbed his face again. From the corridor outside the office came a regular squeaking noise, like a bird call, growing louder then fading as a trolley passed by with unoiled wheels. A door was slammed somewhere many rooms away.

'He's just shy,' Ursula burst out. 'Very shy actually. You've got the wrong idea thinking he's an idiot because he's not.'

Herr Esterbauer looked at her sharply. The doctor barely glanced at her and again swung his pen, the pendulum gaining speed, a hectic flicker of metal. Ursula felt as though she'd shrunk in her chair to the size of a toddler.

Then abruptly the doctor placed the pen on the open file that lay in front of him. 'Hillier Schosi cannot be released just like that. His file states that he comes from a squalid home with an absent mother. He's a congenital inferior who's not properly cared for, allowed to ramble free and break the law. His behaviour is subnormal – he was sterilised as a young boy in Brauhausen – I have it in his records. I know what it is that I see.'

'His mother isn't absent!' said Ursula. 'She has a job at the factory, that's all.'

'Shut your mouth, Ursula,' Herr Esterbauer growled, his country accent returning. He hastily addressed the doctor. 'While the mother works, the boy works too, under my supervision.'

'No, no.' The doctor shook his head impatiently. An aggravated pinkness crept into his sallow cheeks. 'He's been found wandering, thieving – we've a report of his antics from a respectable source, the local leader of the League of German Girls.'

'From Frau Gerg who bears a grudge,' said Ursula, unable to contain herself. 'It's a fib! He didn't steal anything!'

'That's merely your opinion!' Dr Klein's eyes flashed irately on to her before focusing once more on the farmer. 'He is clearly a liability and rule breaker. He cannot speak properly – he cannot read or write. He is obsessive and incontinent. It's not appropriate for him to range about unattended, causing havoc.'

Ursula's fingers trembled and her mouth was dry as dust. Now was the moment; a few more seconds and her chance would have passed. Her heart pulsed strong and loud in her ears; she opened her mouth to draw breath. But after all this time – how could she? Herr Esterbauer would despise her. Everyone would. She'd not be believed. The truth stuck like a fishhook and wouldn't come free.

'And he's being treated?' said Herr Esterbauer, changing tack. 'The receptionist said he's having treatment and we can't visit him.'

'That is correct. He's receiving treatment.'

'Treatment for what?'

'To correct his abnormalities.'

A vague response – an evasive one.

'We must visit him,' Herr Esterbauer asserted. 'He'll be very distressed by all this. We can't return home without at least seeing the boy.'

Dr Klein shot up from his chair. 'Sir!' he said. 'I have other appointments besides yours. You'll have to wait for your visit until the boy's treatment is over.'

Herr Esterbauer quickly stood and collected his hat from the back of his chair, gesturing that Ursula should do the same. She did so, fumbling her arms into her coatsleeves.

'But when can we visit him?' she half whispered.

'I don't know!' snapped the doctor. 'I'm not aware of the itinerary of each of my patients. I'm a busy man. You'll need to speak to the receptionist, or the nursing staff. Now, if you don't mind—'

He came out from behind his desk; his polished boots clicked across the room. He opened the door and signalled towards the corridor. A flash of bright metal on his lapel caught Ursula's notice; he wore the Golden Party badge – Anton had shown her pictures in his manuals. It meant he was connected very highly indeed, to the Führer himself perhaps. A chill passed over her skin. She hurried out.

Bleached winter sun came through the hospital windows as they walked down the passageway and they quickened their pace to warm their blood. Ursula was very glad to be out of the doctor's company.

'We should take pains to avoid any further dealings with him,' muttered Herr Esterbauer. 'He's cold as a reptile and with less conscience.'

23

The group of boys from the ward were taken outside and along a path that ran between brick pavilions. Nurses flanked them and to their right was a lofty hedge of fir with skinny trees waving beyond it. Black birds snagged in the branches like scraps of cloth and Schosi shivered with fear. The scratchy twigs in the trees and ragged birds brought to mind the Krampuses. The bundles of sticks gripped in black hands, misshapen silhouettes moving outside his cottage, scuttling and calling in a way that filled him with uncontainable terror. It would soon be December. They'd come. He fought the urge to run.

They were led, wordless and shuffling, into a square courtyard surrounded by inward-looking windows. Beside a door was a cart covered in blue canvas. Its wheels were tall, just like the one that stood outside the freezing room.

As they crossed the yard and neared the cart, Schosi slipped on the algae-green paving stones and nearly lost his footing. Moritz seized his elbow, righting him.

'They put the dead ones in there,' he whispered. 'Arms and legs hanging out, like turkeys at Christmas.'

Schosi looked at the cart in fright. He thought of Aldo. Was he in there now, concealed by the blue canvas? He could feel the tremor in Moritz's grip. Where were the nurses taking them? They'd broken the rules and would be punished for it. He was always caught whenever he did anything bad. Little bear said he should tell better lies.

Inside, the doors had glass panes of bottle green, blue and frosted white, watery colours that made Schosi remember that he was extremely thirsty. There were rows of strong white doors with hatches closed tight. Banging came from behind them as they passed, and weeping. Other than this it was a quiet place – there was no hustle and bustle of nurses coming and going, no rattle of trolleys, no echo of sports in the red hall, only the sound of birds, occasional cawing and the flap of wings, the stomp of the accompanying nurses and rustle of the boys. A voice cried out, startling them.

'Sister!' It was a child's voice. 'Please, Sister!'

They kept going. After a moment the calling stopped. Schosi tried to breathe normally but silence filled the corridor like being underwater and the doors hid blank spaces containing unknown things, miserable creatures rather than children.

There was the slip-slip of soft footsteps and two other nurses approached. They stopped at one of the white doors, jangling keys. They greeted the nurses with Schosi's group then disappeared through the door. As he passed, Schosi peered into the room, no bigger than the scullery in his house. The nurses knelt on the floor, between them a roll of grey material, a misshapen tube about five feet in length. One nurse worked busily to unbuckle leather straps that fastened the bundle in three places. The tube of material shifted, bending slightly.

'Stay still!' the nurse said, leaning on it with all her weight.

Twenty metres down the corridor was another set of glass-panelled doors; the nurses herded the boys through these and into a spacious, brightly lit room with warm pink tiles along the walls, green curtains and a carpeted floor. Weighing scales stood to the left of the entrance where the boys were told to form a queue. There were several nurses drinking coffee at a low table and smoking. Two men stood close together with their backs to Schosi looking at files in a clean and pleasant kitchen area. One was bald and wore a white coat and the other was tall and stooped, wearing a military jacket, red armband and storm trooper boots. Schosi recognised him immediately as Dr Klein. He took a step backwards knocking into one of the nurses. She grabbed his wrist.

'Line up, I say!' she called to the group.

At this the doctor turned and the bald man too. Dr Klein looked directly at Schosi. A disapproving crease appeared between his brows.

The nurse who held Schosi's wrist addressed Dr Klein. 'Apologies, Doctor. These are the maladjusted from pavilion fifteen. We're just recording initial weight on entry to the cells.'

Dr Klein continued to glare at Schosi, his eyes crowded in at either side of his fleshy nose. 'You're the one who stole fruit in Felddorf?' The doctor left no time for Schosi to respond. 'And now stealing blankets from dormitory thirteen. We can't have that.' He stared ahead into thin air for a moment. Then he smiled almost gently and looked at Schosi again. 'A bout of drink treatment. For your own good.' To the nurse, 'See to it, will you?' Then he and the other doctor bent over their files once more.

24

They returned to the hospital every day for the next two weeks. They became so well acquainted with the receptionist of the main building that before they even reached her desk, she'd call out a greeting. 'Good morning! His treatment's not over yet. You may not visit today.'

Herr Esterbauer tried to convey a sense of resolute confidence to Frau Hillier in his telegrams. He'd find his way to Schosi, as a tenacious dog eventually suffocates its larger prey by clamping over the throat and refusing to release. But neither he nor Ursula were so unwavering and sure. With each cajoling lie from the hospital staff about Schosi being perfectly well, about his 'treatment', their foreboding mounted, each passing moment the loss of another opportunity to save him. Ursula became hopeless, overwhelmed, exhausted.

Herr Esterbauer too was beginning to flag. He worried about his mother, his farm.

They went a few times to search the Hartburg grounds, hunting for the children's ward amongst the many buildings, looking in at windows, though most were too high and they could only grab the bars and shin up to peep over the sill, seeing little. Herr Esterbauer turned the handles on doors but found them bolted. Twice, a patrolling security guard came and questioned them. They pretended to be lost. The guard, poker-faced, escorted them from the grounds, unresponsive when Herr Esterbauer joked about being a forgetful old Opa with no sense of direction.

'It's time to act,' the farmer said one day as they sat together on a bench in front of the Hofburg Palace, having not long returned from Hartburg. He rubbed his hands to warm them, an agitated motion, then leaned forward, elbows on his knees. 'Our luck won't last, they'll call the police and that'll be the end of it.'

'What would be best?' said Ursula, her mind darting instantly ahead; yes, they must do something, something drastic, anything at all. It was too, too horrible to just sit like this, to go back to the apartment for a meal, to sleep on clean sheets and pillows. She leaned forward also. 'What shall we do?'

'What shall *I* do?' Herr Esterbauer cleared his throat then said levelly, 'You must go home now, Ursula.'

She said nothing for a moment. Of course, she'd known at some point this would come. He wished her gone; she'd been nothing but trouble. She looked up at the symmetrical, curved wings of the Hofburg Palace. This time it sounded like he meant it. But she couldn't go, could she? Without her, all would fail – she felt this rather than thought it, a conviction in her gut. It was she who must make this right. Herr Esterbauer could ask her all he liked, implore, command her. Mama's infuriated telegrams and her own homesickness wouldn't dissuade her either; she'd not go back. In her dreams Schosi called her name, the name he'd given her, little bear, pressing his wristwatch to his ear as if there he'd find an answer, needing her to come. Sometimes he blended with Anton or Sepp, the three merging, becoming one, lost, mutilated, killed, and she to blame, desperate, searching, getting no closer.

'Ursula, this is no task for a young girl. You'd be more help at home, running errands for Frau Hillier.' The farmer's tone was straightforward. 'You make this harder – you do more harm than good.' He tried to catch her eye. 'I need to go into that place and get him out. I need to do whatever it takes. It'll be risky and unpleasant. You must go home.'

She shook her head just a little.

'For God's sake, girl!' He thumped his leg, his voice rising to a bellow. 'I'm sick to death of arguing with you! I expect to be obeyed! Do as you're told!'

'No!' She moved away from him, along the bench. 'I shan't!' She knew she was behaving very badly but she couldn't stop.

He lunged to grab her arm, squeezing hard, eyes bulging. 'Don't you dare speak to me like that! What's the matter with you?'

She gasped, almost crying, though it wasn't from pain or even because of his anger. He'd strike her and she'd deserve it. Her blood thumped. She pressed her fingernails into her palm. 'It was me who stole the fruit. I didn't say a thing! Not a thing!'

Herr Esterbauer was silent. He released her and turned in his seat. She wanted him to shout – to clobber her as hard as he could. His gaze roamed over the palace, pausing on the central balcony that dominated the building – imperious, exultant. This was where the Führer had stood and given his first speech to the Austrians, welcoming them to the Reich, to Germany.

After some minutes he looked around to check they were alone, then spoke. 'What has happened to Schosi—' He shook his head. 'It makes me think . . . it's a cruel time. That you would take it on yourself—' He rubbed his moustache, looked again at the palace. 'You're not to blame.'

He drew out his smoking kit, placed a cigarette in his mouth, struck a light. Tobacco smoke rolled over Ursula, the burnt smell of the match. The farmer leaned back on the bench and continued to puff, white rags curling away on the breeze. They watched two passers-by with a chocolate-coloured dog. The dog scampered into the nearby park and the owners followed, calling it. Herr Esterbauer raised his eyebrows, smiled a little. There was something about the companionable hush that made Ursula feel almost like the farmer's equal, instead of the defiant brat of a moment ago. Her anxiousness abated; her guilt calmed, stirred with the smoke and dispersed slightly.

'Such a good lad,' he said eventually.

She nodded.

'He's like a son to me.'

'Perhaps he will be your son one day,' she ventured, thinking of the farmer and Frau Hillier as man and wife.

This time he didn't seem uncomfortable. He exhaled, long and slow. 'I do hope so.'

She realised it wasn't strange any more to imagine them together, to picture them as lovers. It was true that their love was very different from that of the courting couples outside the Gasthaus who were laughing and beautiful and free. It was heavier and slower. It seemed to her that Herr Esterbauer carried his love like a weight on his back, dragged it everywhere in hope, to the hospital each day and to his bed at night. She thought she knew the feeling of such love, which pulled downwards and was more important than anything, but unhappier than anything too because it was lonely. She had to love her brother even though he hated and mocked and drove away every friend she made, and told her she was no good. She kept expecting him to appear somewhere in the city. Several times she had glimpsed his tawny hair, square shoulders, the sharp slope of his cheekbones. From the head of Gütteldorfer Hill she had scanned the skyline for the bald angular flak towers, ignoring the serrated needle of Stefansdom, the pale copper domes of the Belvedere, the double spire of the Rathaus. Was he amongst that great sprawl? Or in Hungary on the flat plains, dodging bullets, forgetting her angrily, not caring like the other young men did whether he saw the miraculous future that Zara Leander promised in her songs, hurting because of his sister, hurting himself?

Her tears fell easily. Dark spots quickly covered her lap. She bowed her head to conceal the sobs that shivered through her. She wondered if she ought to get up and move away. But she didn't want to leave Herr Esterbauer's warm presence, the muddled closeness she felt and needed.

'Why so sad?' he asked. 'All too much?'

'No.' Then after a few steadying breaths: 'I'm just worried about my brother as well.'

'He'll be fine. He's a strong boy.'

'He's not,' she said. 'Not really.' She sobbed then, overcome with remorse for everything.

Herr Esterbauer crossed his boots as he always did when he was waiting. He let her cry. 'He's very dear to you,' he observed when she was quieter.

She wiped her face and nose. 'He's my best friend.'

'Are you sure about that?'

'What do you mean?' She looked at him, hot-cheeked.

'I worry about you holding him up so high. I don't think it's good for you. He's not so perfect, not so . . .' He trailed off.

She sniffed. She couldn't think what to say. 'I know,' she said finally.

'He's a troubled young man. I don't want you to get hurt. He's wild.' He compressed his lips, as though keeping words at bay. 'I never told you about when he shot that Russian.' He glanced at her and saw that she was paying attention so he kept on. 'The prisoner never cut him. Anton went for him like – like I've never seen. The cut happened in the struggle, perhaps even by mistake.'

Ursula swallowed and fixed her eyes on the grit in front of the bench.

'He was so hungry to pull that trigger. And the worst thing – how he watched the poor man kick and twitch on the floor. Greedy. He stared and stared till I forced him away.'

In Ursula's chest a space opened and pushed everything outwards; nausea rushed in.

'You probably don't want to believe me,' the farmer continued, tapping his cigarette repeatedly with his fingertip. 'But I'm telling you because I worry. About you holding him up like you do.'

When at last she responded her voice was slow and thick with anger, the words forcing out of her mouth as if through dense cloth.

'You're wrong. You don't know him.'

She shut her ears, shut her mind, and let fury burn with a blinding light so it used up all the air.

25

It was early the next morning, around five o'clock, when Ursula, Herr Esterbauer and the people from the Gütteldorfer Strasse apartment block descended the stone cellar steps into cool underground air. A cacophony of sirens called from near and far in an eerie discord and Ursula shivered in her nightclothes, overcoat, socks and shoes. There was a strong musty odour in the basement, unpleasant. Someone flicked the light switch and a large low room appeared, partitioned here and there with arches in the plasterwork; boxes were arranged along one wall and there were a couple of old sofas, wooden chairs and stools in a circle; and there was a wardrobe with no doors, which was stacked with cans and jars of provisions. There were blankets rolled up on the sofas, and cushions. A rug had been placed amongst the furniture and a gramophone on a table; a rocking horse peeped from behind the wardrobe and a football waited in the expanse of the floor. Families claimed their patch of cellar by dumping their bags or by dragging a stool or chair into position. Residents of the apartments continued to arrive and there was soon a gathering of about fifty individuals.

Ursula sat on the edge of an upright chair and watched the fuss and busyness. Blankets were unrolled and tucked over the knees of the elderly, several of whom took out rosaries and started to pray. Some of the small boys and girls began a rowdy football game in the empty section of the cellar; the rocking horse lunged to and fro with a girl astride its back. Ursula tried not to think about bombs falling from the bellies of planes, blown off course by strong winds, bricks and mortar thrown to the heavens – bodies and limbs and God knows what amongst the mess. Raids here were different to those that might happen in Felddorf where the only targets were the munitions factory and the freight railway line that connected the factory to the rest of the Reich. In the city, houses were packed tight alongside government offices and other important buildings. The bombers came often.

A woman in a flowing dressing gown put a record on the gramophone – sweet strings trembling faint as gossamer – then perched on a stool and puffed on a slim cigar. She was willowy and tall, with narrow eyes, attractive even with rag knots tied in her hair. This was Frau Wilhelm, about whom Ursula had heard much tittle-tattle from Frau Petschka: apparently her baby had starved and her man had been killed in the East. The tragedy had turned her peculiar. She never replied to a 'Good morning' any more or stopped to chatter or to pass on news.

Eventually the children were lured to their seats with morsels of food. The rattle of flak began, distant and massive. The hairs on Ursula's arms rose. It was a hellish sound. She imagined Anton on a parapet, a dark drop beneath, his slender arms straining to control the great gun muzzle, to swing it in arcs across the sky. And Schosi deafened in his hospital ward, not knowing if the world was ended, with no one to comfort him. Herr Esterbauer eyed her from the opposite sofa; he'd probably have tried to reassure her if she didn't prickle at his every approach. She wondered if he'd made a plan about Schosi – he'd said nothing, and nothing more about her going home either, but then she'd not met his eye or spoken to him since the previous day. She felt confused; he'd been kind and yet she couldn't bear the things he'd said. She didn't want to remember. Her thoughts returned to Schosi continually, to her helplessness. Did Herr Esterbauer feel no sense of urgency? He seemed not to now, squinting down at the newspaper folded on his knee as if it were an ordinary morning. Wasn't he anxious that the raid would drag on and keep him from Hartburg? Was she the only one distracted for Schosi's sake? And yet she must rely on Herr Esterbauer for everything.

She wrapped her coat more tightly around herself, juddering in the cold of the basement, imagining a nondescript container arriving by post, ashes inside; Frau Hillier would see the name tag then howl and howl. Ursula banished the horrifying thought. She glanced at Herr Esterbauer. Perhaps he did fret. Late in the night, not long before the raid, she'd heard his slow footfalls and sighs through the wall. She clung to the hope that he'd lied about Anton. But she knew it wasn't so. What reason had he to be dishonest? And added to his cautioning voice was her own inner one; it whispered a warning, had always whispered such things. She began to feel too warm, despite the chill, and her anger flared again. But why was he delaying? Why was he doing nothing? Couldn't he see that there was no hope of getting Schosi out without breaking the rules? He thought he was important, a Party member, and that that was enough, but nobody cared or listened to him. He treated her like a nuisance and tried to bar her from everything. He knew how much it meant to her – her friend – *her* friend . . .

The flak settled into continuous fire, like hail on a tin roof, and eventually she breathed more normally and heard it less.

She must have dozed because she woke from a dream of Sepp, of soft, warm skin and tingling pleasure, to find herself one of the only occupants of the circle of chairs. A couple of the oldest people slept with white hair disarrayed and clinging thinly to the sofa cushions under their heads. Children were curled beneath blankets. The adults stood near by, including Herr Esterbauer, their talk loud enough to have woken her. The sirens still called. The record was at its climactic finale; the hammer of timpani and shout of horns resounded in the cellar and people were laughing, a couple of bottles circling the group. Frau Wilhelm danced alone, raising her arms and swinging her hips. Her dressing gown hung undone revealing the ripple of chest bones. Ursula was fascinated. She'd never seen a woman behave like this. She got up and joined the group. Herr Esterbauer, his stubbled face a shining half-moon in the lamplight, nodded a greeting and raised his beer bottle. She ignored him.

Frau Petchka watched the swaying Frau Wilhelm and spoke in a voice that was a little too loud. 'When the Soviets come she'll get more trouble then, mark my words.'

'They say that they're just too many,' remarked an old man.

'We'll take the brunt of it all right,' said someone else.

'Unless the Yanks intervene.'

'Not if Ivan gets here first.'

'Which he will.'

'They'll save the worst of it for Germany.'

'D'you think they know the difference?'

'It won't be safe to walk the streets.'

'There'll be hangings,' asserted Frau Petschka.

'Don't start your scaremongering!' somebody snapped.

Frau Petschka bridled and fell silent, as did the others.

A quiet voice spoke. 'She's right though.' It was Frau Wilhelm. She had stopped dancing and cradled one of the bottles against her skinny chest; she was statuesque beside her neighbours, her forehead glistening after her exertions. 'They'll make us suffer. And if you knew what'd been done to them, you'd understand.'

'Whatever can she mean?' said a woman who stood beside Ursula.

Frau Wilhelm turned to face her questioner. 'My Walter saw many horrors in the East, committed by Germans.'

Someone tutted and an old man took a step forward, holding out his arm as though to chaperone Frau Wilhelm away, to hush her. But she waved him off.

'Why shouldn't you hear it?' she said. 'They burned villages. They hanged civilians. It's true. In plain view on the signposts of the town. He sent me photos taken by his comrades. They posed for pictures as if they were on holiday, in front of the swinging bodies.' She shook her head. 'It was too much for him to bear alone, he had to show what they did, what he was forced to be part of.'

Ursula realised she'd been holding her breath, thinking with horror of Papa and wondering if he too had done such things. She told herself that of course he hadn't, would never. She released her breath slowly. People began to shift and whisper. Ursula supposed Frau Wilhelm was drunk. She could be denounced by any one of them for speaking against the Wehrmacht.

When Frau Wilhelm spoke again, as if to herself, the party was immediately quiet in order to hear her. 'They pulled off the uniforms to make the dead ridiculous. Stood the frozen corpses in the fields against trees, or propped them upright with sticks. My Walter was one.' She faltered. 'Well, he might've been. They laughed at how the cold defeated us. They were vengeful *then*—' She grew quiet. Every eye was on her. She looked up at the gathering and her attention paused on Ursula, her expression sad, wistful as if she gazed into a mirror rather than at another person.

Ursula dropped her eyes to the dusty stone floor; she couldn't stand to think of her father dying in that terrible way, being derided.

'Not all our boys can have been so cruel,' said a woman.

'Not all,' said Frau Wilhelm.

Far off, a bomb dropped and Ursula felt the rumble beneath her feet. Frau Wilhelm leaned against the side of the wardrobe and wouldn't say anything more.

26

The silence was the most awful thing about the cell. Not long after the morning light had arrived in the frosted window and woken him, there was a brief period when Schosi heard water running, echoing sounds – quiet voices – which sounded like a washroom. There was clanking inside the wall or ceiling but then nothing else for a long time. Later, while he ate a slice of rubbery bread and a small bowl of broth that had appeared through an opening in the cell door, he heard hatches being lowered and raised on the adjacent cell doors, and snippets of conversation.

'Get up, Ulrich!' came the voice of a nurse.

'I can't,' said a child.

'You must!'

Then some whining and scuffling, the clanging of a door and the rattle of keys.

Schosi watched the birds beat their wings against the wind outside – there was a tiny section of unfrosted glass in the window allowing him to see out. They cried loudly as they flew and he found the noise exciting and unsettling all at once. The birds had ragged black feathers and sharp grey beaks that opened and closed. They were the same as the birds that had reminded him of the Krampuses, the ones he'd seen in the trees alongside the path. They'd frightened him then but now they were a comfort. Birds like these roosted in the trees at home. His mama called them rascals because they gobbled seeds in the soil before they had a chance to grow. She threw stones and tied tin cans on strings to scare them away. But he was glad to see them here, never more than two or three perched in the snowy branches at a time, their heads swivelling to and fro, dislodging crystalline showers as they launched themselves free into the sky. If he closed his eyes and tried very hard, then he could almost feel he was back in his loft, the birds squawking, the hornets bumbling in and out of the window in summer, moths on the walls and beetles on the floor, dormice scampering in the roof and the sound of his mama chopping logs outside – her warbling songs. When the owl made his wooden echo in the evening his mama pulled funny faces to make him less afraid. He missed her cosy body, nestling next to her in front of the wood-burner. He missed the smell of her. She'd be alone in the house, getting the wood into the basket, wearing her housecoat and felt shoes, feet propped on the embroidered footstool.

At dusk the birds became very loud, many returning to the trees near the window, to their lopsided nests. While airborne they wheeled in a cloud above Hartburg, darkening the sky, calling harshly. Schosi prayed for a while – he prayed that his mother would come to fetch him. He prayed that he would soon go home. He thought that God and Jesus and Mary couldn't know about this place because they wouldn't let him be stuck here when he'd done nothing bad. Then he lay on the low bed, the clamour of the birds becoming strange and otherworldly, like the furious babbling of a brook, and in the hubbub there seemed to be many voices, though he couldn't make out the words.

The hole in the door snapped open and an eye looked in. Two nurses entered. They were big and fat, or at least big and wide, their arms as broad as a man's and their necks filling their starched collars. One of them tugged the blanket from Schosi's body and tossed it aside. Then they took hold of his arms and propelled him from the cell and out into the corridor. His toes brushed the floor; their hands clamped tight and the light in the corridor was sharp so that he had to close his eyes. The nurses crushed against him and when he turned his head he saw only their cheeks and ears and caps. They conveyed him down several corridors and through wide dormitories to a short passageway, which finished in a blank wall. A large clock hung overhead, suspended on a stiff iron rod; its second hand ticked as he looked at it. He remembered his wristwatch and wished he could hold it.

The nurses took him into a small washroom with a couple of sinks and a large bath. One immediately bolted the door from the inside. Pipes scrambled along the walls and ceiling; there were cabinets on the right-hand side, which were glass-fronted and contained files of different colours, and there was a set of extremely shallow drawers, too thin to contain anything at all, and going on for ever. On each skinny drawer-front was a label. Schosi was able to recognise that each label had two words on it and that the words were names.

The bath in the washroom was magnificent. It was long and deep and white and already filled with water. He'd never been in a proper bath – the one he used at home wasn't much bigger than his own backside and flakes of metal came adrift while he washed. He wondered whether he'd be given clean shorts, or something warmer to wear.

'Get your things off,' said a nurse, donning thick rubber gloves of liverish red. The other woman dragged a small chair to the head of the bath. Schosi undid his buttons and took off his dirty shorts – he removed his shirt and vest and socks and put them in a heap on the floor near the strange chest of drawers. One of the nurses patted the seat of the chair. He went over to it, covering his private parts with his hands. He didn't like to be naked in front of anyone apart from his mother. He began to shudder because it wasn't very warm in the sparse washroom. He glanced around for a towel or blanket but there were none. The nurses' strong hands closed around his arms, another hand was placed on his back, and finally the back of his head was gripped firmly. The women moved in unison, shoving him forward over the edge of the bath. Head first he plunged below the surface of the water, his stomach and chest bashing the side of the bath. His feet left the floor and his knees knocked against the enamel rim. Breath left him in a violent stream of shock – the water was icy cold. His lungs were emptied and he opened his mouth. Cold water rushed in and he swallowed instinctively, only for more water to flood in. He fought but there was no hope against the burly nurses. The coldness of the water was completely disorientating; he swallowed more water and breathed some down his nose – it felt like fire and he coughed underwater again and again. His skull began to thump and his chest burned so that he thought he would die any second. His legs kicked thin air. He knew that he was drowning.

They wrenched him upwards and out. He gasped and coughed and coughed. Then he was being forced downwards again, submerged, his face this time pressed against the gritty base of the bath. He clamped his lips shut and opened his eyes: whiteness. The nurses pummelled his back until he released his breath in a spew of bubbles, gulped water and kicked and writhed, and only then did they drag him heavenwards and allow him a snatched and desperate breath, before dunking him once more.

The sloshing surface of the bath enveloped him countless times, the interludes so brief he could scarcely draw air. The cold was so intense that his body was soon beyond his control – he coughed convulsively and was hardly aware of whether he was above water or below it. His stomach expelled the swallowed water in a rush of transparent vomit, and he was swallowing and swallowing again. He stopped struggling and each time he went under his head crashed against the enamel. After a while he no longer felt the blows.

The drink treatment was discontinued after the seventh day and Schosi was allowed to sleep, told that he could rest providing his behaviour improved. He slept through a whole day and night and partway through the next day too, before he finally woke and needed to pee in the chamber pot.

He couldn't think of much once he was awake, except his hunger and the cough that had taken hold of him and racked his body by the minute. His thoughts were blurred. He'd been given no food or water for some days. He thought about frothy milk after working hard on the farm, about good *Schwarzbrot* and apricot dumplings and bilberry pancakes. He loved bilberry pancakes more than anything. Bilberries cooked with sugar into sweet, staining syrup, served with cream. He dreamt of *Eierschwammerl* mushrooms and *Knödl* with smoked pork and *Sauerkraut*, hot and good and filling, potato salad and tomatoes with onions, boiled sausage with mustard, and liver dumpling soup. He chewed on the corner of his grey hospital blanket and saliva flooded his throat and ignited a coughing fit so violent that he clutched himself in agony. He went to watch his friends in the tree, the black birds with grey beaks. But the branches were empty and there was nothing to see.

27

'They put you on drink?' asked Moritz. 'Or wrap?' He'd materialised beside Schosi holding a dustpan and brush just as Schosi opened his eyes. Schosi looked around at the room – green bars over the windows and high walls, many beds and the blinking light on the ceiling. He was back in his old dormitory in pavilion fifteen. He leaned forward and tried to embrace Moritz but his friend drew back.

'They put you on drink or wrap treatment?' asked Moritz again.

Schosi shrugged, uncertain.

'Thought you were done for. Thought you'd definitely had it.'

'Where's Paulin?'

Moritz shook his head and grimaced. 'And we're next,' he said. 'Starting on the four thirty.'

Schosi regarded him blankly; sometimes Moritz made no sense at all. Moritz scowled and his knuckles went white from gripping the brush handle very hard. 'Feeding up! You and me!'

'But where's Paulin?' Schosi persisted.

'I told you already! Wheeled off in one of them barrows. Poor bastard. Ain't coming back.' He watched the door. 'No point wishing for it, no point at all.' There were footsteps in the corridor. Moritz dropped quickly to the floor and began to sweep beneath the bed. The steps passed by. 'No point praying for ourselves neither.' His voice rose from below the bed. 'God's a heartless bastard – a bloody mean, heartless bastard.'

Schosi was shocked. Moritz spoke about God as though he hated Him. He wondered whether he should warn his friend about Hell and blasphemy.

A couple of other boys passed Schosi where he lay. He didn't know them. They crouched on the floor with cleaning cloths and brushes. They tickled the tiles and wiped the legs of the beds, sidling, their bodies low, their gaze malicious.

A nurse stood over Moritz until he placed his spoon in his mouth and chewed and swallowed the contents.

'Finish the bowlful,' she said.

Schosi's semolina was already gone and he longed for more; the sweetened cocoa powder that had been added by the nurses tasted delicious and his stomach contracted around the measly portion, which had been nowhere near enough to sate him. The other children at the four-thirty mealtime slurped greedily, loudly. Chocolate was smeared from chin to cheekbone and fingers were coated in brown mess. A girl with sparse dandelion-seed hair lolled on to the table, her hands draped near her bowl and her scrawny spine knobbling through her tunic. She heaved and vomited on to her arms. A nurse shouted and the girl was taken away.

When all were done the nurses scrubbed the children with cloths, then ordered them to their dormitories. Schosi went to lie down and remembered the boys that used to sleep during the early evening instead of doing chores. He was glad now that he was one of them. He'd envied their rest.

Once they were unsupervised Moritz grasped Schosi's sleeve. 'They poisoned it!' he whispered. His eyes popped unnervingly in their sockets. Schosi cowered away. Moritz shook him a little bit. 'Don't you see? Don't you understand? Damn it!' Some of the other boys looked over from their beds, curious. 'No one does, 'cept me,' he hissed, releasing Schosi. 'I s'pose that's why you're in here. Damn idiot!'

He went to his bed and Schosi climbed into bed too. A strong wind pulsed the closed shutters. Schosi was very sleepy. His chest hurt and he couldn't stop coughing for a long time even though Moritz told him to shut up and said that if he were a dog he'd be put down for barking too much. Drowsiness quickly overtook him and he slept till morning, dreamless and still.

Schosi's days became bleary waking dreams; his sleep was as deep and empty as a chasm that he could never fully climb out of. Moritz was subdued and drooping most of the time but often prodded Schosi gently and tried to look into his face as though searching for something.

One day, Schosi's slumber was disturbed by the scream of his friend.

'Murderers!' came Moritz's voice. 'Murderers!'

He kept calling, though Schosi couldn't be sure which was dream and which reality. The ripples spread and travelled, the surface of sleep smoothed and closed above his head once more.

Schosi barely noticed Moritz's absence. He was shepherded by unseen hands to seats and bowls of food and back to bed again, always in the same echoing corridors, with flashing light through the windows and swinging doors and squeaking of the nurses' black shoes keeping rhythm. He heard lots of talk, women's voices. They spoke about Christmas and holidays. They spoke about food, potatoes and no goose this year, at least not a whole one.

Schosi felt pressure on his arm and saw the needle push in. He wanted to struggle but he couldn't feel his limbs and his brain was fogged, a dreadful aching in his skull. He felt icy breath on his legs, the ruffle of blowing air. Moritz was near by again, strapped to a mattress, still and white, hair scrambling across his features, his lips dark like a sealed wound. Schosi wrapped his arms around his body and drew his knees high, but still he shivered. Sleep tugged him downwards. He dropped like a stone.

Ursula knocked on the door that belonged to Frau Wilhelm. Herr Esterbauer was at the post office. After he'd left, she'd dawdled a while in her room then dashed on to the landing with coat on and down the stairs to the floor below. She'd been thinking about an idea ever since the air raid. She knocked again, eager. She was just about to knock a third time when a bolt clacked, a chain rattled and the door cracked inwards. A long narrow eye, red-rimmed, peered through the gap. The door opened further.

Frau Wilhelm wore trousers and a loose man's shirt. She looked tired. Her face showed the unreadiness of someone who was expecting to be alone and was suddenly faced with conversation.

'Can I help?'

'Sorry to disturb you.' Ursula spoke in her most adult voice – she mustn't be shy in front of the elegant woman. 'My name is Ursula. You might have seen me in the cellar, during the raid, I mean.' She was unsure if Frau Wilhelm would remember; she'd been far from sober and it was some time ago. 'I just wanted to ask a question.'

'Right.' Frau Wilhelm sounded weary. 'Come in then.' She wandered into the flat leaving the door wide open.

Ursula hesitated. This was uncommonly lax – slovenly even. Where was the woman's hospitality? Should she not offer to take Ursula's coat, provide her with a drink and something to eat, apologise effusively for the mess in the house, fuss her to a chair? This was so uniformly the case when she was invited into someone's home that Ursula wondered whether the woman was indeed peculiar. Had she judged right? She was suddenly unsure. When Frau Wilhelm had spoken in the cellar – the defiant words asserted boldly for all to hear, their ring of truth – perhaps it had been momentary recklessness. She might be quite different to that normally, quite the opposite. Her heart began to patter as she stepped inside the tiny hall, found a hook beside the door and put her things there. Frau Wilhelm was nowhere to be seen. She passed through a kitchen where a single lamp burned atop a cluttered worktop strewn with onion skins and cups, the remains of meals clinging to a lopsided tower of dirty crockery.

Frau Wilhelm was standing near the window in the spacious living room looking down at the courtyard. Ursula guessed at once that she did this habitually, that this was the spot where she stood and gazed and brooded. Frau Wilhelm gestured to two low and flaccid pieces of furniture with olive-green upholstery.

'Sit down.'

Ursula chose the smaller sofa that faced the window.

Frau Wilhelm lit a cigarette. 'Well?'

'I wondered . . .' The words dried and cracked. 'I thought you might be able to help me.' She had no idea how to continue, how to explain. Frau Wilhelm made no move, her thin back draped in the folds of her shirt. 'My neighbour's being kept in the Hartburg Hospital.' Ursula shifted forward until she teetered on the very edge of the sofa. She glanced back the way she'd come, through the living-room doorway to the way out; she'd run if Frau Wilhelm showed disapproval or reached for the telephone. 'Supposedly he's been thieving. But it isn't true.'

There was no reply. Perhaps she was shocked at this brazen openness; perhaps she was frowning, suspecting treachery.

'We're here to get him out.'

Frau Wilhelm snorted. 'Good luck with that!'

Startled, Ursula almost jumped from her seat. The woman was clearly in no mood to be helpful; perhaps she'd been drinking again. It would explain why she was so ill mannered. Ursula fiddled with her hem. She mustn't back out yet. She must stay calm.

After a moment, Frau Wilhelm flopped into the other seat with a worn sigh. 'Sorry.' She smiled. 'I'm very solitary these days. I forget to be nice. Please carry on – I'm all ears. Smoke?' She held out the tin.

'No, thank you.' Ursula wondered if she might borrow some of that poise, that serene air, if she were to accept. 'My neighbour – he's in danger.' She swallowed. No sign of tension in the woman's face – she must speak frankly now, for Schosi's sake. Her voice trembled; she couldn't level it. 'You know they're killing them?'

Frau Wilhelm's gaze steadied and met hers. She nodded.

'Can you tell me anything?'

'Not much. Though people talk.'

'We're not even allowed to visit. We've been going for weeks. Does anyone ever get out?'

'I only know of one person released. A young woman whose boyfriend travelled the length of the Reich to fetch her. He persuaded them he'd be her guardian and in the end they had him sign a disclaimer and he took her out.'

'How do you know?'

'An old man at my work used to be a gardener there. The boyfriend made them nervous, through sheer insistence. The Party don't want another outcry.'

'Outcry?' Ursula pictured a hundred wizened faces at the hospital windows, all crying and shouting at the top of their lungs.

'There was a lot of protest,' said Frau Wilhelm. 'A couple of years ago.'

'And when did the boyfriend—?'

'Last year sometime. But there's only so far you can rely on such an approach – after all, it continues because the Führer wills it. Does it really matter what's legal on paper?

They sneak and lie and cover their tracks but they know they're protected, right from the top.' She blew a plume of smoke into the air; Ursula struggled to breathe, the windows sealed tight. Still, it was pleasant to be spoken to in this way.

'Letters telling parents their kid died of pneumonia or appendicitis arrive after a fortnight in that place. Even if the kid had their appendix out years before and the parents know it's a lie they can do nothing.'

'I can't even find out where he is. I was going to ask you.'

Frau Wilhelm propped her face in her hand, pushing her fine skin into thin folds. 'There are lots of different wards. How old is he?'

'Fifteen.'

'Mentally deficient?'

'I suppose.'

'I saw some youngish boys in a first-floor window. It could be there. I heard children playing another time near the same place. By the thick hedge that runs along the western edge of the grounds.' She rose and returned with an old envelope, which she scribbled on. 'If this is the main building and the main gate—' She ran her pencil along the small road she'd drawn inside the grounds. 'These are the buildings I walked past, three in a row and I think it was the one at the end.' She tapped her pencil on to the relevant square.

'Thank you.' Ursula took the envelope and studied it. 'Thank you so much!'

'Will you go today?'

'Right away.'

'You'll go with the man? The farmer?' Frau Wilhelm watched for confirmation. 'Not alone.'

'Yes, with him,' Ursula agreed, standing hastily. She was lying but it didn't matter. She'd been to Hartburg many times. And now she knew exactly where to go. She didn't need Herr Esterbauer. She'd show him how much she could accomplish by herself. She'd rush there straight away, before it got dark. Even if it was just to see Schosi through a window, to know he was alive.

'Do be careful.' The woman helped Ursula on with her coat. 'They need no excuse to lock you away along with your friend.'

The warning fell on heedless ears. Ursula congratulated herself. To have some information! No longer at the mercy of the mean-minded receptionist who blocked the way and told them nothing.

'Thank you,' she said again. She shook Frau Wilhelm's hand. 'I'm so grateful!'

The woman pulled away and opened the door. 'Not at all.'

Ursula stuffed the envelope into her coat pocket and clattered down the stairs to the courtyard, two steps at a time, springing like a kid goat, gripping the handrail; she bounded outside and across to the street door.

Frau Wilhelm watched her go with a concerned frown.

28

Schosi dreamt very little, but when he did it was of Krampus. Sometimes it was in the hospital, a dark shape moving from doorway to doorway, pursuing him to a dead end, a room with a bath and a cabinet with a thousand shallow drawers. The drawers were open to reveal labelled glass slides containing pieces of flesh and brain, red and purple, like the offal of Herr Esterbauer's slaughtered pigs. He was trapped, with his back pressed against the pipes, and the chains of Krampus dragged across the floor towards him. The basket creaked, heavy with its contents; Schosi saw the hands and feet of children hanging over the rim; they twitched or waved and the captives cried but couldn't escape from where they were slung on the creature's back.

At other times he was in his home and his mama was nowhere to be found. The house was empty and the doors open wide and the windows too, and there was no way to keep Krampus out, no one to protect him. Krampus arrived and a fierce icy wind blew from its jaws like the cold fires of Hell. Schosi ached and his heart slowed to almost nothing. He hid in a deep hole in the middle of the house, but he couldn't close the hatch and the roof was gone; there were branches above him that moved against the sky – they shimmered with snow and the nurse's pinafore was the same colour white. The needle jabbed Schosi's arm again and he sank.

Ursula walked briskly within the Hartburg grounds. She'd almost reached the main building when Herr Esterbauer arrived, pounding up the grit behind her, beet-red and panting. He snatched her arm and swung her round. She ducked, expecting a cuff to the head.

'You were going to go in' – he was breathing so hard he could barely speak – 'without me.'

She shook herself free. 'How did you find me?'

'Where else? And anyway—' He gulped air. 'Frau Wilhelm. She told me. Saw me come into the courtyard and waited on the landing. Said you visited – went running off. What were you thinking? Talking to her like that.'

'It's fine. And now I know which building he's in.' She drew back from him. 'She's trustworthy – like us – I knew she would be.'

'You knew no such thing! One wrong step, Ursula, and it's the end for him. For us. I can't believe you'd be so stupid!'

She fought the urge to shout – something, anything. The main building sprawled close amongst the lanky trees. She mustn't attract suspicion. 'It's not a wrong step! It's better than no step at all.' She set off along the path again; Herr Esterbauer hurried after.

'What will you do? This is foolish.'

She broke into a trot.

'Ursula!'

A guard emerged from behind the main building, quite far off. He wasn't facing them. She darted into the bushes and squatted low. Let Herr Esterbauer be thrown off the grounds, she thought. She continued onwards at a crouch. But he might be arrested – she didn't want that. She paused, looked behind. He was stationary, staring towards the main building, seemingly frozen, mouth ajar. After a couple of seconds he hurried on to the grass and joined her in the undergrowth.

'So, this is it?' he growled when he reached her. 'We're sneaking like thieves? If we're caught there's no excuse this time. You realise?'

She shrugged, scurried off, her dress tucked into her underwear to free her legs. Herr Esterbauer struggled to keep up, his body bulky, his movements stiff.

Another guard paced the gravel in front of the pavilions that Frau Wilhelm had drawn. Ursula withdrew the envelope. She could just about see the furthest ward where Schosi might be. Shielded by leaves and branches, they watched as the man crunched back and forth. He looked mostly at his own meticulously polished boots, lips moving as if counting his steps. One hand rested nonchalantly on his truncheon, the other swung flamboyantly. After five such lengths, during which time snow began to fall, he branched off down the narrower path that stretched in front of the three pavilions. To his left was a deep coniferous hedge – the one Frau Wilhelm had mentioned. After the guard passed the first pavilion, he turned abruptly out of view, presumably down a passageway between the buildings.

Ursula stepped quickly out of hiding. Herr Esterbauer followed, eyes flashing in both directions. His tall, thick frame was utterly conspicuous compared to hers. She crossed to the smaller pathway and progressed fast along it, stooping to remain below the level of the windows. Herr Esterbauer, legs bent nearly double, coat wrapped around himself to prevent it flapping, came behind. At the turning the guard had taken, Ursula slowed and peered with half an eye around the corner bricks. No one in sight. Had he passed through into the hospital? Would he appear presently, ahead of them? There was no way to deduce it – they must trust to God. She sprang across the opening and continued. There was a sign protruding from the third building. It displayed the number fifteen. She could see the fenced-off area with toys strewn about where Frau Wilhelm might have overheard children playing. There was a miniature wheelbarrow mildewed green, building blocks swimming in rainwater on top of a small table, a meagre and dirty sandpit. Sweat prickled beneath her arms. The snow fell more quickly and more heavily now. She thought of Schosi in one of those high-windowed rooms, the fear he must feel every moment. She reached the gap separating the last two wards, again peeped stealthily for the guard. Herr Esterbauer grasped her arm, held her still.

'Wait!' His whisper was taut with anger. 'Just you wait a moment! What can happen here? Except we get caught. This whole thing . . .'

She kicked his shin as hard as she could and ran on.

After trying two doors and finding them locked, she found a third, around the corner from the fenced area with the battered toys, a cobwebbed entrance. She pushed at it – it took some force because the door was heavy – but it was open. It moved stiffly inwards. She stared into the gloomy interior: it was difficult to make anything out. Should she explore a little more, find a window to check what was inside? She looked back down the pathway; Herr Esterbauer neared but thankfully no guard. If they didn't act now they might lose their chance entirely. Schosi needed her to be brave, to be hasty. She glanced again through the gap, saw no one, took a breath. She slipped inside ignoring Herr Esterbauer's hushed expostulation. She was in a long grey corridor. She immediately recoiled at the stench of illness. Behind her, Herr Esterbauer quietly entered, jowls flushed with alarm, reclosed the door and came to her side. He shook his head at her, jaw clenched. To the right was a flickering overhead light and to the left a corridor which ended in a window. They turned left, walking close together, an immediate truce descending. They passed open doorways and glanced into them. Two of the rooms were filled with cots containing small children of toddling age or thereabouts, another was lined with beds occupied by larger children and young adults – they looked very much handicapped, not able to move. There was no sign of Schosi.

They reached a staircase. Frau Wilhelm had mentioned a ward on the first floor. Ursula beckoned to Herr Esterbauer and they ascended, treading carefully. The place seemed abandoned. Where were the staff? Once at the top, Ursula spied an opening into what looked like a larger room. They crept to it. This dormitory was big with high windows barred on the outside. It was full of boys. They lay on beds, or sat up against the walls. They silently watched Ursula and Herr Esterbauer, apart from those who slept. Ursula couldn't spot Schosi. A boy near the door hugged his knees and rocked like a wind-up toy; a cable of drool swung from his lower lip. Ursula wanted to ask him about Schosi but was too afraid to speak to him. She was repulsed by the boy's dull eyes and skin; they suggested terrible sickness. The state of the children was even worse than she'd pictured when she'd tortured herself with imaginings. Panic began to drum in her body. They might already be too late. 'He's not in here,' she managed to say despite the queasiness washing through her.

'Can I help you?'

A woman's voice came from the corridor behind them. A nurse with arms stacked high with sheets.

Ursula turned, shocked – she was sure she must look as ghastly as she felt; her face tingled as blood sapped from it and she leaned heavily on the doorframe.

'We've come to collect someone,' said Herr Esterbauer, attempting a polite smile.

The nurse frowned. 'Mein Herr – Fräulein, please come away from the dormitory, the patients mustn't be disturbed.' She moved towards them with hand extended to usher them away; the tower of sheets teetered unsteadily. 'We'll continue our conversation in the office, if you please.'

They followed her – she put the sheets on a nearby trolley and trundled it around the corner. She abandoned it outside a narrow door marked *Nurses' Station* and went inside with a beckoning wave. The office was cramped and edged with two skinny beds. The nurse took a seat at the desk and gestured that they should perch somewhere.

'We're here to collect Hillier Schosi,' said Herr Esterbauer. 'I'm his guardian.'

Ursula clenched her teeth. She longed to escape the confined room to find Schosi. She forced herself to be still.

'His guardian?'

'Yes. I've been trying to visit him for weeks, but I've been refused at every turn. I'll be taking the boy into my care.'

'I really must ask you to wait outside the ward until the other staff return. They're in a meeting at present but will finish shortly and will see you then.' She smiled tightly.

Herr Esterbauer ignored her. The warmth of the office provided by a small heater revived Ursula a little. She began to feel more competent.

'We must at least have a visit,' said Herr Esterbauer, his voice rising. 'I insist. I've left all my duties at home in order to bring him back. I have lost a lot of money! This is completely unacceptable! We must at least see the boy today.'

She shrank back a little. 'I am sure that's not permitted, mein Herr.'

'Well, check his file or something, will you?' He gestured sharply.

The nurse blinked, gave an anxious sigh, took a file from the shelf and leafed through the dense papers, labelled in alphabetical order. She reached the letter 'H'. 'Hillier. Yes, you've been refused, sir, because he's unwell. He's been receiving intensive treatment. He's contracted pneumonia.' She turned to them with a slight frown. 'To remove him now would be to endanger him unnecessarily.'

'Come, now!' Herr Esterbauer scowled. 'We'll just look at him – we won't disturb him. What possible harm can that do?'

She sighed again, gazed here and there. 'He's really not strong enough to have visitors, mein Herr. It must be done by arrangement.'

'I told you, girl – it has been arranged!'

'Well, I've not been informed.' She muttered this, almost inaudibly. Her slim hand reached towards a grey telephone that crouched on the filing cabinet.

Herr Esterbauer abruptly stood.

The nurse paused.

'If you don't allow a visit' – he spoke commandingly, with authority; he squared his shoulders, raised himself tall – 'I'll involve your superiors. Dr Klein himself assured me just last week that I'd no need to worry, his staff would attend to me. So far I've seen *no* sign of their obeying him.'

The nurse now lost her guarded air. Her clear round eyes took in the threat. Ursula noticed for the first time that she was very young, just a teenager of a similar age to Dorli. She had pretty blonde hair arranged in soft buns over her ears. Perhaps she was new here and more afraid of the doctor than some.

'But I was sure he would have informed us.'

'Perhaps you were inattentive.'

She wavered for a moment then went slowly to a wall cabinet. She retrieved a large garland of keys. She handled them noisily for a moment; the pink of new petals had appeared in her cheeks. 'Follow me,' she muttered.

Ursula stood and glanced quickly at Herr Esterbauer, hope and excitement buzzing in her veins. He'd done it. The nurse was going to lead them to Schosi.

Outside a door, beside which a large-wheeled cart was parked, the nurse stopped.

'Wait here.' She sidled in.

A few minutes passed. There came a clattering noise. Ursula wondered what she could be doing. She stared nervously down the passageway, picturing the arrival of Dr Klein, his mask of cool detachment gone, his wrath unleashed. The place was like a warren, all gun-metal grey and cream with an unpleasant reflective sheen to each surface, a colourless glare that did nothing to dispel the darkness but highlighted every lump and dent in the plaster. A desolation and eeriness pervaded – oppressive, quiet. On the wall near by, she noticed something written. Words scrawled messily along the plasterwork in pencil or charcoal, almost invisible. She squatted in order to read it: *Dear God, get me out of here. Dear Führer, get me out of here. Utta Mayer.*

She shuddered – that pleading voice, forlorn, desperate.

The door reopened. 'You've two minutes. The staff are due to finish shift handover – they come straight to this room to do medications. I'd rather they didn't find you. Please be quick.'

Inside they found many beds crammed together with barely space to squeeze between them, each with a sleeping occupant covered by a blanket. A cupboard stood open and empty against a wall, its bare shelves exposed like ribs. Schosi was lying on a high bed with wheels, positioned against one of two tall windows beyond which was a balcony. Another bed was end-to-end with Schosi's, the toes of the two boys almost touching.

Ursula ran forward, pushing through the gaps between the beds, dislodging one or two blankets as she did so and stopping to replace them. Herr Esterbauer followed close behind.

'Excuse me!' cried the nurse. She hastened after them. 'You said you wouldn't disturb him.'

Ursula reached Schosi's bed. God, he looked so different, deathly thin and grey-skinned. Beneath his eyes were inky stains and his lips and fingers were dark as though he'd been eating bilberries. She was overwhelmed with emotion – she reached for his hand. The fingers were cold and wet.

'Why's he so cold?' she exclaimed.

Herr Esterbauer touched Schosi's hand and swore in shock.

'Come away, please. He's resting now. He's very sick.'

Ursula touched Schosi's arm and then his cheek. Both were cold and wet. 'Why is he wet?'

'It's part of the illness. The patient becomes chilled and suffers with poor circulation. And perspires – heavily perspires. Come away now!' The woman tugged at Ursula's shoulder. She shook her off.

'Good grief!' said Herr Esterbauer. 'Move him away from the draught then and give the boy an extra blanket. He's frozen. Shouldn't someone be at his side, to mop the sweat away? He'll freeze to death the way he is.'

Ursula turned to stare at the nurse. 'He'll freeze to death,' she repeated.

The nurse dropped her gaze. There was guilt in her look, deep and untended. Ursula returned to stroking Schosi's face. There was no risk of waking him – he slept heavy as lead. She glanced at his arm and saw marks in the crook of his elbow.

'Drugged,' said Herr Esterbauer.

Ursula closed her eyes. She rested her head briefly on Schosi's shoulder. The clothing there was also wet. Sodden and cold. Perspiration? She looked at the other boy who lay on the adjoining bed. His long fringe was slick to his forehead and in his hair were dark flecks of something stuck there. She looked more closely at Schosi – there were the same dark flecks in his hair, not so apparent at first because of his colouring. Leaves, or pieces of leaf. She looked out at the balcony beyond the glass. Leaves of the same colour lay on the concrete, the snow still falling. 'God!' she shouted. 'Look! The inside of the glass is wet – the doors. She's just brought them inside.' She felt the nurse's presence behind her, her silence and her breathing. Near to the wheels of the beds watery tracks expanded into a puddle. 'We're not imbeciles!' She spun to face the nurse. She'd probably done it herself; shut him out alone and helpless. She had a sudden urge to pounce on the woman and throttle her, to frighten and hurt her and make her suffer – the coward, the torturer. She should be made to die in Schosi's place.

Herr Esterbauer swivelled too. 'Why?' he demanded. 'Why's he put out there?'

The nurse looked behind her, as though thinking to escape, or listening for the other nurses.

'Sister?' Herr Esterbauer barked.

She jumped and flinched away, her hands clasped in front of her skirt.

'Answer us!'

'I can't!' she almost wailed. 'I'm not permitted to!'

Herr Esterbauer stood and approached her. 'Did you start this job to be a fiend? Hmm? They'll die if we leave them. They'll die.'

She breathed heavily, her face rigid; faintly she shook her head.

'Help us.'

The nurse gaped.

'You have to,' he pressed. 'It's barbaric. We must save him.'

Ursula was confused; what was he doing? This nurse would never help them – she was part of this awful place.

'No, no, I can't! They'll be here any minute. It's too dangerous.'

'For them it's dangerous!' Herr Esterbauer pointed at the boys. 'Do you think about that?'

One or two tears landed on the nurse's uniform. 'Yes.'

'Then do it!'

'How?'

'Out the window.'

'If I'm caught?'

'Say he escaped. Open these windows. Hand him down. I can catch him.' The nurse winced – fear sweated from her. 'Are you strong enough? Can you lift him?'

'I expect so.'

Ursula turned to look at Schosi again – his gaunt face and skeletal arms. Could it be true that this woman had taken pity? Ursula hurried to the window, terrified that the other staff would appear before they could free him. Something was sure to go wrong.

'Then do it,' said Herr Esterbauer. 'Allow as long as possible before sounding the alarm – say the boy disappeared.'

'They'll never believe me.' A slight noise came from somewhere; a faint bang. The nurse whipped round to face the door, eyes wide. They all stared but no one appeared.

'They will. They'll have to,' said Herr Esterbauer.

White-faced, she ran past them and rolled the two beds away from the windows. She unbolted them, her hands shaking so terribly she almost couldn't do it, then threw them open.

'Ursula,' said Herr Esterbauer.

Ursula went on to the balcony and swung her leg over the rail. The nurse hurried to check the corridor, opening the door to the dormitory just a crack then closing it again. Herr Esterbauer watched her, eagle-eyed. Ursula brought her other leg over and then looked down. A six-foot drop or so. No one about. The snow falling side-swept and thick. She lowered herself with care, the paint slippery. She dropped, struck the ground with a thud and fell on to her backside. Herr Esterbauer followed, coat waving in the wind as he hung from the perilous rail. When he landed he staggered but remained upright. The nurse approached the railing; in her arms lay Schosi, swaddled like a pupa. She edged forward until he overhung the drop.

'Oh God!' she hissed. 'I can't do this!'

'You can. I'm ready.' Herr Esterbauer stretched out his arms.

Ursula bit her lip hard, scarcely daring to watch.

'I can't throw him!'

'It's all right. Just let go.' Herr Esterbauer stepped forward a little more, widened his arms, braced his legs. 'Go on!'

She released Schosi and he fell, blanket unfurling. Herr Esterbauer caught him with a stumble and an involuntary grunt, managed to right his footing and keep his hold. He turned to Ursula, snow coating his hat. They began to walk.

'Wait!' The girl's voice quaked with panic. She waved them to stop. She disappeared inside and reappeared carrying another child, the boy who'd been on the bed end-to-end with Schosi's. 'Take him too.'

'Are you mad?' said Herr Esterbauer. 'We can't do that!'
'Please. He has no one at all. And they're friends. Please.'
Ursula plucked at the farmer's sleeve. 'Come on! The other nurses . . . Come on!'

'We can't take him!' Herr Esterbauer repeated.

'Then catch him at least.' The nurse dangled the boy over the edge. Her grasp looked even less secure than when she'd held Schosi. Herr Esterbauer placed Schosi on the ground, hurried forward. Ursula squinted upwards, flakes catching on her lashes, blurring her sight. This was crazy. They'd all be caught.

The nurse dropped the child and Herr Esterbauer managed to receive him.

'Hang on! I've got to get my bag,' she whispered. 'I won't be long – I'll carry him!'

'What? No!'

But the nurse didn't hear; she closed the window and was gone.

'We can't wait!' Ursula was frantic. Someone would come, someone would see! After getting so close, Schosi would be snatched away. She went over to where he lay, braced herself then lifted him from the ground. He wasn't as heavy as she'd expected, though he was too big for her to hold for long. She clasped him tightly, leaned back to take his weight against her front. She tried to shield him from the driving snow and edged into the bushes.

Herr Esterbauer did the same, holding the other boy. 'Can you manage him?' he asked.

Schosi already slid from her grip. She shook her head and squatted, out of breath.

'We'll be more than conspicuous trying to lug these two,' said Herr Esterbauer. 'We'll be noticed.' His breath came heavy and fast, steaming in the cold air. 'But we can't just leave this other boy.'

'He was outside anyway.'

'That's not the point.'

But why was the nurse taking so long? Had she run to Dr Klein? Was he right now on his way? She shook with cold and hugged Schosi close. She tried to lift him again, her back straining, arms fatigued. 'She might not come back – she might report us.'

Herr Esterbauer looked at the nameless boy who lay unmoving in his arms, then up at the balcony.

A figure appeared on the nearby path. They huddled deeper into the shadows. As the person drew closer they saw it was the young nurse, with coat and bag, and nurse's cap removed. She stepped on to the grass.

'Hello?' she whispered.

Herr Esterbauer echoed her and she located them amongst the branches. Without saying a word Herr Esterbauer handed the boy to her then lifted Schosi and enfolded him in his coat. They set off into the trees.

The nurse fell into step with Ursula, looking apprehensively behind and panting with the effort of carrying the boy. 'I made an excuse of not being well,' she said. 'I told them I'd done the meds in that dorm, which should allow us some time.'

Ursula said nothing. She scowled suspiciously, her anger and disgust still potent. Snow billowed about them like a veil; the daylight was poor, dull as twilight beneath the storm cloud. They heard a motor and yellow headlamps glowed between the trunks. They crouched in dense undergrowth and the lights swept across them.

'I didn't know,' murmured the girl as they hid close together in the greenery. 'I didn't know what they'd ask me to do. I couldn't change it. The orders are direct from the Führer. Direct from him! I would have been killed.'

Herr Esterbauer raised a finger to his lips and they waited in silence until the vehicle was gone.

Once they were out of the gates the streets and pavements were deserted and there were very few vehicles. A man struggled past them going up the hill, bent double over the handlebars of a bike. He didn't even glance their way. Herr Esterbauer led them – the nurse stopped now and then to jog the boy she was carrying into a better position. Ursula walked close beside Herr Esterbauer and Schosi; she could hear the wheezing of Schosi's breath. She kissed him on the cheek, glad to have him near, however limp and quiet, and she kept a sharp eye out for the black-and-white hospital uniform amongst pedestrians and cyclists. They passed a couple of shops still open with their light spilling weakly on to the snow. An aerated blanket of white now covered everything, light in texture but treacherous when compacted beneath a foot; the telephone and tram wires caught flakes and held them along their length in a balancing act, and a person went by with an umbrella white with snow. As they drew level, the person stopped and shook off the snow, then raised the umbrella again, black once more. The woman – squat and elderly with a Jew's nose – looked at Ursula.

'*Grüss Gott*,' she said.

'*Grüss Gott*,' replied Ursula, her lips numb, searching for a glimpse of the woman's clothing beneath the heavy mackintosh, for a sign of the dreaded uniform. The woman passed on.

They reached Gütteldorfer Strasse.

'It's not far now,' said Herr Esterbauer to the nurse.

What had they done, allowing an unknown woman, a nurse from Hartburg, to join them? Ursula hoped upon hope she'd not bring the Gestapo direct to their door. But at least they'd got him out – there hadn't been a moment to lose. She felt another leap of joy and relief.

At the top of the road where their apartment was situated a policeman walked with his cap pulled low. He cocked an eye at them but kept walking, his stoical tread taking him up and over the brow of the road.

They arrived at the entrance to the apartment block.

'The key's in my pocket,' said Herr Esterbauer.

Ursula fished it out and unlocked the door, pushed it cautiously inwards and Herr Esterbauer ushered the nurse inside. The hallway was empty, the opening into the courtyard criss-crossed by scurrying snowflakes. They hurried over to the inner entrance, which required another key. There were no footprints in the courtyard – no one had been outside since the snow had carpeted it.

'He's heavy,' said the nurse.

'We're nearly there.'

Inside, Herr Esterbauer led the way up the spiralling stairs, passing doorways, thankfully closed. They heard voices above – the residents often stopped to gossip on the landings whilst watering the communal plants, mopping the steps, or smoking from the windows. Ursula tensed in readiness. There was always someone ready to make trouble. Self-righteous snoops like Frau Gerg, or informers exploiting the times by passing on information in exchange for a few Reichsmarks. 'Be bold,' said Herr

Esterbauer. 'Stay next to me and smile. We'll pass them without stopping.'

Ursula and the nurse nodded. Ursula's teeth chattered and her whole body juddered with cold and nerves.

'Try to be calm. Try to stop shaking.'

They set off up the steps. Two old men stood talking beside the toilet on the next landing, filling the area with pipe smoke. Just as they passed Schosi began to cough. The cough sounded very deep and hollow and unhealthy. The two men stopped talking to watch them.

'Quite a chest, hey?' said one.

'Yes,' said Herr Esterbauer, beginning up the next flight of steps. 'Keeps me up half the night!'

The man cackled. 'Right you are!'

The nurse struggled up the steps behind the farmer and Ursula tried to partially shield her from view by walking close to her back. The men stared after them, curious, silent.

'Watch your step, Fräulein,' one of them called.

Laughter echoed. Ursula knew that they were joking about the country farmer and his two young girls – speculating. She supposed there weren't often strangers here to make comments about. She hoped they could avoid direct attention or questioning before they set off for Felddorf.

On the third floor, she unlocked the door to Herr Esterbauer's room and they went inside. Schosi was set down and the nurse lowered the boy to the bedclothes. They lay together like a pair of new lambs, ill born and scrawny. Neither boy shivered, but their flesh was deeply chilled, like dead flesh, refrigerated flesh, and Ursula knew that they were beyond shivering, worse than that.

'Fetch some dry things,' said Herr Esterbauer, still catching his breath. He went to his wardrobe. Ursula ran to hers. She returned with clothes then watched anxiously as Herr Esterbauer removed the damp blanket from around Schosi and tossed it to the floor, rolled him over and peeled the wet vest from his torso. Ribs protruded and hip bones jutted like handles from his wasted frame. The nurse put her hand to her mouth and turned away.

'Can't you help?' snapped Herr Esterbauer. 'Change the other boy!'

She obeyed, flustered, and soon both were clad in warmer garments and wrapped in new blankets. They didn't stir even for a moment while they were jogged and twisted about on the eiderdown. Ursula tried in vain to drive dread from her heart.

'Wait here until we get back,' Herr Esterbauer instructed the nurse. 'We have to visit a neighbour who can help house us for the night.'

The nurse agreed, still shivering, her lips bluish pink.

'I'll see if I can borrow an outfit for you also,' he added. 'It might be advisable to lose that uniform.' He left the room and Ursula followed. 'No, stay here,' he muttered. 'I don't trust her alone with them. She might have a change of heart and run off.'

Ursula re-entered the room, glad for a chance to show obedience; she closed and locked the door and pocketed the key. She perched on the foot of the bed and glared fixedly at the nurse until Herr Esterbauer's return.

29

Ursula knocked quietly on Frau Wilhelm's door, the boys lolling in the arms of Herr Esterbauer and the nurse, shielded by blankets. Their laboured breath gargled in the silent landing, magnified by bare stone. It was two in the morning. The door to the opposite apartment stood sealed and dark. Above and below, the spiral staircase curved away into blackness. Ursula's ears strained to catch any sound and she prayed that Frau Wilhelm wouldn't turn them away, that there wouldn't be an air raid, forcing everyone awake and out of their beds. She raised her hand to knock again but at that moment there was a soft rattle and the door opened. Frau Wilhelm's face appeared, eyes stretched wide and scanning the lightless landing, hair pinned into curls along her forehead. She ushered them inside and locked the door at their backs, staring at the nurse, who looked comical dressed in Frau Wilhelm's things, too long for her by far. They were taken into the living room where the full-length, heavy curtains were drawn and tasselled lamps lighted the corners. 'You must stay quiet,' whispered Frau Wilhelm. 'The walls aren't so thick.' She indicated a low bed on the floor made from sofa cushions, blankets and pillows. 'For the boys.'

Herr Esterbauer and the nurse lowered the boys on to the bed; the instant this was done, Frau Wilhelm barred the nurse with a stiff hand. The nurse backed away and lingered near to Ursula, nibbling her fingernails, eyes darting; Ursula could hear her quick breath and, though she now wore dry clothes, her incessant shivering continued.

Frau Wilhelm covered the boys with several blankets then helped Herr Esterbauer to tuck the layers tightly beneath them.

'They'll wake up soon,' said the nurse. 'The Luminal will wear off.'

Frau Wilhelm shot her a hard look then came to stand beside Ursula and leaned close to her ear, her breath stale with smoke. 'What on earth happened that you brought one of those gorgons with you?' She spoke just loud enough for the nurse to hear.

Shortly, the boys began to stir. They blinked glassy-eyed, writhed and grimaced. They kicked the blankets away. Ursula went to replace them but they kicked them off again.

'Why are they doing that?' she demanded.

'They're hypothermic,' said the nurse. 'They feel too hot but their temperature is still too low. Wrap them again.'

So Ursula did. Schosi whimpered and woke, eyes crusted with sleep – he stared at the ceiling with a taut expression.

'Don't worry,' she murmured, stroking his arm through the covers.

He looked at her blankly for a while, recognition dawning vaguely, but not completely.

'It's Uschi. Remember me?'

A faint frown appeared between his brows; his eyes shone too brightly, his skin glistened.

The nurse stood. 'Let me examine him, Fräulein.'

Frau Wilhelm pulled her back into her seat. 'Stay where you are. You're the last person they want to see.'

'Do you live near by?' asked Herr Esterbauer, glancing at the nurse. He'd so far refused to sit, despite Frau Wilhelm's impatient pleas, preferring to stand, slightly stooped, his hands resting in his pockets, his face ash-grey and cheeks hollow with tiredness.

'In Heizing, district thirteen.'

'Will anyone notice you're gone?'

'I don't think so. I live by myself. I've paid my rent for the month.' She watched nervously as Herr Esterbauer turned to address Frau Wilhelm.

'They'll look for her there first. She'll have to stay here.'

Frau Wilhelm nodded. 'At least for a day or two.' She faced the nurse who looked anxiously back at her, like a creature that expects a beating. 'What is your name?'

'Eva. Kuster Eva.'

'Eva, there'll be ground rules. You don't leave the apartment. You stay away from the boys.'

The nurse nodded quickly.

'Do not touch the curtains – they stay closed at all times.' Frau Wilhelm looked at Ursula also. 'If any of my neighbours ask about it, I'll think of something. They're bound to notice. Not that it matters much.' She gave a short laugh. 'They think I'm queer already.'

'We'll go back to the rooms, do you think? Ursula and I?' Herr Esterbauer said. 'So we're not missed?' His hands fidgeted in his pockets. 'No. You must go to work. Someone has to look after them – and watch her.'

'Yes,' said Frau Wilhelm. 'I should go as normal. And you should pay Frau Petschka each day, just like you usually do. Come and go here very carefully.'

A knot of fear began to accumulate in Ursula's throat; she thought about all the residents here, the watchful eyes and bored, gossiping tongues. She remembered the policeman topping the rise on Gütteldorfer Strasse, the old men in the stairwell, the woman with the Jew's nose who'd greeted them. Somebody might suspect, somebody might talk; it would only take one. She swallowed, feeling strangulated. Her palms began to dampen as she imagined a rap at the door, SS with batons and black boots, or Gestapo – rough hands, raised voices, a prison cell, a concentration camp, the tall barbed-wire fence curving inwards like claws. Her voice broke out, high and thin. 'Where do we hide? If they come?'

'Shh!' Frau Wilhelm swiftly put a finger to her lips. Her eyes looked unnaturally large in her face. 'Stay calm, will you!'

But later Ursula heard them talking, huddled in the kitchen while Frau Wilhelm boiled the kettle.

'There's no back door,' Frau Wilhelm said in a low voice. 'That's the problem with these city hutches. There's no hiding – no escaping.'

'Well, we've got no other choice,' said Herr Esterbauer.

'And your people? Back home? They know what to say?'

'I think so.' Herr Esterbauer sighed. 'I hope so.'

That night, Ursula, Frau Wilhelm and Herr Esterbauer tended the boys at the nurse's direction. They tipped and rolled them each hour to dislodge mucus and massaged their backs. Whenever there was a sound in the landing, Ursula froze, held her breath; footsteps on the stairs, voices approaching, rising from below – she braced herself and stared towards the door. But the sounds passed by – so far. Frau Wilhelm prepared mustard presses and placed them on the boys' chests, the skin growing reddened and pungent beneath. Ursula held Schosi's hand, which felt lifeless and cool, like uncooked meat. She prayed for him, repeating endless times, 'Spare him, Lord. Spare him.' She fretted continually about Mama and Dorli, about Frau Hillier. Of course the authorities in Felddorf would be contacted, would be searching and questioning their families. She and Herr Esterbauer were the obvious suspects; they'd visited the hospital every day, asking for Schosi's release. Herr Esterbauer had given his home address. He'd had no reason not to, thinking all would be accomplished above board. Dr Klein wouldn't hesitate – he'd want them punished, would want to ensure they kept their silence. Herr Adler would've been dispatched, a hound on the scent. Ursula hated to think of Mama and Dorli being taken in, marched to the station, the house ransacked. Would they be locked up or sent to the camp? They'd done nothing wrong, but still, that was no guarantee.

Before Frau Wilhelm went to bed, she smoked from the window, the curtains enclosing her to keep the fumes away from the room, to let the boys breathe. When she'd finished, she bade them goodnight and went to her bedroom. Ursula curled up on the sofa beneath a musty eiderdown and lay looking at the shadowy shapes around her, the chairs and table and Frau Wilhelm's bookshelves. She missed Anton though she couldn't picture him; he seemed more remote than ever. She knew she should try to get a few hours' sleep. She closed her eyes but her veins buzzed and her mind kept moving, running ahead of her like a tireless animal over a landscape that went on and on, full of danger. Eva lay on the other sofa, her face turned away, her knees drawn up. Herr Esterbauer kept watch, another dark outline in the nearby chair.

By day, the glow of sun through the dark curtain fabric stained the walls tea-brown. Ursula played with Schosi's hair and sang his favourite hymns under her breath to comfort him. She wanted to be there whenever he woke. She kept thinking he'd stopped breathing. She watched for the rise and fall of his chest; she bent close to his face, waiting for the tickle of exhaled air.

Eva hunched in a chair in the corner of the room, feet tucked under her skirt. Her expression was downcast; her fingers played gently and incessantly with the ends of her hair. Her melancholy added to the gloom of the sunless flat, and to Ursula's apprehension. Herr Esterbauer read the paper, often staring at one page for ten minutes at a time. Frau Wilhelm had left early that morning and wouldn't be home from work till dinnertime; she'd bring food and an extra blanket for Ursula, who'd shivered till dawn. But now it was too stuffy. The oil heaters blazed to warm the boys, the oil giving off a rancid smell. Ursula longed for the window to be opened, for a fresh breeze. It was like hiding in a linen cupboard, she thought, stifling, breathing the hot, dry air. But noise travelled with remarkable clarity from open windows across the courtyard. She'd listened many times to the sounds of other lives over the weeks. She'd heard the old couple from their ground-floor apartment bickering and slamming doors; the boisterous family above, singing, crying, whistling, belching; wireless radios playing different tunes one on top of the other; the man who sneezed like a huge dog barking.

'I hope Frau Hillier keeps her head,' said Herr Esterbauer from behind his paper. 'I hope she's had the good sense to burn my telegrams.' He couldn't risk sending another to her – it might be tracked. 'She'll fear the worst. But she's a sensible woman.' He took his tobacco pouch out of his pocket with shaking hands then put it back. He couldn't smoke, not until the early hours. 'I thought I'd be able to talk them round.' He looked across at Schosi, who'd opened his eyes, one thin arm hanging from under the covers and resting on the floor. 'Didn't I? My little man?' Schosi gazed over at him, as if watching a cloud drifting far away. 'But it's all different now.'

Eva broke her reverie and rose from her seat. She crossed the room and disappeared into the kitchen. Herr Esterbauer stared after her. A second later, there was the gush of running water. Ursula's skin tingled all over in alarm. She jumped up and dashed into the kitchen. Eva was lowering a dirty plate into the dish water. Ursula yanked her out of the way and turned off the tap as fast as she could.

'Stupid!' she hissed.

Eva's mouth hung ajar. Suds streamed from her fingers on to the floor. 'I'm sorry!' she said, eyes filling with tears.

'I'm sorry!' She gulped as if she'd run out of air and put her wet hands to her face. 'I'm sorry!' she sobbed again. She repeated the harrowed apology many times, not to Ursula exactly, maybe to God or someone she was thinking of. Ursula wondered whether she should offer her a hanky. She left the kitchen and let her grieve.

Several more days passed and the boys gradually improved, regaining their appetites. The first time Schosi spoke was while Ursula was combing his hair. His weak, cracked tone sounded like an elderly person's.

'Little bear,' he said.

Her heart thudded with joy and she gripped his hand.

'Where's my mama?'

'Your mama's at home.' She gave what she hoped was a reassuring smile. 'You need to rest. Then you can see her. All right?'

She took to lying at the foot of Schosi's bed, drawing pictures to entertain the two boys, leaning on an atlas belonging to Frau Wilhelm. Schosi's friend was awake now too and had introduced himself as Moritz. When Ursula asked which animal the boys would like to see, Schosi always called 'Cat!' or 'Cow!' and Moritz 'Aeroplane!' or 'Car!' not caring much for animals or perhaps not having seen many. She drew the requested thing in an amusing way and showed it to them but the boys coughed painfully if they laughed too much so she couldn't do it for long.

Frau Wilhelm liked to tend to Moritz and called him a poor, dear little thing.

'And Moritz, where's your family?' Frau Wilhelm had asked one evening while feeding him spoonfuls of soup.

He'd slashed a finger across his neck, a strange gesture to use when talking of his own relations.

'Oh dear.' Frau Wilhelm had looked sorrowful. She murmured, 'He's had so little care. Where will he go after this?' Then she read to the boys from one of her mould-speckled books. It looked as though it hadn't been opened for a hundred years. Moritz nestled into the crook of her arm and a pink tint rose into Frau Wilhelm's cheeks. She kept reading and Ursula closed her eyes and listened with pleasure to the hushed narration and whisper of pages.

It wasn't long before Frau Wilhelm decided that Moritz must stay with her.

'I might even adopt him,' she declared one morning as she nibbled her breakfast, leaning against the kitchen work surface. 'I can pretend I found him on the street – a waif and stray – and took pity.'

She beamed at Herr Esterbauer and Ursula, dropped her breakfast things into the sink with a splash, and left for work. They heard her descend the stairs at a brisk pace then, faintly – it might have been she – someone started singing as they crossed the courtyard.

Moritz got up on the afternoon of the fifth day and went to the window. Ursula and Herr Esterbauer were in the kitchen preparing mustard presses when they heard Eva hiss out, 'Stay away from the curtain, child!'

When Ursula arrived in the room, Eva was half raised from her seat. Moritz yelled and dodged away from Eva, tottering perilously. He shouted something at her, but his voice was slurred. Ursula hurried to him and took his arm and led him back to bed, hushing him. His eyes didn't leave Eva for a second; he glared, breathing as rapidly as a cat and it took Ursula several minutes to calm him. But he started off again as soon as Eva got up to go to the toilet and neared the bed. This time Ursula heard what he said: the word 'Murderer!' repeated over and over, with barely a pause in between, a continuous string of sound in a high keening note that made Ursula shudder. Herr Esterbauer came hurrying in. He knelt and clamped his hand over Moritz's mouth. Moritz's nostrils flared and his eyes bulged. Eva ran into Frau Wilhelm's bedroom and hid there, until Moritz was asleep.

Eva left late that night. Moritz had set up his eerie, accusing cry whenever he clapped eyes on her and there was no avoiding each other in the small flat. She must pass him and he would bring the police to their door as sure as anything if it continued. She told them she planned to flee Vienna as fast as possible.

'And where will you go?' asked Frau Wilhelm.

'I suppose I'll try to get back to Germany.' Eva stared around at them briefly, intensely, her eyes glinting. 'You don't have to worry. I'll say nothing. If I'm caught it's my punishment to take.' She straightened her back. 'Thank you for your hospitality – for protecting me.' Her whole frame was stiff and her lips were bloodless. She was trying to sound brave but her voice quaked. 'I'll have to give a false name, or something, won't I?'

'It might be wise,' said Frau Wilhelm.

They wished her good luck then she slipped away.

Afterwards, the rest of them sat in silence, Ursula's mind whirring with worry, her body braced in the chair, alert. Were they fools to trust her?

30

The road was silent, striated black and white with wheel tracks in the snow. The only light was from the moon and stars. Schosi warily eyed the murk that clustered at the foot of walls and trees. Herr Esterbauer pushed the key under the lip of the apartment-block door then looked up at the windows shuttered tight against the weather. Schosi looked too and became instantly dizzy. Were these the pavilions of Hartburg? He gripped Ursula's hand, expecting to see a nurse any moment or a blue-covered trolley. As they set off walking, an image of Aldo flashed into his mind – his friend with palm outstretched, offering his Oma's shell. They followed the steep street downwards, the pavement slippery with ice and uneven lumps of snow.

Schosi had been told he was going home, but he couldn't believe it, nor picture it, nor even think about it yet. He was too tired – his body demanded all his energy just to keep walking and to avoid falling down. When they turned a corner and the view opened out before him he stopped and refused to walk on – the indistinct buildings stretched to the horizon, the moonlight picking out spires and domes amongst an endless mass of walls and roads. He wanted to return to the flat and to his friend Moritz. But Ursula and the farmer made him keep moving, their boots stamping firmly into the snow to find purchase, holding him upright and catching him every time he lost his footing.

Ursula seemed restless. She kept swivelling to peer behind her and averted her face whenever she saw a figure on the opposite pavement. There were few people – it was too early for most, long before sunrise. They aimed to catch the very first train.

'Damn well hope there's no setback at the station,' muttered Herr Esterbauer.

Before long Schosi was too weary to walk. Herr Esterbauer hoisted him on to his back and Schosi laid his head on the farmer's shoulders, which were tilted forward to form a plateau. He felt safe and soon slept, the rocking of the broad body lulling him, reminding him of the time he'd been put on to Herr Esterbauer's white carthorse, its body so wide that his legs couldn't span it, and he'd lain prone as if atop a moving building as the docile creature had plodded across the field.

He woke in the compartment of a train, though he didn't recognise it as such. He was lying on a leather bench and Herr Esterbauer had spread his coat over him as a blanket. Ursula's thigh was beside his head and one of her hands rested on his shoulder. He sat up.

'We're almost at Brauhausen,' said Herr Esterbauer quietly. 'Then we have to walk. Heaven knows how long it will take.'

Ursula smiled at Schosi, a tight, small movement of her mouth, her hands clasped in her lap. After a while, she went to the window and raised the blind; on the other side of the glass was the night.

'Have you ever been on a train before?' she asked him. She brought him to stand beside her and opened the window, admitting a lashing stream of air that took the breath clean out of his lungs.

'Don't get him cold, Uschi! Away from there!'

'Just for a second,' she said.

'*Only* a second. He can't take much more.'

She held Schosi's shoulders and they leaned together out of the window and watched the land go by. He stared, astonished; the whole world hammered and roared under a magnesium moon. Wind whipped his hair, stung his forehead – shapes flickered, trees, hills, telephone poles and white-roofed sheds. Far off, clouds came over the horizon like colossal blue-black fish.

'I almost think Toni might be waiting for me at home,' yelled Ursula above the noise. She wrapped her arm around his waist and held him steady. 'But you won't want to talk about him!' She was quiet for a moment then added, 'You'll be all right.' It sounded like a question.

Uschi, he thought, *Uschi* – he heard her name in the puffing steam that whirled above.

The forest enclosed them, dense as a wall.

There were no policemen waiting at Brauhausen station, no one there at all aside from a wizened old employee who warmed himself beside a small heater in the ticket booth. He watched them pass with hooded, yellowing eyes. Ursula was glad once they were out of the station building and into the street; she'd be gladder still to be in the countryside.

As they set off through the unlit back streets, Schosi's teeth chattered and Herr Esterbauer looked left and right at crossings, not for vehicles but for people, early risers or night-shift workers on their way home. A few passed them, and Ursula pulled her headscarf forward, lowered her gaze to the pavement. She wished they could have caught the bus. She felt exposed, a fierce, gusting wind pinning her skirt to her legs and making her head ache. The journey would take several hours and they'd reach Felddorf after sun-up, a risk she dreaded, but Herr Esterbauer said they mustn't be seen by anyone travelling to Felddorf either. Some factory workers went by bus from Brauhausen to Felddorf and might spot them. People would talk. They must appear to return alone, with no Schosi. The story they'd give when questioned would be that they were turned away at Hartburg and eventually left disappointed. They hoped a convenient conclusion would be drawn: that the Hillier boy had escaped into the city with the other missing child, perhaps with the help of the young nurse who'd disappeared in the middle of her shift.

From the edge of town, the road curved ahead through farmland, a grey ribbon in the pre-dawn light. They walked along it for a wearying time. Ursula's boots chafed and it was very cold, the snow deep on the verges. They took to the fields as soon as the sky began to lighten. Here, they watched for farmers and their dogs that started work at daybreak. They kept to the trees where they could. The soil was solid beneath the snow, hard as stone, clogged with ice, tripping them, sliding beneath their soles. The ground looked as if nothing would ever grow from it again. Schosi walked too but he was slow and after a while he would lose strength entirely and need to be carried. Herr Esterbauer lifted him, panting with fatigue; Schosi slept and coughed.

When they saw the first recognisable houses, the sun was seeping over the mountains with a wintry apricot glow. Herr Esterbauer chose a circuitous route, following a small footpath – a detour of several kilometres that cut through wooded hills. They gave the village a wide berth. Ursula's belly squealed and burned with hunger and she was light-headed but she felt she wouldn't be able to eat a bite; her heart thumped now that they were nearly home. She feared so much – hoped too. She thought of her mother and sister. With God's help, let them be safe. If they could just get Schosi to the storage hut, deep in Herr Esterbauer's land. She quailed on behalf of her friend. He'd hate it – the darkness, the loneliness; he'd be so frightened. But it was the only way. She ignored the pain of her blisters, her steps silenced on the carpet of needles as they passed amongst the pines. She glanced often at the trees behind, scanning for movement – for hunters or gamekeepers. The skinny trunks, straight as javelins, appeared to flicker.

It was almost ten in the morning by the time they neared the camp, the River Traisen curving fast and strong through the valley and forcing them close; to ford the freezing water would be too dangerous. From the top of a long, undulating slope they looked down on the familiar barbed-wire fence, the watchtowers, the huts inside; there were no trees to shield them here. They progressed at a steady plod, Schosi propped on Herr Esterbauer's left hip so that he'd be less visible if a guard were to scan the hillside with binoculars. Ursula kept to his right to provide further cover. From here, the guards in the watchtowers were invisible, the prisoners' huts small as matchboxes, but Ursula felt afraid, a skin-prickling fear that made her throat dry, her body prepared to run; she waited for a shout, a gunshot, sprinting figures. They reached the other side of the hill and passed out of view of the camp.

Schosi woke when Herr Esterbauer stopped outside a small wooden shed. He flexed his fingers, which felt numb, and gazed around. Near by, a bird hopped across the frozen crust of the snow. It stopped a little way off and croaked a greeting. Schosi stared. It was one of the Hartburg crows with black plumage and grey beak. Had it followed him here? The bird flapped away when Ursula unlocked the shed's rattling padlock. Schosi was relieved but at the same time was sorry to see it go. Herr Esterbauer set Schosi down then guided him towards the shed's open door; little bear went through it first, beckoning and smiling. Schosi followed. Inside was a pitch black space and he caught a dank odour that reminded him of the cellar in his house. No daylight showed between the overlapping planks that made up the walls. As his eyes adjusted to the light, more of the interior revealed itself: a clutter of items, tools leaning and hanging from hooks, sagging straw bales heaped in the corner, the golden strands speckled with mould. Sacks like rows of dumpy men hunched along the floor. Herr Esterbauer gave him bread and cheese, a raw carrot.

'Stay here,' the farmer said. 'And be quiet. Don't call out or make any noise. Don't meddle with things. You have to leave the tools alone.' Schosi eyed the spiked pitchforks and soil-clotted rakes, the hoes, dibbers, scythes, sickles and spades. They made unnerving shapes on the wall. He was afraid of Herr Esterbauer's strict tone. 'Can you do that?' Herr Esterbauer was staring sternly at him. Schosi nodded. 'I'll come back after dark. I'll bring your mama.'

'Be brave,' said Ursula, hugging him. 'No crying.'

'Sit there.' Herr Esterbauer pointed to the straw.

The bale was damp under Schosi's backside.

'Good lad.'

They went out and locked the door. Blackness dropped over him like a cloak.

Ursula and Herr Esterbauer descended the hill to the farm. The cows were lowing as they entered the yard and there were the Polish women, scraping away the snow with broad shovels and brushes. Mama was there too with gigantic belly and hair tightly bound in a scarf, arms exposed to the biting air. She stooped over her shovel, heat in her face from strenuous work, and didn't notice Ursula until she stood before her. She swore and clapped a hand to her mouth. Then she wrapped Ursula in a tight hug, the belly between them.

'You stupid girl!' She drew back. 'You're very bad.' Then she looked at Herr Esterbauer, questioning and tense.

Herr Esterbauer gave a slight nod. Mama breathed out.

Dorli came out of the barn. She ran to Ursula and hugged her. Ursula realised that her own face was wet with tears – she must have started crying when she saw her mama. They went into the warm farmhouse kitchen where Herr Esterbauer's mother slept, blanketed, in an armchair and it felt good under the heavy beams with the fire crackling inside the *Kachelofen*, a familiar smell of cow manure, wood smoke and raw milk filling the room. Dorli kept an arm around Ursula's shoulder and offered her a handkerchief.

'You're in so much trouble,' she said happily.

'Is there any word from Anton?'

Dorli shook her head.

Mama sliced bread, gripping the loaf to her pumpkin belly and pulling the blade towards her middle, a method that always made Ursula flinch. Mama told Herr Esterbauer about the visits they'd had from Herr Adler. Dorli chipped in here and there to say how awful it had been. Herr Adler had demanded to know where Ursula was and why she'd gone with the farmer to the city. Was she a particular friend of the Hillier boy? Were they sweethearts?

Ursula blushed. To think people might be saying that about her in school.

Mama said Herr Adler had called her an atrocious mother. She'd been getting plenty of long looks in the village. The house had been searched twice. Frau Hillier was summoned to the station; Herr Esterbauer's mother had been interrogated in this room and she'd wept, confused and frightened.

Ursula sat down in the second armchair opposite Herr Esterbauer's mother; she tucked her feet up on the seat and watched the old woman's slack mouth, which puffed outwards with every exhale. Worry stirred in her belly as she thought abstractedly of what lay ahead, but she was so tired; her eyelids were heavy and her mind fogged, her body incredibly weary. She shut her eyes and allowed herself to drift. She thought about her brother. She imagined he was at home, waiting for her, or tending to his gun in the shed.

Surely she'd see him soon. She'd hear his voice calling her, saying he was glad she was back.

A loud rattle startled Schosi from sleep. He sat up on top of the straw bales and stared towards the entrance of the shed, heart thumping. The door lurched open, admitting a rush of freezing air. He couldn't see anything – the blackness outside was deep – but he heard footsteps and heavy breath coming into the hut and then the door was closed with a bang, stopping the draught. A second later a voice quavered through the dark.

'Schatzi? My love?'

A match flared. He was momentarily dazzled. A lantern was lit, two figures caught in its amber glow. One of them came towards him. He recognised her thick form in its many layers with its heavy-legged, limping gait, the headscarf tied around her face like a bun wrapped in cloth. He felt a strange kind of pain. He couldn't speak. The joy of seeing her paralysed him. He struggled to stand, his muscles locked with cold. Then her breath fell all over his face and kisses rained down on his cheeks.

'My mouse, my dear, dear boy, my little rabbit!' She wept and squeezed him to her.

'Gently. He's frail,' said Herr Esterbauer.

There were more frenzied kisses. 'Oh, my little one! What have they done to you?' She made a loud sobbing sound, gulping as she tried to control the noise she made. She stayed holding on to him, kissing him and crying. Schosi reached his arms around her, which set off more of her wild sobs.

After a while, Herr Esterbauer said quietly, 'I'll go on back to the farm. Stay as long as you like.' He placed an empty bucket on the floor, some pieces of newspaper, a cushion, a thick roll of blankets. From a bag on his back he got out three jars of water, a loaf, some cheese and boiled eggs, a jar of preserved vegetables, a section of salami, an enamel plate and cup, some cutlery. He brought out a small metal churn of milk and set it down with a clonk. He straightened. 'Just make certain you're not seen.'

Schosi's mama disentangled herself from her son; she stood and went to Herr Esterbauer. She put her arms around him and kissed him several times on his cheeks and then on his lips. 'Thank you,' she said. 'Thank you a thousand times.'

Herr Esterbauer bowed his head, buried his face in her neck and closed his eyes.

Part Three

31

It was late March 1945 when people began to talk incessantly about the Russians. Those with family in the Alps bought handcarts from the farmers, loaded them with things, and fled. Rumour had it that the Red Army was already in Austria, the first of the Allies to arrive; there was no chance any more it would be the Americans. The Soviets had swept westwards across Europe in a quickening tide, ferocious, undisciplined, chaotic, absorbing the formerly German territories. One night, the headmaster of Felddorf school packed as much as he could into a truck transporting manure, crawled with his family beneath the canvas that covered the foul-smelling load, and was driven away. Another teacher disappeared the next day, a panicky escape, his house door left open behind him. After that, the school was closed; the church was crammed with rows of kneeling people, spilling off the pews and filling the entranceway. Information was scarce; scraps, sporadic and late, came from the local paper, but that was all. The best place to catch up on hearsay was in the crowd around the water pump. Ursula fetched water daily for the Hildesheims and Frau Hillier, and for Schosi too. The pipes in the houses had dried. Some of the farmers had springs, but they were few.

Much of the news she couldn't understand. People spoke quickly and all on top of one another so that she often gave up and listened to her thoughts instead. But she heard that Wiener Neustadt and Baden were overrun and that Russian tanks would any day now reach Vienna. So close to Felddorf that it was difficult to believe, though the guns could be heard, a constant rumble, the air moving, grumbling. A dull orange glow lit the north-eastern horizon, a dual sunset at dusk. The Wehrmacht and People's Army were under orders to fight till the last. Hitler's deluded conceit, the villagers muttered. Ursula prayed for Siegfried but mostly for Anton, full of terror for him. The SS were executing deserters and hanging their bodies in the streets. In each direction: death. 'And for all this we thank the Führer,' someone remarked at the water pump, the once worshipful slogan turned on its head.

Ursula delivered the water at home then went to the Hillier house where she left a bucket on the doorstep. Every other day she took a bucket to Schosi at his hut. For three months he'd been carefully concealed though the search for him had been abandoned some time ago. The bomb strike on the Felddorf factory and railway line had come ten days after Ursula and Herr Esterbauer had arrived home, and in a grim sense this had been their good fortune. The village was thrown into uproar – several houses had been flattened, killing three families. The factory was partially hit – some of the workers were injured and equipment was damaged. Frau Hillier was thankfully unharmed but production stopped. The calamity demanded the attention of the authorities and so the questioning of Herr Esterbauer and Ursula was interrupted. Ursula waited nervously for Herr Adler's severe knock to rattle the door once more, but it didn't come. Funerals were arranged for the dead; the wreckage was slowly cleared, the factory restored; gossip had veered on to the subject of the bombing, away from the intrigue about the Esterbauers, Hildesheims and Hilliers. And meanwhile Schosi stayed locked in his shed. The war came closer week by week; uncertainty hung over them all. The line of enquiry was never picked up again. Perhaps their story had even been believed.

Along with the water, which Ursula carried to Schosi after dark, she brought him things to eat, toys and pictures she'd drawn to brighten his dingy walls. She took away the bucket he used as a chamber pot, emptied it in the nearby woods then returned, feeling her way in the darkness. She led him in his exercises; he mirrored her: bending, stretching, lifting his knees to his chest, rotating his arms twenty times in each direction. He'd regained much of the weight he'd lost at Hartburg. She kept watch outside while he jumped up and down and ran back and forth inside the shed and occasionally allowed him to walk beside her along the edge of the field to feel the breeze, her arm tight through his, eyes roving the dark land around them. She doubted he'd try to run away, but she couldn't take any risks. She coaxed him back into the shed with a promise to stay for another hour and read to him. He lay on his makeshift bed, pale as a horseradish, not having seen the sun for so long. She stroked his hair, the wiry curls flattening beneath her hand then springing free. He asked her questions.

'Where's Simmy? What's my mama doing? When will she come?'

Ursula replied that his mama would come soon. Frau Hillier visited as often as possible without arousing suspicion.

It was consoling, for the most part, to be with him, a steady presence when everything else seemed to shift and change by the day, but she couldn't talk to him about how much she worried for her brother and sometimes he behaved oddly, shouting as if he didn't know her, or hitting her with reddened face then turning rigid. There followed a lock-limbed, wide-eyed fit of whimpering, tears coursing down his cheeks, which were now speckled with sparse, wispy hairs. He asked for Moritz then, and another: Aldo.

She thought about Anton constantly. She wished more than ever he was here; she didn't want to be without him when the Russians came and couldn't bear to contemplate that he might have been killed. She was always first to meet the postal worker at home in the mornings, heart galloping with hope and trepidation. The house gaped without him, the rooms fusty and forsaken, the balcony now just another area that must be swept free of cobwebs and leaves, a sad place to sit rather than somewhere to meet or a route to Anton's bedroom after nightfall. His eiderdown was smooth and stale, its neatness and the absence of his things striking her every time she looked into his room. Once or twice, she climbed between the sheets and tried to conjure him in her mind, his face, their conversations, many of which had been silent, each knowing the other's thoughts, the other's body. But without his tight-wound presence, his weight on the mattress, she felt small, unsafe, less than whole. She listened to the house cracking as it only seemed to do in the dark and the thought that she might never see him again made her heart swell and thump. What if she forgot him? She pressed the pillow to her nose and breathed the remnant of his smell until she managed to remember, to really remember the sensation of his touch, his voice saying 'My own'. But his imprint on the bedlinen grew faint and an image intruded of him in the Hillier yard springing at the prisoner's throat; his gun bucked, eyes fixed on the inky blood as if he would taste it. She tried to slip beneath in the creaking dark, to enter the pool that belonged to them, to find refuge, but it evaded her, as did her certainty about who exactly he was, this savage brother who'd destroyed so much.

Mama had needed assistance since the birth of the baby, which had left her limp and melancholy; a sturdy daughter named Waltraut (or Traudi for short) had arrived hollering into the bedroom with Frau Hillier as midwife. It was as though the bright-eyed little thing had sapped Mama of spirit, taken everything for itself; it suckled and slept, soft, fat and rosy, while Mama crumpled into the hollow slumber of exhaustion or wept over the smallest trifle, because she couldn't get the shutter properly closed or her blanket slid to the floor. Ursula wondered had there been any point in ridding the house of Siegfried when all Mama did was lament over the fatherless baby; Anton had deserted her in any case, so it all had come to nothing.

Frau Hillier outlined for Mama a list of tasks which must be done before the Russians arrived in Felddorf. She found a trunk in the shed that could be nailed shut and filled it with Mama's best linen and china, the crystal ornaments, gramophone, keepsakes from Siegfried, including the wooden carving of the Alps that had hung on the dresser. Mama wept as these were stowed, showing them to Traudi who put them to her mouth, dribbled and stared dreamily. Frau Hillier also hid a tiny store of old Schillings, just in case they'd ever be of use again. A separate box, full of provisions, was to go to the cellar. In the living room, Dorli cried as she lifted the Führer's portrait from the wall. She chopped the frame using a small axe, tore the portrait and rolled it. Into the Tirolia it went along with the book *Mein Kampf*. The fire belched and roared.

Later that day the sisters took the bike to see what was happening in the village and to collect rations. In the centre of Felddorf, Wehrmacht soldiers loitered around the fountain and went in and out of shops. The two girls sidled as close as they dared. Dorli adjusted her dress countless times, patted her hair and pinched herself on the cheeks to make them colour up, being still rather pale after her fit of grief for the Führer. The soldiers cupped their hands into the fountain, rubbed water across their faces. They didn't speak and were filthy and shattered. Most of them weren't much older than Anton. One or two looked over at the girls and smiled and winked. After a while a stocky sergeant, who'd been snoozing on a bench with a hat over his face, stood and called them to attention. The men moved off down the road in lines with bags and guns dangling.

'My blessing goes with them,' said Dorli. But it was empty talk, fruitless talk.

On their way home they passed the Sontheimer house. Sepp sat on the steps with his forearms resting on his knees. Ursula hadn't seen him since the school had been closed and hadn't spoken to him since before her trip to the city. Not long ago, she'd discovered that Sepp had taken Marta as his sweetheart. She'd overheard Marta's plump friends discussing it one day and took the news with painful resignation, a dart that stuck into her body and produced a dull ache for a while. She'd known it would happen and somehow it felt right, more comfortable, to be sure that Sepp was out of reach, belonging to another.

Today he looked anxious, his mouth downturned. Behind him, the door to his house stood open; from inside came voices.

'*Grüss Gott*,' called Ursula, stopping on an impulse. Dorli stopped too and waited a little way off. Ursula very much wanted to be friendly; she'd been so chilly with him before, so confused.

'*Grüss Gott*,' he replied.

Irate tones flared suddenly from behind him and Sepp glanced nervously around. There was no one visible in the neat Sontheimer hallway or on the polished wooden stairs. She wondered what was going on. He turned back to her with a skittish grin.

'How are you?' she said. The words arrived awkwardly. She couldn't seem to be natural and never had anything worthwhile to say. She rubbed one bare foot against the other. Sepp too had bare feet, but then probably his shoes waited for him in the stair cupboard of his house. Mama insisted on saving footwear as soon as spring arrived and so there were to be no boots as long as the fine weather lasted. Near by Dorli tapped her basket against her legs and looked on, impatient to be home to claim her share of the rations, to lick fat from her fingers.

'I'm all right.' Sepp gave his ready smile, though it was subdued today. The rascally beauty of the dimple in his cheek and gleam of teeth had the same effect as always on Ursula; she grew ill at ease – it was as if something opened inside her without permission, something she didn't understand or know what to do with. She reminded herself that he'd a sweetheart now but it made no difference to how she felt. Anton's words from months ago revisited her: *If he knew you like I do, do you think he'd smile at you then?* She clenched her hands behind her back.

'Inspection,' continued Sepp, indicating the house. 'Herr Adler. Told me to wait outside.'

Ursula quickly scanned the windows – she'd managed to avoid the Party inspector over the last few months, ducking from sight whenever she glimpsed him in the village. She'd heard he was meaner than ever these days, digging his heels in and his teeth too, Frau Hillier said, so as not to look defeat in the face. He was less methodical but more tyrannical; he refused to give up.

Frau Sontheimer's soft voice drifted out into the street and then came a snippet of Herr Adler's hard-edged tones. Ursula shifted warily; she pictured his face, his angry eyes, small and repulsive. She should leave now before he saw her. She should hurry.

'I hate inspections,' said Sepp.

'Me too,' she answered, remembering the sense of violation as Herr Adler had interrogated her about

Schosi, poking and prodding amongst her things. He'd fingered her books and thrust his arms into her wardrobe, into Papa's bureau, barking out questions all the while. It had been truly terrifying.

'Every week he comes.' Sepp rubbed his head, making his hair stand on end. 'There's some reason, Auntie thinks.'

Ursula recalled with misgiving Anton's catcalling to Frau Gerg's house. Would another of her friends now be punished? She tried to imagine Sepp sneaking a starving Russian into his cellar.

Sepp stood and came on to the road; he came close, leaning towards her ear, his lips almost immobile as he spoke, his body near enough for her to feel the heat of it. 'Auntie says that ash is falling on Vienna.' He glanced over at Dorli then continued. 'They set their documents on fire – the Party. They've run like cowards and old Adler knows it.' He gripped her wrist and squeezed it; his eyes were intent on hers. 'The Russians are taking ground in the capital. It must really be the end.'

She thought of Anton and Siegfried in the maze-like streets, adrift in a grey blizzard, faces smutted by charred paper, seeking the enemy, or evading it – she daren't think of the tanks and fire and death, the Mongol hordes, as the Russians were called in the newspaper; that lofty, alien place flooded with foreigners now as never before. And just beyond the doors and walls of the Sontheimer house was Herr Adler and his desperation, his fury that might any moment be unleashed upon Sepp and his genteel aunt. 'I'm sorry,' she said, the warmth and firm press of his fingers bringing unplanned words. 'Sorry for being rude before. And for what's happening – you know, all of this.

Your troubles. And . . .' But she couldn't tell Sepp what her brother had done.

'Come *on*!' called Dorli from across the road. 'I want to go.'

'All right!' replied Ursula.

Through the open door of the Sontheimer house the rotund form of Herr Adler appeared, passing between two rooms. 'You two!' he snapped, glaring out at them. 'Stop talking!' He came through the door and pointed at Ursula with a fat finger. His eyes narrowed as he recognised her. 'You!'

She backed hastily towards the far pavement.

'What are you doing here?'

His small black eyes skewered her from under their swollen lids, his livid cheeks and accusing finger, and in that moment the strangest thing happened – a window in her soul flew open to a long-forgotten memory: Saint Nikolaus above her in the kitchen pointing just so and berating her, saying, 'You!' The reddened hand bloated so that the fingers could barely bend, a pig's trotter. Dressed as the saint he'd sent her out into the night with the Krampus. He'd watched from the doorway as she was pushed into the snow, his coal-black eyes alight; he'd held her brother's arms to keep him back. She felt again the snow through her perforated house shoes with the moon climbing up to watch her as she trembled and froze. She remembered the touch of frightful hands, burrowing, grabbing, fastened round her throat.

The memory knocked the breath out of her and then she was running, heart thudding, away from Herr Adler, towards her sister who'd begun to sidle off. Sepp called after her, an unheard goodbye. Dorli called too as Ursula passed her, forced to run behind with the basket; she yelled to her to slow down or she'd give her a hiding – what on earth was she playing at? Glancing back, Ursula saw Herr Adler descend the Sontheimer steps. He snatched Sepp by the collar and hauled him into the house. She groaned aloud and then Dorli seized her elbow, pinched hard through her clothes, twisting a swatch of her flesh. Ursula slowed.

'What's the matter with you?' Dorli clamped her arm to Ursula's, furious, as they marched towards home.

'Nothing.'

'You're acting completely mad! You behaved like you'd seen the devil. Now he'll think we've something to hide, you silly idiot!'

Ursula fixed her eyes on her own bare toes, dust-blackened and splaying over stones as they turned on to the track, concentrated on the jab of pebbles and prickle of plants on her soles. She couldn't quiet the thoughts that flew in a clamour in her mind. She remembered that Anton had broken free of the saint and followed. He had seen her pushed on to the snow with stones underneath. It would've gone worse, he said, if he hadn't yelled. That blaring shout, oddly muffled, harsh and fierce then swallowed, silenced. She hadn't recalled the sound of it till now.

'You're doing that thing, that panting thing you do in your sleep,' Dorli snapped. 'Stop it! I hate it. You sound like a goat with its throat slit.'

Ursula hadn't noticed her breath rushing in and out so loudly. She struggled to quieten it.

'Was it that Sontheimer boy?' Dorli snatched one of Ursula's plaits away from her face to better see her expression. 'Did he say something bad to you?'

Ursula shook her head vigorously. 'My chest,' she said, putting a hand there. 'It's just my chest hurts.' It was true that her chest felt constricted, without much room for air, and it throbbed awfully as though bruised.

Dorli tutted and said something about her being a weakling. Ursula trudged alongside her and tried not to think about a murky figure and Anton with his hands about her neck, pressing her into the eiderdown, his face above hers. A wrong thing – a shameful thing.

That evening, Frau Hillier and Mama sat with the girls in the kitchen and Mama fiddled continually with Traudi's knitted bonnet although it was perfectly straight. Occasionally she rose and wiped the edge of the sink with a tea towel or picked up onion skins from the floor, and Frau Hillier smoothed the tabletop with her fingertips before speaking.

'When they come you must hide,' she said. 'In the cellar or the hayloft or the woods.'

Ursula watched Mama who stared off into the corner of the room. It was clear she was in another terrible mood; she exuded harsh distress and Ursula knew to be wary. Until being called into the kitchen, she'd taken pains to keep away from her by offering to do all of the outside tasks unaided. She'd wanted to be alone in any case and had spent the time in the yard and sheds thinking about Sepp and Frau Sontheimer and hoping they were safe. She'd hated to see Sepp manhandled and dragged roughly up the steps as if he were a disobedient child. She dwelled on the moment when he'd stood close to her, the warm squeeze of his fingers on her wrist, the way he'd pressed them there for so long, as though checking for her pulse. She'd revisited the memory a hundred times as she swilled cow dung from the shed floor and gathered sticks for the Tirolia. She could conjure the actual sensation, as if his fingertips were still there, making a depression in her skin.

'You must keep together,' continued Frau Hillier. 'Don't speak to them or smile.'

'Do you not hear?' said Mama when the girls only stared, saying nothing. 'The time is over for wandering into town – for trying to look pretty.'

'Yes! Fine!' Dorli replied, affronted, perhaps embarrassed by her interest in the young soldiers earlier that day and how she'd tried to attract them.

Ursula thought regretfully of her yellow ribbons, the only pretty things she owned. She presumed she'd now have to give them up.

Frau Hillier drew out two pieces of cloth from her pocket, rolled them and dipped them into a dish of dark red liquid. The smell of wine filled the air, heady and strong. She handed one to each of the girls. 'Stuff them in your underwear.' She gestured between her legs and looked at them squarely, but her throat gulped visibly. 'They have a terrible fear of women's blood.'

Ursula held the soiled cloth and watched the dark stain seeping, spreading; the edges of the splodge of wine fanned softly out through the off-white material, which was made from a torn pillowcase. She was still waiting for her own monthlies to begin. With so little to eat, Frau Hillier said, it would take for ever. The colour on the cloth had a purple tinge, deep and rich, like the intense smell of the wine that she breathed. 'Is this what it looks like?' she said. 'Will it fool them?'

'It's near enough,' said Frau Hillier. 'They won't know the difference.'

'You must really *shout* it,' said Mama. '*Bleeding! Bleeding!* And run towards wherever there are people.' Her face was tight and her voice stiff. 'Do you understand?'

'Yes, Mama,' said Ursula, fear turning in her belly, growing solid like curd so that she felt sick. Could she run like that? She'd surely be caught. What would be done to her? Anton wasn't here to holler; she'd be alone this time.

32

err Esterbauer proposed to Frau Hillier at the Gasthaus after church that Sunday in front of a few surprised onlookers. They watched amused, assuming that the proposal was all part of the frenzy before Ivan came, a kind of insurance policy against the grasping Russians. The Hildesheims weren't there to see the farmer present the ring but they soon found out that he had suffered public humiliation – Frau Hillier came to the house to deliver shopping and announced in a brusque but not unfriendly tone that she'd refused him. She said that she knew it was the right decision and wanted to tell them now before they heard it from some loudmouth in town.

'But why?' exclaimed Mama, dumbfounded, as she divested her friend of the shopping bags. 'He's a good catch, Gita!'

Ursula and Dorli hung over the banister, watching as Frau Hillier removed her coat, her rounded breasts and belly showing through her work dress. She took out her handkerchief and blew her nose; it made a short honking sound like a goose. 'I've been married once,' she said. 'That's enough for me.'

'Come now. He's rich.' Mama set down the bags in the kitchen and thumbed the fingers of her left hand as she counted off Herr Esterbauer's attributes. 'He's fit for his years. He adores you and your son.' Her voice rose in disbelief. 'And no one else is going to ask you.'

Frau Hillier merely smiled and shrugged. 'Don't nag me,' she said as she went into the pantry and began putting the food away, leaving the dried beans out ready for the evening meal. Most of the food they'd normally receive was missing: the shops were unstocked, the supply disrupted.

'Stop that, I can do that.' Mama shooed Frau Hillier out of the pantry. 'Now, explain yourself.'

The girls crowded into the room and took seats at the table.

'You're all so nosy.' Frau Hillier folded her arms. 'What's it to you?'

'You mean you're not going to tell?' said Dorli.

'No, it's private.'

'Private!' Mama was incredulous. 'I'll ask him myself.'

'Good luck with that.' Frau Hillier brushed her sleeves with her hands and straightened her cuffs. She turned nonchalantly to her coat and put it on. 'I can't believe you care so much. There are more important things, you know.' She opened the door. 'Such as, today I learned Ivan's just thirty kilometres away. I was going to say so. Some poor crazed refugees came through about an hour ago – Hungarians – shouting "Russians coming!" "Lock doors!" "Women, put on all your clothes!"'

'Crazy woman!' said Mama, ignoring her. 'What are you going on about? Not much good fortune happens around here. We want you to be happy.'

Frau Hillier gave an exasperated sigh and left the house.

Ursula grabbed Dorli's sleeve. 'How long does it take to walk thirty kilometres?'

'I don't know. But they have vehicles.'

'Will they come to the houses?' Ursula followed Dorli as she began upstairs. 'What will they do?'

'Don't ask me!' Her voice turned shrill and unkind. 'I don't know everything!' She stomped off then called from the landing, 'Of course they'll come to the houses!'

Ursula shadowed Mama in her tasks. She tried to suppress the churning of her stomach. She helped with Traudi, changing her whenever the hideous green paste appeared in her nappy, bathing her and feeding her on cow's milk. She tucked her into the basket in front of the Tirolia, kissed her belly, soft as rabbits' ears and smelling of soap. Then she distracted herself further by musing about Frau Hillier and Herr Esterbauer. It was such a pity – if they married then perhaps one day Schosi could live safely on the farm. They'd all be happy and Frau Hillier would be much better off. What on earth was her reason? It couldn't be because she disliked the farmer. They loved to be together, to lean against a gate, or sit beneath a tree, enjoying the last of the evening sun while sipping Herr Esterbauer's home-brewed beer. Ursula had passed them on many occasions in the past so she knew they often stayed out until the shadows were long and the temperature fell, talking and watching the view with half-closed eyes. She wanted them to be like this always – a family full of patient love, the kind she'd never known herself. Why couldn't it happen?

She went to wash Traudi's dirtied nappies in the scullery. She scrubbed until her knuckles ached in the cold water and her skin was abraded by the harsh bristled brush, but she couldn't completely remove the stains from the white towelling, nor the trepidation she felt, like pressure building, because all things had descended into disorder and the future was full of unknowable endings made up of who would die and who would not, who would be lonely or sad, who would suffer or be punished, and who would be close to her or lost to her for ever. After a while she stopped trying to think of anything at all because it exhausted her. She went outside and hung the sullied squares in the cherry tree like flags of surrender.

33

Ursula was at the grocer's and had almost reached the counter when she heard a cry from the street. A farmer from the outskirts of Felddorf sprinted with pounding feet, dark-faced with exertion, his clothes in disarray. He'd shouted himself nearly hoarse. 'The Russians! They're here. On the edge of the village. Inside! Inside!'

Ursula registered his words with horror. She'd been sent alone to the shop; Traudi was ill, vomiting and feverish. Dorli too was pale and sweating with a bowl at her bedside. Now the worst had happened. She backed against the counter as shoppers jostled around her. She'd not put the wine-stained cloth into her underwear. She was unprepared. A woman shoved her aside to reach the shop exit then burst into the street. She ran then stopped and whirled about and ran in the opposite direction.

Another woman hurried out also, calling someone's name loudly and repeatedly. Ursula's body jangled throughout; she felt an overwhelming urge to sprint but her legs grew strangely heavy like bags of sand and she found herself standing while others flowed about her. Herr Wemmel, the grocer, craned his neck to watch the hollering farmer, who was heading for the Rathaus and fountain. 'Christ in Heaven!' swore Herr Wemmel. He undid his apron and threw it on to the countertop. He went to the doorway. 'Jesus and Mary!' He seemed only able to curse and gape like a carp. He turned to Ursula, now the only customer remaining. 'Go home!' he said. 'Go to your family.' And with that he shepherded her outside. 'Quickly!' He closed the door, shutting himself inside. He pulled the bolt and dropped the blind in the window.

Her route demanded she walk in the wake of the sprinting farmer, whose figure she could still just about see, legs unsteady as a drunk's, for he wasn't a young man. She wondered why she didn't run too. Others scurried hither and thither. She ought to flee; her blood was quick with fear. But she hesitated. She realised that, despite it all, she was curious. She wanted to see them – the nightmarish villains who'd filled every thought and conversation for so many weeks and months. How would they look and what would they do? They must be more fearsome than anything. But where was her sense? She should go without delay to warn her family. She walked a little faster.

Soon there was no one else in the street, all the doors of the houses closed. Sepp's house too was quiet when she reached it. She looked for a face behind the modest curtains. In the adjacent homes a few people stood in the entrances to their balconies. She glanced up at them and thought that there was an unusual peace in Felddorf just then, in the appealing buildings with spring sunshine striking the bright roofs, the swept steps and trimmed bushes, the dome of the church tranquil against the sky. A leaf caught on a spider's thread hung from a hedge and twirled in the breeze, appearing to float two inches above the ground. She watched its silent rotation.

From the camp, twenty metres away, shouts erupted. Then a volley of shots cracked the air. Ursula jumped and turned round. She could make out little through the trees that lined the fence; she was glad because she didn't want to see what was happening there. Everyone knew that a large hole had been dug in the centre of the camp two days ago; they'd all guessed what it was for. Then there was the low growl of engines and the people on the balcony turned their heads to watch the road. One of them gestured to Ursula, an urgent flapping of hands. The engine sound grew nearer; the leaf on its invisible filament danced. Her heart accelerated in sudden terror. She should have fled with the others! She looked frantically around. Where could she hide? She must find somewhere! A man came round the corner on a bicycle. He rode fast. Another man followed and then another, until there were at least ten men on bicycles, approaching in ragged formation. An army vehicle roared into sight. More came behind until the road was filled with squat dark shapes, the smoke of exhausts. The growling racket bounced off the buildings. Ursula dashed over to a nearby flower border and crouched behind its low wall. A scant hiding place but her only option. She pulled her hands into her sleeves so that her pale skin was concealed. She got ready to cover her face and peered through the manicured conifers that grew in the border.

After a few moments, when it sounded as though the vehicles were nearly upon her, the wheels of the bicycles rushed by, the engine noise drowning out the whirr of their tyres. Voices were raised briefly above the din, a harsh staccato shout and raucous laugh. Ursula had heard that foreign language in the Weekly Update and on the radio. She tried to see the faces of the cyclists but the bushes obscured everything except their long boots that rotated on pedals, scuffed and grey with dust, khaki-patterned breeches tucked into boot-tops. The Soviets rode a random assortment of old and new bikes, some designed for ladies, others rusted and with a German brand name written on the frame. Next, the vehicles lumbered past, their huge tyre treads grinding the stones – stiff gusts of smoke blew into Ursula's face and the ground vibrated.

The Russians continued towards the centre of the village and then the engines grew suddenly much quieter. Ursula peered warily out from behind the bush. The vehicles were parked outside the Rathaus in clear view, their motors running – the cyclists gone. People emerged on to doorsteps, curtains twitched. Then from Sepp's house came a hurrying Frau Sontheimer. She went directly towards the Russians and began to wave; Ursula stared in alarm. Didn't Frau Sontheimer know the Soviets were dangerous? She shouldn't go dashing towards them like that! She'd be shot!

Red Army soldiers jumped from the parked vehicles – the guns they held were large and angular. They met Frau Sontheimer in the road.

'Welcome! Welcome!' She spoke slowly, just audible above the engines. 'I am so glad you have come!'

The Russians watched her in silence.

'I have waited for years. Welcome!'

One of the soldiers stepped forward, a short man with concave cheeks. 'Watch!' He gestured that she should show him her wrist. Frau Sontheimer hesitated then lifted her cuff to reveal her wristwatch. 'Watch! Give!' commanded the Russian. Frau Sontheimer paused again then unfastened her watch and held it out. The Russian snatched it and dropped it into his pocket. 'Bread! Give!' Frau Sontheimer looked back at her house. Sepp lingered in the doorway.

'Have we any bread, Josef?' she called, her refined voice rather unsteady.

Sepp disappeared then appeared a moment later and raised his hands to show they were empty.

'Come, Frau! Bread!' the Russian demanded again.

Frau Sontheimer looked around her in panic. Ursula touched the bread in her bag that she'd collected from Herr Wemmel, heavy and precious; she didn't know when they might get more. But she wanted to help Frau Sontheimer and Sepp, to make amends for what they'd suffered with the inspections. She sneaked closer, keeping to the edge of the road. The rest of the soldiers had begun to dismount and were creating quite an uproar, all talking and calling to one another. A tall Russian who appeared to be in charge shouted directions above the commotion. There was none of the orderly saluting lines and tight-lipped obedience of the Wehrmacht. When Ursula was close enough to see the stubble on the chins of the soldiers, one of them spotted her, pointed, and several heads swivelled to stare. Frau Sontheimer stared too; she licked her lips and shook her head very slightly. Ursula clutched the bread to her front like a shield. When she was a few metres nearer, she took it out of the bag. 'Here,' she said to Frau Sontheimer. She tossed it.

'Go!' hissed Frau Sontheimer as she caught the parcel. 'Go home!'

Ursula backed away and watched as Frau Sontheimer handed the bread to the short hollow-cheeked soldier. The soldier passed it to the commanding Russian who was broad and deep-chested with pale blue eyes and thick barley-blond hair; he wore a long coat and stars on his hat. Below the hat his eyebrows were so light that they looked as if they'd been bleached by the sun. Ursula thought he was like one of Hitler's beautiful men but in the wrong uniform.

The other soldiers observed her from the far side of the vehicles, their eyes set deep and close together in sun-darkened faces, their bony brows giving them a brooding look, intense and serious. They were thin and their uniforms ill-fitting; long belted khaki tunics over breeches that billowed at the thigh. They wore narrow caps tilted forward, pointing towards their prominent noses. One of the men looked very different to the others; he had an ugly flat face, very brown and round like a plate with eyes that were barely open, as if he'd been beaten and they swelled shut. His hat was round and pointed on top like an onion. Ursula had never seen a person who looked like him.

Frau Sontheimer came and took hold of her arm. She led her firmly inside her house. The Russians meanwhile began more shouting and gesticulating and soon a large group of them set off on foot towards the camp, jogging with guns braced. Another party went towards the Rathaus and a few began to manoeuvre the vehicles in the road.

'Why did you greet them like that?' said Ursula to Frau Sontheimer as she was brought into the polished pine hallway. 'Like friends?'

'Come out of the road. There'll be trouble now.'

Sepp appeared on the stairs. He smiled at Ursula where she stood with her muddy feet nestling in the white sheepskin rug, shedding black crumbs and bits of grass. She wondered if he thought her a terrible coward for running away from Herr Adler last time they met. But he wouldn't think of that now.

'I can't stay. I have to go and tell my family.' The disgraceful Hildesheims – and here she was polluting their house. She glanced out of the door to see what the Russians were doing but glimpsed nothing more. Frau Sontheimer quietly closed it.

'It's not safe yet. You must wait here for a while.' Frau Sontheimer tried to usher her into the living room but she refused, feeling far too dirty to step into the smart room. She wanted to escape the plush, ordered house entirely, but daren't. Her sense of shame made her mean. She shouldn't feel so undeserving and low, she thought, because it turned out Anton had been right about the Sontheimers.

'Take these, dear.' Frau Sontheimer held out a box of crackers. 'In exchange for the bread.' Red and purple bruises ringed her wrists.

'Did the Russians do that?' asked Ursula.

'No,' said Sepp, 'it happened during an inspection. That day when I saw you.'

She looked for marks on Sepp's wrists too and felt guilty again, though it became harder and harder to feel true anger towards her brother. Her loyalty stirred now and made her defensive; he'd only done what he thought right.

'Well, let's hope the Russians are a little better than what we've been used to,' said Frau Sontheimer briskly. She moved to the window and gazed towards the camp. 'But we'll see.' Another crackle of shots came, sharp and distant-sounding.

Frau Sontheimer insisted that Ursula come to the table and eat one of the crackers. 'You look very pale, dear,' she said, guiding her by the arm.

Sepp sat opposite, fidgeting and quiet, while Frau Sontheimer seated herself. Frau Sontheimer began to pray. Ursula nibbled the cracker and took pains not to meet Sepp's eye. It would be too bad to be struck by his prettiness at such a time. She listened to the drone of Frau Sontheimer's incantations; the starched tablecloth scratched against her legs. She had to get out of here, to go to her family. They knew nothing at home – oblivious, ill and vulnerable. She tried to be still. The neat, safe, sober room made her somehow more agitated. She put down her cracker, pushed her chair back; before Frau Sontheimer could finish her prayer, she dashed out of the living room and through the front door, bashing it closed behind her, calling 'Thank you!' as she went. She only glanced back once she was some way down the street. Sepp's face was at the window, a smudge behind the net curtain.

Trees swayed along the camp fence, their leaves rustling boisterously. She ran fast, past the Russians in the road, the crowd outside the police station, where Herr Adler hollered hateful words, held by several Red Army soldiers. A thickset soldier belted him across the face but he kept on screaming threats and condemnations. Ursula reached the beginning of the track. She hoped none of the Russians had gone that way. She ran onwards, leaping over stones, dodging thistles. She still flinched with the oppressive anxiety she'd felt in the Sontheimer house. She'd not tell her family about the bread; Mama would certainly beat her for taking such a risk. She passed the Fingerlos place – Gabriel the dog was in the yard, his ears pricked towards the village.

When she reached the house she ran straight into the kitchen. A pot bubbled on the stovetop. Traudi slept in her basket, exhausted from sickness and crying. Mama emerged from the cellar holding a broom.

'Where are the groceries?' With a glance she took in Ursula's flustered appearance, the absence of food in her satchel.

'They've arrived.'

Mama inhaled sharply. She leaned the broom against the panelling. It slithered to the floor with a clatter. 'Right,' she said. 'We must hide. Fetch Dorli from bed. Make sure she dresses warmly.'

They brought the last few bits of food down into the cellar. There wasn't much – potatoes, a small bag of salt (Mama said you couldn't survive for long without it), a muddy swede, and some dried beans. Ursula was sent to fetch a bucket of water from the trout stream. It would do for washing and cooking, and if they got desperate, for drinking. She worried for Schosi and if he would have enough to last an extra day. Outside it had begun to rain and the surface of the trout stream jumped and crinkled so that she couldn't see the stones or the fish below as she dunked the bucket into the water. The twigs of the trees caught raindrops and held them in rows on their underside. The whole countryside had that same tranquil atmosphere she'd felt in the village before the rumpus and frenzy had begun, as if it wasn't real and they wouldn't come; impossible that uniforms and guns might arrive in this place, or one of those monstrous army vehicles. She looked for figures beyond the gate, but there was no one. Rainfall obscured the hills. She went back inside with damp hair and collar.

Mama pulled the wooden bar across the cellar door and they all sat for a while. Traudi vomited on her knitted suit. Ursula tried to divert herself from the smell and the fear she felt – she found small shards of stone at the base of the walls and used them to draw on the concrete floor.

'They say Ivan's bargaining with the Americans and will organise a deal,' said Dorli from amidst blankets, the bowl within easy reach. She was still slightly green in the face. 'At least the Yanks are civilised, so I hope that's true.'

'Heaven help us,' said Mama. 'We won't know till we know.'

Ursula gave up drawing and hugged her knees. Her sister was an insufferable know-it-all and sometimes Mama said such senseless things.

After passing an uneventful night in the cellar, the family gave up trying to hide – by morning they were cold and sore and realised that the Russians might not come to their house that day, or even that week, and Mama said she'd rather not toilet in a chamber pot if she didn't have to. 'Maybe I should go to work,' she said as she stoked the fire into life in the kitchen and prepared some hot food. 'I could take all of you with me.'

But she soon changed her mind – she was certain that Herr Esterbauer would rather she stayed home instead of walking across the fields and risking an encounter.

They all jumped like cats when Frau Hillier entered. She came into the kitchen breathless – she had news to bring. 'They've closed the factory,' she said. 'They arrested the bosses – marched them away down the road with hands on heads and threw them straight in the camp. They told all us workers to go home. And then they made the SS guards crawl like dogs and Herr Adler too.' She leaned forward and clutched Mama's shoulder. 'They've locked him up! The prisoners kicked dirt in his face. You should've seen it.' She accepted a cup of *Malzkaffee* and joined them at the table to continue her report.

Some of the Russian officers had taken the Siedler farm as quarters, she told them. Herr Siedler, the richest farmer, had torn out his expensive wooden floors to try to put them off, but still they chose his house, because it was so large and because he had two plump daughters. More trucks of soldiers had been tumbling out on to the street all morning, and their horses drank from the fountain. At the edge of the village the verges were used as toilets – the Russians squatted in plain view and relieved themselves. 'To think they'd do that! I know they've no barracks but what a dirty thing to do. We shan't be able to walk out that way – the stench is terrible.'

She went on to describe the arrival of a vehicle full of bigwigs – the commander, and one or two others of distinction, who'd climbed out and looked around with serious faces. 'A lot are coming here,' said Frau Hillier. 'The factory is the thing, I suppose. I don't know the ranks. It seems you just look for the red star on the hat or a good overcoat. They're the ones in charge. The rest of them are scruffy enough.'

Ursula remembered the big blond Russian with stars on his hat – he must have been an officer of some kind.

Then Frau Hillier set down her *Malzkaffee* in a meaningful fashion. 'I have an announcement to make.'

Ursula, Mama and Dorli shared a look, sure it would be news about Herr Esterbauer. Ursula tried to see Frau Hillier's engagement finger but her hand was beneath the table.

Frau Hillier drew a deep breath. 'Schosi will be coming home and he'll go to church with me this Sunday!' Her eyes grew wet with tears and a broad smile erased her usually tired expression. 'Can you believe it? At last!' She gave a short laugh. 'I'm so happy. So happy!'

Ursula's heart skipped. Of course, now the Russians were here her friend could go where he pleased. He could walk about without fear. 'Oh, wonderful!' she said. She stood abruptly. 'I'm so glad!' She hugged Frau Hillier, pressed her face into the grease-stained fabric of her work dress, and squeezed tight about her ample arms and chest. She wanted to run directly to Schosi and hug him too. But she couldn't – not alone, not without the wine-soaked rag in her underwear. Now it was she who must be vigilant.

The next day a Russian soldier knocked on the door of the Hildesheim house, accompanied by two others carrying guns. The man who spoke to them was slight and dark-haired with wire-rimmed glasses and a large nose, bookish in appearance and with a bird-like way of glancing around. He was a clerk and wrote often in a notebook. He asked questions in a polite tone, nodding and conciliatory. He asked whether they were hiding any National Socialists in the house, or any Wehrmacht soldiers, or any Germans.

'No,' said Mama. 'We're all Austrians – all women here.'

The Russian clerk smiled and wrote something down again. The soldiers with guns were silent and peered into the house. They wore the same green caps and dirty uniforms Ursula had seen in the village. Their eyes lingered on her till she blushed and backed into the living-room doorway to hide herself.

'Please report to the town hall next Wednesday at eight o'clock in the morning,' said the clerk. 'We'll be registering all adults of working age. That is to say, between fifteen and sixty.' The small man peered at his notebook short-sightedly then continued. 'Until that time please continue attending your work as normal. If you're a factory employee, please resume work tomorrow morning.' He spoke fastidious and accurate German, his accent and pronunciation very good.

Mama nodded and assured him they'd cooperate.

'Many thanks,' he said. His companions shifted their weight and one of them hefted his gun on to his shoulder to rest his arms. 'We come as your liberators, we mean you no harm.'

After this official statement of reassurance, the soldiers saluted and walked off across the yard. Ursula emerged to watch them go. The clerk led the way, diminutive beside his companions who turned to look back, sauntering bandy-legged out of the gate. Their hungry faces and brutal, long-barrelled guns seemed out of place amongst the exuberant pink of the fireweed that lined the track. The plants sprung about in the breeze, tossing their heads as if nothing in the world was amiss, and the soldiers were soon hidden from view but Ursula stayed in the doorway and listened, barely breathing, as the stamp and jingle of their steps grew faint and eventually disappeared.

34

It was late evening and Schosi watched from his attic window while Herr Esterbauer stumbled against the fence below and tried to open the gate. After a while of fishing for the latch he managed to come unsteadily through into the garden, then wended off the edge of the path. He trampled through a patch of flowers that were the only bright things in the dank, unfilled garden. The stems snapped and the leaves mashed into the soil, squashed by the farmer's heavy boots. Schosi was surprised to see him so clumsy – even clumsier than himself. He looked in danger of falling over. Schosi's mama would soon be home and she'd see straight away that the flowers were spoiled.

There came a knock on the door. 'Schosi, lad!' Herr Esterbauer hollered. 'It's only me!'

Schosi didn't answer at first, afraid that Herr Esterbauer was here to take him back to the hut in the field. He never wanted to go into that dark place again. He was very relieved to be home, even though all the space in the rooms made him nervous. The farmer banged on the door again. When eventually Schosi let him inside he seemed happy, patting Schosi on the shoulder and ruffling his hair. 'Isn't your mama home?' he asked.

Schosi shook his head.

'Thought I'd visit you.' He pulled a chair out from the kitchen table and sat. He scratched himself on the jaw and then told Schosi to come to him. 'You pleased to be back?' he asked and put a hand on his shoulder. Schosi nodded. Herr Esterbauer was red in the face and a strong smell of beer was on his breath. He was drunk like Schosi's papa used to be after playing cards at the Gasthaus, when he came home swearing and couldn't unbutton his jacket. Herr Esterbauer spoke in a heavy tone. 'It's a bad time – a bad time for me.' He gave a lopsided grimace that was almost a smile but it fell quickly away so that his cheeks hung like empty pockets. He said gruffly, 'Not so for you, hey? At least those Russkis will hang that bloody doctor of yours.'

Schosi became worried at the mention of a doctor. He began to wind his comfort blanket, squeezing and twisting it round and round until his finger pulsated.

'She's working for them now. Did you know that?' Herr Esterbauer pointed at the door. 'They'll keep her there till *late*.' He took a beer bottle out of his coat pocket, drained some of it then put it on the tabletop. Bubbles scurried to the surface of the tawny liquid; foam settled in a white scum. Schosi leaned on the table and waited – he was glad to be with Herr Esterbauer who made the house feel secure, his anxiety about the doctor fading as the clock ticked and Herr Esterbauer sighed, sniffed, swigged at the drink every few minutes, belched, and shifted his dirty boots back and forth. He occasionally looked at Schosi, a squint from beneath his unruly eyebrows.

'You want to come and live at my place?' he said eventually. 'If I marry your mama you can. We can live together on the farm. What do you think about that? You'd have your own room.'

Schosi liked the idea of living at the farm, but it wasn't his home.

'You'd be in charge of the herd, lad. How about that?' Herr Esterbauer gave his grimacing smile again then drank more of the beer.

Schosi had never been in charge of anything before; he watched the farmer disbelievingly for a sign that he was joking. He'd like to do something like that very much, something important. Herr Esterbauer finished the bottle and looked around the kitchen, at the skinny cupboards and rough floor, at the mildewed walls and spider webs stretched across the window.

'I could make her very happy.'

'But you stepped on her flowers.'

Herr Esterbauer laughed. 'Yes. She won't be happy about that!'

Very late she came. It'd been dark for a while and Herr Esterbauer had made some food that tasted not very nice at all, but Schosi was hungry so he was eating it anyway. She walked into the house and looked shocked to see Herr Esterbauer in the kitchen. He wasn't blundering around so much any more but he was still red in the face, and spoke with a loud voice. Schosi's mama was filthy, her eyes raw around the rims. Her arms were covered in small cuts and grazes, which showed lurid pink through the grime. 'What's wrong?' she said. 'Is something the matter?'

'No, everything's fine,' said Herr Esterbauer. 'I just came to keep this one company.'

'And your mother? You left her alone?'

'She's fine.'

Schosi stopped eating his tasteless dinner, which was cabbage and noodles without any salt. His mama went to the sink and washed her hands and face. She wiped herself with a cloth and smoothed her straggling hair.

'What was it like at the factory?' said Herr Esterbauer.

'I'm very tired.'

Schosi got up so that his mama could sit down.

'We had to strip out the machines and load them straight on to the trains. It'll be the same again tomorrow.'

'You see,' said Herr Esterbauer, 'they'll take everything. Mark my words.' He glared fiercely, and Schosi knew that the glare was meant for the Russians. He often talked about them, or the Soviets, which was the same thing, and when he did he always glared in that way. He liked to say why he hated them, though the reasons he gave never made any sense and it was very complicated. Schosi only remembered the bit about Russians being like animals, which he didn't think was a bad thing.

'They came to my farm yesterday.' Herr Esterbauer withdrew another bottle from his coat, pulled the stopper, put it down. White froth rose and poked above the top like snow. Schosi touched the froth with his fingertip and tasted it but it was bitter and unpleasant. Herr Esterbauer drank and offered it to Schosi's mama; they shared the same bottle, which wasn't normal. Normally there'd be a glass each.

'They've taken part of my land. They've already ploughed one of the fallow fields.' He shook his head and his mouth turned down at the corners. 'They're moving into the house soon.'

Schosi had seen him arguing with the soldiers the previous day at the farm where he'd been brought from the hut to wait for his mother. Russians had been standing near the farmhouse shouting with Herr Esterbauer. Then some of them had gone into the cowshed and Herr Esterbauer had yelled at them to come out, otherwise they'd disturb the cows, which would soon have their calves. The Russians had come out again and gone off into the field.

Herr Esterbauer shook his head again. 'They're moving in tomorrow or the next day. Mother's terrified. I tried to keep a bedroom for her but they're to have the whole of the upstairs.' He talked a lot about this, angrily, and Schosi's mama nodded, slow and weary. In between his ranting Herr Esterbauer sometimes touched her hand, or looked at her. They kept passing the bottle back and forth. 'I can't stand it. All I've worked for, and they take it from me.'

'We're treated lightly, compared to Germany,' said Schosi's mama. 'The posters in town call us "victims". I can't believe it.'

'And we will be, by the time Ivan's finished with us. They burn rubbish in my yard and make a mess of everything. They've taken away the women who work for me.'

'They're to go back to Poland, which is right and a good thing.'

'I'm to be ashamed then?'

'You're to admit what you've been part of.'

'And bear it as they laugh at me – as they rob me? Gita, be gentle.' He took her hand and a begging look came into his face. Her expression softened.

Schosi, feeling sleepy after his meal, rested his head on his arms on the tabletop, the room dim-lit and full of the adults' voices. He dreamed about the man shot in the back yard all that time ago, the body bucking and flipping behind the horse. He slept and when he woke his mama was on Herr Esterbauer's knee and their lips were pressed together. The farmer broke away from the kiss and held her face between his palms. 'Just marry me,' he said.

Schosi watched through one cracked eye, pretending to sleep. If they got married then Herr Esterbauer would be his new papa – Ursula had told him that. He thought again about being in charge of the herd. He would love to have a papa.

But his mama pulled her face free and said, 'It's no good, Erich. I'm sorry.' She climbed from his lap. 'I shouldn't have.' She moved away from the table and leaned against the sink, folding her arms, her body becoming small. Schosi had never seen her look like that, defensive and sad. 'I'm sorry,' she said again. 'It's just not right.'

'But why?' said Herr Esterbauer more loudly. 'You won't tell me. You won't tell me *why*. I want to know.'

Schosi sat upright; both adults looked at him. 'Why, Mama?' he echoed.

'Schatzi, be quiet, we're talking.'

'Get married?' he prompted.

His mama frowned then turned back to address the farmer but no words came, she only looked at him helplessly.

Herr Esterbauer made a noise like 'Bah!' and stood.

'I know you feel it like I do,' he said. 'It's not the reason. You won't say the reason. You kiss me like that – you do love me.' He put on his hat, collected his coat. 'It's not right, Gita, what you're doing to me.' He pointed his finger and shook it in the air. He moved towards her, dropping his arm to his side. He took her hand, pressed it. Schosi thought his mama would cry. 'Just think about it. Please. If you say yes, I can bear it all – all of this.'

35

The following Wednesday the Hildesheims went to the Rathaus as the Russian clerk had directed; Traudi was brought out in the pram, her first public outing. All the way to the village Dorli grumbled and complained. 'But what kind of work?' she kept asking. 'What type of work are we to do?'

Frau Hillier went with them, leaving Schosi at the farm with Herr Esterbauer. Ursula came too, even though she was still too young for work duty. Mama and Frau Hillier walked slowly at the back of the group. They whispered to each other, obvious in their concealment, but Ursula didn't take notice, nor did she care because a letter had come from Anton. It had arrived that morning with her name scrawled across the tattered envelope and a Viennese stamp. Mama had snatched it from her, not reading whom it was addressed to and thinking only of Siegfried. She'd torn it open. After scanning its contents she'd said, 'Stupid boy,' dropped the letter on to the table and walked away. Ursula seized it with shaking hands and pounding heart. The postmark was outdated by several weeks because the postal service was interrupted everywhere and the page was ragged at the edges and water-damaged, but it was legible. Tears trickled from her eyes as she read the thick ungainly hand; it felt good to hold a scrap of him. The message was short:

Dear Uschi
I've gone to meet the Red Army. I've got it all planned
out so don't worry about me. I won't let them get to
you. I'll soon be back. You're still my best girl.
Toni

After reading it she sat down for a while because her knees felt like water. She couldn't be sure what he meant by half of what he'd written. One thing was clear; he'd gone to the most dangerous of places, to the Front. What did he mean by having it all planned? Did he mean he planned to get safely away from the fighting? Or did he mean killing plans, dangerous plans, wild plans? Had he deluded himself that he could single-handedly hold the Russians off? But they were already here. Vienna had been besieged and occupied and many had died, the Soviets filling the city. He'd said he'd come home, but he had not. Did that mean he'd been killed or captured and sent to Siberia? Or was he even now on his way home? But then, if he came here, the Russians would surely seize him. Many boys had been arrested in other towns over the last few months, shot at dawn or sent to NKVD camps. Anton would find some way to make trouble, fight unwisely when he should give up. She saw again an image of his death, his precious body shattered amongst dust and rubble. She re-read the affectionate end to the note. He'd forgiven her; he wasn't angry. She was too relieved and grateful to notice that he offered no apology.

'Mama!' she called, needing comfort. She found her in the scullery, kneeling on the floor polishing shoes, her knuckles white. 'He's gone to the Front.' Ursula was unable to prevent her voice from breaking. 'I'm scared for him.'

'Foolish behaviour.' Mama rubbed furiously with her cloth till the brown leather gleamed. 'He insists on harming himself, on getting himself killed. I won't grieve. I won't.'

Ursula recoiled. How could she be so cold and unfeeling? Those were not the things a mother should say. Ursula was about to declare just this when she saw that tears were trickling down Mama's cheeks.

Things in the village were a little different than they'd been the previous week – there were more soldiers in the street, droves of them, it seemed, unpacking trucks, whistling, bickering over irritating tasks, feeding and grooming horses that stood in lines, the gutters clogged with the animals' droppings, the smell overpowering. Cyrillic lettering had been painted on to road signs beneath the German names and the swastika flags were gone from the houses, Soviet flags in their place, the red material reused by the residents – the angular black symbol had been cut away and replaced with yellow hammer and sickle.

'A spineless gesture,' commented Dorli beneath her breath.

The bakery and grocer's were serving again. Large sacks of beans on the pavement were spilling on to the road in a mess. The people queuing held bags and pots, or paper rolled into cones to contain the beans measured out by a couple of soldiers. It seemed there was a basic rationing system in place. The Gasthaus owner had written a hasty notice and propped it against the outer wall: *Russians welcome – beer and schnapps available.* Ursula peered inside as they passed; the walls were still covered with antlers and boar skins and bunches of dried flowers, but there were no SS guards from the camp smoking thin cigars. Russian soldiers perched on stools amongst the elderly regulars. They looked into their drinks and one soldier twisted a ring round and round on his finger.

On the Rathaus doors were posters in Russian and German celebrating May Day, Stalin, the Russian victory. Inside was a murmuring mass of people. Some were queuing at a table, manned by two Russians, who had papers spread out before them. Others were being organised into rows by a man wearing an armband of the Austrian flag with a hammer and sickle sewn on to it. He was a local and seemed to have been allocated as a supervisor of some description and was counting and recounting the people. Ursula spotted Frau Gerg, Frau Arnold and their friend Emmalina amongst the throng, and some of the Siedler family; the two daughters, round-faced and dark-haired, stood close together. Ursula felt immediately nervous, as she always did when she saw Frau Gerg.

'I'm surprised she's not been arrested for her role in the League,' whispered Frau Hillier. 'The Russkis are nothing if not completely inconsistent.'

'Wait at the door,' Mama said to Ursula as they entered, giving her charge of the pram.

Ursula sat on the steps beside the pram, the marble cold on her bare legs, while Mama, Frau Hillier and Dorli joined the registration queue. She held on to Anton's letter within the pocket of her dress and stroked the furred and rippled paper. Frau Sontheimer stepped past her outstretched legs and then Sepp came after her. He stopped when he saw Ursula. She quickly drew her legs in and pulled her dress down over her knees.

'Hello,' he said in his frank way. 'Are you signing up today?'

She shook her head. His face was sun-browned and lovely. She touched again the edge of the letter within her dress. Anton wasn't here to see her; this couldn't hurt him.

'You're not old enough, are you?' Sepp continued, squatting down beside her. 'I always forget you're a year younger than me.' One of his olive-gold knees almost touched her and she inched away. She could smell him, a warm, sweet scent like roasted chestnuts. 'You seem the same age,' he continued.

'Well, it's only a few months' difference.' She noticed that her fingernails were black with soil and hid them behind her skirts.

'I'm signing up, of course. Dunno what they'll have me doing.' He looked towards the queue. Frau Sontheimer was talking with Frau Hillier, and Mama had reached the front table; the Russian seated behind it was wearing an important-looking hat and smiling expansively. 'I was going to say when I saw you last time, before you ran off, do you fancy coming for tea one day?' He glanced at her then quickly away, gazing out at the street.

She was speechless for a moment. She had a feeling of falling, falling from the clifftop to the blaze of water beneath, disbelieving, overjoyed. But surely it couldn't be real. Marta and Sepp were sweethearts. He was asking only as a friend, nothing more. *Don't imagine he feels the same way*, the shadow in her thoughts cautioned and dissuaded. Why would he? Why would anyone? Anxiety rose in her throat; her heart began to pulse hard and a glow spread to her face. She felt suddenly trapped on the steps, too close, unable to hide.

She folded her arms. 'With all this going on?' she asked abruptly.

'Well, perhaps when it's calmed down a bit.' He looked embarrassed. 'Maybe then?'

'Maybe.' But she couldn't go. Of course she couldn't have tea with him in that tidy, pious house. Even as a friend, it would be dreadful and awkward just as before – how would she manage to be normal throughout an entire meal? Impossible. She'd nothing proper to wear and no idea about manners – she'd have to wash her feet before entering. Despite Frau Sontheimer's good nature, Ursula was sure she must think her whole family indecent. She grew overheated just thinking of it, picturing herself at the Sontheimers' table, trying not to besmirch the immaculate cloth; she'd be an ugly curiosity compared to the poised and pretty Marta who was probably a regular guest. 'But I'm really not allowed,' she added. 'I mean, thanks for asking.'

'All right,' he said, an uncomfortable silence descending. He trailed his fingers along a crack in the smooth marble step. A hint of suspicion came into his eyes. 'Is it because of your brother?'

'No!' She looked at him sharply.

'He doesn't like us talking together, does he? He doesn't like me.'

'Maybe he doesn't, I don't know.' The letter scratched against her leg as she moved and the paper rustled.

'I can tell – he doesn't.'

'Well, he told me you insulted him at the HY so perhaps that explains it.'

'I didn't!' Sepp's eyes were round. He stared at Ursula until her cheeks turned fierce red.

'You hit him or fought or whatever.' She heard the challenge in her voice. 'He said you were jealous because he got promoted. He said you hid a Russian prisoner in your house, and that he fought you about it. You shouldn't have done that – hidden a Bolshevik. That's what Anton said.'

Sepp's mouth opened in outrage. He shook his head, emphatic. 'No! That never happened.'

They were silent for a moment. Ursula tried to hide her confusion and dismay by averting her face.

'He's a ruddy liar!' Sepp burst out after a moment. 'He just wants to bring me down – he wants you to hate me too. He's started all sorts of rumours about me. I could never be jealous of him. I'm sorry for him, in fact, for his bad character.' He scowled, his face marred by a frown that drew his black brows together. 'I never touched him – I never even spoke to him! I didn't want to because he's nothing but trouble.'

Ursula stood and Sepp stood with her.

'He hasn't got a bad character,' she hissed. 'He doesn't *want* to speak to someone like you and he doesn't need your pity either.' Sepp *was* a no-good sort after all and Anton had known and tried to protect her. But even as

345

she thought it and saw Sepp baulk as if she'd whipped him with a fly swat, she knew it wasn't so. Sepp had every right to be angry; his words uncomfortably echoed those of Herr Esterbauer, the counsel he'd given to her in Vienna. But she couldn't say it, couldn't show it now. She stayed as she was, glaring, fists clenched.

'Never mind.' Sepp looked wounded. 'Forget it, it doesn't matter.'

She crossed her arms and leaned against the Rathaus wall, sullen with the beginnings of remorse. She wouldn't look at him; from the corner of her eye she could see that he stood with shoulders hunched, hands in pockets. Just then Marta appeared at the base of the Rathaus steps and began up towards them. She reached the top and immediately fixed Ursula with an aggressive stare, her chin raised like a territorial goose. 'Josef!' she cooed, her expression transforming to a sickly smile.

He turned and waved then faced Ursula again. 'See you,' he muttered. He moved off to join his aunt, Marta in tow.

Not long afterwards Ursula's family arrived, their registration complete, and she went with them out of the Rathaus, shame and regret making her steps slow and reluctant.

'What *is* it about that boy?' said Dorli, looking back and trying to get a view of Sepp. 'Whenever you see him you seem to be miserable afterwards or in some sort of panic.'

'Nothing,' said Ursula. 'It's not because of him. I'm fed up, that's all.'

'Fed up! You don't look fed up – you look ill!' Dorli smirked but didn't persist.

They began discussing work.

'I'm to stay on at the farm,' said Mama. 'Dorli too.'

'I'm back at the factory,' said Frau Hillier with a wry purse of her lips. 'Frau Sontheimer's there also. I'll try to stop them from working her too hard. She's not used to graft.'

'And to think you could get out of it,' said Mama to Frau Hillier. 'If you used your head.'

Frau Hillier gave an aggravated frown but otherwise the cryptic comment was ignored.

Dorli resumed her complaining. 'We get meals then instead of money?'

'We get breakfast and lunch,' said Frau Hillier. 'Which is certainly not to be sniffed at. What good is money after all?'

Emmalina exited the town hall just after the Hildesheims and walked close behind along the main street, scurrying within their shadows as if she was afraid to be seen. Adelind Gerg, Frau Gerg's daughter, was ahead, surrounded by a knot of Russian soldiers. As she walked the men capered alongside her, tugging her clothes and the ends of her hair. Adelind kept her head lowered and arms wrapped around her middle. Ursula felt sorry for her, even though she was a Gerg. The soldiers heckled her and made kissing noises as if to a dog.

Emmalina fell into step beside Mama. 'See that?' She indicated the besieged Adelind and the rowdy soldiers. 'There's worse to come. My cousin in Baden told me to watch out for this new lot, because they're nothing but pigs. The first soldiers weren't so bad. They were good people.'

'These aren't the same soldiers?'

'No. They arrived two days ago and are stationed here now as well. My cousin said many of them are recruited from Soviet prisons. They're a bad sort.' Emmalina continued to walk beside them until she was safely at her house. 'God preserve you,' she said, as she left them.

They went on, staying close to one another. The soldiers blocked the road ahead. Adelind reached her home and the men shouted comments as she climbed the front steps. One threw a pebble at the door as Adelind closed it behind her.

'Hey,' said a soldier as the Hildesheims and Frau Hillier passed. 'You married? Have husband?'

Ursula wasn't sure whom the questions were meant for, or whether they were aimed at the whole group.

'You like Russian kisses?' said another. As Frau Hillier passed he swung his gun like a cane and struck her across the backside. A few of them watched as the women and girls turned off the road on to the track.

36

The day was white above, featureless as a bed sheet, and a cool spring wind blew insistently along the road. Shop signs flapped and jerked and Ursula's clothes whirled around her body, strings of hair clinging across the wetness of her eyes and nose. After distributing identity cards to the residents of Felddorf in the Rathaus, the Russians had gathered the villagers in the road, every person over the age of four, which left the babies and toddlers unattended in their homes. The Russian soldiers were quiet and didn't speak to one another, formidable with guns angled across their uniformed chests, guarding the edges of the crowd.

The soldiers led them in a procession through the wire gates of the camp, which sagged forlorn into the trees after having been battered open the week before. Ursula, once inside, couldn't see much because the villagers choked the pathway with their numbers, slow-moving, their eyes rolling like jumpy cattle. Many of the women shielded their children's eyes beneath their shawls but the soldiers pulled the shawls away and handed them back to the women with shakes of their heads. To their left were the rows of wooden huts, mildewed and dank, creepers growing on the roofs like hair and darkness seeping up the planks from the ground. From the doors and windows of the huts peered the remaining inmates; also some of the Polish labourers, who were waiting to be transported home. Their faces were as bony as ever, there not being sufficient rations to fatten them. They came shuffling out of the huts like rickety marionettes and stood near by with blankets around their shoulders and socks on their feet. Each had the stripe of hair down the centre of their head, and short hair at the sides, which used to be shaved close but was now growing out. Ursula covered her nose with her scarf; a terrible smell of unwashed bodies came from them.

'Move along,' said a Russian soldier with a long coat and stars, one of the officers. He pointed down the grit path in the direction the villagers should go. More ghoulish figures came from the huts, and crowded forward to watch. Around Ursula, the people of Felddorf jostled and whispered and held on to one another – some of the old men who'd been in the Great War walked with regimental dignity, but most were hunched and obviously scared. The tall wire fence shook in the wind; it made the sound of coins in a pocket, a hectic metal clamour that filled the air and disoriented Ursula. Ahead there was a larger building and before it a heap of earth tall as a man and long as a truck. Beside it was the hole. The villagers were ushered into this area and instructed to be still and quiet; they coughed and groaned because filling the air was a sickening smell. The prisoners followed like shadows; there was some talking between them, mostly in Russian or Polish. Ursula thought it was odd to hear their voices now, which had been forbidden before. This time it was she who must be silent.

The soldiers arranged the villagers in a line, with the men in front. Russian soldiers stood ready around the hole at a distance of a couple of metres. 'Walk forward,' came the instruction. 'Single file.'

The men began to move, milling in a knot, none wishing to be in front.

'Walk forward!'

Herr Siedler, the rich farmer, took the lead. He wore his Sunday best with a sharp crease in his hat and a bright sprig of jay and pheasant feathers, which looked too jolly as he stomped towards the hole, his arms held tightly at his sides. The others followed – white-haired men: Herr Wemmel the grocer, several farmers, including Herr Esterbauer. There were a few who were younger and dark-haired. Marta's handsome father was one, and the former guards and men who'd run the factory – they'd been brought out from their imprisonment to join them. Herr Adler too had been brought out, both his eyes surrounded by black skin, swollen like plums just as Rudi's used to be. When the men reached the edge of the hole they were directed to look into it. They did so, a mismatched line, their trousers fluttering in the spring wind; a few put their hands over their nose and mouth. After a couple of minutes had passed, which felt much longer, the Russians moved them on behind the long mountain of earth, out of sight of the waiting women and children. Ursula could hear nothing of the exchange that followed as there was a lot of crying and hyperventilating amongst the cram of waiting villagers. Eventually, the men re-emerged. In pairs they carried bodies, sagging between them, one man gripping the ankles, the other the hands. Herr Esterbauer was paired with Herr Siedler, the corpse naked, thin and mottled, with a lolling head. Ursula watched Herr Esterbauer, his usually ruddy face greenish-white, his mouth stretched into a grin of horror. He struggled with the head of the dead man, which dangled loosely and dragged along the ground. 'Lift him!' snapped a nearby Russian. Herr Esterbauer lifted the arms he held as high as he could; he gasped and panted and his mouth fell open in a slack hole. Some of the villagers began to sob and a few women sat on the ground and yanked their children into the folds of their skirts. Herr Esterbauer and Herr Siedler carried the body to an area alongside the larger building, where soldiers met them and indicated a row of graves dug neatly in a line with crosses at the head. They lowered the body, using ropes, into a grave. They were waved away to wait beside the huts. Herr Esterbauer fell on to the ground, where he rested with face lowered.

Ursula was in the second group called to the graveside. Beside her sister and mother she looked into the hole. The corpses were about a metre and a half below, thirty or forty of them in a heap. The smell that rose from them was not just an ordinary smell, it was a foul soup, cloying and dense, that Ursula could feel in her nostrils. She breathed through her mouth and tried to close her nose to the air, but she could still taste the stench, sickly and awful.

'Our officers!' called a Russian. 'Our men shot here like dogs. You look!'

The skin of the dead people was discoloured and unnatural. Flies teemed across them and the frenetic movement of the insects created the illusion that some of the bodies themselves were moving. Faces peered from beneath an arm or a leg, some of the eyes open, some closed, the cheeks and lips wizened. Along the graveside somebody retched. Ursula thought she herself might vomit. She looked behind to see Herr Esterbauer still lying on his side, a flask of vodka being pressed to his mouth by a Russian. He was pulled upright and made to stand.

Ursula wondered if he was amongst them, the Russian that her brother had killed – and those that Herr Esterbauer had killed too. They might be buried at the bottom of the pile with a dozen bodies on top. At this thought coldness clenched her insides and wrung them tight. She held her breath but the feeling washed over her again and again – she felt faint and light, as though she might crumple or float away. She clutched Mama's arm. Vaguely she registered that she must be wrong, that those particular Russians couldn't be in this grave. The night of the escape from the camp was over a year ago, and the body of the Russian frozen in Frau Hillier's yard would be dust and bones by now. At this she felt relief, but then she thought that these other dead men were just the same, and that her brother had killed one, murdered a person just like this – had been celebrated for it. She began to cry and knew that she was making a lot of noise but couldn't stop. Her voice seemed separate from her, like a distant caterwauling from over the fields. She wanted to look away from the bodies but the Russians wouldn't allow it. Beside her, Dorli muttered and when Ursula looked up at her, her lips were framing Hail Marys.

'Move along!' commanded the Russian close by.

The people shuffled along the edge of the grave.

'Frau, move along!'

There was a disturbance further down the line. It was Frau Sontheimer, Sepp's aunt. She was weeping and not moving along. Sepp was holding her hand. A Russian soldier pulled her forcibly from the graveside and out of the way. She was placed beside the skinny tree near to Herr Esterbauer, still crying and hiding her face. Ursula caught Sepp's eye and he gazed back with a worried frown. Their group was sent to wait with the men, while the next lot of women came to the graveside. While all this went on, the prisoners watched intently, their shoulders touching, as if they found some paltry nourishment in what they saw.

For the rest of the day the grown-ups were made to dig new graves and lift and carry and lower bodies. Some of the younger children could not and stood together and waited, afraid and quiet. Schosi was given a spade but he stopped too often in his work and began twirling his comfort blanket, his mouth stretched over his teeth, and when a flock of crows flew over the camp cawing loudly he screamed and crouched on the ground. Eventually, the soldiers took away his spade. Once the graves were filled and covered and crosses placed at the head, all were directed to shovel soil into the large hole until it was no more. Ursula panted with exertion and her back ached and she observed sidelong as Frau Gerg with haughty disdain refused to cooperate and was hit in the stomach with the butt of a Russian gun, pushed to the floor and made to carry a dead man alone.

'Take gloves off! Take them off!' shouted the young Russian who guarded her. And so she was denied her gloves and handled the body with bare hands.

Ursula felt a flush of horrible triumph and perspired with the guilt of it. Beside her, Frau Hillier and Mama, shovelling silently, watched their enemy's punishment and degradation. Frau Hillier crossed herself and lowered her eyes. Schosi twirled his cloth around his fingers and released it and the material spun and spun.

37

In the early evening there was a loud knock at the front door and voices on the other side of the panels, in dispute it seemed, though it was difficult to tell because the Russian language often sounded argumentative. The door shook and the bolt rattled.

'Hello! Hello!'

The family were in the kitchen.

'Should we open it?' said Dorli.

'No,' said Mama, scooping Traudi from her basket. 'Stay where you are.'

A few minutes passed and everything went quiet. Then there was hammering at the back door, only a few feet from them. Traudi began to cry. Mama hushed her and tried to smother the noise with her cardigan but she kept on wailing, gaining volume.

'Hello!' A man's face appeared at the kitchen window. He stepped out of sight. Another bang on the back door, of something hard like a log or a stone, some loud Russian, then another bang and a splintering sound.

Dorli leapt to her feet. Mama yanked her arm and made her sit. 'Where will you go?' she whispered fiercely. 'Stay here. It's safer together.'

'Open the door!'

'We didn't put on all our clothes,' said Ursula. 'The refugees said we should put on all our clothes.'

'Get into the pantry,' said Mama. 'Quickly!' She pushed them towards the cupboard and bundled them in, closed the narrow door and dropped the latch. She dragged the easy chair so it obscured the entrance and then hurried back to the table.

Ursula pressed her eye to a crack and saw Mama push a cushion up the front of her dress so that she was transformed once again into a heavily pregnant woman. She answered the door with Traudi balanced on her hip.

'Why are you breaking my door?' she said, slowly and loudly. She pressed one hand to the small of her back, her belly thrust forward. The soldiers ushered her inside, talking in Russian and pointing their guns, trying to see beyond her into the kitchen. They surveyed the bare shelves and table, the meagre decor. Mama lifted the pan from the stovetop and tipped it towards them, showing them the contents; the remains of the potato stew from the day before. She smiled, only the tightness at the corners of her mouth giving her away. 'Take it. Take it,' she said.

The men peered into the depths of the pan, suspicious; their eyes flicked here and there. The smaller man sidled forward with his gun jabbing. 'Where is girls?' he said.

Mama feigned confusion. She gestured to Traudi. 'My daughter?'

The soldier shook his head. 'Other girls.' He looked into the hall; his gaze swept over the pantry door and Ursula drew back. Dorli crouched amongst the bags at the base of the shelves.

'No other,' said Mama. 'This is my daughter.'

The men conferred for a moment, tense and displeased, then they turned their attention to the pan on the stove. They made a gesture of eating. Mama darted to the drawer and scrabbled amongst the cutlery. She held out two spoons. With much clanging and banging, the men scoured the pan. When they were finished they slid the spoons into the basin.

'Eating,' said the taller soldier, pointing to his stomach. 'Bread.'

The only other food was in the pantry, which contained Ursula and Dorli. Mama shook her head and shrugged.

'Eating,' said the soldiers, taking a few steps further into the kitchen.

'Ah!' Mama exclaimed, and beckoned the men to follow her, smiling and inching out of the back door. The soldiers muttered to each other and then one of them went after her, while the other stayed in the kitchen. It was the taller soldier that remained. He leaned against the edge of the worktop and crossed his boots, scrutinising one corner of the room then another. The silence was complete and Ursula stayed as still as she could and prayed that Dorli would make no noise. The soldier began to explore the room, opening the drawer in the table as he passed. He rifled through the contents idly, picked out some letter-writing paper, a pen, Anton's pearl-inlaid letter opener and a small leather purse. He pocketed the things.

Mama returned with hair flattened to her skull from the sudden downpour that had begun outside, the soldier behind carrying jars of preserves. They were the ones from the shed, which they'd put aside as an emergency supply. Mama looked pale and shaken and forced her expression back to containment as she ushered both the men outside. The tall soldier touched Traudi's rain-wetted cheek as he left with a sentimental expression and said something softly in Russian. Then they went out of the door and jogged away, casting looks over their shoulders as they went.

'We come back!' shouted the shorter soldier, grinning through the rain, before turning and splashing across the yard, both disappearing into the hiss of the evening storm.

Together in their room, the girls got ready – Mama fully believed the soldiers' intention to return and expected another visit soon. Ursula put on several layers of underclothes, and wriggled into a dress. Her best dress, the one with the fewest repairs, went on next and she didn't care how she treated it, wrenching and yanking the fabric roughly. She put on two cardigans and wrapped a shawl around her head and face, and then several pairs of bloomers.

'Now, help me,' said Dorli.

Ursula buttoned Dorli into various garments until side by side they looked as fat as cooks. Ursula felt a fool in her bulky outfit, her arms sticking out from her sides and so many layers of material between her legs that she waddled when she walked. She quickly became much too hot.

'Do I need to wear all of it?' she asked Mama when they met on the landing.

'Yes! Of course you do.' Mama wore a bed jacket back-to-front and belted with a piece of cord over several skirts and dresses and two pairs of bloomers. She wore Papa's trousers too and the turn-ups showed beneath her hem.

They were all too nervous to have much of an appetite, except Traudi, who cried a lot and needed frequent feeding and changing after her day of being abandoned in the house. But they boiled something up for dinner in any case and the steaming pans were some reassurance. It was raining again and the water flew against the shutters, rushed into the water butts and drilled against the roof – an oppressive sound. Dorli sat at the table with her hands resting on her knees and her eyes cast down. She had an air of doom about her that Ursula found infectious. Ursula listened for the crash of an intruder and couldn't rid herself of the memory of the dead men in the grave. She sweltered in her clothing and almost wished that the Russians would just come, that whatever awaited her would happen quickly and be done with.

There was banging on the door just as they were eating. Ursula threw down her spoon and stood, ready to run. A woman's voice called from outside.

'Frau Hildesheim! Are you there?'

It was Frau Hillier.

Mama laboured in her many layers to the door. When Frau Hillier and Schosi entered the warm kitchen steam drifted from them; drips pattered from Frau Hillier's sodden and mud-splashed dress. Schosi stood almost on top of his mama, teeth chattering, his comfort blanket draped over his shoulder like a dead thing.

'What's happened?' said Dorli, aghast.

Frau Hillier smiled in a grisly kind of way. 'They got me. Sneaked up behind me and hit me on the head. They got me all right.'

Mama put a hand to her mouth and stared at her friend.

'Yes,' said Frau Hillier, but not very seriously. 'He was so young. He didn't even have facial hair. To think – an old thing like me.'

'Were they at your house?' said Mama.

'Yes. They went off with my food. I waited until it looked as though the way was clear then made a dash for it.'

Mama began to fuss. 'You'd better get out of those wet things.' She removed some of her clothes and handed them to Frau Hillier. 'And you, Schosi. You can wear something of Anton's.' She went to fetch a towel and a couple of blankets.

'Did he – you know—?' asked Dorli once Mama had left the room.

Frau Hillier nodded.

'Was it awful?'

'I suppose it was.'

Mama reappeared and showed Frau Hillier into the scullery so she could undress in private. She emerged wearing an odd assortment of Mama and Dorli's clothes. She had on a dress that was too small, undone at the front with a scarf wrapped around her bodice to conceal the gap. Then she put on two cardigans, the outer one on backwards. She turned so that Mama could do up the buttons. Schosi had been given a pair of trousers of Anton's, long woollen itchy things that he wore in wintertime. He'd also borrowed a dry shirt and jumper. He huddled against the stove.

After an hour or so, and Frau Hillier and Schosi had eaten, they all went upstairs. Mama brought the rifle and put it under the bed. The three Hildesheims lay tightly together, Traudi on the rug on the floor beside Mama. Frau Hillier and Schosi used Anton's old bed. Ursula stared at the ceiling and couldn't sleep; her sister squirmed against her. The many layers of clothing were uncomfortable, strangling around her legs, arms and waist. The pinched faces of buried Russians moved against the dark as though lifted on a wave. The more she tried to expel them, the larger they loomed and the sweet smell of decay seemed to enter the room so that she had to draw breath through her mouth. She turned and nestled against her sister, but it wasn't a comfort, because Dorli's body hummed with anxiety and exuded heat. She could feel her rapid pulse and the shallowness of her breath. Ursula turned back the other way. She slipped into dreams and came out of them again, because they were worse than the imaginings. Eventually, she slept.

She woke when Dorli and Mama sat up in bed. There had been a loud noise – Ursula had registered it in her sleep.

Mama swung her legs out of the bed. She twisted to look at her daughters, listening. 'Someone's at the door.'

There was another crash at the front door, and then at the back door. Dorli put her arms around Ursula, which was an unusual thing for her to do, and Ursula supposed she must be out of her wits with fright. She began to whimper. The banging kept on and on and the shouting too. Ursula watched her mother for a sign of what they should do, but she seemed frozen, her profile an unmoving outline in the dark room, like a statue or a drawing.

38

Frau Hillier lifted the latch of the bedroom door and came in while the din from downstairs continued, guiding Schosi before her. He stuttered terribly, winding his piece of material and moving around, pacing in front of the windows. Frau Hillier perched on the end of the bed and she and Mama clasped hands. There was a metallic clatter. It was unmistakably the sound of the bolt flying off and striking the tiles. It skated the length of the hallway. The door crashed inwards and Russian accents filled the house. Frau Hillier went over to Schosi and held him by the shoulders to keep him still but he struggled free and went to Ursula and bent to look into her face, stammering something she didn't understand, about a cart in a yard and being dead under a blue blanket. She pushed him away – he didn't seem to realise what was happening and his frantic eyes scared her.

The voices in the hall gained volume and glass splintered somewhere below, maybe in the kitchen or in the living room, it was difficult to tell. Dorli began to cry – Mama pressed a hand over her mouth as boots thundered on the stairs. Ursula could hear every word spoken by the soldiers but understood nothing.

There was knocking and pounding on one of the bedroom doors, not theirs. A latch was lifted. 'Hello!' a soldier called. 'Women, hello!'

Mama snatched the rifle from below the bed, levelled it at the door.

'Be careful.' Frau Hillier pushed the gun barrel down. 'They'll be armed.'

The floor vibrated with heavy footfalls as the soldiers explored the adjacent bedrooms, including Anton's, where Frau Hillier and Schosi had been moments before.

'Can we not get out of the window?' Frau Hillier darted to the shutters and opened them, then unfastened the casement. Damp air entered bringing the smell of the fields. Schosi tugged Frau Hillier's sleeve repeatedly, stuttering. 'Quiet!' She cuffed him around the head. He fell silent.

Mama got up and lifted Traudi, who was awake and wide-eyed. She left the rifle on the bed and joined Frau Hillier. Frau Hillier put her leg out of the window and began to lower herself, feeling with her toes for a branch of the apple tree.

'Am I close?' she panted.

Mama leaned out. 'A few more centimetres.' She grabbed Dorli's sleeve. 'You next!' The bedroom door opened. Gun muzzles swept over them. 'Quick! Quick!' She shoved Dorli towards the window. Dorli struggled in her bulky layers to get her foot on the sill. Mama grasped her by the ankle, wrenched it higher.

'Stop!' A Russian soldier crossed the room in two strides and seized Dorli. His comrades followed, a jostling crowd, filling the room. There were six or seven men, two of whom Ursula recognised as their visitors from earlier in the evening – they held bottles that were nearly empty; their bodies moved with the slack easiness of drunks and they talked hectically, fingers resting on triggers. One had a torch and pointed it into each face, the beam loitering on Dorli, Mama and Ursula, passing over Schosi as though he wasn't there.

A soldier with a broad flared nose and whiskered cheeks snatched Ursula's arms and held her in a rough grip. She didn't struggle or cry out; she tensed, motionless. He twisted her wrists till they burned and forced her on to the bed, her face not far from the rifle.

Dorli meanwhile was hauled backwards by the skirt, her captor deliberately unbalancing her as she pawed at the windowsill, hopeless as a spider in a bathtub.

'Get off!' Mama slapped at the Russian's arms, a wobbling Traudi clinging to her shoulder. 'Let go!' Another soldier barged Mama out of the way. She staggered and cupped the baby's head. Ursula wanted to call to her but there were no sounds, only a strange shadowy stillness in her limbs and thoughts.

Frau Hillier was found dangling from the window ledge, balancing on a branch. She was dragged inside, her laughter high-pitched and frightening – the window was violently slammed. Hands gripped Ursula's chest, the sore flesh of her new breasts. The shadow in her thoughts struggled; a writhing shape at the edge of sight set up a cry; her own voice was mute.

Dorli's assailant kicked her ankles from beneath her and she hit the floor with a crash. He drew out a short-bladed knife, knelt and pulled up her skirts. With a few strokes he cut through the layers of bloomers and ripped them entirely away. Ursula averted her eyes from her sister's nakedness. Mama was accosted too – Traudi had been wrestled from her grip and another knife was put to speedy use. She was shorn of her clothes like a sheep in springtime. The flop of her breast set Ursula's face ablaze. She'd never seen Mama without underwear – the flesh was pale and the nipple dark and rude. There was an atmosphere of awful inevitability, dirty like going to the toilet in front of each other.

'Shame on you,' said Mama as she was struck to the ground.

Dorli's young soldier was clumsy and his uniform impeded him, a water bottle dangled and got in the way and he kept swinging it behind only for it to come windmilling back around to strike his front or the side of Dorli's hip. A magazine of bullets sagged from his chest and snagged in Dorli's cardigan so that he had to pull the bullets off over his head to free himself. They rattled on the floorboards and lay around Dorli's head like a crown. The Russian holding Ursula called to the younger soldier, as though giving instructions. Within a few seconds he fell from Dorli, leaving her exposed and grappling for clothes to cover herself. The man holding Ursula howled with mirth and exclaimed boisterously to the exhausted young soldier. He pressed Ursula deeper into the mattress.

When the man pulled her underwear to her knees she remembered in an instant how it felt to be a baby, manhandled and bared – a hot-cold fire burned across the surface of her body. Was it shame, anger, fear? The shadow grew larger, clearer, driven from hiding. The soldier's uniform was rough as coarse hair, sharp as twigs, as stones beneath the snow; her face was pushed into the eiderdown; she fought for breath.

The sensations that followed were a vivid blaze of pain. Through her mind flashed past injuries, the kitchen knife that cut her finger, the flesh parted and bloody as though it would never fit back together. Or when skin and tissue had ripped when she'd fallen from her skis, a gory hole in her knee that swelled and wouldn't heal for weeks so that she walked with a stiff leg. She couldn't mount the stairs without someone to steady her, hopping like a crippled frog. Perhaps it was the same, she thought, screwing shut her eyes. A bad thing happening to her body that afterwards would mean nothing at all, like a beating or a tumble down the riverbank. The shadow pressed close and whispered, accusatory, that it was more than that; it was sin. Much worse than the time she'd skinned her palms, scrabbling to be free, had escaped calamity, but only after he'd given his blaring shout, swallowed by the snowdrifts. She'd let it happen then too, lain still. Why didn't she struggle? he'd demanded, furious. But what would struggling do? She twisted her head to look out, to glimpse the freshness of the air outside. Framed by the window was a bright moon caught in the branches of the apple tree.

𝔍𝔢

The house was smashed; anything expensive or decorative was taken or destroyed. The food was gone, what there was of it. The Hildesheims and Hilliers gathered after a cursory wash in the rain butts and a change of clothes, though Dorli refused to get out of her torn things. Mama repeatedly professed the wish that she was dead, spoken through thick and bloodied lips. Ursula was afraid to look at her and avoided her eye – her face was much worse than when Papa used to bash her. Frau Hillier took the lead. They'd go to Herr Esterbauer. He'd know what to do. They put on warm things and set off.

The fields were a soggy expanse, no longer a familiar place but a landscape drained, as they all were, and full of danger and disorienting things. Ursula couldn't walk fast because there was sharp pain between her legs and each time Schosi shuffled near to stroke her shoulder she withdrew abruptly and her heart began its feverish drumming – her very skin recoiled from touch after the stifling and crushing of the soldier's body.

'Little bear,' he murmured. 'Little bear.'

They went onwards in fits and starts, Frau Hillier quietly offering encouragement, and finally came to Herr Esterbauer's place. They paused behind the barn in a patch of black shadow. Many Russians were billeted here, maybe even some of the ones who'd attacked them. They went together to the front door of the farmhouse, tiptoeing like fugitives. The shutters weren't closed and the unlit windows reflected their faces as Frau Hillier tapped on the pane. The farmer now slept in the kitchen area on a stack of cushions and blankets; Ursula saw a bulky shadow detach itself from the floor and approach the window. Herr Esterbauer's face appeared then disappeared; he opened the door.

'What's the matter? Are you all right?' He was fully dressed with thick woollen socks pulled high over his trouser legs.

'Please can we stay here tonight?' said Frau Hillier, voice quivering. 'We've had a terrible time.'

'What happened?' He sounded angry and stared at Mama's swollen face. Ursula felt nervous in case he called them names or sent them away.

'Please don't ask,' said Frau Hillier.

He said nothing more.

The next morning he waved them off from the top of the hill. He found it difficult, it was clear from his grave expression and his lengthy goodbye, but they couldn't stay amongst the Russians at the farm; they all felt they must slip away soon after dawn. 'We'll meet again tomorrow,' he said, 'and share a drink.' He regarded Frau Hillier with a tragic frown; she looked everywhere but at him. 'You mustn't be alone – stay together in one house. And keep a gun to hand.' He looked truly wretched. 'I'd come with you but Mother can't manage without me. I'll call on you later today.'

They set off along the forest edge, back through the fields cottony with mist, and on to the track, walking in a tight knot and glancing around all the while for signs of trouble. At the turn in the track Dorli tripped and grazed her knees. She knelt on the ground for a full minute with her head in her hands like an overwrought child.

There was a lot to be done and the morning was taken up with chores – no time yet for sleeping or bathing. They couldn't rest until the house was theirs again; broken glass must be swept, the bedroom scrubbed clean. Traudi was the only one who was happy and played amongst the mess. Ursula found it a comfort to watch her and tried to stay in the same room as much as possible, but Mama often took her off and kept her to herself, cuddling and feeding her for long periods of time. Ursula noticed that Mama showed her breast when feeding the baby, which she'd never done before, and there were red marks all over the white skin, bruises and dried blood.

Afternoon came and Herr Esterbauer didn't call. Ursula and Dorli collected edible things from the verges – sorrel, dandelions, chickweed and nettles. They added them to the stew that Mama and Frau Hillier made. The only foodstuffs that the Russians had left behind were half rotten and needed laborious preparation. They'd even stolen the rabbits. Frau Hillier lit the oven, which took an age as it kept dying as though it too was tired and confused. Eventually the fire was built, and it felt good to have the warmth and crackle of the spitting logs. Dorli crushed herbs on the board with a stone, hair hanging in ropes. Frau Hillier and Mama picked through the potatoes, whittling away bad flesh and throwing the misshapen remains into the stew pan. No one went to fetch water: they'd settled for drinking from the trout stream, or the river. It needn't be said that they wouldn't venture as far as the village.

Ursula ate hungrily that day. She wanted her strength for whatever lay ahead. They hadn't collected any rations so they broke into their storage box in the cellar and opened a few jars of preserves. They devoured the stew, which was hot and thick and filling. Frau Hillier ate with them and apologised many times for being a drain on their resources; she promised that as soon as she could bring a contribution she would do so. Mama silenced her with an impatient hand, though Ursula watched the food disappearing into Frau Hillier's mouth with regret.

At about five o'clock two Russians forced the door with an iron bar. At first Ursula thought it was the same men from the previous night, but these were older, grizzled and grey-haired. One of them, with a thin face and scabbed lip, dragged a bandaged foot. The other had bristling grey hair and a square-shaped jaw. They located Ursula and Dorli. Gusts of alcoholic breath came from them. The larger soldier seized Dorli and the other wrenched Ursula's arm behind her back. The man holding Dorli pointed his gun, one-handed, directly into Mama's face. Ursula was terrified he'd accidentally press the trigger: he didn't look very much in control of his movements.

Mama raised her hands, kept still as stone. The girls were marched to the cowshed where the animals chewed and gently knocked their hooves on the straw-covered ground.

As the Russians left, the larger man slung one of the kids, bleating and struggling, over his shoulder, then the sisters lay for a while before going inside, listening to the fading cries of the baby goat separated from its mother.

Mama bathed them in the kitchen, washing their bodies with warm water and soft cloths. They were helped into bed. Frau Hillier prepared tea made from mint she'd harvested from the watery ditches.

'This will make you safe,' she told them, brushing hair from their foreheads. 'It's best to be careful – even you, Uschi. You must drink it regularly for a while.'

Dorli sipped her drink. 'I'm thirsty,' she kept saying, 'I'm so thirsty,' her face oily with sweat, and then quickly she was asleep, her breath leaving her in abrupt, deep exhalations.

40

Over the next week there were two further attacks, both at night. They drank the mint tea four times daily and deliberated about whether it would be best to hide in outdoor places, especially the girls; it might be safer than the house. In the daytime, Ursula accompanied Schosi, Mama and Dorli to work so as not to be alone; she minded Traudi while they laboured on the farm.

Herr Esterbauer went to one of the commanders to complain about how the soldiers behaved, but he was dismissed. 'Come! Our boys only have a little fun. It's a hard war for them. Do they really hurt anyone?' Herr Esterbauer assured the sardonic, black-haired commander that the soldiers did very much hurt his neighbours, who lived far from any witnesses – that the troops were drunk and dangerous. He was sent packing with a warning not to make trouble again.

Whenever the Hildesheims were at the farm Herr Esterbauer asked them how Frau Hillier was. How they all were. And they learned to tell him nothing because he became mad with anger, shouting, 'If only I could do something!' and raged and cursed against the Russian rapists, slammed his fists, said he couldn't bear to think of it, lapsed into depressed silence. Schosi sobbed in alarm when this happened and Herr Esterbauer growled at him to dry his tears. 'Just speak to that mother of yours! And make her see sense.'

'You should have said yes,' said Mama to Frau Hillier over breakfast one morning. She took bread from the basket and spread fat across it, fat that Herr Esterbauer had sent the previous day. Schosi had delivered the gift along with another plea for Frau Hillier to reconsider. But Frau Hillier wouldn't eat the fat or agree to the marriage. Mama muttered something about her stupidity, her cruelty, that Herr Esterbauer couldn't be expected to understand seeing as she'd explained her reasons to no one. 'You could be away from here. You could be protected.'

'You want me gone then?' Frau Hillier's eyes burned.

'Don't be such a *Dummkopf*!' Mama set her knife down with a clang. The two women faced one another like cats. Ursula allowed Schosi to take her hand beneath the table, his palm clammy. 'I just feel sorry for him. You don't tell me anything. It's so stubborn!'

'And why would I, when you blame and make judgements? Perhaps you miss your man and think I'm ungrateful. Is that it?'

'I can't listen to your stupid talk.' Mama sounded rather childish. 'All I know is you've made him miserable – I see it every day. It's pitiful. You can't—' She glanced at Ursula and Dorli then continued. 'You can't lead him on with kisses and God knows what else and then—' She stopped again. Schosi was transfixed, rocking in his seat. 'Your son needs a father. You should think of him.'

Frau Hillier threw down her napkin, stood up and walked halfway towards the door. 'You've so many opinions! My son is everything to me. I do everything for him.'

'You can barely feed yourselves – you rely on us.'

'We'll go then! It's clear we're no longer welcome.' She swept from the room.

'Madness!' exclaimed Mama as soon as Frau Hillier slammed the front door to make her way to the factory. 'What I wouldn't give!' She seemed to be squawking, amongst the subdued and listening children. 'He gambles and neglects his work, even his mother, and all because of her.'

Ursula wondered if this was quite accurate. There were other reasons Herr Esterbauer was unhappy. And it was unfair to make Frau Hillier feel unwelcome when she'd nowhere to go. Her house had been spoiled by the Russians; they'd broken in, smashed the windows, set fire to the kitchen, perhaps by accident, no one knew, and taken what little was there. Frau Hillier and Schosi wouldn't be able to go back until it was repaired.

They got ready for work and Ursula dressed in her ugliest clothes, concealing her figure with large shawls. She helped Dorli to push a pillow up the back of her coat to imitate a hunchback. Schosi became more cheerful – he always found this process hilarious, especially when they scooped redcurrant jam with their fingers and rubbed it over their faces as though it was a lotion. It created the look of weeping sores. He observed Ursula closely as she tied a scarf over her head in the style of an old woman and screwed up her eyes into as many wrinkles as she could; he wrinkled his eyes too and she was glad to giggle with him, to forget for a moment what the strange attire was for.

'I'm going to have a new papa!' he crowed, his voice cracking between the tones of a man and a boy.

'You're not!' She pushed him playfully. 'Cos your mama's a silly goose.'

He lunged for her and licked her sweet-tasting face.

'Have some decency, girl!' snapped Mama. 'You're not an animal.'

Ursula pushed Schosi off and told him not to. She stung from the rebuke. How could Mama care about such things after all that had happened? To her it felt only right to be squalid. Her mood plummeted sharply: she was oppressed by her unsightly clothes, the repulsiveness, inside and out, and wished that somehow she could become nothing – wiped away – nothing at all.

That evening Mama took her daughters to one of Herr Esterbauer's remoter fields where a haystack stood far from any house. They went under the cover of darkness with a small lantern to see their way across the ditches.

'Don't be scared, my dears,' said Mama, petting them. 'Use the hay to keep warm and stay quiet till morning.'

Ursula took one of the blankets from her knapsack and arranged herself amongst the damp hay; she tried not to think about slugs, snails and spiders. She wrapped the blanket tightly around her body and tucked it beneath her behind. Dorli pressed close and Ursula was glad of her sister's solid presence. Mama handed them the lantern, a jar of stewed apple and a portion of bread, then kissed their heads. 'Don't use the light if you don't have to. Be invisible.' She said goodbye before setting off into the night.

Ursula sat awake a long time, listening; it grew cold and dewy and there were creatures in the field, hares and foxes and mice, and the stars increased in number until the sky was full, pregnant with milky light, and they looked cold and unforgiving, surveying what was below, not caring about their plight. A moon glided upwards, free to sail, no longer trapped in apple branches, she thought. She studied its shadowed face, its shadowed eyes; was it God gazing down at her, listening to her like she was listening? Or something else? The accusing stare – her brother's blaming look. They hadn't kept her safe, she realised, neither God nor Anton. They watched over her, not kind but jealous and judging, just as Mama was jealous and judged Frau Hillier. But this was a much darker thing.

Wings flickered. A bat gave its almost inaudible call. Dorli huddled closer, took Ursula's hand; it felt good to be held. They stayed with arms entwined beneath the blankets, the outside of the wool now coated in moisture. Mama would come at first light and then another day at the farm. Who knew what would occur? Would a Russian wait outside the outhouse again and when Ursula emerged sidle near and show her a palm full of money?

'I have somewhere to go,' he'd said.

'Bleeding, bleeding,' she'd replied, running as fast as she could to her family.

As the shadow-eyed moon climbed Ursula drifted, half waking, half sleeping, her thoughts on her brother and the letter he'd written, which was stowed in her knapsack. She prayed that God would at least not abandon him. He must come back, she thought blearily. But she was afraid too. Could she keep such secrets? Would he see how she'd changed? And if he didn't come back? If he never returned, what would that be like? The rock that had smashed the ice at the river pool, the black scar after it sank: it would be like that, she thought. Exactly like that.

'Good day,' said the officer, lifting his hat.

It was a Sunday afternoon and the family were in the Hildesheim garden. Frau Hillier stopped her work and straightened.

'Grow vegetables,' said the man with a smile. He was big as a bear and his thick blond hair stood up in tufts. His eyes were light blue and his eyebrows white. Ursula remembered him from the first day the Russians had arrived – he was the broad officer who'd taken her loaf for his men. He came around the fence to stand closer to them. 'My name Efim.' He bowed slightly, the introduction directed at Dorli who stood beside Ursula wearing muddy gardening gloves. 'I have record – play music. I have food. Chocolate.' He gave a hopeful smile. 'I come tonight?'

What could he be thinking of? thought Ursula. Talking to them as if they were chums. Dorli looked at Frau Hillier with a silent plea.

'No, no, sir. Go away!' Frau Hillier flapped her hands.

The officer bowed again. He backed away. Frau Hillier continued to shoo him. Eventually he walked off down the track at a leisurely pace, throwing glances over his shoulder. Of course he'd persist, thought Ursula, because it didn't mean anything to say no.

Later, as they cleaned their tools in the stream and Ursula began to watch the sinking sun fearfully, Frau Hillier broke the silence.

'You girls wouldn't have to sleep in the field any more,' she said. She was contemplative as she scraped soil from the trowels. 'It's making you ill.' It was true that Ursula had developed a harsh cough and Dorli was always on the verge of being unwell. 'He'd bring food and at least some safer companions.' She eyed them, her expression furtive. 'You've heard about the Siedler daughters.'

Dorli drew back. 'I don't want to be like them! They're as good as prostitutes.'

Ursula wondered what Frau Hillier could be driving at. The Siedler girls were despised and called Bolshevik whores.

'Would you rather be fair game for the whole pack?' said Frau Hillier. 'He's one of the better ones.'

Dorli's cheeks flamed. She didn't reply.

At dinnertime Mama was informed about the encounter. After eating she went into the living room with Dorli. They were in there for half an hour and when they came out it was obvious they'd both been crying. Dorli appeared persuaded, though she was dejected and ate very little. Frau Hillier commented that it was a good job Dorli was naturally well built, because the officer preferred her over the rest, who'd become scrawny and unattractive. At this Mama straightened in her chair and glared. Frau Hillier fell silent.

The following evening Efim the officer returned with three more Russians; one of them Ursula recognised as the bookish clerk who'd called at the house about work duty. His small stature and calm bespectacled face were unthreatening and Ursula was surprised to find that she liked him immediately. Everyone in the household had dressed and washed in readiness. Mama had braided Dorli's hair and wrapped it around her head in an elegant style. Ursula stayed close to Schosi, linking arms with him as he twisted his comfort blanket and let it loose to tickle her legs. In the living room the soldiers seemed oversized and awkward amongst the low chairs and settle and what was left of the decorative trinkets. The glass in the cabinets was gone, but Mama had chipped away the broken remains so you could hardly tell there was nothing in the frames. When the soldiers sat, their knees bent double and the springs squeaked and groaned, especially under the bulky officer. Ursula hung about on the edge, the situation unlike anything she'd known. She spied some tins of fish in the clerk's satchel and when he opened his bag further she saw two records and a bottle of clear alcohol with a Cyrillic label. Mama dragged the small table in front of the chairs and the clerk set all the things on it, nodding and smiling. Ursula crept closer. She tried to see what the records were but they were in their card sleeves and she couldn't tell. The officer picked one up and offered it to her.

'Play! Play!' he prompted.

She was too shy to take it; Frau Hillier went with it to the gramophone, which had been retrieved from its hiding place in the cellar. She wound the handle for a while and put it on. Brassy Soviet music filled the room. Meanwhile Dorli arranged herself on one of the empty chairs. The men smiled at her and at Ursula and at the rest of the women but there was no leering or attempt to touch them. They got out a pack of cards and Mama produced the schnapps glasses. Soon drinks had been poured and cans of fish were opened and dished out on to plates. With the music and the clinking of glasses the room gained quite a pleasant atmosphere. Ursula was sure the music was doing her good, healing her like a kind of medicine; it reverberated in the floorboards and at her side Schosi hummed tunelessly and bobbed up and down. The men spoke in Russian amongst themselves but generally made an effort to converse in German. Mama accepted a glass of alcohol. Frau Hillier did likewise. It wasn't long until Dorli was smiling. The clerk, who was called Pasha, sang and stamped his boot to a particularly rousing section of the music. Ursula began to enjoy herself; it would be wonderful to sleep in a bed tonight. She'd come to dread the cold, quiet haystack and never resting well; her body ached with tiredness and her head longed for a bolster.

'You like cards?' said the officer.

'Oh, why not?' said Frau Hillier. 'You have to take fun where you find it these days.' She looked at Mama. 'Isn't that right, Frau Hildesheim?'

Mama smiled slightly and Ursula hoped that they'd soon be friends again – a tension had remained between them since their row about Herr Esterbauer. The Russians dealt amongst the fish bones and tails, and they began a complicated game, which produced some restrained laughter. By the end of the game, the others had had several more glasses of the alcohol and there was quite a bit of chatter. Ursula perched on the arm of Mama's chair, sipping some schnapps of her own, and watched her sister trying to avoid the glances of the increasingly tipsy officer. At one point, the soldier called Immanuil, a young man with prominent eyes and bad skin, put his arm around Ursula's waist but the officer instantly became stern, rebuking the soldier in Russian. The arm was withdrawn.

'No have fear,' Efim told Ursula.

She tried to relax. But she couldn't, not entirely. The snaking arm had reminded her that, despite the merriness that now prevailed, something less pleasant awaited. She monitored Immanuil closely; he seemed to be getting drunk. The soldiers who'd attacked them had invariably been drunk. She watched for signs that he might be transforming. At one point a cigar rolled off the table and nearly set light to the rug – Mama dived to retrieve it and there was a black mark where it'd fallen.

'Sorry,' said Immanuil. 'Sorry, Frau.'

Mama laughed and said it was really the least of her worries, and as long as they didn't burn the house down they could do what they liked.

After a few hours, when most of the alcohol had been consumed, the officer began to mutter restlessly to his companions. The three other soldiers stood and said thank you and could they please have a bed for the night downstairs. Mama went off to fetch blankets from the linen cupboards, and some bolsters. Frau Hillier bundled Schosi off to bed saying she'd see them all in the morning. She gave Dorli a meaningful look before going upstairs. Ursula was nudged painfully in the ribs and told to get to bed. It was past midnight and she was very drowsy, struggling to keep her eyes open.

'Will she be all right?' she whispered to Mama as they went together up the stairs.

'Hush, now,' said Mama, trying to seem cheerful and unruffled. 'She'll be fine. We'll all be fine tonight. Get some sleep, Schatzi.'

But it wasn't fine; a while later Immanuil came to Ursula's bed.

41

The war ended officially in early May, though there wasn't much sign of it. It felt as though the battle had been lost weeks before. Mama and Frau Hillier prayed that Siegfried's life had been spared, kneeling together before the crucifix, and Ursula added her own plea for Anton. Dorli's reaction was euphoric. It was Klaus, Klaus, Klaus each minute of the day as she set about preparing for Herr Oberndorfer's return, which was downright peculiar in Ursula's opinion, given the situation. The Russians had moved in the previous week bringing boxes and crates full of personal equipment, clothes, alcohol and food; the bedrooms had been reorganised. Initially, the officer and his men had used Anton's old room but it wasn't long until Dorli was poached and installed in the officer's bed and the men displaced to makeshift quarters on the living-room floor. Ursula slept in with Mama to be out of Immanuil's way and Frau Hillier and Schosi shared what had been the girls' bedroom.

Much of Ursula's time was taken up with trying to avoid Immanuil. Whenever he passed her and there was no one to witness him, he put his hand between her legs. She'd learned to dodge him with an abrupt twist of her body. He stalked her through the house and his heavy breath at her back took on a nightmarish quality, a constant menace and intrusion. She was often too busy to evade him. There were chores to be done and animals to care for and Mama wouldn't stand for shirking. If ever she left the house for the cowshed, even as she took the first few strides across the yard, she could predict the click of the latch behind as he slipped out to follow. If she was quick she could reach the shed ahead of him, push the door closed and drop the bar from the inside. Safe then until she'd finished her milking. Best of all was if she could bring Schosi with her. Still Immanuil would wait, patient as a hound as she perspired within, other memories filling the cowshed, the hush of the animals mixed with the grunt and rustle of men, their curses and spit and the unclean smell of them amongst the straw. Having Schosi near helped to ease it, restored the tranquillity of the place somewhat, even when Immanuil's fingers appeared beneath the door, travelled the wood like the ponderous legs of a spider, searching for an entrance, gripping and lifting the cracked and worm-riddled planks, thankfully to no avail. Schosi would point and whisper, 'Look!'

When she emerged Immanuil would snatch her arm. 'Come to bed,' he'd say, and her heart would sink, feeling it was somehow inevitable, remembering his puppyish pleading on that first night, which when she'd ignored it had turned to threats and hands pinning her legs apart. She'd silently borne it. What other way was there? Then she thought of Anton when he'd pushed her into the bed with his hands around her throat. They'd only been children then but both had understood; he throttled her for doing nothing. She fought a little after that, clobbered Immanuil's shins with the milk churn, making him hop backwards. If there was no way of doing this, if he held her too tightly, burrowing at her private parts, then she had to wait until he released her, his pimpled face flushed, eyes sly. He always did release her – so far – allowed her to walk away, his fists clenched. He was a coward. But if he ever did find his courage, or his chance, she feared he'd use a wire around her neck or some other gruesome thing.

The other two men were no real bother. Pasha liked to lie in the living room, reading a book and picking his nose when he thought he was unobserved. He had a box of fine-looking volumes, some of which were in German. Frau Hillier said this meant they were stolen, which made him a scoundrel. He sometimes read aloud to Ursula and she sat, captivated, not having been read to in this way since Frau Wilhelm had done so in her city flat. She enjoyed the novels best, but she also liked the essays, even the parts she didn't understand. She enjoyed the shape of the words, lovingly strung together into pleasing garlands of sound, and the serious way Pasha spoke, glancing at her to check she was paying attention. Pasha also befriended Schosi and invited him to smoke each evening in the yard. One day, he presented Schosi with a wristwatch, which delighted him and sealed the bond. Frau Hillier was indignant about the tobacco at first, but she soon saw how much it pleased her son and how he loved to stand with the Russian, his hand thrust in his pocket in imitation of him. They spoke little, but stood under a cloud of exhalations and watched the sky. Schosi seemed to grow as a direct result of these new freedoms; the sustenance they brought to his soul also nourished his sixteen-year-old body. He became noticeably taller and thicker in the limbs as the weeks went by.

The other soldier was Viktor, a stringent, anxious fellow with a high fluty voice, who hadn't been here on that first visit and spent much of his time doing army business over the Russian military radio now housed in the shed. He always gripped the mouthpiece very tightly so that his knuckles went white, and Ursula noticed that there was rarely a reply, no sound came from the receiver, apart from a dry hiss. Viktor didn't speak a lot of German and kept his mouth shut in the evenings, a quiet uneasy presence. Efim had told Dorli that Viktor was shell-shocked. Ursula knew this had something to do with bombs, and that the sheer noise of a blast could send a man out of his mind. He did seem to live in another world. He wandered in the night, dragged the table flush to the wall in the kitchen and sat beneath it till morning. She found him there once when she was the first to come downstairs. He peered from between the table legs, wearing his helmet. He said nothing so she left him alone. Soon after, Efim came to coax him out.

At the farm, Dorli chattered to Ursula about Klaus. She'd beckon her to accompany her on her next task and Ursula would sigh, knowing that she was to be a listening post again. While she helped to clean out the chicken shed, to net the fruit bushes, to knock a wasps' nest from the cowshed wall, she was subjected to Dorli's fantasies about married life in the adjacent valley. She supposed her sister was trying to ignore what was happening to her, eyes fixed on the future as though her time in Felddorf was already history, as though everything that occurred here could be erased as easily as the stains made by the officer's boots on the bed sheets.

'I'll have my own house,' she babbled. 'And I'll go every week to church. I'll have children – two boys and two girls. The eldest will be Klaus, after his papa.'

Ursula swept, sickled, swilled, and made obliging sounds, only partly paying attention to the endless monologue, her mind more inclined to wander to thoughts of Anton or Sepp. She hadn't seen Sepp for some time and wondered if she'd still find him beautiful and if they'd argue again. The trembling, leaping pleasure – the March hares in her belly – she couldn't feel that any more. She seemed incapable of longing these days. She felt not quite alive, her flame stamped out. But she remembered it and perhaps an ember survived. She considered what her sister would do: what if she married and Klaus wanted to kiss her and sleep with her? Could she be happy? She thought of her own happiness, her future; there were no painted fences, dumplings bobbing in a pan, a tableful of children, a life of church and pinafores and never telling. Nothing so simple. It refused to take shape, wisp-like, blowing and shifting like flimsy fog dispersing on a field. She could only think as far as Anton's return, and she clung to the belief that other things would return with him, times gone by, those days when they'd lain in the meadow collecting grass seed to throw into the wind, flown a kite made of one of Mama's old slips, the string looped around her foot. She closed her eyes and pictured the flash of material against the sun, the tearing flutter of air across silk, June bugs like pieces of chaff striking her head and body. She felt again the heat and drowsiness, barely able to open her eyes against the glare, not worrying at all, stupefied and content.

'I hope he's on a train already.' Dorli paused in her polishing of the farmhouse window. Ursula was inside and her sister out; they'd cracked open the sash to converse while they worked. Dorli inspected herself appraisingly in the glass and attacked snarls in her hair with her fingers. Ursula was invisible to her sister in the dim interior of the kitchen. 'He'll be thinking of me, I'm sure,' she continued. 'But what will I tell him? What will I say?'

Ursula stopped polishing and wandered away amongst the mess of the kitchen while Dorli talked. The worktops were spotted with mouse droppings, mould grew on dirty crockery in the sink and the basin was splattered with scraped food; a crumpled spider lay drowned near the plughole. Herr Esterbauer didn't make time for housekeeping now and the stove was so full of clinker it barely burned, coughing faint heat into the room. Ursula opened some of the drawers – cutlery mixed with tools, rags and tea cloths, a whole drawer full of odds and ends, scraps of paper. A small square box in the back corner, its lid covered in ornate carving. She opened it carefully. In it was jewellery: necklaces, rings, earrings, a gold watch for a woman's wrist, glittering stones, emeralds, diamonds, rubies. Ursula knew Herr Esterbauer's mother had once been very wealthy: a Prussian aristocrat who'd lost everything after her imprudent marriage to Herr Esterbauer's father. She lifted a ruby necklace, draped it across her palm. It snaked over her fingers, weighty and smooth, the jewels that hung from the main strand large and gleaming. She tilted it so it caught the light. The glorious depth and darkness of the colour struck her in a deep red place of her own and she felt quite breathless looking at it; vivid light leapt from the gems, brilliant as flame, dancing and licking across the many faces, rich as wine, as blood. She brought the jewels nearer to her eyes, inspecting their clarity; they warmed her, made the ember glow.

'Fräulein?' came a voice from the far end of the room beyond the half-wall. She hurriedly replaced the necklace, closed the box, her nerves jangling with guilt. She hadn't thought to take it, she told herself. She'd only looked. A man stood in the doorway that led to the stairs, a young Russian, slim and with a clean-shaven face, dust-coloured hair and narrow chin. It was the same man who'd offered her money outside the outhouse. He leaned against the doorframe as if he'd been watching for some time, arms crossed, deep-socketed eyes unblinking. 'You like them?' he said, with an upward nod. She stared at him for a moment then hurried to the window, collected her polishing cloth and joined her sister outside.

$$42$$

The Allied powers divided the country as they saw fit; Russia, America, Britain and France occupied the provinces, the capital carved into four sections like a great Sachertorte. The country's de-Nazification was to be closely supervised. Winter arrived and clamped grim cold over the land as tight as the lid of a funeral urn. In Lower Austria the Russians stayed and in the Hildesheim house too. Worst luck to be under Soviet rule but there was little to be done about it and the people of Felddorf and the surrounding area plodded onwards, learning as best they could to tolerate the drunken, disorganised Easterners. Ursula grew accustomed to the smell of the protecting mint tea, herrings and tobacco smoke, a pungent blend of odours that filled the house, and to the sound of muddied boots clattering up and down the stairs. She accepted the ever-deepening disapproval in the village, all eyes following once she'd passed so that it felt as though a string of cans was tied to her foot and trailed behind, growing heavier, noisier, and more difficult to drag with each step, collecting whispers and condemnations. She'd even accepted Immanuil's tireless game, though he came closer and closer to serious violation. He bared his private parts, gripped his peter and shook it. Old resentments against Mama surfaced as Ursula found she was unable to keep him away; when she sat at the table and cringed at the touch of his fingers on her neck and Mama stared into her soup, ignoring what was happening in front of her, long-forgotten feelings rose anew, returned to Ursula from another time when Mama had done nothing to protect them, had invited the beasts inside, allowed the house to become a trap, a place without safety.

She prayed often for Anton, fretted and hoped. If he'd fallen into Russian hands there was no knowing what punishment would be decided. Some were let go with a reprimand, others put to death. She stopped often at holy shrines to light candles. She developed superstitions. If she could carry her washbowl down to the scullery without spilling a drop then he'd be saved; if she could leave one potato uneaten despite her hunger, or find a face in the clouds and point it out to Schosi, then Anton wasn't dead or on his way to the East, a prisoner in rags, but near by and thinking of her. She waited for another letter but none came. She tried to take the advice that Frau Hillier gave to Mama about Siegfried.

'It's best to ready yourself,' she counselled. 'Don't make it harder by wishing.' Mama grew stiff-faced at this and the two women bickered, Mama unable to bear Frau Hillier's pragmatism, her capability, how vital she'd become. Frau Hillier had developed a kind of matronly authority with Efim and his men. She enlisted Pasha and Viktor in household tasks, sent Immanuil on as many errands as possible and told Ursula to keep her eyes peeled when he was due to return. She devised prayers to help them feel less wretched after another radio broadcast about the death camps, all listening in speechless horror to the news – the sheer number of Jews, gypsies and others, the abominable thrift and macabre system of the exterminations – mattresses stuffed with human hair, soap flakes of fat and meticulous removal of gold fillings, awful experiments conducted on children, on the weak. Ursula thought about Schosi and his close escape, of the pleading message pencilled in the Hartburg corridor. Frau Hillier spoke about inhumanity and godlessness and the need to now make amends, to do God's work, to bring hope again to the Austria she'd known and loved, to tolerate no more of this vile cannibalism. They must think of the future. Her presence was a warming fire around which all could gather and for a moment heat their hands and ease their conscience. In comparison, Mama was unneeded, dependent and inept in her own home; she commented sourly on the one subject that would hurt her friend:

'Don't get too attached to your new job, Uschi,' she'd say, within earshot of Frau Hillier. Since Ursula had turned fifteen she'd been officially employed at the farm. 'He likely won't keep you on for long. Perhaps we'll all be laid off.' She glanced at Frau Hillier to see if her barb had stuck. 'He's already fired several workers because he can't afford them. A desperate man running out of money is never reliable. And what can be expected when he's treated so heartlessly that he's lost his will?'

'Ah, leave off!' was generally Frau Hillier's flippant response, but Ursula could tell she felt it bitterly. Even Schosi attacked her. Herr Esterbauer often shared alcohol with him at the end of the working day, his arm about Schosi's shoulder, as though they were two men of the world, the farmer muttering in his ear and Schosi nodding. Ursula wanted to tell Herr Esterbauer to stop it, to stop planting ideas in Schosi's head that would never come true. But she knew that nothing she said would make a difference.

'He's doing anything for you,' Schosi hoarsely echoed, once he'd wended his way tipsily home. 'I want my own room.'

'No, Schatzi.' Frau Hillier tried to pacify him. 'You mustn't say that.'

'I want to!' Frowning, he'd clumsily pull at her sleeve and repeat his demand.

'What is he thinking of, getting my boy drunk like this?' Frau Hillier fretted. 'He's not in his right mind. I'm not ungrateful. I'm not. But this . . .'

Her defences, eventually, were overcome, besieged as she was from all sides. One day Mama accused her of using Herr Esterbauer, and said that she couldn't truly love him if she tormented him like this. Frau Hillier, who was drying dishes, dropped the plate she was holding, quite on purpose, and watched it smash.

In the silence that followed she shouted, 'Will you shut up? Will you? Will you leave me alone?' She drew a shuddering breath, her usual contrary mildness entirely spent. 'I can't marry such a man! A Nazi! Have you never felt troubled? Have you never thought about what he did? Executing helpless men. I suppose you don't mind at all!'

Mama looked shocked, then eventually said, 'But he was trying to protect us all, Gita. And isn't the whole country full of old Nazis now? If you care for him . . . He risked everything for you – for your son. Who else would show such kindness?'

Frau Hillier began to cry. 'One kindness, yes. Amongst so *much* unkindness—' She wiped her tears as they fell. 'Of course I care for him. I care for him very much. But it isn't enough. He followed blindly that lunatic, that dreadful, demented man.' At this Dorli stood brusquely, walked down the hall and upstairs. Frau Hillier carried on, glancing at Schosi. 'It was only because of how he felt about me – because he's my son.' She leaned close to Schosi. 'Don't worry, little rabbit,' she whispered and kissed his cheek. 'But how can I make vows before the eyes of God, when he stands for everything I don't believe in?' She looked at Mama with genuine appeal in her eyes. 'How could I take his name? Give his name to my son? I want to be *with* him, but I can't.'

Mama fiddled with her fingernails. There was a period of quiet; Frau Hillier breathed heavily.

'Well, if you won't explain this to him, I will,' said Mama softly. 'He deserves to know.'

Frau Hillier caressed the thick curls at the nape of Schosi's neck, her forehead wrinkling as she thought.

'All right,' she said. 'If you think it best.'

Mama spoke to Herr Esterbauer the following day. They wandered in the orchard and she put her arm through his. Afterwards, she told Ursula that he'd cried.

'She doesn't know how much he regrets – how he's changed. He thinks of that day in the camp. He said he'll never be able to forget.'

After that, Herr Esterbauer drank as if there was something he wanted to scour away. His nose turned dark as a rotted strawberry. Ursula didn't like to see him weak and sorrowful; so utterly depleted; she tried to speak with him several times. She'd her own reasons also; she was ready at last to hear the truth about Anton, but Herr Esterbauer was unapproachable. His fits of rage built daily to great thunderheads, unleashing and tearing through the farm; he'd curse the Soviets and argue with them, convinced they claimed more than their share of the harvest, or bring to tears some unfortunate farmhand. The fury dwindled to sodden grief, his sight clouded, his mind closed in with loneliness. His mother had died in the first cold of winter; his evenings were now entirely solitary, apart from the Russians who he refused to converse with. Ursula waited for him to recover, to return to himself.

The Russian with dust-coloured hair waited again outside the outhouse and his palm this time revealed a coil of ruby fire. Such colour when everything else was grey – the snow, the soldier's dirt-ingrained hand, the grey-green uniform on his back. It seemed to Ursula that the necklace shone more brightly than any imaginable thing. It didn't matter that he unwrapped her much as he'd unwrap a loaf, a quick, perfunctory, necessary act, and lowered her to the floorboards of the upstairs Russian quarters, his coarse uniform against her skin resurrecting memories of other encounters. She thought of the jewels, the borrowed fire, and even let him hold her afterwards, his hand stroking her shoulder. He sang in Russian a wistful tune and smoked between verses.

'Only one left,' he lied, indicating the cigarette. 'No more.' But she didn't want it anyway. When she dressed she put on the necklace and hid it beneath her collar, enjoying its heaviness, a yoke of gold and stones that slid on her breastbone and gave a faint clink when she bent forward to fasten her boot. She wondered whether for such a lavish offering the Russian would expect more, or tell Herr Esterbauer she was the thief. She was sure in any case that Herr Esterbauer would soon discover it was missing. A rather painful, hollow sensation arrived in her body as she slid from the back entrance of the farmhouse and returned to her tasks, self-loathing mixed with the fading thrill of acquiring the necklace and the perturbing knowledge that she'd crossed a line, made a choice she feared would alter her for always. She didn't understand why she'd done it, only that she'd had to – she'd *had* to.

That night her dreams were filled with boots at the door, chest-crushing weight, stillness in her limbs. She saw herself at a table, napkin tight to her throat, drinking red wine from an upturned bottle, rivulets spilling down her chin. Opposite, Immanuil picked slivers of toothpick from his tongue and eyed her with satisfaction. She woke sweating despite the cold and couldn't be sure whose body it was that lay beneath the blankets, a horrid polluted thing, a hostile thing, like a nasty strangling coat she needed to struggle away from.

In Felddorf she clasped Schosi's hand firmly in her own. They walked through spaces where people moved hastily aside. Behind her, scandal flared. *Do you see her hair, so matted? I suppose she's always on her back! Her skin, how grimy! And just fifteen. A crying shame, but she brought it on herself, no doubt. Do you think she's having it away with the handicapped boy? There's no excuse for it. They were always ungodly – always strange.*

Sepp and Marta were outside the grocer's when she exited, her shopping complete. Schosi had shielded her deft actions from the view of Herr Wemmel and the other customers – he'd stand wherever she told him to without complaint. In her basket was flour and sugar, and a container of coffee substitute, none of which had been on her ration card. Marta's giggle reached her like a silver dinner bell. Ursula glanced morosely at her; Marta gave an impudent smirk. Sepp raised a hand and said hello. She hadn't spoken to him since the spring. She'd only glimpsed him about the village with Marta or his aunt, and he'd tried to come close to her several times but she'd pretended not to see or hear and dashed away. Today she was too tired to do even that; she trudged slowly on. Sepp jogged to her side, pushed a hand through his hair and swept it over to create a kind of jutting fringe. He'd probably been listening to the American pop tunes that played endlessly on Vienna Radio and was aping some of the Yankee flair.

'Are you all right?' He reached tentatively to touch her thick coat sleeve. 'You look terrible.' For Ursula this was too intimate a gesture and she snatched her arm away with a faint sense of insult. She hid her eyes by looking at the ground. There was no way to hide the rest of it – the filth.

'Answer me.' He peered into her face.

'Leave me be.'

'But, I just want—'

She didn't care what he wanted.

'Look at that!' Marta suddenly flanked Ursula on the other side. She pointed at the ruby necklace, some of which showed between the buttons of Ursula's coat. Ursula fumbled to conceal it, her fingers frozen in the November air. She was so used to wearing it that she'd forgotten to be careful; several times her secret had nearly been discovered. 'She must have stolen it! Where would she get such a thing? Watch out, Josef! Keep an eye on your pockets!'

Sepp's gaze returned to Ursula's wind-bitten face. 'I just want to help you,' he said softly.

'I don't want help!' Ursula glared ahead. 'Not from you, not from her!' Marta tittered in shock. 'Just stay away!' Tears spilled and she ran as fast as she could towards home, Schosi sprinting after her.

She took something each day, either from the farm or the village shops, food and trinkets of no worth – a comb or shaving brush that she thought Anton might like; money from the tin stashed beneath junk in Herr Esterbauer's scullery cupboard, or from Frau Hillier's purse at home. She took from the farm grain store and the mound of potatoes in the shed and traded with the malnourished city mothers who wandered through Felddorf bartering their last adornments, books and underwear. She hid behind hedges and made the exchange. The women breathed hotly and their mouths were dry and cracked. Sometimes they brought their babies and they too appeared feverish. Ursula was careful not to touch them – the city was rife with typhus. At home she stored the loot in her wardrobe and pored over it in moments of privacy, the secrecy and risk heating her blood, her exhilaration at owning such items pushing her worries aside. Thoughts of Siegfried sometimes dogged her, the high price he'd paid for his theft, and thoughts of Sepp and his devout aunt and what they'd think of her. The rest of the time she refused to reflect, or else there wasn't the opportunity amidst her busyness. She gathered wood for the Hildesheim stove, tugged the stubborn-wheeled handcart to and fro, tying bundles of tinder. Gas and electricity flashed through in a sporadic Morse code and they needed more wood than ever. She wrestled with the tinder-cutting machine in the shed, the handle seizing up with age – she'd grown weak, thin, her kneecaps protruding like the knobbled hocks of a horse. It was on one such occasion that Immanuil slid his hands round her sharp hips, pressed a knife to her ribs and had his way. Afterwards he pulled the handle down on the cutting machine as if gloating at his own strength; the blade beheaded the sticks and the trimmings fell to the floor with a clatter. She staggered off with the basket full.

'I have food for you,' he called, leaning against the shed doorframe, his belt undone. She ignored his offer, anger sustaining her, her hunger erased; perhaps that was what the ember now consisted of, anger almost gone, like her energy, like her resolve.

One late November evening the family had finished eating but remained at the table. Mama breastfed Traudi, Dorli seated herself on the officer's lap, legs swinging, his thick arms around her waist. She shared his cigarette and tapped ash on to her dirty dish. Frau Hillier coached Viktor in the washing up: 'You're only tickling the plate – make an effort, man! Don't put a bowl to dry that way – you must turn it over.' Ursula, Schosi and Pasha began a game of cards and Immanuil pretended to join them but spent his time creeping his fingers into the folds of Ursula's skirt. She moved closer to Pasha who said something sharply in Russian and Ursula was thankful for the look of shifty disquiet it brought to Immanuil's face and the hasty retraction of his hand. She loved to play cards with Pasha. He was friendly and patient, especially with Schosi, and became utterly absorbed like an energetic child. Most nights they found time for a game.

'We must go soon away,' asserted Efim suddenly. 'I go to Vienna – have duty there. Pasha, Viktor, Immanuil go to Felddorf barracks.'

Dorli twisted to look into the officer's face.

'When?' asked Mama.

'Three days.' Efim stroked Dorli's arm.

An awkward feeling filled the room. Frau Hillier finished the dishes and came with Viktor to the table. Ursula was shaken; her mind leapt immediately to the horror of the night in the bedroom, then the haystack, waking criss-crossed by slug tracks, the constant apprehension when the house was open to all-comers. But then Immanuil would be gone, so she'd have some respite. Schosi and Pasha continued the game. Ursula tried to play but she was distracted. Pasha whooped in celebration and Schosi leaned on the table with elbows splayed, forgetting to conceal his hand of cards. Immanuil sloped out of the front door; he preferred to smoke in the privacy of the shed and Ursula breathed a little easier. Frau Hillier and Mama spoke in hushed tones, Traudi suckling noisily, and Viktor bent studiously over his pocket notebook, filling it with Cyrillic scribbles.

The back door opened. Ursula was disappointed Immanuil had been so quick to finish. But when she looked up it was Anton who stood in the frame. For an instant she felt pinned to her seat as she stared at the angular symmetry of his face, the burnished colour of it, in so many ways different to how she remembered, but still, it was he and she dropped her cards in shock, in sheer joy. He was taller, thinner, grubby as a chimney sweep. He wore thick trousers belted high above his waist, a shirt with collar hanging on one side, a long coat and top-heavy rucksack with straps trailing from it. He looked at her directly and her heart boomed. But his expression was stony. His eyes slid from her and took in the rest of the scene, all faces turned towards him: the Russians around the table, Dorli sprawled across the huge officer, Traudi guzzling at Mama's nipple, Ursula, dishevelled and huddled close to Pasha, Schosi sitting in Anton's place.

'Toni!' Mama stood and rushed to him, pulling up her blouse to cover her breast. 'My God, Toni! You're all right, you're all right!' She tried to hug him but he stepped away with a look of incomprehension. His boots unbalanced him on the lip of the doorframe; he teetered and wobbled, his face creased, his eyes ranging around the room, as if they couldn't stand to rest on one spot for too long. Cold sweat broke out on Ursula's forehead. Her tongue became sticky and dry. She could barely breathe, let alone speak, a sensation like a balloon expanding huge in her chest, threatening to burst with the incredible intensity of her relief. He wasn't killed. He'd come back to her! She wanted to run to him and hug him as hard as she could. A wide smile cracked her face, the most sincere and irrepressible thing she'd felt in a long while. Anton gave her another cursory glance but again with such coldness that she felt it like a blow. Her smile faded.

'Toni,' said Mama. 'Are you quite well?'

Again he swayed on the threshold breathing hard as a runner. 'God!' he said, a ragged, strangled sound. 'You shameless bitches!'

He left the way he'd come, backpack lolling, boots rapidly crunching the grit. Ursula scrambled out from her place at the table and ran after him into the dark yard, past the firefly glow of Immanuil's cigarette in the shed entrance.

'Anton!' she called. 'Wait!'

It was too cruel, to get only that brief glimpse – she'd had no time to adjust, to his older face, his long hair and the patches of stubble on his jaw – certainly no time to see what was beneath, his heart, his thoughts, to hug him, shake his hand or kiss him on the cheek, to remember what it was. She saw his dim outline climb the field gate and drop down at the other side. Shadow swallowed him. She pelted after him, climbed the gate, hurried into the field, directionless because he was already gone, she could see nothing; he could easily outrun her. Should she try to guess where he'd go and pursue? After a while of struggling uphill, she stopped. 'Anton!' she hollered again at the top of her lungs. 'Come back!'

But he wouldn't.

43

The next day she shirked farm duties and searched for him. She wandered the fields and woods and went to the river pool, returned to the house as the light faded to wintry green on the horizon, and put on her coat and headscarf against the cold. She planned to walk to the church to check for him there – perhaps he was sitting in the porch or visiting Opa's grave – but Mama forbade her. It wasn't safe to be out alone. If Anton was coming, she said, he was coming. And if he wasn't, he wasn't. And that was that.

Later, Pasha read aloud to Ursula and Schosi, curled on the chairs in the living room. Ursula listened more for the opening of the front door, for the scuff of footsteps in the yard, a telltale clatter from the shed. Perhaps he'd cool off and come to talk to them then she'd explain to him the Russians were soon leaving and everything in their home would be normal again. If only Efim's deployment could have come the previous week, she thought, Anton wouldn't have seen them here, would never have known.

'Going to sleep,' mumbled Schosi in a stupor, accustomed to a much earlier bedtime. He heaved himself upright, collected his comfort blanket and bade them goodnight. Pasha finished the chapter then began organising his books into his packing chest. Ursula realised she'd be sorry when he went. She'd have told him so, except she was too unhappy. Heavy torpor filled her limbs and her thoughts were slow with misery; they felt somehow sticky, like drowning in syrup.

'You want to keep this one?' Pasha held up the novel he'd been reading. Lamplight reflected on his glasses in golden semicircles; the lid of the chest obscured his body and he peeped over the top like a funny, long-nosed dwarf. Ursula nodded. She'd like it to remember him by. Perhaps he was even a friend. This thought added a further layer of sorrow so she felt quite buried. Maybe it showed on her face because Pasha said, 'Your brother is angry?'

She sighed.

'Why?' He came out from behind the box and sat near to her. 'You cannot help what happens in this house.'

She looked at him and saw he meant it. 'He doesn't know that,' she said, with difficulty, struggling against the syrupy thickness to say what she meant. 'I'm his sister.' And brothers love sisters with hot fury, try to rule them, to keep them. 'I disappoint him,' she added. But this wasn't the right word; she couldn't think what it was, but she felt it: it was that she hurt him, wounded him. And he wanted to wound her too because she no longer belonged to him.

He was afraid. She thought this vaguely, uncertainly. 'He's troubled.' She repeated Herr Esterbauer's words.

Pasha rubbed his knees and nodded. It was quiet in the living room, in the whole house, aside from some shuffling on the floorboards above. She felt sorry again for stealing from Herr Esterbauer, for lying. She wished she knew why she did it and how to stop. 'He likes to kill things. And people too.' Pasha's dark eyes blinked thoughtfully at her. 'I don't know why.'

'Difficult, I see.'

This was the most Ursula had ever told anyone. It felt good. But such honesty was unfamiliar and it was as though she was breaking the rules, cheating by confiding in this man, the enemy. She plunged onwards.

'He tried to kill Schosi – to have him killed. He hates him because he's slow.'

'Hate that boy? Hate everything if he hate that boy.'

'Something bad will happen.' She swallowed against the lump that clogged her throat. 'He'll do something.' Something ferocious. She looked at Pasha. 'I have to find him.'

Pasha insisted they accept a farewell gift: several fine handkerchiefs embroidered with the initials *FS*, which they all knew he'd pinched from Friedrich Siedler.

'We'll have to pick the stitching off,' Frau Hillier commented.

Pasha gave a rueful smile. 'He has too much – you have too little.' He patted Traudi on the head and his eyes were wet. 'This sweet one knows nothing about it. I am sad to say goodbye to you, *devotchka*. You make my heart feel lighter.' Then he ruffled Ursula's hair also. 'Be careful – yes?'

She nodded. The previous night someone had taken a sledgehammer to the Red Army vehicle parked in the yard, a shocking racket that resounded in the early hours. When they'd run outside, lanterns flashing, they'd found no one, but of course they'd all known who it must have been. The head of the hammer was buried in the windscreen, the handle protruding like a curious animal horn; the tyres were punctured. Ursula had been glad to know Anton was still close by; her daily searching had yielded nothing. But beneath this she was afraid.

Dorli and Efim said goodbye to one another in the hallway. There was uneasiness in the officer's look as he bowed, the rest of the family watching. Perhaps he felt himself a foolish figure who'd lost his head, an interloper who'd forced himself on a stranger, a young girl. Perhaps he feared the attack on the vehicle was meant especially for him. In any case, he appeared half glad to go, half maudlin. He seized her hand and asked haltingly for a photo.

'I haven't got one,' she replied.

'But how I will remember you?'

Dorli looked at the floor.

'I carry picture here.' He tapped his forehead. 'I take to Russia. I not forget.'

He leaned forward as though to kiss her. She drew back.

'That's enough,' said Mama.

Efim released Dorli's hand, cast a look of reproach then left the house.

Meanwhile, Ursula met Immanuil's stare from where he waited in the yard. She frowned with as much energy as she could, her face contorting, eyes blazing with the urge to blink. She concentrated, held his eye until he glanced away. She savoured the feeling.

Efim, Pasha, Immanuil and Viktor shouldered their bags, bent to lift the packing chest, and departed.

Mama announced her intention to go to Vienna a few days later. She planned to travel alone, a kind of pilgrimage to look for Siegfried's apartment where he'd lived with his wife.

'I need to know for certain,' she said, but what she needed to know exactly she didn't explain. She hurried about the house gathering things for her trip, stocked her rucksack with snacks and a flask of water, her identity card, which she'd need to pass between occupation zones. She strapped Traudi to her front using an old pinafore, a fat, drooping bundle. 'Don't try to talk me out of it!' she called in a high voice. She refused to look into the dismayed faces of her daughters or to acknowledge the dry expression of Frau Hillier. 'Don't make a fuss now! I'll only be gone for a day.'

Why couldn't she wait like the other women? thought Ursula. Plenty of men had disappeared and their women didn't go searching. Why must she be so reckless? And if she found Siegfried and he began to visit again Anton would never come home. She found herself gritting her teeth. 'You shouldn't go, Mama. We need you here – at the farm. Herr Esterbauer can't manage without you.'

'Pah!' she replied, stuffing a spare scarf into her bag and pulling on her gloves. 'For one day? Don't be silly.' She set off down the hallway.

'A woman by herself in the city, full of troops and pickpockets and rapists,' Frau Hillier cried, going after her. 'It's ridiculous!'

'It's safer in the city. More people about. It's for Traudi's sake.'

'He might have been captured,' said Ursula. 'No one will have news of him.'

'Then I'll come home.'

'It's too dangerous,' pleaded Dorli.

Frau Hillier put on her coat.

'No, no!' said Mama. 'You don't have to come with me. What about work?'

'It's beside the point. You can't go alone.' Frau Hillier finished doing up her buttons then regarded her friend for a long moment as if waiting for Mama to re-evaluate but Mama only looked back at her with her jaw set. Frau Hillier sighed then addressed Ursula and Dorli. 'She'll clearly not listen to reason. Stay at the farm until we're back – we'll collect you as you soon as we can.'

Ursula stared, aghast that Frau Hillier had given in so easily. But then, she knew Mama well.

After Ursula and Dorli had been escorted across the fields and deposited at the farm, the women left for the city. Ursula went cursing to her tasks. Why didn't Mama stay and help seek Anton? Why must she run after Siegfried like a madwoman with the child slung on her belly, with no thought in her brain? So selfish – so careless. She dismissed the realisation that she herself had done a similar thing in her search for Schosi. How could Mama leave them at such a time?

In the barn, she and Schosi worked side by side. She sat on folded sacks and washed dried sweat and mud from the halters and harnesses. She attended to every seam and stitch, scrupulous in order to deflect the anxiety that threatened to absorb her. The regular sound of Schosi's whetstone divided the minutes like a hypnotic clock, the slithering sweep of the blade always the same volume

408

and duration, six strokes on one side of the blade, six on the other. But the repetitive work did little to calm her; her mind slipped into confused thoughts about Mama and Siegfried, Anton, Immanuil, Herr Esterbauer and Frau Hillier, Sepp's concern and Marta's pointing finger, her silver-bell laughter at seeing the necklace, absurd in its glory against her soiled dress. She felt now for the gems against her chest, pressed the stones to her flesh. It belonged to her – she'd forgotten that in fact it did not. Her fingers trembled as she worked and she wrestled with fury and also with fear because she realised she'd grown up bad inside, like a rotten fruit. She glanced at Schosi. He bent close to his work, face rapt; he dipped his whetstone into the water pouch at his waist. Even to him she'd been unfair, wicked. She'd used him as comfort, much like he used his blanket. She'd let him come into her bed and they'd lain with arms around each other's middle, or she'd traced shapes on his bare back, muscled nowadays and peppered with spots. She'd let him touch one of her breasts through her dress. He was careful and kept his hands still, cupped over the small mound as though he'd caught a cricket. She knew he had the same stirrings as any man, as her own for that matter – except whenever she felt that stirring, the almost-ache between her hip bones, she'd push him out of bed and tell him to go away. And now she'd push him away even more because Anton was back.

By late evening Mama and Frau Hillier had still not returned and Ursula, Dorli and Schosi were put to bed in Herr Esterbauer's hayloft, there being no space in the house. They huddled beneath dusty horse blankets, amongst owl pellets, bat droppings, the skeletons of mice, tickling chaff and spiders' webs. Dorli was paranoid that the lantern oil would run out so she plunged them into darkness as soon as they were horizontal. Ursula itched and scratched and wriggled and eventually slept, only to wake hours later with a dull pain in her lower abdomen, her skin hot to touch, her breasts tender. She felt wetness between her legs and put her hand there to check what it was – an oily substance. She tried to rouse Dorli but her sister only grunted and turned away. She clambered from under the blanket, put on her skirt and cardigan and climbed carefully down the ladder. Outside, she inspected her hand in the pale dawn; her fingers were stained dark. She went to the animals' drinking trough, which was frozen over with a thick crust of ice. She broke the ice with a stone and dabbled her hand until the stains washed away. She was disgusted and cried suddenly, unexpectedly, suppressing the sobs as best she could so as not to be heard. She didn't want it to begin. She didn't want any of this. She crept into the barn again and found the rag she'd used to wipe the tack. She put it between her legs – she should go back up to the loft and try to sleep but she didn't think she'd be able to rest with the strange feeling that pulled downwards, like a weight was attached to her private parts, dragging her earthwards. Instead she walked into the field. All was hushed, the hill veiled with frost, the sky a tentative ash blue, the sun not quite up, the birds beginning to call, one here, another there. She noticed the moon, ghostly, floating above the trees as if unsure, the face – the shadowed eyes – invisible. Her back ached too and it was soothing to walk; she guessed it would be another hour before the others woke. She wandered towards the woods, thinking about how she used to long for her monthlies, to know how it felt, to be like her sister, to be grown-up. She wondered why it felt so desperate now, so much like grief.

In the forest a skin of ice covered the ground. The woods were secluded and suited her mood. It was just habit to look for him; she searched for a sign of someone having been there, snapped twigs, battered ferns and grasses. She daydreamed, spotting grey snails as big as fists moving like slow tongues across the log stacks; hoping to see deer at the huntsmen's mangers. She soon came to the top of the steep slope that ended at the river pool. She'd go down to the water, bide her time until work. She descended, grasping ferns for a handhold. Amongst the plants were streaks of exposed earth, as though someone had skidded down not long ago. She went to the edge of the pool. On the beach in the shelter of the overhang was a heap of charred logs encircled by stones. Someone had built a fire since her previous visit. She scrambled down to inspect it. The waterfall trickled, most of it frozen in a white column, the surface of the pool also solid. The smell of wood smoke tinged the air. She inspected the logs – warmth emanated from them and fresh splashes scattered the stones. Near by was the small red bucket she and Anton had used when this was their special place. She picked it up. It was wet and the rock inside was gone. She looked around; she wandered further along the beach, which narrowed and continued beside the river.

She saw the boys when she was only metres from them. They weren't moving and had very likely been standing amongst the tree trunks for a while, watching her. There were seven of them, all different ages, wearing an assortment of scruffy clothes. Some wore Hitler Youth shorts or the Hitler Youth shirt minus the necktie. Their faces were blackened by dirt, their legs also, and they were very thin, almost as thin as the prisoners in the camp, with kneecaps like bulbous turnips. She stopped and stared. They weren't local; she didn't recognise them. She waited for one of them to speak or move; the hairs on her arms and neck prickled and rose. She'd heard of Hitler's Werewolves, a network of Nazi fanatics living in hand-built shacks in the Alps, resisting the occupation, plotting revenge. Or so the radio had proclaimed before the Reich fell. But these boys weren't as she'd imagined the Werewolves to be; they were too small, emaciated and threadbare. They looked more like guttersnipes.

'Hello!' she called. None replied. If she offered food maybe they'd realise she was no threat. But she didn't have anything with her. 'Have you seen my brother?' The question came before she'd thought, urgent and involuntary. The boys inched forward, moving as a group, treading softly over the brambles and sliding their hands around the skinny trunks of saplings. Should she offer them something even though she had nothing? They'd be distracted and then she could escape. 'I'm looking for my brother, Hildesheim Anton.'

The boys reached a patch of nettles, walked amongst them without seeming to feel, their legs already scabbed and stippled with insect bites and stings.

'Go away!' called one small boy. He wore a large shirt torn at the shoulder and was covered in what looked like soot. He bent to pluck a stick from the forest floor. The other boys copied him.

'I won't hurt you.' She tried to look harmless and kept her expression calm – she wouldn't easily be able to get away if they attacked her, stuck as she was below them on the river beach. What on earth did they want? 'Don't be afraid. I won't tell anyone you're here.'

'Got any food?' croaked the biggest boy. 'We know you earn plenty extra. And your sister!'

They snickered and looked at one another.

Ursula blushed. How did they know about her family? Had they been spying? Had they been speaking with others in the village? But she couldn't imagine that. Suddenly, she recognised the tallest boy, though he was so changed she had almost failed to do so – it was Rudi, his once-pudgy face hard and thickly shaped, his cheekbones so prominent it looked like he'd been bludgeoned. He stooped to collect a bulky stick. Ursula stepped back; her feet crunched through ice and sank into the shallows of the river.

'Anton!' she yelled as loudly as she could. The nearest boy jumped with fright. 'Anton! Where are you?' She waded into the flow of the river, testing the depth. She'd cross and climb the bank. The water was icy, a muscular current swirling above her knees. 'Anton!' she called again.

A stick flew past her head and struck the water, immediately whisked away by the flow.

'Shut up,' said Rudi. 'He's not coming. Go away. Don't come back.'

'Why's he hiding from me?' She was close to tears. Her fear receded – she could feel the blood throbbing around her eyes. She didn't care if the whole pack assaulted and drowned her. 'Why are you hiding from me?' she shrieked towards the trees, which whispered and waved, revealing nothing. She snatched a stone from the riverbed, submerging her arm to the shoulder, flung the stone at the boys. 'Get away!' Her heart hurt like it was being wrung. 'He's *my* brother. He wants to see me!' She scooped more stones from the riverbed and launched them at the group. Water clutched her waist, painfully cold, the current nearly too strong for her. She kept her feet braced wide; she could hardly breathe because of the cold. Another stick, Rudi's hefty one, windmilled by, hit the river surface, splashing her face; she made for the opposite bank. Something struck her on the back of the head. She ignored it, reached the edge, crawled out. Her dress was heavy as chainmail – she squeezed some water from it then clumsily scaled the muddy bank. When she stood her dress was smeared brown all along its front; the rag between her legs had come adrift and bloody water streamed pink down her legs. The boys threw more sticks across the river. None hit their target – they weren't really trying.

'Go to hell!' she hollered.

'Whore! Jezebel!' More sticks sailed overhead.

She left with their jeers nipping at her heels, reminding her of a time when she and Anton had called Mama those same names. The blood reached her ankles; there was no way to stop it. She rushed up the slope, the treetops making a hullabaloo in the wind. Once she was out of the forest, rain spat across the field. She must go home and get clean and dry – she couldn't be seen at the farm like this. She ran with teeth chattering down the hill towards her house.

44

About the only thing she recognised were the plump lips. His black moustache was replaced by ravaged skin, shiny and mottled. Black and grey hair sprang upwards in a frizz where it used to be neatly barbered and smoothed with lotion. A crutch was propped beside his chair. Traudi was on his lap and he cuddled her carefully, his expression vibrant with joy. Every time he smiled his burned cheek folded like a concertina. A large suitcase stood near the pantry door.

'Hello, Ursula,' he said. She could barely return his gaze. The whole of the right side of his face was blotched with violent purple scars, his neck too. The terrible welts descended below his collar. But worst of all was that where his right ear had been there was only a hole the size of a pfennig coin. His head looked like a mug with a missing handle. She ate breakfast while the adults talked and guilt leaked through her like a terrible ointment, searing her stomach and her guts, making her throat dry and cheeks glow. She couldn't eat much at all.

She'd seen Siegfried as soon as she'd come into the house. She'd barely had time to register that he had returned before there was a shocked outcry from Mama and Frau Hillier; her blood-streaked legs and skirt brought them running. They heard her mumbled explanation then bundled her upstairs. Mama helped her to peel off the wet dress and wiped her legs clean with the rolled-up garment. Ursula felt like a pony being rubbed down. Then Mama dug out an old sheet already stained and wrapped it around her body. Warm water was fetched and Mama helped her to wash properly at the washstand, gave her rags for her underwear and told her to put on her darkest-coloured and least favourite skirt. 'Siegfried's quite different,' she said, as the water in the bowl blushed pink. 'Don't be upset. It was tank fire.'

Over breakfast, Siegfried described the seige of Vienna, the high death toll, the hopelessness of the fight, starvation all around. Mama sat close and they both looked at Traudi. Mama kept welling up and smiling. After a short time Siegfried went upstairs to rest; he limped badly and was slow. Mama took Traudi and the three retired to the bedroom. Ursula and Frau Hillier washed the plates. Ursula experienced a moment of jealous exclusion: baby, mother, father – the other papa. Would Mama always choose to resurrect Siegfried instead? Would she prefer to live with him and Traudi as a happy threesome? She sighed, knowing that soon she must set off for work and still her belly ached. 'Where did you find him?' she asked.

'At his apartment,' said Frau Hillier. 'Such a stench! Rotten food in the kitchen, dust an inch thick, living off nettles the neighbour left on his doorstep. Dismal. His wife's dead. Jumped out of the window apparently. They lived on the fourth floor.' Frau Hillier grimaced. 'No doubt to avoid the inevitable. I asked him why he didn't come here, to Felddorf. But I suppose it's hard to be less than you were.'

Ursula dried the rest of the dishes in silence; Siegfried's wife might have lived if he hadn't been conscripted and was at home to comfort her. She tried to put the thought out of her head. She and Anton had done an appalling thing.

A different weight, however, had lifted from her. Here he was, alive, and Mama made happy again. Would he stay? He mustn't go back to that squalid flat, that isolated existence. From now on, she vowed, she'd be unfailingly kind.

old air nipped Schosi's nose as he came down from the hayloft; Dorli was still sleeping but Ursula was gone from her place beneath the blankets. He wondered where she could be as he crossed the yard and took a walnut from the box in the shed; he always ate a nut each morning before beginning work. Herr Esterbauer said it was good for his bones. He squatted and placed the nut on the concrete and cracked the shell with a stone – it wasn't rotten, which was good. The walnut tree that grew near the farm was a gift from God, Herr Esterbauer said. Schosi believed that was true. He chewed and enjoyed the bitter oily taste.

He made his way to the outhouse; the hooded rascally crows patrolled the field beyond the fence, and further still the horse chestnut tree with bare branches made a shrugging shape, spindly fingers fanning out at the ends like the hands of a priest turned upwards to the sky. He thought about the time he'd climbed in the flowering tree, the aroma so thick and sweet he'd got drunk and had to call for Herr Esterbauer to lift him down; later, he'd had a dream about it, but the blast of a nurse's whistle had torn him from the branches and back into that harsh place where no one knew him and everyone was cruel.

Schosi walked along the side of the farmhouse, past the water butts and back into the yard, empty except for a few chickens dawdling near the barn door. The cows lowed now and then; he wondered where everyone was. He went to the rabbit cages, which were clean and bedded with fresh straw, but their dishes were empty. The rabbits twitched their velvet noses. Outside, he sat on the tree stump that was carved into the shape of a chair. He waited – he supposed that Herr Esterbauer was late to rise and would soon emerge to milk the cows. Schosi would help him and they'd talk to the animals and to each other. He picked at a scab on his knee and squinted up at the leafless creeper that tumbled from the top of the barn. Birds' nests, now empty, clotted the underside of the eaves and white droppings streaked the wood. In summer he liked to watch the house martins flit with their thin wings, emitting high cheeps that echoed off the buildings.

Ursula arrived, swinging her arms and legs, her feet loud on the concrete. She greeted Schosi, sat beside him and gave him some of the bread she was eating. They chewed in silence. Ursula frequently looked up at the windows of the Russian quarters but there were no lights on. They were probably already in the fields. She ate the rest of the bread and then dusted the crumbs from her hands.

The chickens came close to their feet, pecking the morsels. They groaned to each other, like unoiled hinges. She kicked at the chickens and they scattered, flapping. Why did she do that? wondered Schosi. The birds had done nothing wrong. But he knew Ursula was unhappy – she was always either angry or sad.

'I found out Toni's hiding in the forest,' she said. 'And Siegfried's back.'

'Anton?' said Schosi. He became nervous. 'In the forest?' He'd rather Anton stayed away – he remembered him only as someone who was rough and unkind, who'd played mean tricks, called him names, had thrown a helpless cat into the river.

'He's living with Rudi and some other boys. Like an animal.' She tempted another hen forward only to kick at it again. 'Perhaps they've got a treehouse or a burrow or something. They look half starved.'

Then she asked Schosi if she could please have a nut and he went to fetch it, cracked it for her. She thanked him.

'He won't speak to me,' she said, chewing, resting her elbows on her knees and frowning. Schosi did the same so that their heads were close together. He vaguely recalled something his mama said about ragged boys scavenging in the village. People had seen them thieving from shops and farms and also from delivery lorries when the delivery men weren't paying attention. They'd even stolen from the Russians, someone had said.

Ursula stood. 'I'm going to see who's in the field.' She wandered off.

Schosi continued to wait. He checked his wristwatch repeatedly. Eventually he became too restless. Perhaps Herr Esterbauer had already done the milking. He went to the cowshed and pushed open the heavy door. Some of the cows were lying in their stalls, broad humped backs visible, tails swishing in lazy circles, while others stood and ate from their feeders. Their udders were full and the animals trod fitfully from hoof to hoof. He'd make a start. He went to the adjoining shed. He lifted the milking pails from their hooks. He looked down the length of the shed.

Herr Esterbauer hung from the rafter, his boots dangling above the floor. A chair was overturned not far away. His face was dark and his tongue poked from between his lips like a slug. Schosi dropped the milking pails. They clanged and rolled at his feet. He knew that Herr Esterbauer was dead; the red eyes and swollen neck and thrusting tongue could not be mistaken. His heart lurched painfully and beat with unstoppable speed. He ran out of the house and down to the fields, his stutter stifling his cries.

Ursula was standing amongst the Russians who were busy sawing a fallen tree trunk into pieces. The smell of resin filled the air. Schosi waved frantically. She came to meet him. 'What's wrong?' she said.

He could only point and stammer, 'Esterbauer!'

She shouted to the Russians to come and everybody ran, Schosi floundering behind, his legs weak and chest hurting.

The soldiers were used to death. They shook their heads and crossed their chests to save the farmer's soul. They murmured about what they should do. Ursula hugged Schosi and told him not to worry, to come away, to step outside, but he wouldn't leave the shed and one of the Russians righted the chair and made Ursula sit because she was crying so much. Then two of them held Herr Esterbauer's legs and lifted him slightly to slacken the rope, while another cut him down.

46

Schosi milked the herd twice daily. His mama and Frau Hildesheim spent a busy week organising Herr Esterbauer's things. Lawyers were called to the farmhouse; they made mounds of papers, spreading them everywhere so that the kitchen was covered in snow just like the land outside.

Herr Esterbauer was buried in the churchyard, his suicide concealed. Many villagers came to the funeral but he didn't have family – there were no cousins or nephews to see him off. Some of the Russians attended and stood stiffly at the back. Siegfried wore a finely tailored suit that made his wounds look all the more monstrous, the sleek fabric contrasting starkly with his ruined skin. Eyes turned to fix on him and a murmur passed through the gathered crowd.

Schosi's mama cried very hard and said she was sorry as she went past Herr Esterbauer's coffin. She also told Schosi she was sorry as they walked home, together with the Hildesheims. 'He's gone,' she said, rubbing her son's broad, stooped back. 'But you'll see him again one day.'

Ursula's eyes were gritty from crying and she felt worn-out from holding herself rigid and proud by the graveside. The others in the village gave no thought to how well the Hildesheims and Hilliers had known Herr Esterbauer; to them it was merely unpleasant to share his departure with two such families. She hadn't known whether to wear the necklace or remove it. In the end she'd taken it off and laid it under her things in the bottom of the wardrobe, feeling little and drab without it.

It made her sadder still as she watched Schosi walking ahead of her with his rickety gait, his reaction to the loss muted – hapless. Outside the church he'd mentioned again the blue blanket and cart. He'd said something about a friend called Aldo – about freezing in a yard and going to the graveyard. This time she'd allowed him to insistently repeat himself until he was soothed. Some thing from that hellish hospital, she guessed. She shuddered, thankful for both their lives.

A little further down the track, Mama, who walked arm-in-arm with Siegfried, called to Frau Hillier. 'I think it's important for me to say,' she announced, 'that none of this . . .' She shot a glance at Siegfried. 'I've been very unfair.' She cleared her throat, her tone not entirely willing. 'This isn't your fault.' She glanced at her friend. 'You do know that, don't you?'

Frau Hillier cried even more after that.

December came and soon after, Krampus night. Frau Hillier told Schosi not to be scared because Saint Nikolaus and his band of followers hadn't visited Felddorf since he was a child. Schosi believed what his mama told him and even forgot which day it was. After work, as a special treat, he was allowed to play with the wireless in the Hildesheim living room. He positioned himself in front of the bureau. The women laboured in the kitchen and scullery, Ursula too, while Siegfried read in the kitchen, harrumphing now and then, his boots resting on a chair. Outside, snow stuck against the doors and windows and congested the cherry branches. Schosi thought about the cats huddled in the woodshed, tucked tight against one another – Simmy had settled here now; wherever Schosi went was his home. He twisted the knobs on the wireless. His mind drifted as the stations drifted, his mood as restful as the white hiss in between. He loved the oiled motion of the knobs, the needle jerking on the dial, thin like a whisker, the dial lit with a warm yellow radiance, and when the needle struck the right point music leapt from the speakers straight into his heart. He hummed and tapped his feet, turned the knob again until the notes were swallowed by nothingness. A tap on the shutter made him jump. He listened. There it was again! A slow tap-tapping on the shutter.

'Mama!' he called. No response. From the scullery came the banging of hard objects being washed in the sink. 'Mama!' But no one heard his cries. He daren't go into the hall. He'd have to pass the front door, which had a small window near the top. He didn't want to see what was outside. He grabbed a blanket from the settle and cloaked

424

himself. He climbed on to the padded seat and pulled the blanket over his head, creating a cavern – he pressed the wristwatch Pasha had given him to his ear. From outside came metallic rattling, another tap. His mama had lied to him. He began to panic and thought about all the bad things he'd done. He'd drunk beer and schnapps with Herr Esterbauer; he'd listened to the farmer swearing and copied the swear words under his breath. He'd had unclean thoughts, lain with Uschi under the sheets, touched her. He began to cry quietly. He curled into a tight ball, his knees beside his face – dread huddled with him beneath the blanket. 'Mama!' he wailed.

There was a terrible bashing and clattering against the shutters. Schosi leapt from the settle and ran out of the living room. He headed for the scullery, praying loudly as he went. He begged forgiveness for all his bad deeds. He kept his eyes averted from the door. He careered around the corner and collided with his mama just as she was tipping a bowl of suds down the sink. She slopped some of the water on to her feet.

'For God's sake!' she said. 'What are you playing at?'

But she quickly saw he was frightened and put the bowl down. The women stepped into the hall, Frau Hillier holding Schosi's hand. Outside the door, chains battered against the wood; someone laughed and then there was the gibbering squeal. Schosi clamped his hands over his ears.

In the village, lamplight threw shadows into the potholes on the road. Groups gathered outside the Gasthaus and on doorsteps, or staggered, inebriated, against fences and hedges. The family made their way slowly through the throng towards the beer hall where a band played. Schosi grimaced and twirled his blanket incessantly but Ursula was sure this was the best thing; they all thought so. Everywhere were merry people, the quickening of alcohol in the air. Ursula felt it in her own blood though she hadn't drunk a thing; the atmosphere of fun and forgetting seemed to soak through her skin. She relaxed a little. It had been so long since she'd seen festivities and it felt precious, a rare spectacle that she could view as if from a high-up window. Some way off a group of Krampuses called at a house near the bakery – they crept the length of the shovel-scoured path between mounds of soiled snow, postures exaggeratedly hunched and menacing, predators trailing chains and rattling bunches of sticks, dressed in sheep-skins, rabbit skins, black and brown with tails sewn on at the rump. They assembled behind Saint Nikolaus who stood on the doorstep, forming a tight semicircle, their dark shapes melting one into the other and their horned heads pressed close so they appeared to be one great spiny beast.

At the Hildesheim house Siegfried had gone to the door and shooed the mischief-makers away, a ragged trio of masked Krampuses who'd jabbed their sticks into his belly before bounding off with calls of, 'Cripple!' and, 'Who toasted you in the fire?' Schosi had grown hysterical, piercing sounds erupting from his mouth that were unlike his usual voice. He'd shouted repeatedly about not wanting to go to Hell; he'd struck his mother across the face when she tried to touch him and looked at them all with such terror it was as if he couldn't recognise them. Ursula had seen this before, but not so bad. Not even the music on the wireless could pacify him. The family had set out to the village as a last resort. They'd go to the Gasthaus, somewhere bright and lively – the music would cheer him and they'd show him that the Krampuses were nothing to be afraid of. Before they'd left the house the adults made a big show of being light-hearted, cajoled Schosi until he began to quieten, coaxed him into putting on his coat and told him not to worry, that there was nothing outside any more and that they were going to a party. Siegfried exaggerated his limp as they crossed the yard and acted the clown. Schosi watched him but didn't laugh like he normally would.

In the beer hall, the adults drank at a long table near to the band and Ursula, Schosi and Dorli munched on apricot dumplings and watched the antics. Russians crowded against the bar or slid from their stools with drink, and there were one or two scuffles between them, ending in laughter and loud singing. When they'd finished eating Frau Hillier hoisted Schosi out of his seat.

'Come,' she said, businesslike.

Ursula followed them into the street. They walked as far as the low wall of the fountain then Frau Hillier swept the snow from the stones and sat. Ursula and Schosi sat beside her.

'Look.' She gripped Schosi by the shoulder and pointed. 'They're just boys in costumes. They can't hurt you.'

Not far away a group of Krampuses showed off to passers-by their masks of carved wood with angry eyeholes, gnarled horns and long red tongues, which stretched beyond the tips of their chins into a lascivious point. The shaggy, dark shapes were goat-like, bear-like, misshapen and monstrous. Ursula felt an echo of childish fright as she observed them – they did look evil. How silly, she thought. There was nothing to be scared of. But something tugged at her consciousness, tried to make itself known, a memory just out of view, fear that was real and rooted deep. Beside her, Schosi put his hands partly over his eyes, a white dusting of dumpling sugar on his lips. He mumbled to himself and Ursula felt a surge of protective love. He was tall as a man but with all the innocence and credulity of a child. She put her arm around him. On each doorstep parents appeared with their little ones and the saint and Krampuses were handed glasses of schnapps, which the demons upturned on their horrific lips. At other houses they went to the windows where parents had left the shutters undone, leering through the glass so that errant children would see their gruesome faces. They shook their chains and made their signature gibbering noise until shrieks and sobs came from within. As Ursula watched, three more Krampuses arrived to join the group, running from the unlit alleyway beside the bakery, shouting and jumping over flower borders, crashing into one another. They immediately joined the terrorising but from these three came a different feeling: they weren't only unruly and mischievous but aggressive and destructive. They swung their chains against the windows so roughly that she worried they might shatter. Ursula recognised them as the Krampuses who'd come to their house.

'Silly boys,' she told Schosi. 'They're just silly boys.' But she watched them with wide eyes, trying to make sense of the raised and rowdy voices, disoriented by the leaping figures everywhere.

'Good God, they're lively,' said Frau Hillier with a laugh. 'A schnapps too many, I think. I'd smack their bottoms if that was my house.' She rose from the wall, warming her hands by blowing into them. She hugged Schosi. 'You'd never fit in their baskets, Schatzi, so don't you fret.' She kissed his hair. 'Bring him inside soon, before he gets cold.' She went back into the Gasthaus.

As Frau Hillier left, a house opened its door to Saint Nikolaus' knock and a woman beckoned the whole mob inside. The saint and his companions crowded in and Ursula imagined the horror of the children who lived there. It was palpable even now: Mama and Papa welcoming the saint, the group of Krampuses in the kitchen. They'd surrounded her, whipped her, hissed in her ears. Anton had been ready to strike them, he'd told her afterwards, to throttle the whole lot. But instead his thumbs had pressed into the centre of her throat, cutting off the air, his face crimson above hers. The saint had read a list of her transgressions, pronounced her a thieving, sinful girl and she'd wept, kneeling on the flagstones. She remembered the throb of her heart and the cold air blowing from the open door into the kitchen – it had wrapped around her neck and drawn goosebumps from her skin. The deformed faces craned close, hungry to suck on her soul. As a finale they'd lifted her into the basket and she'd known she was condemned to burn for all eternity.

Beside the fountain, her heart started to anxiously thud, blood beating as she relived the shame, as she again faced Herr Adler the punishing saint, old and ill and cruel, contempt swelling in his ruddy jowls, glinting in his eyes. He'd eaten death rather than face punishment for his own sins, she thought, poisoned himself in the camp before he could be hanged. She remembered how one Krampus had crouched to take the weight of her in the basket on his back. Outside into the night she'd been taken, crying, seeing only black sky and stars, the basket around her hard and scratchy, smelling of mould. From behind she'd heard

Anton call and could see through the creaking wicker that Saint Nikolaus restrained him tightly so he couldn't follow, his struggle futile. The Krampus left the yard and loped away down the track, moving fast, rattling her brains inside her skull and bruising her against the basket. She could no longer see the house. After running a little further along the track the creature dumped the basket on to the verge. The impact jarred her teeth and she bit her tongue so it bled. She clambered out, the Krampus standing tall beside her, his matted fur lifting softly in the night air. Her feet sank into the snow, straight away cold and wet because she wore felted house shoes that were broken along the seams. Then the Krampus took a handful of her dress and pulled her close. His bulging eyes locked on to hers and her limbs turned leaden, useless with terror. The Krampus struck her with his bundle of sticks. She was sure that at any moment the ground would open like a fiery throat and there would be the entrance to Hell. A scream threatened to tip out of her mouth but silence rushed in to smother it, to protect her, to warn that to make a noise was to make this worse. The sticks lashed her calves again and again and blood began to smear and spread from the many scratches. Her voice had vanished, the dagger-like tongue and glaring eyeballs inches from her face. Her legs burned – stinging, raw. She clenched her teeth. The Krampus pushed her down into the snow, knocking her breath out. He quivered his chains in threat and emitted a long growl, alcoholic breath puffing from his jaws in a cloud. *Penance*: she heard the voice of the saint and the priest in the confession box, the two men frowning in judgement. Penance was to suffer – perhaps pain would cleanse her and she'd be forgiven, would have another chance. A heavy foot pinned her to the ground, pushed downwards, crushingly, so that it felt as though her ribs would break. Sharp stones knobbled her back. She screwed her eyes shut, tears squeezing between clamped lids. This was when she heard the shout, blaring like a horn, and saw Anton running, the sound he made a hard blast of fury, deadened by snow. His thin arms flailed as he came across the uneven drift-covered track, his legs too short, too puny. He stumbled, eyes fixed on his sister. The Krampus looked behind; the pressure of his foot lessened slightly. The sharp yell had jolted Ursula out of inactivity; she struggled, twisted, and scrabbled for purchase on the rocks with her fingers, pulled herself out from under the foot of the Krampus.

She and Anton ran, the Krampus pursuing. She lost both slippers, wallowing through the snow. Anton was caught. A howl of fright escaped him. He cowered and almost fell, his face con torted and tear-streaked as the demon gibbered and hissed and cornered him near the gate. He whimpered, 'Please! No!'

Ursula barged the Krampus sideways with all her bodyweight, almost toppling him. Anton dodged from the trap. They ran into the yard. The Krampus raised his black arms but didn't follow, sticks in one hand, chain in the other. The rest of the Krampuses were gathered near the doorstep. They caterwauled as the children passed. The adults – Mama, Papa and the saint – called from the living room, 'Let that be a lesson!' Their laughter rose up the stairwell as Ursula and Anton dashed to the bedroom, crying with fear, panting hard.

The next part of the memory arrived fully formed, a story that was familiar yet strange. Details presented themselves like objects she could reach out and touch, somehow overlooked until now, though she'd always known, had woven them into her dreams, into her unthinking moments, worn them as skin and, in that way, forgotten. Anton had pulled her into his room. He'd yanked her dress off over her head, tugged her petticoats down, stripped her to shivering nakedness. She'd felt humiliated as he looked at her body, her bloodied calves. His expression was a mixture of many things she recognised but didn't understand. He grabbed her chest, pinching with wicked force, and told her she should have screamed, fought, done something to save herself instead of relying on him.

'I can't look after you. Not always.' His voice was a harsh whisper and his cheeks were wet. He was angry because he'd been made to cry, because she'd saved him from the Krampus. 'Come here!' He pushed her until she sat on the bed, her flesh mottled blue and purple with cold. He removed his trousers and his peter poked upwards in his underpants. He was often vindictive when it was like that, tormented her or was tense and cross. 'Lie back!' He clambered astride her and her teeth began to chatter. 'Come on, silly,' he said. She kept still, numb and wretched; he covered her with his body, his fingers travelling, prodding, grasping, his peter within his underwear pushing against her with insistent pressure. She was worried for him because he looked so afraid, his face pinched and body humming with distress. The pressure increased, upsetting her. A hot-cold sensation spread all over her, like the crawl of red ants and the ache of ice all at once and it was this feeling that seemed to prevent her from moving, that made her limbs lifeless and without resistance. She allowed him to rub against her, cramming and shoving, until he gave a small cry. He sat up.

'You shouldn't have done that!' he said, his cheeks dark and eyes bright, gasping like a dying thing. 'You're not allowed. It's vile! It's disgusting!'

He placed his hands around her neck and squeezed until her breath came in a thin wheeze and his in irregular gulps. Glittering dots flew busily across her vision. 'You shouldn't let me. Why didn't you struggle?' His eyes were pockets of shadow in the lamp's glow. He would punch a hole with his thumbs! 'You didn't stop me. You should've struggled. Don't talk to me!' Not that she could. She began to squirm, head thumping. She thrashed until eventually he let her breathe, slid away and under the coverlet. He hugged her then and she stayed silent, swallowing again and again against the hard knot that hurt in her throat. The cold bite of air around her face and ears was filled with his love as he whispered tenderly, repeatedly that she was his best girl, best sister, best friend. Still she shivered, danger beating in her like a drum, a slice of pain between her legs when she moved, a splitting stab that made her catch her breath. She drew her knees gingerly towards herself to get warm, her brother's arm thrown heavily on top of her, restricting her. He slept after a few minutes. She lay awake until light glowed between the shutters.

Ursula shifted on the wall. The queasy heat and sinking coldness revisited her from all that time ago with astounding power. She put her hand into the snow of the flower border to dislodge the disturbing thoughts. Near by, the Krampuses yowled and emerged from a house; the smiling pink-faced mother with sniffling child waved goodbye. The voices of the disguised men and boys merged like baying wolves. The three who'd frightened Schosi at the house swore loudly and kicked at each other's legs, at the snow, at signposts and fences. One tore a branch from a young fir and used it to thrash his companions. He wore a brown woollen costume with patches sewn roughly over frayed holes; his two friends were similarly unkempt, one sporting a grey fur-lined coat turned inside out, again with great rents in the fabric, and the other wore a mask he'd carved himself by the crude look of it. The wood was whittled into bulging cheeks, long spear-like tongue and splintered mouth. Misshapen eyeholes had been hurriedly cut. The effect was grisly.

'Just silly boys,' said Schosi, cowering close to her.

'Yes, that's right.' She lowered her face and pulled her headscarf forwards so they wouldn't notice her as they passed.

The Krampuses began to clown for some of the villagers who were gathered near to watch the fun. They hit the legs of the young girls and smacked them smartly on the bottom. The girls shrieked and huddled together. Ursula spotted Marta amongst them – she was accosted, her backside swiped hard enough that she yelped, jumping, and Ursula didn't know whether to feel glad or envious because Marta was there, as ever at the centre, while she was at the edge. The trio of ragged Krampuses shoved Marta to the ground – the sticks connected, singing as they flew, producing deep muscular thuds that would certainly cause pain. Marta braced her arms over her face and head.

'Stop!' squealed her friends, surging forward. 'Get off, you brutes!' The main group of Krampuses hung back – some yelled to lay off, but the three wild Krampuses

434

ignored them. They landed more vicious thwacks then sprang away into the ranks.

'Damn you!' Marta struggled upright, her fine coat dirtied, blood on her cheek. 'Disgraceful louts!'

Pushing and shoving erupted amongst the boys, Krampus masks waggled, chains tangled around ankles, and bundles of sticks were used in earnest. As the boys fought, Ursula waited for an opportunity to get Schosi back into the Gasthaus – the brawling Krampuses were now blocking the door. One of them shook off his attackers and came straight towards them. The glint of eyes moved behind the eyeholes. The mask was lifted away and Sepp appeared, scarlet and rumpled. He rubbed a hand through his hair.

Schosi yelled, in fright and half in jubilation, 'Sepp – it's Sepp! Just a silly boy!'

Sepp sat on the wall and removed the rest of his costume; he tugged the long furry garment off his body and tossed it aside. 'Hello,' he said, once he was done.

Ursula was confounded, a mixture of shock and embarrassment, remembering her outburst in the village and the exposed necklace, her unkempt appearance, her degradation. She glanced about for a sign of Marta. The group of girls some distance away fussed over the scratch on her cheek. Why hadn't Sepp dashed to her aid a moment ago? Courtships had been terminated for less.

'They're all mad,' he said. 'Drunk.'

She nodded, wishing she could borrow his mask to hide her confusion.

On the outskirts of the fray a couple of Russians pitched in; the three ragged Krampuses flew instantly at their backs, gripped their necks, punched their ears. The Russians, intoxicated, reeled and fell. The Krampuses laid into them, stomping and lashing. The Russians lay inert. Ursula watched in distress; they'd be trampled, badly injured. Hostility crackled in the air, an electric charge she was sure she could feel. It was fearsome the way the boys attacked each other, catapulting high in the air like battling goats, heads clashing, legs kicking, not caring if they were hurt. Where were the police? Somebody should stop this.

'What the hell are you playing at?' Saint Nikolaus bellowed from the periphery as the noise rose to a cacophony of screams and yells. His bishop's hat was askew. 'Boys! Boys! Stop this at once!'

Ursula recognised him as the irritable shopkeeper, Herr Wemmel, from whom she'd stolen countless items.

The thrashing bodies and limbs whirled suddenly in their direction. She grabbed Schosi by the hand – if they dodged around to the right and behind they'd be able to reach the Gasthaus. Frau Hillier peered worriedly from the doorway. Another cluster of Russians came out of the beer hall and hollered for order. One was Pasha; Ursula caught a glimpse of his wire-rimmed glasses and hooked nose. He tried to keep his comrades from the rumpus, but five or six shouldered past him and joined the fight.

'Quickly!' Ursula pulled Schosi from the wall. They hurried around the outskirts. They'd almost reached safety but the throng abruptly swirled like a river in spate, and surged on to the pavement. The punching and swearing boys collided with Schosi. She lost her grip on his hand. He was dragged into the pounding of the crowd, was snatched and set upon. Bewildered by the churn of bodies, she tried to locate him. She saw his legs, outstretched on the floor; the next moment she glimpsed him again, standing this time with his hands raised to protect his face.

'Schosi!' But he couldn't hear her. Sepp joined her in shouting for him. 'Pasha!' she yelled above the hubbub. 'Help him!'

Pasha, across the crowd, began searching too and calling.

Ursula wanted to dive into the fracas but daren't. She imagined herself with incredible strength, wrenching the boys apart, throwing them to the floor or knocking their heads together.

Schosi burst from amongst the windmilling fists. He didn't see Ursula or Sepp; he didn't see anything, he hurtled down the street with several Krampuses at his heels. Ursula gave chase as fast as she could, the ruby necklace rattling. Schosi's long strides and the sprinting Krampuses outpaced her.

'Pasha!' she yelled as she went. She recognised the grey fur coat and the ragged brown garments of the most aggressive Krampus – the one with the rough-hewn mask led the charge. She took deep gulps of air, willed her legs to move faster. She glanced behind for Pasha. Instead, Sepp followed.

Ahead, Schosi turned off the road on to the track – he'd try to reach home. The three Krampuses tangled their sticks between his feet to make him trip. Sepp soon overtook her; he too reached the turning and disappeared. When she got there the whole lot had vanished into the night. She laboured on, the snow deep. Sepp all of a sudden was at her feet, holding his head. She almost fell over him.

'They hit me,' he said. His hand when he withdrew it was wet with blood.

Ursula dropped to her knees beside him. 'Oh God!' The blood frightened her. 'Do you need a doctor?'

437

'I don't think so. The stick was sharp, that's all. It wasn't a hard knock.' He stood with her help.

All around was darkness, the way ahead black. They raced on, aiming for Ursula's house – it was the only thing they could think to do and if Schosi was leading the way he would have gone there. But what if he'd been captured? The Krampuses could have taken him anywhere.

The house when they reached it was dark. There was no one in any of the outbuildings. They stood in the yard, undecided.

'Maybe he went to his old house,' said Ursula. But she already knew that the boys wouldn't be there – something gnawed at her awareness – she tried to pinpoint the feeling, to decipher it. She'd met those vicious Krampuses somewhere before – shabby, damaged and intimidating.

When she realised who they must be she was truly afraid. The boys in the forest – Rudi. And two others, one of whom, she was certain, was Anton. Who else would so purposefully target Schosi? They'd called at the house to petrify him and now they were hounding him, forcing him away into isolated dark. This was more than just a prank, more than tomfoolery fuelled by too much schnapps. This was hunter and quarry. 'I know where they've gone,' she said, her voice high and urgent, beginning to run. She led into the fields. Why did the whole world torment her friend? People like her brother. This time there was no Herr Esterbauer to help. They laboured uphill. Her legs ached, her muscles wasted and underfed. It seemed time itself slowed, thumping in a sluggish tempo that matched her lunging steps, the stab of frozen air in her throat, the convulsions of heart and blood, a lagging pulse, her mind reciting a rhythmic command: 'Go to him, go to him, go to him, go to him.' Like madness, she thought, the strange sensation, like dragging a spoon through molasses. She recalled Anton's stranglehold, him wringing her neck, her thoughts drawling, airless, as he mouthed a mixture of love and violence.

At the forest edge she found a trail of broken snow, the footprints of several people. They followed it, entering the trees, gripped each other's arms as they stumbled over tree roots treacherous with ice. Ursula forgot to feel shy; she wiped her streaming nose on her sleeve. They skidded down the steep slope towards the river pool. She spotted movement – light flickered from the pool. There was fire on the beach and figures on the bank above with guttering shadows. Almost no sound came from the river, which was ice-bound and coated with snow. Only a muffled burble came from beneath the surface, the waterfall choked. Raucous voices rang clearly in the quiet. As she and Sepp approached, cautious and concealed, she saw several boys seated beside the flames, wrapped in thick coats and hats. The whole beach was covered in what looked like hay. They sat on mounds of it, or on sacks stuffed full, to keep themselves off the freezing ground. Icicles fringed the bank; the pool was a white circle, the snow on its surface dimpled and pitted like the moon's face. The boys called up to the people above – Ursula could see Schosi now, clasped at the elbows by two of the Krampuses, his back pressed to a tree. Sepp gestured that they sneak behind. But how would they free him? How would they get safely away?

Glass clinked on the beach. Boys were retrieving bottles from the snow.

'Is he the simpleton?' one of them shouted, bottle in hand. 'He looks like one! Head like a potato!'

The Krampuses holding Schosi laughed and shook him from side to side. Ursula and Sepp skirted the firelight by some metres, cloaked by shadow and undergrowth. They positioned themselves not far from Schosi, behind the needled branches of a pine fallen across the forest floor. Here they waited and watched, leaning forward with hands on knees, breathing softly through the bristles. The third Krampus pushed his splintered mask on top of his head so that it perched like a peculiar hat, and turned towards Schosi. Ursula saw Anton's face lit by orange firelight. His cheekbones were thick-looking as Rudi's had been, his nose bloodied, his lips lean over his teeth. Schosi moaned, recognising him.

'Look at that!' Anton played to the gallery. 'He's wobbling like jelly.' Some of the boys sniggered and came closer to watch the display. 'Did you miss me? Come on! Don't be rude. You're living in my house, for God's sake. You ought to be grateful.'

'Where's the rent?' called one of the boys. 'Go on! Cough up!'

'He's shit his trousers!'

'He's pouting like a fish!'

Anton put a finger on to Schosi's underlip and jabbed so that the flesh gave way and the shaft thrust into his mouth. Schosi flattened himself against the trunk, eyes bulging. 'No crying!' Anton removed his finger, wiped it on Schosi's coat-front. 'Are you a baby? No. You're old enough to touch my sister.'

Ursula's stomach lurched and she shifted uncomfortably beside Sepp.

Anton aimed an abrupt kick at Schosi's middle and he doubled over, gasping. He kicked again and Schosi fell, the two Krampuses releasing their hold. He made an alarming hooting noise with each attempt at breath. Anton kicked him again.

'Stop it!' Ursula scrambled from beneath the fallen tree and into the open, Sepp following. Anton registered their presence with a short stare and a few blinks. His eyes slid over Ursula sideways.

'Rudi!' he said. 'Tomas!' The two Krampuses came forward and seized Sepp. They forced his arms behind his back, scuffling until he was fixed to the tree as Schosi had been.

'What are you doing? Why are you doing that?' said Ursula.

Anton looked at her but didn't reply.

She dropped to her knees beside Schosi. He was breathing hard, wheezing. She put a hand on his shoulder – his whole frame shuddered. His left eye was bloated and split across the brow, and he nursed his aching stomach. Anton grabbed Schosi by the coat and yanked him to standing, knocking Ursula out of the way.

'Don't you hurt him! Don't you dare!' Her veins filled with scalding broth.

'Or what?' said Anton. 'What's so brilliant' – he knuckled Schosi in the ribs. Schosi jerked and yelled – 'about this stinking, flea-bitten spastic?'

'He's my best friend.' Anger opened in her, hot and deep, bringing strength, a thirsty energy, a sense of her own power, an ability to hurt him as she'd never dreamed of doing. 'A better friend than you've ever been!'

Anton snorted. 'You're wrong – you don't think – you're wrong!' He spat words like pieces of rotten food. She studied him; he could barely form his sentence. Her blow had struck home. The gaping mouth of anger began to slacken and close – too easily filled, too easily satisfied. Pity crept in.

'What on earth are you doing out here?' she said. 'Just come home.'

'No!' he shouted. 'For Christ's sake, I won't! With those Russkis all over you? And now that cripple and his bastard brat?' His eyes were half-eaten by his narrowed lids. He released Schosi's collar. Schosi tottered away and stood near by catching his breath.

'I didn't want to,' she said. 'You don't know what it was like.' She couldn't explain to him about the Russians; there were too many things. He never thought about how she felt, only himself. 'It was terrible, Toni.'

'Don't!' He raised an imperious palm. 'I know you're lying. I saw you—' A bubble of rage burst. 'I know you!' He kicked at the pine needles, gouging the soil. Ursula readied herself to dodge his fist. 'I fought them. I tried to keep them back so they wouldn't reach you. I did that!' He glared at her, his eyes wet. Tears began down his cheeks. 'You just forgot me!'

'You forgot *me*!'

He shook his head. 'Such a liar. Always like this. Always.'

'Ursula,' said Sepp quietly. 'It's all right. Don't listen to him.'

Anton lunged, but didn't strike. 'Hold your tongue, traitor! I know what you're after.' He snatched his mask off altogether and flung it at Sepp's feet, the splintered eyeholes turned to the treetops. He put his hand around Ursula's throat. His fingers dug deep.

'Don't, Toni,' she said. Her belly grew rigid with threat. He pressed deeper. His tears had dried. Her breath became shallower, the air curling wintry around her face as she stifled. Her voice hissed out flat and dry: 'Bully!' Glitter drifted, little splinters of ice that swam in front of her brother's face, fragmenting him. Sepp shouted from behind but she couldn't quite hear – around her, vaguely, more boys floated, silhouetted by stuttering light. Pain sent her throat into spasms. 'You—' She tried to speak. He shook her by the neck. The rubies rattled softly. 'You shouldn't have done it.' His fingers gripped tighter so she could say no more; fingers thin and long and hard at the tips, fingers that had travelled over her, taken what they wanted, accompanied by threats, smothering, tenderness. What *did* he want from her? She used to think she knew.

He released her abruptly. 'Uschi, I had to.' His tone was cajoling. 'It wasn't right for you to be so much together.' He'd misunderstood her – he thought she was referring to Schosi. 'You know he really wasn't—' He touched her hand.

'Not that.' Her voice was hoarse; she pulled her hand away from his. 'You weren't supposed to do those things to me.'

Anton tried again to take her hand; it was as if he hadn't heard her.

'What about what I've been through?' he entreated. 'What about that? I loved you, always.'

'You loved me wrong.' She spoke loudly so that he couldn't ignore her this time.

'Hold your mouth!' one of the boys yelled.

Anton looked at her for a moment. He glanced at Schosi and Sepp. 'You'd rather have them? Would you?' His lips closed in a soft line. 'Well?' He searched her face. Sadness surfaced in his expression, reminding

443

her of another time, of the many occasions he'd brought her here to escape the battles that raged in the house, of the ripples that glided when he swam, suffused with melancholy light.

'Well?' he said again then he reached towards the red glint that showed between the buttons of her dress.

Schosi hit Anton from the right, a sudden flurry, a long arm raised, fist swinging with a downward crash on to Anton's head. Anton staggered, almost collapsing, steadying himself with a hand on the ground. Schosi dropped the rock and stared. The boys moved closer and stared too. Anton was white-faced. He seemed unable to stand. Blood rolled slow and black down his temple. He tentatively touched his skull. He sought Schosi and his eyes cut like blades. He sprang up. He pushed Schosi again and again; he kicked and clobbered and whirled him about. The boys scattered. Ursula was bashed aside by a spinning arm or leg. He dragged Schosi by the coat so that it half peeled off him, Schosi's white back exposed, then forced him with great powerful tugs on to one of the oval rocks that overhung the pool. With a precise, deliberate strike Anton sent Schosi over the edge.

He hit the ice with a crash and went straight through, leaving a large black hole at the centre of the white. Ursula screamed. The boys on the beach yelled and jumped from their perches. A second later Schosi surfaced with arms splashing. He gulped air; the broken ice clattered around him. He sank again, hands reaching, unable to swim. Ursula ran to the overhang, looked down. Anton was beside her. He watched her, an unwavering, questioning gaze, face painted with blood. She met his eye. She felt no love for him then, only dread, and could think of nothing but Schosi, panic almost sending her off the edge in a flying leap. But she wasn't a good swimmer. She'd drown.

'Hey!' A loud voice called from the top of the slope; light scissored through the trees, a torch beam. Someone careered downwards through the undergrowth, ran to the edge of the riverbank and flung the torch on to the ground. It was Pasha.

Cold water enveloped Schosi. Breath left him in a plume of bubbles. When he opened his eyes there was blackness. The cold was pain in his head and he tried to paddle but couldn't. His waterlogged coat constricted his limbs; his movements were heavy and difficult. He kicked, looking upwards, seeing nothing. There was no way out, something blocked his way at the surface. The ice above him formed a lid. He inhaled water and it was agony in his lungs. He tried again to surface but strong arms kept him down, liver-coloured gloves. His body grew numb. He remembered Krampus in the corridor, the bathroom, the freezing room; it had followed him and waited for him to die. It had chased him here. He tried once more to reach the air, moving faintly. But he couldn't fight against the brawny arms, the vice-like hands. He stopped trying and bobbed beneath the ice. The deep bath water sloshed above his head. From somewhere the birds with grey beaks croaked, 'Hartburg! Hartburg!' There was no way out this time.

Pasha threw off his overcoat, hat and glasses and plunged into the water. After a couple of seconds he reappeared with eyes screwed shut. He took several noisy breaths and dived beneath the thicker ice that was unbroken at the edge of the pool. He stayed under for quite some time. The disrupted water began to still and the reflections of firelight joined to form an undulating glow. Ursula hoped the Russian was strong – she thought about Tobias Messer and Mama's account of the lethal effects of ice-cold water, how it could deaden muscles, stop the heart. Pasha popped up like a cork, sucking air, sweeping hair from his eyes. His mouth opened wide and then he dived again. This time he didn't come back up for what felt like minutes and Ursula began to fear that two lives would be lost. She looked around for Anton but Sepp had replaced him – Sepp picked up Pasha's torch and shone it on to the pool. The two Krampuses who'd held him were nowhere to be seen.

When Pasha reappeared, he held Schosi in his arms. Schosi floated limply as he was towed shorewards, hair straggling over his face like riverweed. When Pasha reached the beach the remaining boys bounded up the bank and away leaving their bottles behind. Pasha pulled Schosi clear of the water, laid him flat, listened for breath, placed his lips over Schosi's and blew. He did this a few times then tilted Schosi on to his side, limbs flopping lifeless and sodden. Pasha struck him on the back. Schosi coughed; water sprayed from his mouth. He kept coughing.

'Bring clothes!'

Ursula and Sepp seized Pasha's coat and hat and delivered them to him. The fire heated the air beneath the curve of the bank and Pasha tugged Schosi free of his drenched garments. His skin was blue-white with only a borrowed glow from the firelight. He looked as dead as he had done in Vienna, except he shook from head to toe and his teeth clattered. Pasha wrapped him in the coat, which was full-length and fur-lined, and placed the Red Army hat on his head. He fastened the earflaps under his chin then shifted him so he was lying on hay and stuffed sacks, rather than on bare stones. Ursula put her arm around Schosi. The bulky hat dwarfed his narrow face. She stroked his chilly cheek. Schosi tried to move but he was stiffened with cold. Sepp gave his coat to Pasha who was grey-lipped and shuddering.

Once he'd recovered somewhat, Pasha lifted Schosi and they hurried together out into the field, towards the house. Beyond the hoop of light from the torch there was no sign of Anton or the boys. Ursula talked to Schosi as they went, trying to cheer him, though tears strangled her and made speech difficult. 'Who's your favourite cat?' she said.

But when he tried to answer he only coughed and Pasha told Ursula to let him be. Sepp tramped through the snow close by and a heavy feeling accumulated in Ursula's chest as she thought of what had occurred, what she'd lost for always. She recognised it; she'd felt something similar when the letter had come telling them Papa would never be home again. It was a squeezing sensation, a spreading ache.

47

There was a note attached to Herr Esterbauer's Last Will and Testament, written in his formal, old-fashioned hand. It said:

Dear Frau Hillier
Make the land work for you. Whip Ivan into shape.
Let the boy be useful – the cattle are his.
Your loving friend
Esterbauer Erich

They moved up to the farm with their few possessions as soon as Schosi was well, Simmy yowling captive in a box. The Hildesheim house was bereft without them. Ursula, Dorli, Mama, Siegfried and Traudi couldn't fill it: the rooms seemed too big and the evenings too quiet.

There was much to do in helping Frau Hillier and Schosi to settle at the farm and Ursula was glad to assist, cleaning and carrying and following Frau Hillier's instructions. Frau Hillier frequently stopped in whatever she was doing.

'I can't believe it.' She'd raise her eyes to stop the tears from falling out. 'The old devil. How can I refuse his last wish?'

On the evening of the second day, she called a meeting with the farmhands and Russians. She announced that she was now in charge. She stood stoutly before everyone and spoke without raising her voice – in the thin pocket of her pinafore the outline of a pistol was clearly visible.

'Be honest, respect me and my son and my property – that's all I ask.' She introduced herself to each farm worker and soldier. Schosi was by her side and looked smart and clean in a fresh shirt that used to belong to Herr Esterbauer and with his hair combed over and swept behind his ear. The soldiers smiled and an amused hum of voices began. Frau Hillier clapped her hands, silencing them.

'A house-warming dinner will be served tomorrow at six. You're all invited.'

When the following evening came, the Hildesheims and Siegfried shared a table with Frau Hillier, Schosi, several of the neighbouring farmers, their wives, the farmhands, the resident Russians, and Pasha. Frau Sontheimer and Sepp came and some other factory workers who were friends of Frau Hillier's. Frau Hillier said if the Russians were to be sharing the land and the house then they must all cooperate – she'd have no prejudice on her farm in either direction and they must eat elbow to elbow. The kitchen was brightly lit with lanterns on every surface and there was the atmosphere of a party; songs played loudly on the

449

wireless and there was soon plenty of chatter. Frau Hillier served a tasty broth and the Russians contributed fish and bread. Sepp was ushered to the seat beside Ursula. She managed to perform the polite kiss to each cheek without fumbling or misjudging her approach. She was determined to keep her timidity at bay. On the night of Schosi's ordeal there'd been no voice in her head that whispered a list of her failings, reminding her she was no good. She'd been free of all that.

She maintained her composure throughout dinner, tried to be unselfconscious about her choice of words, gestures and inflection, her appearance. She tried also to ignore the young Russian with dust-coloured hair who kept smiling and winking. The rubies round her neck seemed heavier than usual; she lowered her eyes to her meal but the Russian was determined.

'Bread, Fräulein?' He shook the basket at her, reaching across the table and trailing his unbuttoned jacket through the butter dish and plate of cheese. He was tipsy. 'Bread?'

'No, thank you.' She studied Frau Hillier's tablecloth. It was embroidered with colourful flowers and pictures of Austrian men in lederhosen holding hands with Austrian women in dirndls. She toyed with the noodles that floated in her broth, pushing them to the sides of the bowl and watching them drift back to the centre.

'You don't like it?' asked Sepp. He'd wiped his bowl clean – perhaps he wanted to finish her portion.

'It's nice,' she said.

'Delicious!' Sepp aimed this comment at Frau Hillier but she was chatting loudly on the other side of the table and didn't hear. Then he said, 'I've a new bike. Well, it's not new actually – it's second-hand. But it's quite good. D'you want me to show you some time? I got it for my birthday.'

'From Marta?' She straight away wished she hadn't said it, it was a stupid question and a peculiar one, but perhaps she wanted to be reminded of how hopeless was her crush, to mention Marta and see his response.

'No.' He looked mystified. 'From Auntie. Why did you think that?'

'I don't know. Because you're sweethearts.'

He shook his head, frowning with haste. 'No. Not at all.'

'But you're often together. You get on so well.'

'No, we don't, I can tell you! She's a snob. And I can't stand gossips. It was just this Confirmation thing. She likes to think we were sweethearts but we never were and now she just keeps hanging about.' He smirked, mischievous. 'Are you glad to hear it?'

She reddened, saying nothing – she felt quite giddy. He knew her feelings; she'd let them be seen just like that; like the contents of an overful cupboard they'd tumbled out. And he'd willingly opened the door. It felt so wonderful all she could do was smile. She felt intensely grateful to him for disliking Marta, and for remaining somehow removed from things like she was herself. She listened and nodded as he told more about his new hike, warmed by his closeness, by their understanding. He'd visit soon, he said. Tomorrow, if she didn't mind. She was glad that this year they'd made an effort and the door of the house showed the chalk scribble of C + M + B. She'd written it herself while Mama and Siegfried burned the blessed herbs, Siegfried with his sleeves rolled flicking holy water over the threshold and asking Caspar, Melchior and Balthasar to protect their house from fire and water for another year. Perhaps Sepp would let her ride on his handlebars and she'd lean against his chest as she'd seen other girls do with their boys, his hands either side of her hips, the bike swerving, whirring, the slab of his fringe lifting in the breeze at the corner of her vision. She'd wear her yellow ribbons. She found she didn't care a jot whether he'd hidden a Soviet prisoner all that time ago, whether he was a Communist or anything like that – perhaps Sepp and his aunt had saved another decent man like Pasha, an honest soul. She glanced at Pasha who was tucking into his third helping of dinner, thoroughly spoiled by Frau Hillier.

'You didn't have to come with me,' she said in a rush, 'to find Schosi.' Sepp stopped, surprised. 'Sorry!' She blushed again, imagining herself pink as boiled ham. 'I didn't mean to interrupt. It's just it was good of you, to do what you did.' She bent close to her soup bowl as though spotting a fly or hair in her food but it was impossible to hide her face entirely. Sepp touched her arm, just for a second.

'I wanted to. Because I like you.'

Her heart somersaulted and her cheeks began to flame all over again. It was hopeless. She needed air. She stood.

'Excuse me a minute.' She got tangled in her own skirts, almost overturning her stool.

As soon as she was out in the yard, she felt better. She wiped the clamminess from her forehead and upper lip. Snow was shovelled into crumbling piles and the stars were stark above the white barn roof. She breathed deeply to rid herself of the wincing feeling that lingered. Sepp was just another person, ordinary, not perfect, no better or worse than she. She remembered Schosi's shout of glee when he emerged from the Krampus costume. Yes, he was just a boy. Not a monster, not someone to run from. She should be happy. She began to shiver and walked about to stay warm. She entered the pocket of blackness near the water butts, momentarily unable to see her own feet, emerged into moonbeams that angled from above the farmhouse and lit the outhouse, chalkily pale. She glanced up at the moon's face, its penetrating gaze. She thought of Anton's last unblinking look, wondered where he might end up. Would he go to the place on that fire-blackened photo he had showed her once? Would the moon shine in the same way on to the African pyramids or in whichever far-flung place? Or was there only sweltering sun?

She ended up at the cowshed. She watched idly from the door – Schosi was inside, leaning into each stall to sweep his hand along the cow's back or to dig his fingers into the dense hair between their horns. This was his nightly ritual. He sometimes slept out here, resting on the ribs of a cow, rising and falling with each breath. She was glad he had somewhere, as Herr Esterbauer had wanted. God must have had reason, Frau Hillier believed, to test her son then reward him at last. But this was just a simple way of making sense of a senseless thing. Schosi still sometimes retreated into a rocking silence, eyes fixed on something only he could see. Ursula couldn't understand how to love a God who'd inflicted such suffering.

Schosi stroked the nose of a rust-coloured cow, carefully lifted the chain around its neck to check that the metal hadn't chafed or broken the skin. He was already planning which special fodder to give the herd for Christmas and had prepared the incense ready to bless the barn and shed.

She called to him softly.

He came, stuffing his handkerchief in his pocket. 'Got a bad bit,' he said, indicating the cow.

She took his hand.

'Got a bad bit on her neck.' He tapped the back of his own neck. He looked at her, waiting, sensing her mood. After a while he said, 'You're a good girl, little bear.'

If a child is good, gifts appear in their waiting boots, oranges and walnuts delivered by Saint Nikolaus. If a child is bad their boots are filled with coal and Krampus comes to beat them and take them to Hell. Just another way of making sense where there was none, a chaos and sickness all of its own. The saint was a devil and the devil her own dear brother. She feared in some instinctive way, as Schosi took her along the stalls and told her for the umpteenth time the names of the cows, that she'd never be entirely mended. That, like a broken packing chest that drops its contents every time it's lifted, she wouldn't be able to hold on to good or hopeful things. She thought of Sepp sitting inside at the dinner table, how in each of his eyes danced a warm candle flame. Then of Dorli lying on her back with her cartridge crown, the noises that had filled the bedroom and everything that happened that night. These last belongings she kept sealed tight, stowed away. She toyed absent-mindedly with the necklace, pressed it to her collarbone then drew it out into her palm. That marvellous red that for a moment made her feel like a queen.

Sepp met her as she exited the cowshed, just as she was stuffing the necklace away. Taken aback, she dropped her hands to her sides.

'They're worse for wear in there.' He thumbed towards the farmhouse, his gaze pausing at her neckline. Lively singing spilled out into the night.

'There's a lot of schnapps in that cellar.' She forced a smile. 'Beer too.' She tried to pass him but he took her hand.

'We're going now.' He was awkward, his face obscured by shadow. He smelled of beer, a sweet bread-like scent that leaked from his skin. 'I'll come by tomorrow. You won't run off this time?'

She shook her head. He stroked her palm, a feather-touch. It was the most exquisite feeling. Then he put his fingers to the base of her throat. Her stomach clenched instinctively but he only rested them there. After a moment he gently pulled the necklace from under her dress.

Acknowledgements

Thank you to my family, friends, teachers and tutors who have supported me throughout. Thanks to my mum for her keen and meticulous reading of drafts, to my dad for letting me plunder his memories, and to Barbara and Ernst for showing me the Austrian fields and pine forests. Special thanks to Mr Ballinger, my enthusiastic, kind and encouraging English teacher who gave me my first shove towards writing, and to Rob Middlehurst, my tutor and friend, who has kept me going and believed in this book from the start. Thanks also to Des, Philip and Maria for their interest, feedback and advice and to my extraordinary agents, Binky Urban and Karolina Sutton, and brilliant editor, Alexa von Hirschberg. Thank you above all to my dear David, for coming with me, for talking, listening and making space.

A Note on the Author

Holly Müller is a writer and musician. She teaches Creative Writing at the University of South Wales and sings in the band Hail! The Planes. *My Own Dear Brother* is her first novel. Holly Müller lives in Cardiff.